Joseph O'Connor

My Father's House

Harvill *Secker*

LONDON

3 5 7 9 10 8 6 4

Harvill Secker, an imprint of Vintage, is part of the Penguin Random House group
of companies whose addresses can be found at global.penguinrandomhouse.com

Copyright © Joseph O'Connor 2023

Joseph O'Connor has asserted his right to be identified as the author of this
Work in accordance with the Copyright, Designs and Patents Act 1988

First published by Harvill Secker in 2023

Map © Mike Hall

A CIP catalogue record for this book is available from the British Library

penguin.co.uk/vintage

ISBN 9781787300828 (hardback)
ISBN 9781787300835 (trade paperback)

Typeset in 11.5/15.76 pt Van Dijck MT Pro by Jouve (UK), Milton Keynes
Printed and bound in Great Britain by Clays Ltd, Elcograf S.p.A.

The authorised representative in the EEA is Penguin Random House Ireland,
Morrison Chambers, 32 Nassau Street, Dublin D02 YH68

Penguin Random House is committed to a sustainable future for
our business, our readers and our planet. This book is made from
Forest Stewardship Council® certified paper.

For Emma, Laurence and Cormac, *un abbraccio*.

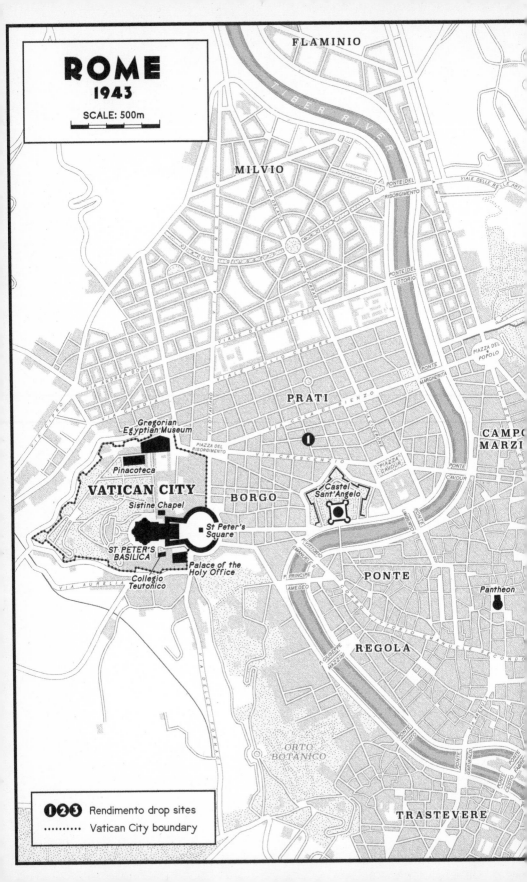

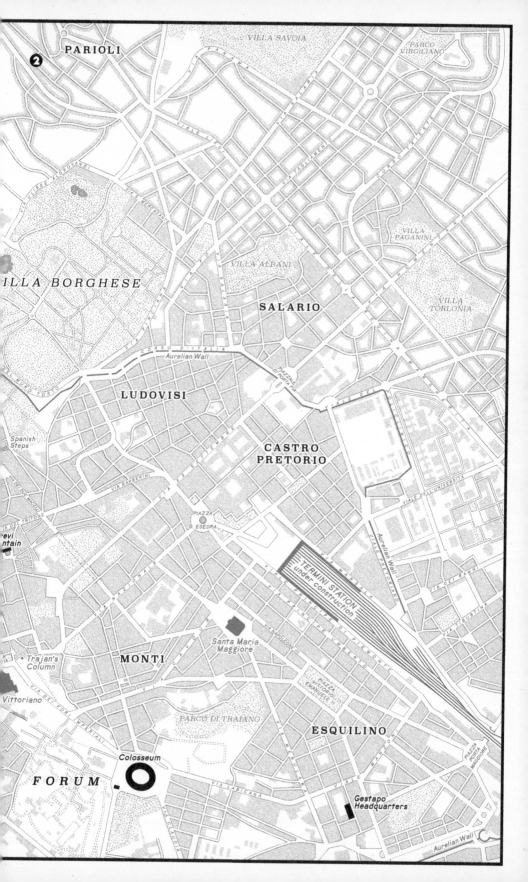

Dear Mother, Father and Family. This is the last letter I will be able to write as I get shot today. Dear family, I have laid down my life for my country and everything that was dear to me. I hope this war will be over soon so that you will all have peace for ever. Goodbye. Your ever loving soldier, son and brother, Willie.

Letter written by a Scottish prisoner of war in Italy

ACT I
The Choir

Sopranos: Delia Kiernan, Marianna de Vries

Alto: The Contessa Giovanna Landini

Tenors: Sir D'Arcy Osborne, Enzo Angelucci, Major Sam Derry

Bass: John May

Conductor: Monsignor Hugh O'Flaherty

September 1943: German forces occupy Rome.

Gestapo boss Obersturmbannführer Paul Hauptmann rules with terror.

Hunger is widespread. Rumours fester. The war's outcome is far from certain.

Diplomats, refugees and escaped Allied prisoners risk their lives fleeing for protection into Vatican City, at one fifth of a square mile the world's smallest state, a neutral, independent country within Rome.

A small band of unlikely friends led by a courageous priest is drawn into deadly danger.

By Christmastime, it's too late to turn back.

1

Sunday 19th December 1943
10.49 p.m.
119 hours and 11 minutes before the mission

Grunting, sullen, in spumes of leaden smoke, the black Daimler with diplomatic number plate noses onto Via Diciannove, beads of sleet fizzling on its hood. A single opal streetlight glints at its own reflection in an ebbing, scummy puddle where a drain has overflowed. Pulsing in the irregular blink of a café's broken neon sign, the words '*MORTE AL FASCISMO*' daubed across a shutter.

Scarlet.

Emerald.

White.

Delia Kiernan is forty, a diplomat's wife. Doctors have ordered her not to smoke. She is smoking.

A week before Christmas, she's a thousand miles from home. Sweat sticks her skirt to the backs of her stockings as she pushes the stubborn gear stick into first.

The man on the rear seat groans in stifled pain, tearing at the swastikas on his epaulettes.

The heavy engine grumbles. Blood throbs in her temples. On the dashboard, a scribbled map of how to get to the hospital using only the quieter streets is ready to be screwed up and tossed if she encounters an SS patrol but the darkness is making the pencil marks difficult to read and whatever hand wrote them was unsteady. She flicks on her cigarette lighter; a whiff of fuel inflames his moans.

Swerving into Via Ventuno, the Daimler clips a dustbin, upending it. What spills out gives a scuttle and makes for the gutter but is ravaged by a tornado of cadaverous dogs bolting as one from gloomed doorways.

Squawking brakes, jouncing over ramps, undercarriage racketing into pot-holes, fishtailing, oversteering, boards thudding, jinking over machine-gunned cobbles, into a street where wet leaves have made a rink of the paving stones.

Whimpers from the man. Pleadings to hurry.

Down a side street. Alongside the university purged and burned by the invaders. Its soccer pitch netless, strangled with weeds, the pit meant for a swimming pool yawning up at the moon and five hundred shattered windows. She remembers the bonfire of blackboards, seeing its photograph in the news-paper the morning of her daughter's eighteenth birthday. Past the many-eyed, murderous hulk of the Colosseum like the skeleton of a washed-ashore kraken.

Across the piazza, gargoyles leer from a church's gloomy facade. She flashes her headlights twice.

The bell tolls eleven. She feels it in her teeth. Wind harangues the chained-up tables and chairs outside a café, wheezing through the arrow-tipped railings.

A black-clad man hurries across from the porch, damp raincoat clinging, abandoning his turned-inside-out umbrella to the gust as he scrambles into the passenger seat of the ponderous, boat-like car, trilby dripping.

As she pulls away, he takes out a notebook, commences scribbling with a pencil.

'What do you think you're doing?'

'Thinking,' he says.

Pulling a naggin of brandy from his pocket, he offers it to the groaning pas-senger who has tugged off one of his leather gloves and jammed it into his own mouth.

The man shakes his head, scared eyes rolling.

'For pity's sake, let him alone,' she says. 'Give it here.'

'You're driving.'

'Give it here this minute. Or you're walking.'

An eternity at the junction of Via Quattordici and Piazza Settanta as a battle-scarred Panzer rattles past, turret in slow-revolve as though bored.

'What does it mean for the mission?' she asks. 'If he's gravely ill?'

'We'd have to find someone else. Maybe Angelucci?'

'Enzo couldn't be trained up. Not in the time.'

Hail surges hard on the windscreen as they pass Regina Coeli prison. She lights another cigarette, veins of ash falling on the collar of her raincoat. He has his eyes closed but she's certain he's not praying.

'For the love of God, Delia, can't this rust-bucket go any faster?'

Steaming blue streetlights, alleyways snaking up hills, ranked silhouettes of martyrs on the rooftops of churches. It comes back to her, her second morning in Rome, when she climbed the staircase to the roof of St Peter's, every feature of every statue worn away by time and storm. Soot-stained, weather-beaten stalagmites.

Now, a farm gate blocking a driveway. He steps out into the furies of rain and tries to haul the gate open, trilby falling off with the fervour of his shakes. In the glim of the headlights, he wrenches at the bars.

'Tied closed,' he shouts. 'Would there be a toolbox in the boot?'

'Stand out of the road.'

'Delia—'

Revving, foot down hard, she *bolts* the massive car through the splintering, wheezing smash as the gate implodes and he clambers back in, shaking his heavy, wet head as a man wondering how his life can have come to this pass.

Through the long, flat grounds, where soaked sheep bawl, then the road climbs again and the hospital buildings loom, three blocks of brutal concrete bristling with empty flagpoles and monsters that must be water tanks.

A fluorescent yellow road sign commands in black:

'*Rallentare!*'

Up a short winding drive where the gravel is wearing thin, past a trio of diseased sycamores and the concrete hive of a machine-gun turret, to the floodlit portico by which a khaki-and-red-cross-painted ambulance is parked, engine on, three orderlies in the back playing cards. Inexplicably, on seeing the Daimler approach they pull the doors closed on themselves. A moment later, the floodlight is extinguished.

She exits the car but leaves the engine muttering.

The hospital doors are locked, the lobby beyond them in darkness. She tugs the bellpull three times, hears its distant, desolate jangle from somewhere in the heart of the darkened wards.

Stepping back, she looks up at the shuttered windows, as though looking could produce a watcher, the hope of all religious people, but no one is coming and as she approaches the shut ambulance for help a wolf-whistle sounds from behind her.

An orderly in his twenties has appeared from some door she hasn't noticed. Sulky, kiss-curled, cigarette in mouth, he looks as though he was asleep two minutes ago. The smell of a musty room has followed him out. The flashlight in his left hand gives a couple of meagre flickers, diminishing whatever light there is. In his right hand is an object it takes her a moment to recognise as a switchblade. He looks like he'd know what to do with it.

'I've a patient who needs urgent assistance,' she says. 'There. Back seat.'

'Your name?' he sighs, peering into the Daimler's chugging rear.

'I am not in a position to identify myself. I am attached to a neutral Legation in the city. This man is seriously ill, I had our official physician attend him not an hour ago. He says it's peritonitis or a burst appendix.'

'Why should I care? I am a Roman. What are *you*?'

'Matter a damn what I am, send in for a stretcher.'

'You come here with your orders expecting me to help a son-of-a-whore Nazi?'

'You've a duty to help anyone.'

He spits on the ground.

'There's my duty,' he says.

The man in black steps out of the car, heavy hand on the roof, gives a grim stare at the sky as though resenting the clouds, slowly rounds to where the youth is standing.

'You kiss your mother with that mouth?'

'Who's asking?'

'Name's O'Flaherty.' Opening his raincoat, revealing his soutane and collar.

'Father. Excuse me, Father.' He crosses himself. 'I did not know.'

'The German uniform that man in the car is wearing is a disguise. He was running a surveillance mission and became seriously ill.'

'Father—'

'Tough Guy, here's a question. Is there a dentist in that hospital behind you?'

'Why?'

'Because you'll need one in a minute when I punch your teeth through your skull. You ignorant lout, to comport yourself before any woman in that fashion. Go to confession tomorrow morning and *apologise this minute.*'

'I beg forgiveness, *Signora.*' Bowing his florid face. 'I haven't eaten or slept in three nights.'

'Granted,' she says. 'Can we move things along?'

'Our passenger is escaped British prisoner Major Sam Derry of the Royal Regiment of Artillery,' O'Flaherty says. 'The lives of many thousands depend on this man. If you love Italy get him into an operating theatre. This minute.'

The youth regards him.

O'Flaherty hurries to the ambulance, hauls open its doors.

'*Andiamo, ragazzi,*' he says, beckoning towards the Daimler. 'Off your backsides. Good men. We need muscle.'

Derry lurches from the car, blurting mouthfuls of blood, clutching at his abdomen and the night.

2

THE VOICE OF DELIA KIERNAN
7th January 1963
From transcript of BBC research interview, questions inaudible,
conducted White City, London

I probably drink too much. Which is the main thing to say. They'll have told you, no doubt. You needn't sham.

We were after setting up a mission – a 'Rendimento' was the code, the Italian word for 'a performance' – for that Christmas Eve, starting at eleven o'clock that night. But on the Sunday five evenings beforehand, Derry, our mission-runner, got sick while out on reconnaissance, and Angelucci was sent for, to stand in.

But you're wondering what led to it. As well you might.

Old age has made a bit of a hames of the memory, I'm afraid. Not that I forget things, but sometimes I remember them the wrong way around. So I'm not entirely certain when I first met the Monsignor. It was in Rome during the war. Don't ask me to work it out more than that or I'd need a long lie-down.

No, I didn't keep a diary, love. Never had the patience.

You wouldn't happen to have a cigarette? If we're going to get into it.

Thanks. No, I'm grand. I've matches.

As the wife of the senior Irish diplomat to the Vatican, you did a lot of standing about at official receptions being talked at by Archbishops and pretending to listen. But I suppose you felt it a sort of duty to do what little you could for the young Irish of the city, most of whom were in religious life.

Oh, I'd say a total of five hundred or so, priests and nuns. Many seminarians. What with rationing, you didn't have much of a good time in Rome during the war – you wouldn't see a head of cabbage or a bit of chicken in a month's travel. Scabby bits of turnip. Hard-tack biscuit tasting of sawdust and ashes. Sausages with that little meat in them, you could eat them on a Good Friday.

And so many of the youngsters I'm talking about were barely out of their teens. These days we'd call them teenagers. That word didn't exist back then. So they seemed – how to put it? – a bit lost. And exhausted. A religiously minded kid will often be good at lying awake all night because you need an imagination if you're going to believe.

One or two were scarcely into long trousers and they staring down the barrel of priesthood. Some of them, you wondered had it maybe been more Mammy's idea than their own. And, often enough, though some won't like me saying it, a nun was the youngest daughter of a poor family, with no other prospects. Or she's impressionable in adolescence, like most of us were. Some ould gull of a Mother Superior goes prowling for vocations into a little school in Hutchesontown, Glasgow. Annie raises her hand and she barely gone thirteen. Annie loves Our Lady and the flowers on the altar. And that's Annie despatched to the convent, for the rest of her life. Not in every case, obviously, but you wondered. You wondered.

Anyhow, there was all of that, just fellow feeling for these youngsters. You'd see an awful lot of fear and plain hunger in Rome at the time. It was also a hellishly hot summer, scalding, sapping heat. The gardens of our beautiful Legation villa had a swimming pool, and I let it be known at every function I attended that all Irish youngsters in the city could use it, and the numbers of the trams that would take them there from Piazza del Risorgimento, which is right next door to the Vatican. My poor Tom nearly lost his mind with me and insisted, at the very least, that the sexes must attend on different days. 'You're no fun,' I told him. 'But sure that's why I married you.'

To be serious, of course I was happy to agree to his compromise. Seeing their poor, scrawny bodies leapfrogging and splashing would have brought tears to a glass eye.

So, I started putting on a weekly evening for them, an Open House, if you like, at the Residence of a Thursday night.

I'd have tureens of delicious minestrone and that lovely long Italian bread, you know, a bit of fruit if I could get it on the black market – the Legation maids used to help me in that respect – a few bob will get you most things in Italy. Great cauldrons of pasta; a quid's worth of spaghetti will do you to feed

11

a whole battalion. If you'd olives or a cheese or two, that was nice for them as well. A dirty big beast of a lasagne, piping hot. Also, sausages and rashers from Limerick the odd time, if I could get them brought in in the Diplomatic Bag. A table of ices or poached peaches with zabaglione, maybe a lemon tart. Yes, wine, too. Why not? I wanted them to feel welcome in my home. If they felt like *un bicchiere di vino rosso* or a bottle of stout, which most of them didn't, I wanted them to enjoy it, and to share anything we had ourselves. That's the way I was brought up.

I'm a Catholic, I love the faith as best I can, but I wouldn't be a great one for kissing the altar rails. Not at all. Wouldn't be a Holy Mary. There's good people of every persuasion, and there's 24-carat bastards. Life schools you the way no catechism will.

There was a modest enough budget provided for entertaining guests at the Legation. I drove my misfortunate liege demented by exceeding it every week. And then, Dublin could get a bit snippy, too, as I recall. There'd be these urgent cablegrams from the Department of Foreign Affairs demanding a receipt in triplicate for that bottle of Prosecco: viz, heretofore, moreover, block capitals. Oh, I didn't give a fig, dear. We'll be a long time dead. Here's a girl wouldn't be too renowned for doing what she's told. Some little jack-in-office of a penpusher thinks he'll lord it over yours truly? Take the back of my arse and boil it.

This particular evening, I'd plenty on my mind. I was after spending the morning in the recording studio at Radio Roma because I was making a record of two songs to be released back in Ireland. Yes. I was a professional singer before I was married. I didn't want to give it up fully.

That day? Oh, I can't remember now, love, I think 'Danny Boy' and 'Boola-vogue'. Maybe 'The Spinning Wheel'. I'd have to check.

I'd a grand little career going back at home and I got such fulfilment and excitement from that. To be honest, I missed it dreadfully, the concerts, the travelling around. But by '41 I'd had to take a break from it, between one thing and another, the war getting worse, Tom's posting to Rome. I was singing in Belfast the night the Luftwaffe firebombed the theatre. That's what you call a mixed review.

Wasn't a town I didn't perform in the breadth and length of Ireland. In the summers, the Isle of Man, Liverpool, Manchester, often Dundee or Ayrshire, maybe a couple of nights in Cricklewood at the dance halls. I've sung in Durham, Kilmarnock, Northampton, all over. A woman can lose her confidence in the house all day. And I always think, if singing's in you, you have to sing.

Anyhow, in comes this polite sort of fellow to my get-together that evening and introduces himself as Monsignor O'Flaherty of the Holy Office. Chilly words.

'Monsignor' is a title conferred by the Church on a diocesan priest who's been an administrator five years. So, it conveys a bit of importance. As for 'Holy Office', that's the department of the Vatican where they keep a weather eye on what's called 'adherence to doctrine' and ensure everyone's toeing the line. It's what used to be called 'the Inquisition'. So that carried a bit of weight, too. There's few of us want an Inquisitor at our party.

Normally at my evenings I didn't like too many high-and-mighty sorts, because the youngsters weren't able to relax and enjoy themselves if the quare ould hawks were along. Once, for example, a certain Cardinal who shall be nameless pitched up; a long drink of cross-eyed, buck-toothed misery if ever there was, he'd bore the snots off a wet horse, and the effect was like turning a fire hose on a kindergarten. He'd a way of smiling would freeze up the heart in your chest. As for smug? If he was a banana, he'd peel himself.

But this Monsignor fellow was different, down to earth. Affable. You get that with Kerry people, a sort of courtesy. Too many priests at the time saw themselves not as a sign of mercy but as grim little thin-lipped suburban magistrates. Hugh wasn't too mad on authority.

Another different thing, his means of transport over to us that night was his motorcycle. Here he's ambling up the steps to the residence and he grey with the dust from boots to helmet, huge leather gloves on him like a flying ace, and he blessing himself at the Lourdes water font on the hallstand. As though a priest dressed like that was the most everyday sight you ever saw. And the bang of motor oil off him. Unusual.

He spoke in beautiful Italian to my servants. I didn't know it yet, but I would never meet a brainier piece of work: Hugh had three doctorates and was fluent in seven languages, his mind was like a lawnmower blade; he'd shear through any knot and see a solution, if there was one.

Around the party he sallies, anyhow, tumbler of *limonata* in hand, a word of chat here, a joke or two there. Two Liverpool students were playing chess; he watched them for a while, and, when they finished, asked the winner to explain what the strategy had been. He didn't touch a drop but not a bother on him about anyone else having a glass of beer. Fire away. Whatever you're having yourself.

There was a young woman from Carrigafoyle, a Carmelite novice, they'd a great old natter; didn't it turn out he'd known a late uncle of hers through golf back at home. Hugh was brought up on a golf course as you probably know. His father, a one-time policeman, was the club professional in Killarney. Then Hugh and the young Carmelite – I can see them clear as you like, still, from that night in my living room – the pair of them demonstrating to the company how to putt with a walking stick. There was a bundle of talk about happy subjects and none of the war.

Oh, I forgot to say, when, later, we started having code names, his name was 'Golf'. He was obsessed with the notion the Germans were listening. Escaped prisoners were known as 'Books', their hiding places 'Shelves'. We never used the real names of the Roman streets but gave them names of our own, based on numbers, like the streets in Manhattan. Or we named them after the great Italian composers. And we had to keep mixing the codes to stay ahead of the Gestapo. But more of that, anon.

Tom was out that evening, visiting a trio of Dubliners who were after unwisely giving lip to the Fascisti and getting themselves chucked into Regina Coeli, the jail in Rome, after a hiding; and, anyway, he rarely attended my get-togethers. He enjoyed pretending to disapprove of them more than he actually did.

A point came in the evening when the youngsters started asking would I sing. Some of them had my 78s back at home in Ireland, or, likelier, their parents had. There was a recording of mine was after being played all that summer on Raidió Éireann, 'The Voice of Delia Kiernan', even on the Third Service and American Forces Network. The great Richard Tauber himself had said in an interview he liked it, so that was a feather in my cap. The Monsignor encouraged me to oblige them. 'Go on, Mrs Kiernan, before they start breaking up the furniture.' I answered that I had no accompanist and would feel nervous without that safety net. In truth, I'd a couple of whiskeys on me.

He answered that he was no Paderewski but would vamp along as best he could if I would tell him the key. What I had in mind was written in A-flat, which isn't easy for an improvisor, but I told him I could hack it in A. So, over with the pair of us to the piano, a lovely old Bösendorfer, and off we went. It was an old love song, an arietta by Bellini I've long had a place in my heart for – a lovely loose melody like a soft-rolling folk song. It always brings my father back to me, Lord have mercy on him, it was a great favourite of his. As a girl I learned it off a 78 he had in the house, John McCormack's version – and some of the younglings joined along.

Vaga luna, che inargenti
Queste rive e questi fiori
Ed inspiri agli elementi
Il linguaggio dell'amor

It wasn't false modesty from Hugh, I must say, about the level of his musicianship. Dear knows I've heard bad pianists in my time but he was cat altogether, God love him. He'd grand big hands on him like a pair of shovels but he was clumsy. All the same, it was a lovely experience. You'd remember it. In recollection, Rome comes to me always as everyday music: the clunk of a shutter on a sweltering afternoon, the gasps of wonder when you're inside the Pantheon and rain starts to fall. The hot pigeons warbling, the way the drinking fountains chuckle. But there was never music sweeter than hearing the room sing that night.

Something happens in a room when people are singing. It changes the air, like rainfall, or dusk. You've those say it's escapism but, to me, life seems realer, then.

Forgive me. Makes me emotional to think of.

Well, that's how we met, and we were soon good pals. He'd come along to my evenings the odd time, bring a chum or two with him. Priests, yes – a Japanese Franciscan came once – or pilgrims from the homeland or his beloved United States, and always a bottle of excellent Chianti, the dear knows how he laid hands on it, though he didn't drink himself, as I say. Often, he'd bring a naggin of brandy.

A well-placed Papal Count was after gifting the Irish Legation an expensive subscription to a box at the Opera House, to which we'd often invite other diplomats and their families. You've to remember that independent Ireland was still a very young country, having only won her freedom in 1921. The solidarity of others was needed and valued. Hosting was something a diplomat's wife was expected to do. Verdi sometimes proved an ally, you could say.

This one particular occasion the plan was for a party of seven, but the Portuguese Ambassador was under the weather with the awful heat, the filth of which brought headaches that would cripple you and made it hard to breathe, so I invited along the Monsignor to join the group, for I knew he loved Puccini, and *Tosca* is set in Rome as you know. We were the Swedish Ambassador and his wife, the Swiss Cultural Attaché – there's a part-time job if ever there was – and a lady friend, then the Monsignor and yours truly and my husband. 'A riot of neutrality,' Hugh joked, shaking hands. 'We lot couldn't shoot our way out of a mousetrap.'

Which the Swedish Ambassador laughed at. But not the Swiss Cultural Attaché, as I recall, who seemed understandably put off by the fact that Hugh had a little notebook in which he kept scribbling, all the way through the performance. It was an oddity of Hugh's: if a thing wasn't written down, it hadn't happened. Even his Bible, he'd be scrawling all over the margins. Anyhow. Another story. Where were we?

Yes.

Late in '42 it must have been, a kind of darkness I hadn't seen before came over him. For a while he'd been visiting the Axis prisoner-of-war camps in Italy as an official Vatican observer. But something happened to him that autumn. He wasn't the same. He stopped attending my evenings, went to ground a while. Someone told me he'd been sick, was after being in hospital with cancer or was considering going to Massachusetts to do parish work. My Tom heard on the Vatican grapevine he might be leaving the priesthood. But when at last he agreed to see me, he said that wasn't so; he'd been preoccupied with what he called a private matter.

It was after raining for days as we spoke, and the river was rising, one of those nights when the Tiber was tipping the tree-roots. Was he in trouble? I remember asking him. Was he in need of a friend?

Because, I'll be honest, sometimes you heard of a priest where a woman had come into the picture. Human nature is what it is. We won't change it this late in the day. There's many a good man discovered the celibate life wasn't for him, but they'd be shunned by the Church when they left. The routine was you'd be told to go to a particular room in some shabby back-street hotel, on the bed there'd be a suit from a pawnshop and three pound-notes. You took off your priestly clothes, folded them on the bed, got into the dead man's suit, left the hotel by the back door. It was understood no one from your old life would ever contact you again. They made it hard for you to leave. So, too many stayed.

I can say now, after all this time, I had a particular lady in mind, a young Contessa recently widowed who'd been seen in Hugh's company at art galleries and the like, around Rome, each of the pair for different reasons clad in black. A beauty she was, with something of what the French call '*gamine*', slightly boyish film-star looks, like those of Leslie Caron. She and I became great friends; indeed, I was speaking with her on the telephone not two hours ago. The Vatican, like all kremlins, is a hive of whispers and envies. I know for a fact that her friendship with Hugh didn't merit the way it was sometimes talked about. 'No smoke without fire' is the way gossips put it. I always say, maybe it's not smoke, maybe your spectacles need a wiping.

Anyhow, he gave a laugh when I mentioned her name. The private matter he was after mentioning was nothing at all of that nature, he assured me. 'But thank you, Delia, for the compliment.'

When I persisted, he showed me a scrap of a letter that had been smuggled to him from a poor Scottish boy, a soldier in a prisoner-of-war camp, about to be executed. The lad wanted it sent to his mother. The words of it, the fact of it – forgive me a moment – had been coming between Hugh and his sleep.

I wept when I read it. Handed it back and wept. There's never a single day of my life I don't pray for that mother.

We'd go through American bombing attacks the following summer. Those I'll never forget. Because unless you've lived through an air raid, I don't think I can convey the terror. There's no film could capture it. The screaming. The smell. The nerves would be at you weeks afterward.

A B-25 Mitchell bomber is the size of a London bus. You look up and there's forty of them raining 500-pound bombs. So, a street isn't damaged, it's obliterated. Gone. A rubble of stinking smoke and pulverised bricks. The planes would come the night before, drop eighty thousand leaflets saying what would happen the next day. So you'd plenty of time for the dread to build up. One night an air raid came during one of my evenings. I'll never forget the young people's fear; they were weeping, terrified.

By now, Hugh had become aware that certain individuals in Rome – a person here, someone else over there – were helping escaped Allied prisoners and Jews get out of the country, into Switzerland, and he'd been giving them the odd bit of assistance on the QT. Things like buying train tickets in false names, getting clothes, nothing much more. It was ad hoc, you know, not organised. Hugh had a lot of friends in the city between one thing and another; he wasn't one of those priests that eat and sleep and die in the chapel. He was half-thinking of putting together a proper group that might raise a few bob for the escapees, the odd handout, at a distance, on the quiet.

Discreet. Nothing formal. All very hush-hush. Perhaps best not to mention it to Tom or anyone else at the embassy. There wouldn't be any danger, it would only be in the background, like a charity fund.

I didn't know what it would lead to or I'd have run for the hills.

He was after thinking of a cover for it.

The Choir.

3

Monday 20th December 1943
6.47 a.m.
112 hours and 13 minutes before the Rendimento

In the hours after the dash to the hospital, a head cold assails him. Racking sneezes, hacks, shivers, hot eyes. The fear looms that this is the onset of the dreaded Roman flu, which killed a dozen of his African First Years and nine of his Chicagoans last winter.

Minutes before dawn, exhausted, he forces himself to sleep. The Daimler roaring through his nightmares.

Somehow it becomes the Mercedes of Hauptmann, the Gestapo commander. They're driving long spirals of impossibly narrow streets in a city that is and is not Rome. Oak trees. Lightning. Bloodstains on sand. Rain patterning a window. Vast towers. A well as deep as the moon is high. Faces turning to stone as a Chopin nocturne plays, the settled, broken blankness of those without hope. Now Hauptmann is at his bedside, a presence, a virus. You'd be afraid to breathe in case you inhale him. *Tell me who you met. Tell me why you met them.* The Nazi's grey eyes. Grey infantry braid on his cuffs. Grey smoke of his grey cigarettes. The wolf feeding Romulus and Remus in a fresco comes to life and slobbers at her starving babies before devouring them.

At ten o'clock, he leaves his room, walks uneasily to the School of Divinity, starts into the three-hour lecture he must give on Aquinas, in Latin, to a class of ninety seminarians. Last night's sleet still beating in his head as he clutches the lectern for steadiness, the bleached-out yellow windows of the lecture hall throbbing. This term's Third Years are bright. Their questions swarm like wasps. The glass of hot water and lemon he has brought with him to the dais tastes of mud and pencil shavings.

Afterwards, wrapped in a blanket, he begins grading their end-of-term disquisitions but makes it through only thirty papers before retreating to his sickbed. The remaining sixty scripts he marks between bouts of flicker-lit half-sleep and fits of angry coughing. His wheezes cast a seething dog into the corners of the room. His ribcage is made of fire.

No word from Sam Derry.

Bombers overhead.

Perhaps news will come tomorrow.

Transcript of memorandum recording made on Allgemeine Elektricitäts-Gesellschaft AG Magnetophon

This is Obersturmbannführer Paul Hauptmann speaking. For the attention of Dollman, confidential. Twentieth of December, forty-three, Gestapo headquarters, Rome.

Himmler telephoned again. Ranting, threatening. Furious that enemy prisoners are escaping Italy-based camps in large numbers. Says most are heading towards Rome, seeking asylum in the Vatican. I appreciate you're busy but I have changed my mind and want you to look into a couple of suspects we discussed recently, including that nuisance of a priest I mentioned before. I know you think he's nothing. Let's find out.

Poke around. Bang heads. The usual informants. See if he's using a false name.

I'm sending you a dossier on him, into which I have written what I already know. Complete its currently empty sections and return it to me before Christmas.

Be discreet. Stay in backstage.

Let's get this weed uprooted.

We don't need trouble.

Heil Hitler.

Awakening in the early hours, he realises that today is the eighteenth anniversary of his ordination. Fevered, his thoughts skim oceans. He sees himself prostrated before the altar that morning in the cathedral, then walking back down the aisle, hands bound, the hawk-faced, candlelit Bishops.

Around sunrise he drifts into some zone of pulsing, crackled redness that is not sleep, some land where candlestands have voices. Surfacing, he stirs the tumbler of medicine someone has placed on his locker and manages two sips before dry-retching.

The lemon wedge in the copper spoon beside the alarm clock is the strangest object he has ever seen, so yellow it's green, so green it's blue, its aroma creeping up his sinuses like a midnight burglar until it sprouts a thousand insect legs and scuttles around the pillows, emitting a sordid, irksome buzz that becomes the reedy drone of an oboe.

A dream of words slithering out his ears like worms.

The air in the room is rank. He pushes open his window.

In the rainy street below, Hauptmann's black Mercedes.

As he watches, its headlamps are killed.

Transcript of memorandum recorded on Allgemeine Elektricitäts-Gesellschaft AG Magnetophon

Twenty-first of December, forty-three, Gestapo headquarters, Rome, Hauptmann speaking, for the attention of Dollman. Confidential.

Tonight, I was driving near the Vatican. On a hunch, decided to reconnoitre the College where HO'F lives. Forbidding-looking building. Own graveyard. Rather Gothic. Sort of place one imagines vampire priests. At midnight the porter came out but did not lock the door. Taking a chance, I entered. The hallway was dark. Religious pictures, a lurid crucifix, the usual tat. A pile of mail for residents; I looked through it but could find nothing intended for HO'F. I began to ascend the staircase, but the sounds of men talking (I assume the students) dissuaded me. See if someone working there can be compromised. A servant or skivvy. Maybe another priest. We'll pay.

———————

Wednesday 22nd December
11.49 a.m.
59 hours and 11 minutes before the Rendimento

When he wakes, the fever has broken. His skin feels new. The air in the room smells of woodsmoke and beeswax.

The bells in St Peter's clang dolefully for noon. Women are singing the Angelus.

Pages from his jotter lie in flitters around the eiderdown. Horrified, he sees they are covered in his handwriting: names of the Choristers, locations of hiding places. He gathers and rips them, washes the ink from his fingers. The bedsheets and pillowcase are smudged with black, too. The tell-tale pen on his locker.

Some winter days in Rome have ice-blue eyes, a freezing stare.

From the bedside drawer he takes his darts, stands shakenly to the dart-board on the back of his door. The darts cold and weighted, *heavier* than they are, threading flight paths from his fingertips to the sockets of the board.

Fthunk.

Thrunk.

Double top.

One hundred.

Then the livid red iris of the bull.

Like writing something down. Nailing air into numbers. Little wonder it assuages his dreads. Pull the darts, they come out. Throw them sharp, they go in. A cork-and-wire battlefield where a squint is a rapier and the points stab nothing worth adding.

Long minutes, he plays. An hour disappears. Measuring, thinking, planning out the shots. Trying to think like Hauptmann, to reason like him, to *be* him. Trudges a thousand metres of linoleum between the mark and the board, the board and the mark, the oche and the door, feathered flights in his hands, hidden routes in his mind, and every time he throws one, a fugitive is rescued and the *fthunk* sends Hauptmann stone mad.

From his desk he takes the file of cuttings he assembled in the Germany section of the Vatican Library, clippings mentioning Hauptmann from the German newspapers: the regionals and locals, the Party publications, a one-line reference here, a brief paragraph there, even the entry from his School Yearbook back in Stuttgart. Know your enemy, they say. See through his eyes. A photograph of him leading a Hitler Youth hike. The announcement of his engagement to be married. Wife's name is Elise. Two children, one adopted. Joined the SS, '34. Graduated from the Führerschule der Sicherheitspolizei, '38. Former Kriminalkommissar. Boy Most Likely to Succeed.

From time to time, he dons a threadbare dressing gown and inches barefoot down to the hall, on the pretext of expecting a Christmastime letter from home, but no message about Sam Derry – about anything – has arrived.

He tries to place a call to the hospital, then to Delia Kiernan or the Contessa, but the Vatican's telephones are dead; no one knows when they'll be fixed. The editorial in this morning's *Messaggero* is hinting that the Nazis have cut the lines, that the invasion of Vatican City will happen within days.

Three weeks ago, at the start of December, he applied for a haircut pass, as all Vatican residents must, a complicated process involving a letter in triplicate to the Curia. Usually, he cuts his own hair in a shaving mirror, badly, but the students have begun to pass remarks. If granted, the permission to leave the Vatican and enter Rome will be for one hour and ten minutes. Armed guards will conduct him to the barber's and back.

At two, he goes out to the loggia to see if the pass has arrived and is surprised when the *portiere* finds it.

'You look poorly, *Monsignore*.'

'I'm improving, Giancarlo, *grazie*.'

'*Con rispetto*, I can cut your hair if you wish, *Monsignore*? To save you the trouble?'

'I could do with getting out.'

'Very good, I will send a message to say you're ready. Three o'clock?'

'Three o'clock it is. *Grazie*, Giancarlo.'

'*Prego*.'

The two troopers sent to convey him are clumsy and young. Helmets loose, grimy tunics ill-fitting. They stumble on Rome's cobbles, seem uncertain of the direction, their confusion occasioning halts and bleak, muttered squabbles over the blurrily printed military map they've been issued, itself twenty years out of date. He could indicate to them the right road, with gestures, a pointing finger, but he feels they'd resent it, as they about-turn and double-back, and he longs to happen into someone who might get a message to the hospital, but suddenly, as he and the soldiers pass through an arch into a high, cold piazza, they are moving through a party of black-clad SS officers taking photographs of the statuary on a church's facade, their death's-head cap badges shining. Now he sees that Hauptmann is among them, but alone, looking distracted, out of sorts, scrawling in a wire-bound notebook, conversing with no one.

The barber, Orlandi, wrestler fat, damply breathless, must be the only one of his profession in Rome with little to say. From the mirror a taped-up newspaper photograph of the Lazio soccer team stares down on his sink, beside an icon of the Black Madonna and a postcard of Betty Grable in a swimsuit.

'You're a Lazio man, Orlandi?'

'For my sins, Father.'

'I never saw a better striker than Piola.'

One of the troopers emits a hiss, puts a finger to his lips. No talking.

'These sausage-munchers think they can boss us,' the barber sings quietly, in Italian, as though half-remembering an aria he heard a long time ago. 'The kid's half my age, impudent prick, and he's telling me when I can talk? In my own place, too. You want me to shave you while you're here, Father?'

Mixing the soap in a pewter mug, he strops the razor seven times and croons onward. 'Turn your face for me, Father. That's it.' Shaving his nape hair. 'Be done soon. Kick this sausage-muncher's ass. Alleluia.'

Opening a package of Old Golds, Orlandi lights one, drags on it, places it in a scallop-shell ashtray – as an afterthought offers a smoke to the troopers.

'Go ahead, help yourselves,' he says amiably, in Italian. 'You ugly sons-of-bitches.'

'*Danke schön*,' they reply, understanding his gestures but not his words. Not that you can ever be sure of their ignorance. Some pretend not to understand; it's a part of their training, another way of listening to the conquered.

'And your mother,' mutters Orlandi. 'I hope you get shot.'

24

Through puffed smoke, they grin, nodding, coughing gratitude.

'*Allora*,' he says, 'Been to the movies lately, Father?'

'Not in a while.'

'Only, I wouldn't go tonight. If you know what I'm saying. Little birdie told me the picture house in Prati might be best avoided.'

'Why so?'

'Certain out-of-towners frequent the place. I hear there's a welcome planned. The kind of Christmas present where someone lights a fuse and starts running.'

On the way back to the Vatican he sees Hauptmann again, now seated outside a café with a man in plainclothes. The soldiers salute as they pass but Hauptmann and the other don't notice, Hauptmann taking minuscule sips from a tumbler of water, the subordinate drinking red wine and operating what appears to be an addition machine as he listens, nodding, unpicking a paperclip, pausing to smoke. A beggarwoman approaches. Hauptmann gives her a coin.

Half an hour after the priest and the soldiers have departed, the barber, whistling and cursing, goes to his till to fetch some change. On a banknote, six scrawled figures he didn't notice when the Monsignor handed it to him:

'Bach 21.'

In the code known to the Choristers' supporters, '21' means 'urgent'.

'Bach' means Enzo Angelucci is to make contact by any means available.

Orlandi shutters his shop and starts walking.

———

Thursday 23rd December
7.00 a.m.
Exactly 40 hours before the Rendimento

Fthunk.

Thrunk.

He pulls the darts from the board.

Throws again.

Still no message.

Last night's grenade attack on the cinema is not mentioned in the newspapers but he is certain it happened, one of the younger priests was called to the scene. Three German soldiers, a Roman woman and the projectionist were killed. He wonders why the news has been censored, what Hauptmann's reprisal will be.

Perhaps a deathbed summons will come today, a legal reason to leave the Vatican, the fifth of a square mile to which he has been confined for so long. It seems improper to pray that someone would be close to death, although many in Rome are closer than they know. Many more soon will be.

He lobs volleys of unseeable darts across the city to Angelucci. *Come to the Piazza. You are needed urgently. Derry is sick, for all I know may be dead. We need you to run the Christmas Eve mission. Come to the Piazza tomorrow at noon. Wait by the colonnade. Do not leave.*

Opening his Bible at random, he allows his fingertip to find a verse. Matthew 27:52. 'And the graves were opened; and many bodies of the saints which slept arose.'

He shaves in a bowl, dresses, hurries the rainswept hundred metres across the courtyard from the Collegio to the Holy Office, where he switches on the lights and climbs the marble stairwells and says Mass alone but for his lamplit shadow in the private chapel off the seventh landing.

His left hand is shaking. A flicker in his eyelids. A headache is creeping around his boundaries; he dreads its return.

The fox of his fears prowls a carpet of broken glass.

Some say the Renaissance crucifix on the altar has been seen to move. This morning, that could happen. Others claim the miraculous cross was swapped for a fake many years ago, that the real one is hidden so deeply that no one remembers where.

Glancing out the chapel window, he sees three German tanks nudge into place on Via Rusticucci. Troopers crowbarring up cobblestones, hefting sandbags into clusters around machine-gun posts. A *Panzerjäger* anti-aircraft cannon being aimed along the three hundred metres of space that ends at the doors of St Peter's. Last night Radio Algeria broadcasted 'on cast-iron authority' that an incursion into the Vatican is 'absolutely imminent'. The servants have stopped coming to work.

'*Look again*,' his shadow cackles. '*The crucifix does not move.*'

Mass said, he leaves the Collegio and crosses the passageway to the abandoned Annex, a quattrocento *casa del pellegrino* whose long-planned demolition was delayed by the coming of war. The Rector, a German, is given to joking that he wishes a bomb would be dropped on it. 'The expense saved would be considerable and welcome.'

Up the staircase, through a long corridor where dilapidated statues are stored, to the loft he has made his private nook. For months he has managed to put off the task, but several documents must be written now.

He will limit himself to what can be written in forty minutes, what might be read in thirty. If the invasion does come, he wants his family to know his mind at the last.

So as not to exceed the allotted time, he takes from his pocket and winds his alarm clock, its rusted ratchets rasping. The cockerel down in the yard gives a disconsolate squawk.

He writes hurriedly, in Latin, placing the papers one by one in a metal box, like a cashier's, which he locks with its fat, short key. In an hour, the key will be mailed to his sister in Ireland, with a coded message in mirror-Gaelic, the play language of their childhood, as to where the box is to be found.

He does not know that the key will be lost on its journey, that for decades the box will squat behind the loose wall-plank where in forty minutes he is about to place it, until many years later, when renovation work on the Annex will be halted by a pandemic, and a sinkhole will open, causing a buttressed section of the eastern gable to collapse, vomiting slates and ancient bricks and stained-glass window frames and ancient codices and Bibles and a crucifix said to be miraculous and a rust-blackened metal box and plaster haloes of statues into the mosaicked courtyard below.

MY LAST WILL AND TESTAMENT
23rd December 1943

Since I own almost nothing, I have little to bequeath. My books I ask be given to my sister, Bride, my brothers Jim and Neil, and my parents, James and Margaret, 11 Henn Street, Killarney, County Kerry, in Ireland. I request that, for three years, on the date of my ordination, a Mass for the forgiveness of my sins be offered in the church where I was baptised. The above is the entirety of my Will.

As to my Testament, I should like to tell of a man I never met, an orchestral conductor, a Roman by birth, whose presence in my life — whose absence from it, really — altered how I understood the world and how we are to act in it, if any single event other than the Resurrection may be said to have done that.

In my twenties, once a schoolteacher, now a student for the priesthood, I came to undertake doctoral study in Rome having never previously left my home place. With a cabbage for a brain and the stones of rural Kerry in my shoes, I gaped as the train pulled into Tiburtina.

The multitude of steeples, that pincushion skyline. I can never forget the exhilaration of those first weeks. That quartet of great and majestic basilicas in the gloaming, the hundreds of dark and beautiful churches, the food, the art, the zestful life, the many languages, the glories to be encountered in the Vatican Library: it was like awakening in a land of wonders.

Rome for me is a painter's palette, a chiaroscuro of burnished pinks, old copper, walnut, honey, ivory, mocha. It is also its own music, a piano sonata. I can never hear Clementi without the sight of my beloved adoptive home and the pierce of a spear of longing.

After periods of ministry in Palestine, New York, Haiti and other places, in my early thirties I was summoned to return here. On the evening when I arrived, it happened that a small electrical fire had broken out at the dormitory intended to house me, in a poorly modernised medieval friary, and so I and seven fellow priests were lodged in an old *pensione* on Via Pompeo Magno in Prati, not far from the Vatican. But far enough.

As is the case with all marriages, priesthood has its seasons and tides, the gravities no one warns you about. Yes, there are summer evenings when the stars in the sky may be stirred by the outstretch of a hand, but there are Februaries, too. You'd want to father yourself when those happen. The lonesomeness of priestly life can at times freeze the heart. My Rome thawed it out, helped me breathe again.

I lived in a boarding house for pilgrims, managed by Congolese nuns who had taken the holiest oath of all, an oath of silence. They would point you to the dining table or the sitting room in which we had a wireless, or with a pencil indicate on the map the ancient church you sought. Gentle, unsettling ladies, they ruled with their eyes. I pray God for their safety in the coming days.

Joy it was to live in that house with my good-humoured Mauritian and Romanian confreres and the travellers who came and went. As Chaucer knew, only rarely are pilgrims the drearily spotless saints we imagine; usually they are people who have lived with whole heart. I loved my lecturing work at the College for the Propagation of the Faith, the intelligence of my students, their courage and simple likeability, but, more than that, I loved the Rome I had been given, the bell-song for vespers, the faces of travellers from every land, their languages so strange to me that one wondered *were* they languages, how any two people ever born could have even begun to learn them, the theatre of going through the streets.

There was an ease to Roman life, a taking-in through the senses, the very name of the city a metaphor for patience. The place that wasn't built in a day.

My walk would take me by way of the Spanish Steps, where I would say a silent prayer for that haunted man, John Keats, who died in a house nearby. A sinner, as who is not, but a greater poet than Wordsworth, whom I was never able to forgive for the daffodils.

The place names and direction signs were as jewels set into a mosaic: the Quirinale, the Orti Farnesiani, the Fontana di Trevi, the Arco di Costantino, Santa Maria Maggiore. To say those words aloud was to fizz.

To walk the Via Cola di Rienzo or the aisles of the Mercato Rionale, the great beauty and profusion of the produce, the sweet *prosciutti* and bursting cheeses, the intense sensuousness of any place in Italy where food is bought or sold, to watch the handsome women going about, the mocking way they argued with the stallholders, hefting an avocado here, a stem of luscious tomatoes there, or to cool by the cascade in the Piazza Navona, to sit a while by the Tiber, not a half-hour's walk from my room. Ardent lovers, hand in hand, glitter-eyed and gesturing, alive in the radiance of their need for one another, or the youths full of peaceful silences, as Italians against expectation can be, staring contentedly into a fountain. Romans are like people stepped out of a Caravaggio, long-nosed, alluring, courtly. The street singers, the vagabonds, the bawling men arguing. A painful difficulty about happiness is that we so rarely notice its arrival. In Rome, we would soon know it was gone.

In those days, for a couple of coins, one could attend the Opera on weekday afternoons to watch rehearsal. It was something that gave me immense pleasure. I liked seeing the young music students, their attentiveness and seriousness – we are all drawn to those skills that we do not ourselves possess – and I found it fascinating to hear but also to *see* the orchestra. Once you did not interrupt or make your presence too intrusive, you were permitted to walk right up to the lip of the pit and watch. Their carefulness touched me, their meticulousness in small things. It interested me, for example, to see that the musicians had a particular way of turning the page of a score, double-tapping it with a finger or a violin bow, so that the breeze would not turn the page back.

Such occasions were often used by the company to try new, young conductors from the Conservatorio. Their role enthralled me in a particular way.

What is the conductor doing? I had little idea. Despite what we think, erroneously, when we are children, he is not providing the rhythm or beating out time, but is editing, italicising, adding emphasis, a style. His version of the piece will not be the same as anyone else's on this Earth, though both orchestras are playing from identical sheet music. For that reason, his knowledge of the score must be total, more even than the composer's. Is there any more difficult calling?

The chief tutor of these young conductors – all of whom, notwithstanding his strictness, adored him – was a professor named Vittorio Proietti.

Proietti, an imposing man in his early forties, was a figure one would notice in a room. He was what was termed in those days 'a confirmed bachelor' and had the sensitivity and great graciousness one often encounters in homosexual people. An artist of courtesy and distinguished, dignified fervency, he was the sort of person for whom the Latin noun *gravitas* was coined, a word that has entered many languages because we know it when we see it. Once, I was outside the Teatro, just passing the stage door, when I saw Maestro Proietti step out of his long black Maserati, in his long black cloak, long black cane in hand. It was a sight to make the waves dance.

That evening, I had gone for a simple meal at a trattoria near Piazza Mazzini with two companions, my visiting friend and fellow Kerryman, Dr Maurice 'Moss' Trant, with whom in happier days I studied as a seminarian, and another man whose name I cannot quite recall now, a Chicagoan, a Father Valentini, I think it was. Often when people came into my orbit who were new to Rome, I felt it a pleasant obligation to show them one or two of the little museums that are not in the guidebooks, the hidden chapels and galleries, to break bread with them in the wider city.

Not long before that night, the Fascist emblem had been nailed onto the crest in the Royal Box at the Opera House, a desecration that caused offence to many regular attenders, and gladness, I would hazard, to others. As for me, in those days, I saw all political systems as more or less the same, forms of foolishness, the prattling of apes, designed to keep the lesser chimps down. This was a shameful foolishness of my own. I have come to see that neutrality is the most extremist stance of all; without it, no tyranny can flourish.

When my two companions and I arrived at the Teatro that evening, many of the orchestra members were already in the pit and there arose that special sound that brings such joyous excitement, appealing as it does to the child in every heart, the noise of an orchestra tuning up. The sound that says Reason may be left at the door, Wonders are about to witnessed. A stately, bright trumpet. The seethe of impatient violins. A crescendo of harp arpeggios arising like wavelets and the answering foghorn of a bassoon. God, to be alive at such moments.

A coven of Fascist roughnecks now appeared in the Royal Box, ostentatiously smoking, opening a jeroboam of Prosecco, making self-important nuisances of themselves, but people pretended not to notice. The house lights were extinguished. Out strode Proietti. He stalked to the podium like an early Roman king, half-nodding to the audience with that curious mixture of acknowledgement and disdain that the greatest performers evince.

The overture began, then the first act of the piece, Bellini's *I Capuleti e i Montecchi*. All progressed sumptuously until fifteen minutes into the performance, when from the box came brays of loutishness; the Fascists were drunk. They had brought along as guests certain ladies of the pavement; the misfortunate women themselves were embarrassed by the Fascists' inebriated catcalling and entreated for it to stop, a plea that only seemed to stir the boors on.

At a certain point, one of the yobs called out '*Me ne frego*', a slogan of the Fascists, 'I don't care', and the imbeciles about him whinnied into coarse laughter and bleary cheers. The remark, hitting its target, was shouted a second time. Again, the explosions of glee. The fleeting appreciation of his fellow nonentities is always a powerful fuel to the bullyboy, living as he must with his greatest fear, the dread that even among nobodies he is nothing.

The third time the Fascist motto was howled, Proietti rapped his baton eight or a dozen times against the lectern. The orchestra stuttered to silence, the soprano stopped singing; Proietti folded his arms. He had the air of a person awaiting a tram but not in desperation, a nobleman not bothering to look at his watch. Some in the audience began to hiss, others murmured or shushed. Without turning to face the auditorium, he called out with brisk sternness, '*Signore e signori, silenzio! Abbiate rispetto per gli musicisti!*'

Applause and cheers arose. The orchestra resumed.

As he left the theatre that night, Vittorio Proietti was seen getting into a car at gunpoint.

His body has never been found.

In dreams, I'd often see Banna Strand or the rocks of coastal Kerry, the tiny islands like inkblots splashed by a careless cartographer. The corner of the world where I was reared is known for its stern, stark mountains and mirroring lakes, its raggedness on a map, the attack of its fiddle style, for an imperiousness of character that is sometimes mistaken for mere pride, though it is something far stronger, a pagan identification with place. There's a notion of land and person as expressions of one another, translations.

Kerry people are Kerry people first.

In my childhood the neighbouring counties were lampooned and done down, their indigenes, often our own relatives, the butt of only partly good-natured quips. Corkonians? Arrogant. Limerick people? Sanctimonious. As for derision of the capital city, that was part of the weather. Dublin was 'West Britain'. Her citizens had sold themselves. Prancing like show ponies for their overlords across the water, while the overlords snickered at the effort. My father used to joke that there was only one circumstance in which he could ever bring himself to cheer for England; that would be if an English team were somehow opposing Dublin in the All-Ireland Gaelic football final. 'I'd be draped in the Union Jack.'

Otherwise, England was despised, Perfidious Albion, a despotism. As my poor, ardent grandmother, God be good to her, used to vow into her teacup: 'I'll burn everything English but their coal.'

No matter that our uncles were digging the streets and drains of Coventry, our aunts nursing the sick in Poplar and Camden Town. Their youngsters, our cousins, had the accents and outlooks of England, as how would they not. Money sent home from the kingdom of the conqueror bought shoes for children that were otherwise patriotically barefoot, saved many a widow from famished destitution or the assiduously rationed mercy of the ratepayers. But we in my homeland have a limitless capacity for self-delusion, as all once-conquered peoples have.

England's junta was hated; being hated was its purpose. Hating it drew us together, gave us a banner under which to congregate, when we feared, indeed were coming to see what some had long known, that there was little but clichés and superficialities to bond us. Differing from your enemy is the illusion of a powerful unifier, the moonshine passed around the campfire as the cold dawn comes.

Tens of thousands in my townland had been permitted to starve, whole families my grandmother knew in her girlhood; a million starved throughout the island. They had been informed to their surprise that they were not Kerry folk at all but something called 'British', whatever that meant, subjects of a family living five hundred miles away in one of its many palaces, claiming your allegiance despite doing nothing to earn it. You had never seen any of them. They had never seen you.

But your contract with this London-based family of unemployables was binding. You would work every hour; they would do literally nothing. The fruits of your work would be sent to their acolytes in the form of rent so as not to inconvenience them too much. Had you land, it would be stolen and given to their henchmen. Your religion would be crushed, theirs raised; your language outlawed, theirs established; but when hunger arrived to destroy you the picture would become clearer, that you were not British in the same sense as were the good people of, say, Hampshire. You were a surplus, a sort of trash, the sooner exterminated the better. In every one of her dozens of colonies the whole world round, England and her owners toiled hard at being hated. In Ireland, they received their due.

For this hatred, as constant and intoxicating as the turf smoke in October, we may blame proximity or history or everyday human feeling; but that history sharpened malignly in the years of my youth, when a force of reprobate mongrels, the scum of England's jails, was sent to assist Ireland's constabulary in pacifying the colony, by the jackboot and the noose if needs be. Not for the first time in the star-crossed story of the archipelago, the bout did not come out as planned.

Their viciousness against the people of the countryside was infamous. If one Tan had a stone thrown at him, a village was burned. Prisoners were shot without trial, Catholics arrested without cause, women aggressed, men beaten. Once, in my twenties, a friend and I were walking back to the seminary having paid our respects at a funeral in Limerick city, when a Tan patrol happened along the street and dragged us away to a cell, getting in a good rake of rifle blows and cannonades of cockney spittle along the way. Next morning, an urgent telegram from the Abbot secured our release. It was not a night one would quickly forget.

Hatred of England was deep as the graves, hatred of her armies, deeper.

Thus, when two years ago I was ordered by the Papal Secretariat to serve as an official Vatican visitor to the Italian concentration camps for British prisoners of war, I found myself not wanting to comply. I was in favour of the Vatican's neutrality, and in favour of Ireland's, not that, in either case, anyone outside the rulership was asked. Spells of ministry in London and the New Forest had planted a fondness, indeed a love, of those places and their people in me. But it wrestled with inherited darknesses. And Vanity, the siren of ego, goaded me like a leashed dog: these Vatican appointments are rarely given to non-Italians. But how could I dishonour my home place? I was on the point of writing to His Holiness to ask that I be released from my obligation when the Rector of my college gave me stern, correct counsel. A priest takes a vow of obedience.

The appointed day came. I set out with the Vatican driver, an official photographer and another priest, a Milanese, to the Passo Corese camp some thirty kilometres from Rome, in the countryside. I will say that I had not slept well.

The lands immediately beyond my beloved city are some of the loveliest a weary pair of eyes will ever see: olive and lemon groves, fields of aubergines, vineyards, the ruins of aqueducts, scenery like the background of the *Mona Lisa*, roadside stalls piled high with artichokes and pumpkins. The hot musk of citrus and pine nectar as you open the car window on the winding, high-hedged lanes in summertime. You imagine that if you stuck an old man's walking stick in the earth it would sprout into a gorgeous willow.

I was raised among country people; to me, there is no glory like a farm. Those of the Roman hinterland are so beautiful and pleasing, with their red, loamy soil and well-kept fields, little barns painted ochre, and fat, peaceful cows, the countryfolk handsome and strong. On another day, one's spirit would have soared to the skies. But what was coming would be scorched into me like a branding.

I had ministered in jails before. Not like this. In Durham prison, I once sat a terrible night with a man who was to be hanged at dawn. In Haiti, I saw unspeakable things. But the afternoon that I spent at Passo Corese took five years from my life in as many hours.

Four thousand frightened prisoners crammed like abused beasts, half starved, into a couple of barbed-wired stony fields. One doctor, a drunken pervert. No letters. Two latrines. Compulsory hard labour. Frequent beatings.

Perhaps cruellest, nothing to do, as a matter of policy. No newspapers, no writing materials, not a playing card or a prayer book. Possession of a chessboard meant ten days of solitary confinement in a punishment cell scarcely larger than a coffin. No curtains on the shed windows, so that the wretched men could not even attempt to sleep away their boredom. Each inmate was given one litre of water daily, about two pints, and no more, so that he could not even clean himself, again a deliberate policy. The guards' leader was a vicious, dull-eyed brute, one Müller, later commander of the regional Gestapo before he was sent to the Russian front. One imagined him as a disturbed schoolboy hacksawing the legs off cats.

The photographer and I walked in silence as he made his pictures. I found I was incapable of speech.

What could one say to those emaciated, skeletal men, some of whom were in age no more than boys? I entered their sheds, the yards, saw their bunks, their gaunt bones, their good-fellowship to one another, their dread. The rule was that I was not to speak with them on any matter but might make notes if I wished to and could offer Holy Communion. My notes would be compiled into a report.

The priest who was with me, I do not judge. He had family in Milan and did not want Nazi trouble for them, so he looked away towards the olive groves and the ruins of the aqueducts, his spectacles misting with shame. I am no better than him, as God knows, and might well be worse. I burned to look away, too, but was unable to.

It would have been evident to a blind man that the prisoners had been threatened that they must lie to us. This all of them did, insisting they were in good spirits, well treated and adequately fed. I nodded and uttered my platitudes. There are times when we must permit one another to lie. I wanted none of them to suffer a beating for telling me what I already knew.

The stench in those sheds, I shall never forget, and the fear in the eyes of those prisoners. Their dignity had been systematically stripped from them; they were as whipped orphans. Even some of the guards had the decency to appear ashamed, refusing to meet my stare. Presently a seventeen-year-old boy from Liverpool came to me. About his throat was a medal of St Michael, patron of airborne warriors, and he requested me to bless it, which I did. As we conversed, it transpired that the boy had in fact the same name as my father. He asked to receive the Eucharist.

I knelt there in the filth, and we prayed, James O'Flaherty and me. The German guards did not like this, sent me angry glowers and coarse whispers. Some began barking at me like men trying to take bites out of the air. But the courage of the boy gave me strength, and I continued.

We offered a decade of the rosary together, him counting off the prayers to Our Lady on a length of knotted twine, then he began gently to sing the old hymn 'Abide With Me', and despite having the voice of a jackdaw, I joined him.

A moving custom of the crowd at the Cup Final in England is the communal singing of this hymn before the commencement of the game. Never has it been sung by anyone in Wembley Stadium as stirringly as by Private James O'Flaherty of Bridgewater Street, Liverpool, that day.

God bless that boy, wherever he is as I write. He showed more Christlike manliness in one moment than I have shown in all my life.

Soon, his bravery strengthened his fellows, too. Some limped from their sheds, in nervous twos and threes at first, blinking in the painful sunlight, helping one another along. One prisoner, a Dundonian who was unable to walk, was taken to me in a wheelbarrow. Before the war, he had been a schoolteacher. Others had improvised crutches from tree branches or broken planks. Their accents were of Birmingham, Manchester, Coventry, London, Tyneside, every corner of England, and among them the intonations of Scotland and Wales. They had been captured in North Africa, a good number at El Alamein or in the desert south of Tobruk. Many men, intending respect, addressed me as 'Padre', a term used in their own Church if not mine. Some spoke with hesitant affection of Ireland or of sporting contests between our two countries, in football, steeplechasing, rugby, boxing; others said nothing because they were dumbstruck with fear but looked at me with pleading glances.

I found myself telling them the war was going well, that the Allies would soon wrench Italy back from Fascism; that before long they would be home again with their families. In my pockets I had bars of chocolate and a couple of packs of American cigarettes – I do not myself smoke but they are a currency in Rome, as in all prisons, and I make it my business never to go out without them – and I distributed these among the men, who fell upon them. I had brought a bottle of Sulfaguanidine, diarrhoea medicine; this was received with pitiful gratitude. We spoke again of football and cricket. Some of the prisoners had boxed. A middle-aged man who had been blinded, his head wrapped in russet, bloodied bandages, held my hands as we spoke of Everton, Stoke and the Kop, the glory days of Freddie Steele and Tommy Lawton. A bantering argument began about the ill fortunes of Manchester United, and it was good to see the prisoners laugh and mock one another, pointing and mimicking, to the bemused chagrin of the guards.

Too soon, the appointed time came for us to conclude the visit, this fact being communicated to me by a Nazi sergeant who tapped on his wristwatch and briskly jerked his thumb toward the tall iron gates, which he stalked off to open. I said to the prisoners that we might gather in a circle and say the Lord's Prayer together, that everyone was welcome to stand with us, men of all creeds and none.

One prisoner, an East End Londoner, a fighter pilot downed in Tunisia, whispered to me that he was of the Jewish faith, was being protected by his comrades who told the guards he was a Methodist, but he wanted me to know the truth, he could not pray with us for he did not know the words. I said the greatest Being ever to set foot on the Earth was born a Jew, that it was not important to know the words, we would each of us pray in our own private manner or simply be silent together in examination of conscience and the will to do one another good when we were able.

Now one of the guards ordered me in angry, bitter German to cease what I was at, jolting forward and aiming his rifle at my face. I asked if he would like to join us in the prayer. For one moment, I thought he might.

'I offer you my hand,' I said. 'Take it. Let us pray.'

'I do not need your prayers.'

'Soon enough, you will.'

'What is that supposed to mean?'

'What it says, no more.'

'Are you threatening me?'

'With a prayer? You are easily threatened.'

By now, the camp's commander, Müller, had been summoned from his office, which, I recall, was in the foot of one of the watchtowers overlooking the main gate. He strode towards me with the false bonhomie that is always the mark of the secretly gutless, raising his right arm in the Nazi salute.

'*Heil Hitler*,' he uttered, attempting but not quite succeeding to click his heels.

I offered no reply.

'*Sie sind willkommen*,' he said.

I said nothing.

'Your papers, Father.'

'I presented them on arrival.'

'You will present them on departure, please. To me.'

'Why should I be asked to present my papers on departure?'

'To ensure that you have not given them to a prisoner.'

'You are accusing a representative of His Holiness of breaking the regulations?'

'I hope I never have to.'

'Your discourtesy to an emissary of His Holiness shall of course be noted in my report.'

'No discourtesy was intended. The Reverend Father will excuse me.'

From my briefcase, I produced my wallet of Vatican credentials, and I watched as he pretended to read them, now also pretending to make notes. I could see that he was worried. This pleased me.

'Reverend Father is an Irishman,' he said.

'My nationality is of no concern to you or anyone else. I am here as Envoy Representative of the Vatican City.'

'The Party and the Führer have many admirers in Ireland. Your people have of course fought the British dogs many centuries. Ireland's struggle is well known and admired among all right-thinking persons.'

I did not accept the invitation.

'The prisoners have made no complaints, I assume,' he now remarked, handing me back my documents, refusing to look me in the eye.

'No one has told me he is being ill-treated,' I said. Which was true.

'Good. Excellent. That is gratifying to know. We are not of course –' he gave an unctuous, buttery grin – 'a luxury hotel. That much will be obvious.'

'Yes,' I agreed. 'That much is obvious.'

'Nevertheless, we do our best. With straitened resources. My requests for food and medical assistance are often not listened to, by Berlin. And I have not enough men, as you will have seen for yourself. I send a telegram once a week. One may as well throw it in the river. Many in Berlin are of course careerists and bureaucrats, nothing more. They have no understanding of war. One may as well be dealing with women.'

'You dare to criticise the Reich,' I said. 'That fact, too, shall be entered in my report.'

One could almost hear the cogs squeal in the private hell of his mind. Crows on the barbed-wire fence squawked bleakly.

'Of course not,' he replied. 'I am a loyal servant of the Reich. It was merely that I wished the Reverend Father to know of the background to the work we are doing here. It is not easy, you know. Wartime, so on. Often our hands are tied.'

'I am to inform His Holiness the Pope that wartime means these men may not be given water?'

'There must be discipline,' he said.

'Must there?'

'Of course.'

'Where do you see the line between discipline and torture?'

'No man here has been tortured. To say so would be a slur.'

'Five minutes ago, I was ordered to leave. Stand out of my way.'

'But in honour of the Reverend Father's visit and as a mark of respect to the Vatican, I shall increase the water ration to two litres today. There is no need for undue harshness, after all.'

'You are a disgrace,' I said, then. 'You miserable, pitiable coward. You would be wise to un-holster your pistol and shoot me, this minute. Because, if it is the last thing I ever do, I will have you dismissed. I give you my solemn word. You vermin.'

'Reverend *Father*—'

'I shall return in one week. Have this abattoir in decent order. And make certain you're not here. *Auf Wiedersehen.*'

I visited many more of the prison camps, some eighty installations across Lazio and beyond. If there were occasions when I witnessed the prisoners treated properly in accordance with international law, I am sorry to say they were few. Fewer still were the times when I saw anything like the simple human decency that should not need legislating for, but usually does.

Mostly it was a matter of dismal, everyday belittlement, guards lording it over prisoners, standing in their way, making schoolyard remarks about their wives and mothers back home and so on, rather than outright physical violence. But there were times when one encountered a little Göring who needed putting in his place. At any rate, thus I saw things.

Meanwhile, things in the city were worsening.

It was my habit at that time, for the sake of my health, to walk briskly every day from the Collegio to the Victor Emmanuel monument ('the Altar of the Fatherland') and back, a trek of six kilometres or so. If it was hot, I broke the ordeal with an orange juice at a little bar on the Via del Portico d'Ottavia, in the quarter of the Jews, one of those places where you stand at the zinc and engage your neighbour in the talk of the day or are pleasingly left to mind your own business.

One noontime, I was at that counter, reading a copy of the *Chicago Tribune* someone had left behind, when a commotion out in the street took my attention. A group of the Fascist police had stopped and emptied a tram and were forcing a Jewish lady and her husband, a Rabbi, to their knees, mocking these elderly people and calling them vile names. One swine handed the old couple a toothbrush and instructed them to clean the pavement, his fellows having a mighty laugh at his brilliance. I went out and demanded the bullies' names and that of their superior officer – I had on priestly clothing, which fact I thought might soften their cough for them – and, during the noisome squabble that ensued, the old couple managed to make away into a side alley. But it was a sickening piece of casual cruelty. The fact that these innocent Romans had been abused in a busy street, at noon, as hundreds passed by, was itself a sort of poison.

One afternoon in late '42, just over a year ago, not long after I had returned to my quarters in the Vatican from a prison-camp visit, the Rector of the College, a good man now deceased (he died of influenza two months ago; Lord have mercy on his soul) sent a message requesting my presence. I was hungry, weary, dishevelled with dust, had been on the road nineteen days and was low in my spirits, wall-fallen a little, the camps having brought this about. The pleas made to me by the prisoners had kept me awake many nights. But I washed at the sink as best I could and put on the cleanest soutane I could find. Seeing the Rector, a learned theologian and exegetist if a somewhat humourless Berliner, was rarely an occasion of light chat.

As I entered his study, he appeared troubled, more anxious than I had seen him. It disturbed me a little that he was smoking. He beckoned me to his desk, gestured that I was to be seated. We had always got on civilly enough, the Rector and I, despite my lack of capacity in German, perhaps *because* of it, in an odd way. Sometimes, I have found, when people are not fluent in one another's languages, conversations become limited to bald pleasantry.

On his desk was an unruly stack of the reports I had compiled on conditions in the camps. It struck me as odd that the Rector had read my despatches, that someone must have had them translated, for I had written them in English. I had not sent them to him. I wondered who had.

Addressing me by my forename, he said he was *in Schwierigkeiten*. Which I knew meant 'in difficulties'.

I indicated as best I could that I saw distress in his face, that I was sorry to know he was burdened and would consider it a blessing to share the weight if he would permit me.

He began speaking to me in Latin, quietly.

Was it true that, some time ago, I had interfered with an attempted arrest of a couple in the Jewish quarter? An official complaint about me had been made by the authorities.

I answered that the elderly Rabbi and his wife were being victimised in the street, that I would interfere again if such an outrage required me to do so.

'You would?'

'Yes, Rector.'

'I see.'

He made a note.

'You surely know,' I said, in Latin, 'what is being planned and done to the Jews.'

Refusing to answer appeared to give him almost physical distress. Eyes shut, he rocked a moment, inhaling through his nose.

Was it also the case, as the official complaint asserted, that I had distributed books and food among the Allied prisoners of war in the camps on dozens of occasions, in defiance of the agreed regulations?

'I suppose so.'

A further note was made.

Then pausing, he tore out the page on which he had scribbled, carefully shredded it to pieces, and looked at me.

'These are not the correct answers, Hugh.'

'With respect, Rector, what are?'

At this point he picked up and rang a handbell that sat on his desk. A very young nun I had never seen before came into the office and stood by the window. She explained that she would be acting as interpreter for this meeting.

Adding to the surrealism of the moment was the terrible detail that the young Sister's right hand was missing.

The Rector touched his fingers together and told me he was not a Nazi.

I did not know how to reply.

He despised the National Socialists and all they were doing. 'To my Germany, to Europe, to the People of the Book.' Everything about them was *schrecklich*.

'Horror,' said the Sister.

'Abscheulich, entsetzlich, fürchterlich,' he continued. *'Grässlich. Schauderhaft. Widerwärtig.'*

As she translated these words, all variations of the same word, the Rector's whole face became slick with grief. He wept.

The Papacy was neutral, he continued. This must be respected. It was a matter of international treaty, was not open to debate. The Vatican ('our Mother') must be protected from Nazi invasion or bombing. Beyond the pastoral realm, visiting the sick and so on, what happened in wider Rome or Italy was none of our proper concern. In any event, there was nothing we could do about it.

But the Vatican, we must defend, as was her God-given right and our solemnest duty as Christ's ordained soldiery. Provocations of even the smallest kind were to be avoided. The Nazis were burning for a pretext, 'like a dragon lusting'. Imagine what would happen were *they* to disrespect the treaty, perhaps cross the boundary, roll their Panzers into the square. The Musei Vaticani might be burned to the ground. Or worse.

'Picture it, Hugh,' he said, 'the swastika flying from the dome of St Peter's.'

That would be a special obscenity, I agreed.

'So, you will give an assurance that you will desist from doing anything that could cause difficulty. Won't you, Hugh?'

'It has never been my intention to cause difficulty,' I said.

'Does that mean yes?'

'I would rather you did not ask.'

'Why so, Hugh?'

'Because I should prefer not to tell you anything that would bring you distress.'

He nodded.

'Stand up, please, Hugh,' he said, and he crossed to the door of the anteroom. Into the study strode the Holy Father.

The young nun genuflected. I was unable to move.

His face always has austerity when one observes it in photographs but is capable of tenderness, too, when one sees it in person, which I had only ever done once, from a fifty-metre distance, while assisting with a hundred other priests at High Mass for Easter. But there was nothing at all of kindliness that evening in the Rector's study. He looked as one carved of granite.

Like a slow-moving cold front he walked to the leaded window, now peering into St Peter's Square below.

I swallowed beady tears. Blood throbbed in my eardrums. A sudden and dreadful thirst possessed me, so that I would have drunk from the blackened ocean I found myself picturing.

He turned.

For what seemed a long time, the Holy Father looked at me without blinking, an expression of stony disapproval flinting his eyes, long arms by his side, like a soldier's in an honour guard. The gold crucifix about his neck caught the twilight. From far above us, I heard a bomber, then the dull wail of the air-raid siren from Parione. Even these did not cause him to flinch. The young Sister brought a chair. He nodded gratitude to her but ignored it. When, finally, he moved, it was to brush something invisible from the skirts of his impossibly white robe.

'The celebrated Monsignor O'Flaherty,' he said. 'We are honoured to make your acquaintance.'

I approached and kissed his hand but felt him draw away.

'Do you know Shakespeare, my son?' he asked, quietly, in Latin, and I said I knew a little, had read some of the plays as a young man training for school teaching.

'Which ones?'

'*Macbeth*, Holy Father. *The Merchant of Venice.*'

'You would appreciate that one,' he said. 'It being about a Jew.'

The air in the room seemed to be changing colour.

'We used to act,' he said now, with an icy smile that unnerved me. 'In High School. We were not very gifted.'

He paused as though providing a space he expected me to fill, but I felt that, if I did, he would interrupt immediately, which I had heard him do many times

44

during the wireless broadcasts of his weekly audiences with the faithful. It is a thing done by men as a way of italicising their power.

'And then,' he continued, 'in the seminary a little. We were permitted a Drama Club. Supervised by the authorities, of course. The milder classical plays. Things like that.'

I was lost as to what response was required.

'Did you ever act, my son?'

'No, Holy Father.'

'Truly? Never? That seems odd.'

'In the Christmas play as a boy, nothing more than that.'

" 'In the Christmas play as a boy, nothing more than that,' " he repeated, another tactic I have witnessed him deploy.

'Yes, Holy Father.'

'I have the feeling that you are acting now,' he said.

'Holy Father, forgive me, I do not follow.'

'*NO, YOU DON'T!*'

I had never heard him shout. Hearing it shocked me. It was not a raised voice but a furious bellow, almost a scream, that made something glass in the room vibrate. The Rector bowed his head, the young Sister appeared terrified. The Holy Father dried his mouth with a handkerchief.

'Do you wish to ruin everything?' he said. '*Answer when we address you.*'

'Holy Father—'

'You wish to see our Vatican, where repose the bones of our greatest pontiff, a saint who knew Jesus Christ *in person*, a man who witnessed the very transfiguration itself, in smogs of flame and poison gas? The storm troopers' jackboots trampling the martyrs' graves. Two thousand years of Christ's dominion destroyed in a single night of firestorms.'

'No, Holy Father.'

'No, *Holy* Father. No, Holy *Father*. The sour, black irony of your pretended respect. But why do you address us thus, when you are evidently the only priest in the world never to have undertaken the vows of submission? When you have a special dispensation to formulate your own rules and procedures. To ignore decisions and orders deliberated by your betters. Surely it is we, the Bishop of Rome, who should genuflect before *you*. *È bene.*'

At this, he put his hand on the desk and made to kneel down, until the nun

45

and then the Rector hurried over and pleaded with him not to do such an appalling thing. The young Sister's lips were trembling, her face contorted in shocked sorrow.

'Surely the Saviour Himself and all the saints should offer prayers to O'Flaherty,' he continued. 'We beg you, O'Flaherty. *Ora pro nobis*, O'Flaherty. Intercede for your inferiors from whatever pulpit of vainglory you preach from. *Have you an explanation you would like to offer for your filthy arrogance and insolence?*'

I began to speak. He interrupted me.

'We hereby strip you of your authority as a Vatican representative. Until further notice you will remain in this college or go one hundred metres to your work in the Holy Office every morning and home from it every evening, nowhere else, I say *nowhere*, without written permission in advance. You will not set foot outside the walls of Vatican City again until we permit it. You will reflect on the gravity of your errors and atone for them. *Do you hear me?*'

'Yes, Holy Father.'

'Because of *you*, those prisoners are to have no further visits.'

I felt that he was about to strike me across the face.

'How sharper than a serpent's tooth it is, to have a thankless child,' he said, bitterly. '*King Lear*. Act One. Scene four.'

With that, he swept from the office. The Rector said nothing. His silence, his very decency blazed me like a furnace, as he looked at his hands and the floor. He was merciful enough not to say that I had brought shame on the Collegio as he murmured that our meeting had concluded.

I went at once to my room and tried to sit with the shock of what had happened, as well as the grave sin of my disobedience. The Holy Father's words had scalded away my egotism, and I prayed that his indomitability would be rewarded. It came to me that what we find convenient to call charity is often vanity in camouflage, merely a way of floating up smoke signals of superiority about ourselves, or *to* ourselves, so that the smoke will conceal our ugliness.

Weeping, I pictured the men in the camps, their worn faces and wounded hands as they had reached to me in supplication or simple friendship. I prayed hard for all prisoners, as hard as I could, for the circumscribed of the world, this wretched sinner included.

For six months I remained in Vatican City. In time the Rector took pity and mitigated my sentence. Following the commencement of aerial bombing in July this year, I was permitted to attend the Irish Legation fortnightly, then weekly, there to offer pastoral support to the young Irish Religious and their hosts, if solemnly I undertook not to speak with anyone else and not to come to the attention of the authorities.

I can say with honesty that I gave the latter undertaking every effort I could. On the former point, I need now to confess that, while en route to or from the Legation, I would sometimes permit myself to converse with individuals whom I knew were in small ways aiding escaped prisoners and other fugitives to make their way to the coast. It was at that time a matter of a few lire here and there, sometimes a change of clothing. I knew I was in contravention and nevertheless continued. I ask prayers for the forgiveness of my disobedience.

On 13th September, a couple of days after the Nazi invasion of Rome, an urgent note came to this house that many of the Dominican friars at San Clemente had fallen gravely ill with the consumptive flu, which of late seems rampant around Italy. There being a contingent of pilgrims trapped in the city at that time, an English-speaking helper was needed to hear confessions. A pass to leave the Vatican and enter Rome for two hours would be arranged for the acceptor of the message.

That Monday was on the roster as a day of rest for me. I had intended to study and pray, for I was very afraid of what the German incursion might mean, but I decided that I would instead offer to volunteer at San Clemente. At the back of it, I think, was the hope of perhaps encountering someone from home. Perhaps, too, I wished to test if I had been forgiven by now, if the sentence of internal exile imposed by the Holy Father might receive official parole. I telephoned the Papal Curia and explained the pressing need of the Dominican Brothers. An hour passed before my call was returned. Permission was given for me to accept, but I was to speak with absolutely no one outside of San Clemente. Would I promise before God not to do so? I did.

Setting out on my motorcycle, I saw many German soldiers in the streets around the Vatican, dishevelled and unshaven, a rabble. Some were manhandling women or roaring for drink at the proprietors of cafés. Others were older than me, gaunt men in their fifties, or were boys in ill-fitting grey drabs. At one point I saw a man I know, John May, on the street, and our eyes met in greeting but neither of us made to stop and engage the other in talk. He looked fearful and exhausted, and this pained me to see, for usually he is a cheerful, bright Londoner.

Chillingly, as I passed one alleyway, I heard an abrupt burst of machine-gun fire.

Arriving at the church, I went directly into the sacristy. Often, I think of San Clemente as my most beloved Roman place of worship. It is far from the most beautiful, the largest, the most ornate, but always seems cooler and airier than it is, an atmosphere that raises the exhausted spirit, like a ladling of cold water after a banquet. There were indeed many people coming in and out, praying quietly, some admiring the frescoes or waiting in lines at the confessionals, but none of the monks was about, so I entered the first available confession box I saw and began to minister.

For an hour, all was normal enough. It felt a blessing to offer the mercy of the confessional. There arose the unearthly beauty of the choir and organist practising a piece I have loved since boyhood, Perosi's *Missa Eucharistica*, beautiful baritone timbres thickening the sound. And then, a thing occurred that was so frightening that I must commit report of it to paper. Should anything happen to me in the coming times, this event may explain it.

I opened the small, grilled hatch separating priest from penitent. As is the best custom, I did not look through, but continued facing ahead of myself, eyes closed. There was silence for some moments, an occurrence not all that unusual. People can be troubled before confession.

'Friend,' I said, at length. 'Leave anxieties beyond. Know you speak to the Unending Compassion, not to me.'

The voice, a man's, commenced reciting the introductory prayer monotonously, as though reading it out from a card.

In the usual way, I asked how long it had been since the person's last confession.

'I am not here to answer questions,' came the reply.

'My brother,' I responded. 'You are a long way from home.'

'So are you.'

'Come with openness. Our sins are a tomb. Roll back the stone.'

He said nothing.

It was so quiet that I could hear the ticking of his wristwatch from the other side of the hatch. To my astonishment, I now saw, when I glanced through the grille, the livery of a Gestapo commander.

'My name is Paul Hauptmann,' he said in English.

I made no response.

'We have not met,' he continued.

'This is a place of worship.'

'The door was open. I entered.'

'How dare you.'

I went to slam closed the grille, but his gloved hand stopped it.

'I have not finished speaking, Monsignor.'

'I want nothing to do with you.'

'I should like you to know something. A fact that is important. When two years ago you were selected as Vatican Envoy to our prisoner-of-war camps, it was I as Gestapo Officer overseeing Lazio who made the appointment, from a list of suggested persons.'

'You?'

'I wanted an Irishman leading the delegation. For reasons that are obvious.'

'Such as?'

'Unlikelihood of undue sympathy with the enemy.'

'Leave this holy place.'

'I misjudged you. You were weak. I had forgotten that an intelligent man can also be – in fact, usually is – naive.'

'I have nothing to discuss with you.'

'Nor I with you, Monsignor. But I will offer a piece of advice. *I* run this city now. You would be wise to remember it. In future do not go making trouble, for yourself and others.'

'Meaning?'

'Meaning we must have responsibility, cool heads. Respect for realities. Your addiction to belittling Wehrmacht commanders of the prison camps in front of their soldiers made you feel better, perhaps. I am aware that you did this often. Know, the commandant who succeeded Müller when your report recommended his dismissal is the most brutal thug ever to don a uniform. All your stunts ever accomplished was the worsening of conditions for those prisoners. The measurable worsening of thousands of lives. When there was no need for that. A pity.'

'Have you finished?'

'Ask yourself sometime, who brought about your removal from the delegation.'

'The Papacy brought it about.'

'You think so?'

His question, which was not a question, floated between us for a moment.

'I know there is an Escape Line,' he said. 'I will crack it. Believe me.'

I offered no reply. His voice became quieter.

'Berlin has ordered, no Escape Line. Or I shall suffer harsh consequences. Which means my family would suffer in turn, and I do not permit that to happen. I do not suffer consequences. I inflict them.'

'So I notice.'

'Order in Rome is my duty,' he continued. 'Do not make further difficulties, Monsignor. The slightest cooperation with an Escape Line would result in sentence of death. If you find that your friends are tempted – if you are tempted yourself – remember this conversation.'

'There are people awaiting confession. Again, I ask you to leave.'

'Your stubbornness, Monsignor, is standing in your way. Clouding your thinking. You are drunk on false virtue. Our movement will not be halted. Indeed, we have many priests, many Roman Catholics who support us. You would be amazed if I told you.'

'I would be disgusted and ashamed but not amazed.'

'My own wife is a Roman Catholic.'

'In that case she, too, should be ashamed.'

'Of her husband? Of her country?'

'And herself.'

'Rome fell, Monsignor. The British Empire will fall. So, too, the Soviet Union and the United States. All empires will fall. But one.'

'Yours will fall, too. Sooner than you think.'

'Not certain, are you, Monsignor? I hear the doubt in your voice. It is part of my training, to hear the doubt in the voice. But it is part of your own training, too, no? To listen to the poor captives? As they stutter their little failings in this box.'

'There is no captive here but yourself.'

'Be part of the march, Monsignor. Or don't stand in its way, I warn you.'

'You are part of nothing at all but your own self-hatred and irrelevance. Parades and processions and games of dressing up.'

A sob of grim laughter. 'Says a priest?'

'You are each of you alone in the pit of your inadequacies.'

'Rhetoric, Monsignor. Get down from your pulpit. I am not one of the sheep to be impressed by old women's prattle, and in truth you're not much of a sheepdog.'

'Get out,' I repeated. 'Before I kick you out.'

'You like hearing yourself say that, don't you, Monsignor? Not that you'd try it. All posturers are cowards. And all priests are afraid of life.'

'We'll see who the coward is when they're dragging you up a gallows.'

'Only know that you can be liquidated at any instant, Monsignor. It would be like snuffing out one of the candles those deluded outside pay a few lire to light, as they cower before gilt-stained idols set up by you and your ilk to frighten them into doing your will. You are alive because I tolerate it. You are the candle I burn. And I can choose my moment carefully for when your extinguishment is most useful. In the meantime, good day to you, Monsignor. Consider yourself advised.'

'I am not afraid of you,' I said.

'You will be,' he replied.

After he left, I stayed where I was for a couple of minutes, trying to calm myself. When I went outside, my motorcycle was in flames.

From the distance, the stutter of machine guns.

As he walks away from the burning motorcycle outside the church of San Clemente, Paul Hauptmann wipes his fingers on a scrap of paper he rips from a
loose-flapping poster, 'DEATH TO THE FASCIST INVADERS'. Glad he
didn't take the car. A good day to stroll a few kilometres.

The September sunshine is warm and golden, autumnally Roman; laurels
sweeten the air as he crosses the little park near the marble staircase on which,
people say, Christ once walked. Nonsense, of course, but let them have their
stories. A line from Shakespeare arises at the thought. 'What fools these mor-
tals be.'

From time to time, they stare at him, the conquered Romans and their children. Let them stare. They'll get used to him. No choice. He is new, unfamiliar,
only a few days in command of their city; they can be forgiven a slight sullen-
ness; their situation is not easy. He could go about with a bodyguard but that
would be seen as weakness. The Luger on his hip is all the bodyguard he needs.
That, and the reputation he's been careful to stoke through his leaks to the
Fascist press. Should a Roman attack the Gestapo, the reprisal will be the
dynamiting of seven city blocks and the hanging of the attacker's parents.

At the headquarters he's established at the German Cultural Institute on
Via Tasso, he issues a directive to his men: no looting, Rome's businesses are
not to be thieved from. Women are to be respected. Proven rape will be punishable by death. The enemy shall be permitted to bury his battle-dead with
dignity. Furlough will be allowed, but you will behave as a soldier of Germany.
I am proud of you. Commander Paul Hauptmann.

It rankles, the priest's accusation about being alone. He shouldn't let it
bother him but when one is tired and under strain, nonsenses can hit home
harder.

Typists have arrived, radio engineers, Nazi clerks. Wehrmacht masons are
mortaring bars into the windows of the smaller rooms on each floor, installing
manacles and leg-irons, draping the walls with horse blankets for soundproofing.

A dentist's chair has been requisitioned and is being bolted to the floor of the cellar, restraint straps and a strangle-wire will be added soon. His second-in-command, Dollman, wants a gallows erected on the stage of what used to be the concert room, more for the dread its sight will induce in prisoners than for every-day usage, but that might be a bit much, the room adjoins the typists' office after all. The electrical supply to most of the building has failed; men are coming to get it reconnected. It pleases him to see the work being done, the set-up of governance. A lick of paint would be good; he records a memorandum on the subject. Perhaps a bit of new furniture. Those curtains are shabby. The sundial in the garden is broken.

As for those cheap, horrible reproductions adorning every wall, have them removed, he tells a secretary, we are in the city of Michelangelo. Fresh flowers and a borrowed Madonna in every public room of the headquarters. 'My wife says I'm inhuman,' he deadpans, 'before my coffee in the morning. Be sure I never need wait too long.'

At three o'clock, a captured deserter is brought before him, a young soldier from Bremen. He listens to the weeping boy's case, wishes there was an option for clemency. 'I will write to your parents to say you died in battle,' he says, 'so there will be no disgrace. It is sad we've come to this, be brave at the last,' shakes his hand before sending him downstairs to the yard to be shot. The sordidness of war. The wretched, filthy waste. When *all* of us have moments in which we would desert our lives if we could, if only it weren't too late. But it is. The crack of the pistol volley appears to upset one of the typists, but that can't be helped. Christ, the squalor things come to. War is war.

An idea has been nudging him, to bring the family to Rome. Is it feasible? Where would they live? Would the danger be immense? It's a balance, but isn't everything, now. The warmth, the sunlight, the statuary, ancient temples. Perhaps good for the children, to live a season or two abroad.

On the telephone from Berlin, his wife seems distracted. Their daughter has a cold, their son is in trouble again at school, very slow with his letters, disobedient, introspective. In her voice, he hears anxiety, a sort of false glee she attempts when he calls. He wonders if she's drinking again. She sounds tired.

'Are you eating properly, Paul?'

He tells her he is.

'Is your barrack all right?'

'It's good.'

'I miss you,' she says. 'I wish you were home.'

'*Wenn ich mir was wünschen dürfte*,' he whispers, the title of an old love song they associate with their courtship. 'If I could wish for something.' The phrase has become a sort of private tenderness between them.

'You're sweet,' she says.

'Because I love you.'

'Paul, did Himmler call again?'

'I can't say on the telephone.'

'Are we in trouble, Paul?'

'No.'

'Then, why does he keep calling you?'

'There's no need to worry. It's only a difficulty.'

'That's why they pay you the big money, my darling,' she jokes. 'To solve them.'

'That's why they pay me the big money, you're right.'

A line from an American gangster movie they saw while on honeymoon in Guernsey. Somehow it became part of their couple-talk.

'Have those prisoners stopped escaping?' she asks.

'Sweetness, I can't discuss it.'

'So unfair of them, rotten nuisances, causing problems for my Paul. You'd tell me the truth, wouldn't you? If we were in trouble with Himmler?'

'I'd tell you the truth. We're not.'

'If those prisoners keep escaping—'

'Elise, let's not speak of it.'

'Are the Roman women beautiful?'

'Not as beautiful as you.'

'Liar.' She laughs. 'I wish I could kiss you.'

'I wish that, too, darling. To cover your body with kisses.'

'Don't say such things, Paul, when I'm lonely without you.'

'Sweet girl, get some rest. I adore you.'

'I, you.'

'Goodnight then, little dove. Let's speak again tomorrow. I've an idea to put to you, might be a nice thing for the family.'

'One last time, can you tell me we're not in trouble with Himmler? Because

I'd worry myself sick, Paul. Those rotten, escaping troublemakers. Why can't they *stay* in their prison camps, must they always cause a problem? Don't they *want* their wives and girlfriends to know they're safe, away from war? If *you* were in a prisoner-of-war camp, I'd be glad you were safe.'

'Elise—'

The line goes dead.

On his desk, Himmler's telegram:

'Führer incensed by these recent escapes. STOP THIS EMBARRASS-MENT. I warn you.'

From a drawer he retrieves a file of photographs he's been collecting in recent months. People worth looking at again, possible collaborators, suspects. Placing them painstakingly into alphabetical order by surname, he pauses from time to time, to extract a photograph from the folder and pin it to the cork board above the desk. Persons of Particular Interest. His Portrait Gallery.

He pauses at 'O'.

Pins that photograph to the board.

'O'Flaherty, Hugh' is the name on the label. In pencil he adds the words: 'Troublemaker. Stubborn.'

He blows out the candle.

To bed.

But hard to sleep tonight. Difficult to say why.

It isn't quite anxiety. Not wakefulness alone. It isn't the solitary church bell that tolls the hour through the night, or the silence that follows it, the wait-ing. Some unease for which he has no name has entered him like a splinter.

Darkness.

Fox bark.

Three-in-the-morning Rome.

A man in a box, saying, 'I'm not afraid of you, Hauptmann.'

The silence that follows the bell.

— 6 —

THE VOICE OF ENZO ANGELUCCI
7th November 1962
From transcript of BBC research interview, tape 1,
conducted Bensonhurst, New York City

Speak in here? Like this? You hearing me okay?

So, my name is Enzo Gianluca Alessandro Angelucci. Age, fifty-four. That's right.

I'm living seventeen years in Brooklyn but I was born over there in Rome. People in the States call me Johnny.

Italian-American? Sure. Put the 'Italian' in bold.

When I first came I worked construction, a sheet-rocker, good money. My three brothers and me lived in one room over a deli on the corner of Mulberry and Broome, on boloney and cans of tuna.

Later, things came up. I done good. These days my wife and I got a used restaurant-equipment business on the Bowery and a hardware store on Mott Street. Angelucci Paint and Tile. We don't owe nobody nothing.

Before the war I had a newsstand on the corner of Largo del Colonnato and Via di Porta Angelica, right there on the edge of St Peter's Square, a good sit. You got a lot of passing trade with a sit like that. It was hard, honest work. I liked it. My parents established the business. Their names were Sandro and Antonella, *che Dio li benedica.*

And my mother was the toughest business person you ever met. Her thing was work hard, God gave you two ears so you'd listen twice as much as you talk. Get up early, love your family, don't bullshit.

My old man built the stand from old oak barrels that was rescued from a winery on the Principe Pallavicini estate out in the countryside, the Castelli Romani, so the walls was kind of curved, a nice talking point. The people liked that. It was good for trade, a conversation starter.

Me and my sisters and brothers worked there on weekends and in the summers or after school, and when my parents got too old, I took it over. I guess I was twenty at the time. Young punk. Full of piss and vinegar. I built it up over eight, nine, years, something. I was married on my twentieth birthday, my wife died in a bombing raid on Rome in March '44. We was only kids when we met. Yeah, I still think of her, sure.

Kind of stuff on the stand? Oh, everything, everything. All the newspapers we sold. Italians are crazy for newspapers. Even second-hand, I'd sell those if some guy was buying. Even a week or ten days old, you might get five lire for it. Sure.

Fashion magazines. Guidebooks. Crosswords. Dirty books for old men. Tickets to the Vatican. Biographies of the Caesars and saints. Holy pictures. Old maps. Everything.

Yeah, that was how I met the *Monsignore*.

He starts coming by my stand every other morning for the *Gazzetta dello Sport*. Tall fella, well built. Little red in the face. We true Romans are small-boned. But this guy's the size of a door. Stands out. This blue-and-white golf umbrella, huge thing, when it's raining.

'I got a spare ration card for today,' he tells me. 'You want it? Take it.'

I tell him I don't need nothing, I'm good.

'Take it for your children. Get a little extra milk. Or bread. It's going to waste right now.'

Hair's a little thin but it's black as the Sicily grapes, as we say. These old-fashioned, horn-rimmed glasses, bifocals. Sense of humour he got. Made you grin.

'Say, friend,' he goes. 'How much are your postcards?'

'Five lire for two.'

'How much for one?'

'Four.'

'I'll take the other.'

Sometimes he whistles as he looks over my stock. Or he sings to himself.

I like a man who sings. I'm Italian.

Another thing I remember, he got this strong, distinctive walk, manly, you know, head up, swinging his arms. Confident. When we introduce ourselves, one day after he's been coming to my stall for I guess a week, his handshake is firm, like a farmer's selling you a cow. His eyes don't move while he's talking to you; the guy scarcely blinks through them glasses. There might be fifty, sixty thousand people in the Piazza; you're the only one there. You can tell he's taking you in, with the cash-register eyes. In Italian we got a word for it, *sprezzatura,* that's a word I like. Means knowing how to come across casual.

Stands to reason in St Peter's Square, you're seeing priests all day long, right? I was Communist at the time, but they didn't bother me none. You want to buy a newspaper, brother, I'll sell you a newspaper. I want confession? I'll let you know.

And this one, the *Monsignore,* he's hard to dislike. Such a big, laughing countryman, got no airs, he talks to you like an equal, in Italian. *Come sta, Signor Angelucci, amico mio? Come stanno sua moglie e i suoi figli?* Oh, swell. No, we didn't talk politics or religion, just the everyday shoot-the-shit.

Soon afterwards I found out, from the other guys in the square, he's giving away his ration card every other morning. What's happening – we figured it out – is the guy's only eating every second day. The other, he's hungry. Swear to God.

Another thing I liked, he was crazy for sports. Boxing was his thing. Regular encyclopaedia of fights. The Cuban fighters he loved. Also football as we call it in Italy, by which we mean soccer. Then tennis, cycling, the Tour, any contest. The ponies not so much. I don't know why. Because plenty of priests, let me tell you, they go nuts for the ponies. But the boxing, oh, baby. He adored it.

Talking your arm off about the great heavyweights. Joe Louis, guys like that. Loved the welterweights too, he seen Rocky Graziano fight amateur. Graziano was born right here in Brooklyn but as a kid moved to East 10th Street and First, over the bridge, a big Italian neighbourhood, where my own sister and her husband lived. She cleaned house for a family called Barbella, which was Graziano's born surname. The *Monsignore* loved hearing all that.

For a foreigner, he had an incredible, I mean incredible, knowledge of Rome. This street, that block, the little '*vicoli*' as we call them, *vicoli e incroci,* the passageways and criss-crossings between the old houses and around the backs of churches, some of them too narrow to ride a scooter through. Rome is like a cheese, you know, full of holes. You could live in Rome a thousand years and not know every alleyway. But this guy came close, let me tell you. His hobby was studying old maps of the city; if I came across one on the stall, I'd give it to him. Always he tried to pay me, but these was just pages cut out of books, not originals. You'd frame them and hock them to Americans. His big thing was breaking my balls that the guidebooks I was selling on the stand was garbage. He wanted to write a guidebook himself one day and maybe I'd sell a thousand copies at twenty lire a throw and we'd both get rich and have ringside seats at the fights. Type of guy he was. Down to earth.

We'd pass the time, have a conversation, compare the reports of the bouts in the different newspapers. If I was making coffee on a cold morning, he'd take a quick cup with me, sure. When war came, the coffee was horrible, you couldn't even call it that. Made of acorns. But we'd force it down, it was something, at least it was hot, right? We'd have a bet now and then. It was part of his playfulness. One morning he says to me, 'Angelucci, you're deluded, Armstrong won't last four rounds against Montañez, let's bet on it.' Now, I'm joking back to him, just bouncing the ball. 'Brother, you're a priest, ain't betting a sin?' He says, 'Not with invisible dollars.'

So, he bets me fifty invisible dollars, like a yank, and I give fourteen to one, like a bookie. Next day he says to me, 'Angelucci, you made me a Rockefeller, hand over my invisible winnings,' or 'Enzo, you broke my bank.' We actually kept account, in a notebook. He never went nowhere without his tiny notebook and a pencil stub behind his ear. And we'd bet, like two dukes. It was ridiculous, you know. Just a way of passing the time. I'd write him an IOU for a million dollars and change. He'd say, 'Give me a cup of your rotgut coffee, we're even.'

Well, the Fascisti kicked my stall down and burned what was left. Because I wouldn't quit selling foreign newspapers. But you don't tell no Angelucci what to do. Like we say, '*O mangi questa minestra o salti dalla finestra*,' kinda means you deal with the shit or you jump out the window. My wife had a cousin worked in a chandlery, an old factory in Trastevere where they made church candles, and he'd let me have a box or two, cost. I'd get them blessed and go around St Peter's Square like a pedlar selling them for a couple of lire to the pilgrims queuing in the line. Two babies at home and another on the way? You do what you do. Feed your family. I'd say, '*Buongiorno, Signora*, inside the Basilica these are ten lire each. How about I give you two for five. These were blessed by Cardinal Ventucci.'

Because people like a bargain. You learn that in business. Specially the old ladies, see, they don't have much dough, so you cut them a deal, we're all happy.

'*Nonna*, I give you four for eight, *che Dio protegga tutti.*'

I won't lie, sometimes them candles was blessed by Enzo Angelucci. But if I could find a priest to do it, I did. Strange to say, I don't remember never asking the *Monsignore*. Maybe I didn't want to, whatever, compromise him I guess. But I'm sure he would have done it if I asked.

Allora: here's one hot afternoon I'm down in the square and, hand to God, the sun's beating me like I owe it money. It's one of those Rome days when even your sweat burns. I'm working the line, when I seen, near the colonnade, trying to get some coolness in the shadow, here's this young guy alone, in shabby, dirty clothes, and he's looking so sick, face white as the moon, arm in a sling made of a potato sack. You get tramps in Rome, same as everyplace else. But something about him. His eyes.

Tell you the truth, I'm busy; the people are buying candles – beautiful – but something in his face is so sad, so broken. Only nineteen or twenty. Handsome kid. Floppy hair. Reminds me of my brother, Marco, always getting in trouble. So, what are you going to do?

I go over in his direction and he's backing away scared. Sweating like a waterfall. He's got fever.

'What's the matter, kid? You hungry?'

I offer him a pear.

Kid looks at me a long time before taking it, eats it down in five bites. Tattoo on the back of his wrist says '*Viva l'Italia*'. In my pocket I got a porchetta sandwich she made for my lunch and I give him that, too, and a flask of cold water, and my kerchief for his face and his neck.

'Sit down a minute, *Paesano*. Take it easy. Bathe your forehead. You got sunstroke? You want a cigarette maybe?'

It's like he don't hear me. Eyes rolling like a doll's. I'm thinking he's going to faint. Jesus Christ.

I mean, he's terrified. Shaking. And your heart is going to crack. If I live to be two hundred, I'll never forget what he's about to say.

Forgive me, it still . . . When I think of it.

[*Subject becomes emotional.*]

'For the love of God, brother, I beg you, don't betray me.'

60

Those were his words. Like flames.

He's an escaped prisoner of war, a Jew, half-Italian. They catch him, he's dead. We both know it. It's over.

I mean, what am I to do? I'm some guy who hawks candles. I don't got no powerful friends or money or connections. My place is five kilometres away near Termini and anyhow there's no room, and my wife is going to kill me if I bring this kid home. That's not going to be happening. Impossible.

I mean, I'm tempted to walk away. I got a family, a life. Italy, now, is a place where you're careful. Don't go looking for trouble, you won't find no trouble. All kinds of thoughts go tumbling in your mind. Suddenly you're in a sandstorm. Until you're a grain of sand yourself. Or you're staring at a moment. And you better believe there's consequences. These guys of Hauptmann put a bullet in your head before breakfast then sit down to eat. You're dirt on their floor. But I can't help it.

I'm looking across the square – I'm desperate, confused – and, right then, three hundred metres away, I seen the *Monsignore*, by the fountain, pacing and reading his holy book – the breviary they call it – the holy book a priest got to read from every day. I tell the kid come follow but not to say nothing, just pretend he don't know me, and we cross, in and out of the crowd, and it takes a while because he's limping so bad. Nazis every which way. Fascist police. The works.

The sun is blazing down on the granite like a bastard. The kind of heat you can feel through the soles of your shoes. You'd give a lot to be far away, in a cool room with the shutters closed, and your wife. When I'm maybe twenty paces from him, the *Monsignore* looks up from the book, like he's been expecting me all along.

'Say, Angelucci,' he goes, like good-humoured, poker-face. 'You're come here to rob me on the Sugar Ray fight, you bum. And you owe me four million already. You finagler.'

I go closer and explain what's going down over here.

He looks past me at the kid. Then he looks at me, angry. I ain't never seen this expression in him before.

'Are you out of your living mind?' he says. 'To bring this man to me?'

'They'll murder him,' I say. 'Let's not let that happen. Got to be something we can do. You're a priest.'

I swear to you, I can see the thunderstorms lighting up his eyes. I'm not sure if he's going to agree with me or punch me. We're there two, three minutes. A long time to stand in sunshine. Try it.

Then with his expression he beckons. The kid nods and follows. And off they make tracks, in the direction of the Basilica, this big, tall countryman the size of a door and this limping, broken kid beside him. There's a little bridge to the left of St Peter's, which leads into the Campo Santo. Little bridge I can't remember the name of. That's where they go.

I say to my wife what happened, she goes crazy that night. I'm this, I'm that. She could cuss, for a girl. Rile up an *Italiana*, you'll hear about it. But she'd have done the same thing, is the truth. I know it. She was a good person, full of kindness. She'd have done the same thing. Elisabetta Monti. *Possa riposare in pace.*

Next time I see the *Monsignore*, couple days later, he tells me, 'Angelucci, the kid is safe, in the Vatican infirmary, been given false papers. Only thing he needs to worry about now is some Carmelite falling in love with him. And I've decided to form a choir.'

'A choir?'

'You're one of the members.'

'But *Monsignore*, I can't sing.'

'I can't dance and I'm dancing. You're about to learn.'

'I'll think about it,' I tell him.

'Don't take long,' he says back. 'Storm's blowing out there. I need help.'

No wind where we're talking. Nice sunshine. Calm day. But yeah, course I know what he means.

Was I scared? Bet your ass. Who wouldn't be? Times was bad. Hauptmann finds out you're fooling, it's curtains, *ciao a tutti*. No trial, no sentence, you're dead. But then, that kid's eyes. So, what the hell was your life? Was there anything you ever believed in, any moment you stood up? Because, brother, the day will come when your children be asking, and you better believe you'll need an answer, so what's there to say? In my head I went back and forward, but in the end, I agreed. That was that; I joined the Choir. Once in, I was in. It's like taking a penalty in soccer: choose your spot and aim hard, let the goalie dance around if he wants to, that don't change your decision. So, yeah. I'm on board. *O la va o la spacca.* Better or worse. *Il Coro.*

Every day from then on, as the bells rang for noon, he'd come out from the Collegio and start pacing the Basilica steps. Or he'd stand there, big and tall, in the black cassock and red sash, so anyone coming into the square could see him, couldn't miss him if they tried. He hid in the open. Like a lighthouse.

If it was raining, he'd have that huge golf umbrella with him, like a giant blue-and-white toadstool. He might as well be standing in a spotlight on the Pope's balcony, he's so visible. Like some goddamn soprano up there.

So, in twos and threes they'd appear. Or, some by themselves. Guys escaped from the prisoner-of-war camps. Out the side streets, the laneways all around St Peter's. In disguise as Roman workmen, trashcan collectors, coal heavers, streetcar drivers, housepainters, *muratori* – our word for a stonemason, a wall-guy – farmers in town for market, hawkers, priests, I got no idea where they got the clothes. They'd make their way to the *Monsignore* and he'd lead them through, under the bridge.

Soon it got out among the escapees, don't know how, that I was one of his helpers, and they'd come up to me in the square, saying they wanted to buy my candles but needed 'to get them blessed'.

I thought, I'll bless you in a minute, with my boot up your ass. But then I'd point out the Boss.

That's how it got started. The Choir.

Every day they kept coming, one after the other. Before long, I couldn't keep count.

But that Christmas Eve Rendimento. Christmas Eve '43.

We planned it so careful. All the time, fate was laughing.

Cuts me to pieces to think of it. Still can't believe what happened.

And that was the *Monsignore*. Irishman. Crazy. Type of guy wouldn't listen to reason.

Christmas Eve 1943
9.11 a.m.
13 hours and 49 minutes before the Rendimento

The refectory is empty but for three Japanese priests conversing anxiously in their language over a newspaper. Avoiding them, he fetches an ersatz coffee from the bulbous copper urn on the counter, a steamy blast of chicory odour and potato peelings assailing him, now following him to one of the long tables down the end of the room, over which glowers a reproduction of van Craesbeeck's *Temptation of St Anthony*. A hang-around smell of old mops taints the air. Three fluorescent tubes emit a bile-green unpleasantness no one could define as light.

A Sister he's never seen before approaches and addresses him in German but in a moment apprehends that he doesn't understand and translates herself into Italian. Would he take a piece of biscuit?

'*No, grazie.*'

'We have no other food today, Father.'

'I'm fine. Would there be a sheet of notepaper?'

She brings it.

What he needs is to be alone at the long table with his thoughts, the space to spread out a contingency. Time to think.

At the top of the page, he writes one word:

'RENDIMENTO'

The Choristers' code for a mission.

With no news of Derry, the plan must be recalibrated, and, if Angelucci doesn't show, changed again. One by one, he considers the possibilities, his associates, the understudies. The Rendimento is too dangerous for any of the women to be asked but all of them are too brave to decline it, he knows. Perhaps Delia? The Contessa? What about Marianna? She's tougher than any man, a fast-thinker, clever. May couldn't do it, he doesn't yet know all the back streets. Asking Osborne is out of the question. Or is it?

Yes, it is, Marianna de Vries seems to say, pushing to the front of his mind. *He's too old and he talks too much.* Her Dutch briskness makes him laugh, though not today.

Scribbling, sketching, scoring, cross-hatching, blackening every millimetre with spirals, altered lists. The Rendimento *must* take place tonight, any later is too late. Hauptmann will never expect anything on Christmas Eve. No matter how the sum is done, there is only one answer.

It adds up to Enzo Angelucci.

He gets himself another coffee, thinks toughly about Angelucci. Loyal, courageous, brimming with righteous hatred – but he lacks Derry's cunning, the discipline-under-fire drummed into their officers by the British. Derry can climb facades, get through barbed wire fences, evade a pursuer, disappear into shadow, has seventeen Rendimenti under his belt already. Angelucci doesn't have combat training or counter-espionage expertise. Might he brag a bit in advance or let something slip later? Would his hot head be a vulnerability?

In the credit column, he's a Roman, knows every alley and nook. His impatience to run a mission should be used without further delay, months have passed since it started becoming dangerous. He's bored of being a watcher, a glorified tout, noting the movement of Nazi trucks, counting the numbers in a patrol, smashing streetlamps with a catapult so the police don't see who's entering an apartment building. All Italians talk in emphases but when Angelucci gets frustrated, hands windmilling at the air, his undulations overwhelm him. 'Like a *school*boy,' he often complains. 'I am treated as *a child* here. For *pity's* sake, *give* me a *Rendimento*, Father. A *solo*.'

Captured by Hauptmann, would he break?

Who wouldn't?

Even Derry might break. Always says it himself. *Don't tell me everything, Padre, because they'll start with the pliers and blowlamp. I'll hold out as long as I can but you know what Jerry's like. Once he gets you to Via Tasso, German efficiency's rather efficient.*

The former German Cultural Institute, Via Tasso. As a young seminarian awed by the city, he had often attended concerts there, Brahms, Schubert, the lattice-like fragility of the music. Now there will be no more concerts.

Barbed wire, hooded sentries, the windows bricked up. People living three blocks away awakened by the screams. A baker's truck materialises every dawn to collect the carcasses that were once the bodies of students, Partisans, resisters. The van is said to have been made leakproof by casing its interior in rubber, but even such orderliness doesn't always prevent the trail of scarlet splashes from Via Tasso to the squares and parks of the city, where Hauptmann has the disfigured bodies placed so they'll be widely seen.

On benches. In bus shelters. Hanging from lamp posts.

Would Enzo be one of them?

A married man, could he be asked?

What of his wife and children should the worst thing happen?

Derry knows precisely how many Books are in hiding, and where, has some memory system he learned during his training at Sandhurst, but whenever he tries explaining it, the other Choristers plead with him to stop. The speed of the number's growth is too frightening.

At the table up the hall, the Japanese priests are chuckling, pointing. It seems a mouse has been spotted in the corner nearest the lectern where the Rector, before the war, used to read aloud from the scriptures during supper. The unknown Sister hurries out from the kitchen and a pantomime of mouse-hunting commences, colander as snare, egg-whisks as cudgels, but the mouse, if it ever existed, proves unwilling to appear despite the shrieks and multilingual cajolings.

People would delight you if you let them. Their innocent foolishness. That, and his tiredness, threaten his eyes with tears, face turned to the frosted window.

Via Tasso feels close.

A baker's truck, revving.

He goes to the public telephone in the cubbyhole under the stairs, expecting that the line will be down, but no, it is working, a burr, like a dozing animal.

He wonders why the Nazis have switched it back on. Bait, he supposes. Hauptmann's fishing for something. At this stage, there is no choice but to bite.

Placing a code-call through to the Contessa's private number, he hears her pick up, so he knows she is at home, then he disconnects and dials again, letting the ring sound four times. This is the most urgent of the signals they share.

One ring. Two rings. Third ring. Four.

It's urgent. The usual place.

66

Receiver replaced, he stays where he is for a moment, in the telephone cubby under the stairs, among raincoats and yellowed directories. He prays for her, or tries to, as he does every day of his life, but the words turn to smoke as he thinks them. She feels oddly present, somehow; he can sense her reassurance, *I heard you, I'm on my way, don't worry.* Sees her putting on her gaberdine in the dark old house, running down the marble staircase that's too steep to run down, emerging into the street, the hurting brightness, the noise, and the old door slamming behind her. He's too shy to put a name on the fondness he feels for her and often wonders if it's true. There is an ache in many hearts where a daughter might have been. He never knew it before he met Giovanna Landini.

He returns to his room, collects his breviary and rosary beads, then back across the landing and down the squeaking stairs, through the chatty tempestuousness of the busying male house, students jostling and joking on the ashy cold corridors or hurrying out to the last of this term's lectures.

'*Guten Morgen, Monsignore. Guten Tag. Salve.*'

In the gardens behind St Peter's the stilled fountains have frozen so that the water is the same sooty grey as the marble containing it. Gravel scrunches as he walks, thoughts monkeying at him, mocking; the cold stone bench a taunt.

A dream he had of London looms up from old leaves: mist rolling across Hyde Park, cavalry horses exercising, a young, veiled woman seen as from a great distance across the lake. He wants her to unveil, but she won't.

Farm Street, Brompton Oratory. Old bookshops. Cricket scores. Charing Cross Road in the autumn, dusk bringing on lights in the theatre foyers. The consoling bleakness of slate-grey skies. A night on Leicester Square Tube Station when a woman fell ill, he knelt by her on the platform and waited for the ambulance men to come but she had said with immense gentleness, English politeness, that she would prefer him not to pray, just to converse with her or remain silent, that she was not a believer, and even if she were, 'God has better things to be doing.' They talked of Handel and wildflowers as she died.

From the pocket of his soutane he takes an unopened stack of blank postcards and the fountain pen his mother sent last Easter, bought on a trip to Dublin for surgery, and begins ticking through eventualities.

He checks from time to time that no one is coming. Birds wheel and shriek above cypresses.

Osborne and Giovanna have between them arranged the last of the money – he doesn't know how, doesn't want the burden of knowing – which will arrive in used notes via an unidentified city this morning. Delia Kiernan has a contact at the American Express office who has agreed to look the other way when a certain package comes in. John May will see it delivered to Operations HQ.

If they can find him, Angelucci will undertake the Rendimento. If not, they will gamble on a former soldier known to Marianna de Vries, a tough, committed sniper, knowledgeable of the streets, who's been pushing a long time to join the Choir. A baptism of fire might be the only option. Far better if it were Angelucci.

Three drops, one in Prati, the second in Parioli, then a 'refuelling stop' to take on more cash, then the largest drop in Campo Marzio but no one will know exactly where until the final moment. Then rendezvous with a getaway agent, 'the pilot', for the last kilometres home.

If everyone's still alive.

In the distance, the same distance as the veiled young woman in the dream, he sees the slim, deliberative, white-clad figure of the Pope, walking alone near bare olive trees, from time to time stopping, glancing up at the sky like a farmhand expecting it to tell him something about weather.

Normally there would be guards. Why are there no guards?

He moves painfully, stiffly, as though much older than he is, towards a bower of tied-up roses near which someone has left a barrow with a spade shoved into muck. He seats himself on the rim of a fountain, long arms by his side, before rising again and going to the barrow and shovelling out a hefty spadeful of manure. As he digs and thrusts, steam globing from his mouth, he turns his weary torso in a slow, steady circle.

Two Swiss Guards and a nun hurry out from the palace doorway with an overcoat. The old man ignores them, digging, digging, his skullcap the colour of dirty snow.

Bombers overhead, high above the range of the ack-acks. An old man hoeing at thorns.

— 8 —

THE CONTESSA GIOVANNA LANDINI
From an unpublished, undated memoir written after the war

We had been married less than a year when my husband died. The day after his funeral, I lost a longed-for pregnancy. I was thirty, in storms of grief.

I had servants, gowns by Chanel and Elsa Schiaparelli, jewels, a palace, a villa at San Casciano dei Bagni, a yacht moored at Ostia, a prosperous vineyard. Without Paolo, it counted for nothing.

When war came, I volunteered in the Ambulance Corps as a driver. Without that, I would have gone mad. The irregular hours were a cover for the fact that sleep had become a stranger to me. There was no fire towards which I wouldn't drive. In the end, they had to dismiss me.

For a time afterwards I assisted as a motorcycle despatch rider for the Red Cross, delivering medicines about the bombed parts of the city where a truck could not go. Paolo had taught me to ride the Triumph Tiger I had given him as a wedding gift, a small, fast, good-handling machine. But war made it impossible to find British spare parts, and, following a fuel line malfunction that burned out the engine, his steed had to be glumly stabled in the old coach house at the end of my garden, where the spiders found its wheel spokes the perfect lattice for their webs, and mice gnawed the saddle leather to black lace.

If you know Rome in high summertime, the weeks leading up to Ferragosto, I don't need to explain the vampiric, exhausting heat. My house on Via del Corso, built around a quattrocento courtyard, had a fountain and a colonnade in which bleary peacocks sulked, but I couldn't abide the courtyard, young and jealous as I was, for it had been remodelled by a former lover of Paolo's, a girl who had left him, rather too glamorously I felt, to become a nun and die in China, on the missions.

Instead, on those scourging afternoons of heat, when most of Rome retires to a café or to bed in a shuttered room, I would bicycle to the gardens of the Villa Umberto and lie in the grass between the lordly pines. The heat would coax loamy musk from the earth. I felt close to Paolo then. It was as though I could hear his whisper. The agony of life would abate.

Mostly, what I wanted was to follow him, wherever he was. The only thing I had not decided was the method of my self-destruction. I had a pistol he had given me, a small, jade-handled Beretta. Perhaps that would return me to his side. In the gardens, he would whisper that I was to remain; hope would come if permitted. The heat, the aromas, the earth beneath my body made it possible to believe in a ghost.

There was no need to bring a bundle of his love letters with me; in truth, I knew every one of them by heart. Blushed into my memory, as pomegranate juice tinctures Prosecco in the cocktail we shared on the Terrazza dell'Infinito at Ravello before retiring on our wedding night.

Those gardens were where Paolo and I had met, on an autumn day in 1936. I was walking with my sister when a blazingly handsome soldier approached, pushing a wheelchair in which was a blanketed old gentleman, his father. Elisabetta asked them for directions to the Casina delle Rose – a concert we wished to attend was to take place there – for we were lost and had been going in slightly argumentative circles, as sisters sometimes like to do. His eyes had a fierce gentleness, if such a contradiction is possible, and his manner such gallantry and what I can only call acumen – but enough of happier days.

On those afternoons of my raw widowhood, when I would go again to the Villa Umberto gardens to weep on a park bench with his absence and the sirocco, I would sometimes after an hour or two go into the Galleria to wash my face or to look at the beautiful things. On a hot afternoon, the great rooms were often empty, lending the statues a pleasing sadness in that particular redolence of old, heated dust that, for me, will always be Rome. Or, a couple of students might be sketching them, a tousled boy, a smoking girl; I found envying their youth a healing heartache.

One Thursday (I remember it well), as I entered the Sala Bernini, the only person there was a priest. A tall, high-coloured man, in wire-rimmed spectacles, he was clad in a black cassock that must have been making him broil; his face was red as the monsignorial sash he had on and his thick, black hair looked damp. He was standing before that disquieting masterpiece of statuary, *Apollo e Dafne*, which Paolo had always loved and often bribed the attendants to be allowed to photograph.

Obviously, one sees priests every day in Rome. But something about him took my attention. He was not a particularly striking person to look at. Perhaps it was simply that he appeared hot and uncomfortable or that seeing a priest in an art gallery is for some reason not all that common. Anyhow, he glanced towards me and smiled.

'Did you ever in your life see anything so beautiful,' he said, in good, very formal Italian that had been learned from a book, in that it lacked the jaunt with which we speak. 'If one lived a million years and had lessons from a master every day, one could never do a single square millimetre of that. Imagine, it was once a block of stone in a quarry.'

'*Vero*,' I agreed, '*è bellissima*.'

'*Meravigliosa*. The detail takes one's breath; one would swear they are alive.'

'I have sometimes seen them move and breathe,' I said. 'If you watch for an hour that happens. Or, when you enter the room very suddenly.'

With a look of joyous bafflement, he indicated the most miraculous detail of the piece, where the fingertips of the god's left hand touch Dafne's flesh.

'Miraculous,' he said. 'One doubts one's own eyes. Such softness could not be marble.'

Shaking his head as though in disbelief, he then turned to me again.

'Madame is French?' he asked amiably.

'*Sono italiana*,' I said.

'Forgive me, *Signora*, I misheard your accent.'

'My family are Parisian on my mother's side,' I told him. 'My sister and I attended school in Nantes.'

'The Oblate Franciscan Sisters, I am guessing? Excellent ladies. Not to be trifled with.'

'A little strict,' I agreed.

'Very good.'

By now, we seemed to have steered ourselves into the sort of conversational blind alley that often, among the newly met, preludes a departure. But, oddly, I did not want him to go. Equally oddly, I felt he knew that.

'Have you lived in Rome long?' I asked. 'Do you like it?'

'I studied here as a seminarian in the late Prehistoric era and returned a few years ago for post-doctoral work. I am attached to the German College, do you know it, in the shadow of St Peter's? I like Rome very much. But then, who wouldn't like it?'

'May I talk with you, Father?' I blurted.

Suddenly I was weeping. He did not look taken aback. What I can only describe as a sort of fit assailed me. I had a feeling that I was drowning, and it frightened me. I remember a woman attendant hurrying in but then leaving the room just as quickly, perhaps to seek help. The old, hot dust stung my eyes.

'*Signora*,' he said, gently, with intense respectfulness and grace. 'Of course. Shall we walk a while outside?'

In the garden, I was unable to speak for a time. He cooled a handkerchief in the fountain and gave it to me silently, then led me towards a granite bench under cherry laurels. A minute or two passed before my weeping subsided a little, a minute or two that must have had their difficulties for him, heaven knows; more than one passer-by glanced with what the English call dagger eyes in our direction, as though my tears had been caused by their consoler.

'You are young to be so troubled,' he said. 'I am sorry you are in pain. It walked into the room beside you. Like music.'

My voice would not come, only bitter, anguished sobs. I realised I was tearing his handkerchief.

'Try to believe me, *Signora*, that your burden will pass.'

'I fear it won't.'

'In time.'

'You don't even know what it is and you speak to me of time.'

'That is true. *È vero*. Forgive my presumption. It seems to me that there is only one thing that causes us such pain. To lose someone dear to us. Too soon.'

'*Why?*' I wept.

'I don't know,' he replied.

'Why don't you know?'

'I don't know that, either.'

There was a pause before he added, 'It is not given to us to know. There are those that would say, to share the crucifixion is a great blessing; it is also to share the resurrection.'

'Enough,' I retorted. '*Don't* tell me such lies.'

He nodded, gazed about. 'We need not talk at all if you wish; I can sit with you here and watch the trees.'

This we did for a time, during which we said nothing. I smoked. He did not. I wept. He bowed his head. Presently he went to the railings where a battered old First World War motorcycle was parked, held together with bits of coat hanger and Scotch tape, fuel tank badly dented, handlebars mismatched, puncture patches on both tyres; from its panier he took a pad of notepaper on a page of which he wrote the address and telephone number of his Collegio.

'May I ask that you accept these, *Signora*,' he said, resuming his seat beside me, 'in case I or a confrère can ever be of assistance. I apologise with all sincerity if I have been presumptuous or intrusive. Sometimes I jabber clumsily without thinking. You have heard of the Roman flu, of course?'

I nodded.

'The condition I have myself, you see, is the Irishman's flu.'

'What is that?'

'The brain takes itself on holiday while the mouth works overtime.'

The ridiculous image could not help but make me laugh. I told him my late husband had been a motorcyclist, that I was one of sorts myself. If I am honest, he seemed a little shocked that a woman could advance such a claim but he made a reasonable fist of disguising it.

'Need you go?' I asked.

'Soon enough,' he replied.

'Perhaps you would hear my confession,' I said.

At this request, he looked surprised but without delay he agreed, turning from me, closing his eyes and murmuring the prayer in Latin. I noticed that he had taken a set of wooden rosary beads from his pocket and was holding them as he listened to my words.

A priest may never reveal what is said in confession but of course a penitent may. I had never killed anyone, nor, I hope, had I ever sinned against the most important of all commandments – for me the only truly unbreakable commandment – *Thou shalt not bear false witness against thy neighbour.*

My transgressions against the other edicts, which seem to forbid everything from loneliness to human nature, I listed as thoroughly as I could. I conceive of these transgressions not as sins but as ghosts who draw us in to their orbit. And there was one great ghost that had me in its grip in those days. The high prince of ghosts. Despair.

Despair, in his diamonds of ice and grief, his robes of shimmering mist. In his eyes the strange light that draws ships to the rocks, in his mourning, ten thousand choirs. You may gamble a hand with him but the cards are all marked; he knows he will win at the close. What he's offering is opium, but many times stronger. There is no intoxicant quite as numbing as perfect despair.

You don't understand the fact that hope, if it is ever encountered, is in the small things of the everyday, not an announcement from on high. In the aroma of cooking, a phrase from Vivaldi. A handclasp. A conversation.

This is what happened in the gardens of the Villa Umberto that day. Hope was waiting in the Sala Bernini.

Entering the park, I didn't know him. Leaving it, I had shaken hands with the greatest friend of my life, who in those terrible months would give me purpose, a reason to go on living. We can never know the miracle that is hiding in the everyday. Sometimes, it is a matter of looking.

I handed Hugh the pistol that had been in my haversack, loaded with one bullet only, all I would have needed to put an end to myself. My plan had been to go to the pine groves, to wait until no one was about.

Unloading it, he threw the cartridge in the laurels.

I still think of it, rusting there, all these years later, through rainstorm and sun-blast and the nights of my Rome. Perhaps a scavenger will one day find it and wonder at its journey, the story that brought it to the place where it now lies.

No one will know.

But you, reader, know.

These words would never have been written without Hugh O'Flaherty. Their author would be dust in Rome's air.

— 9 —

Christmas Eve 1943
11 a.m.
Exactly 12 hours before the Rendimento

From far across St Peter's Square, he sees her at the café table. Dressed in black, she is reading a magazine, smoking. She pushes a strand of hair behind her ear. As though sensing his presence, she glances up but does not wave. He sets out hurriedly towards her through a cloud of uprising pigeons but, approaching the barriers at the edge of the Piazza, is halted by a German trooper who holds up a gloved hand.

'Remain inside the Vatican, *bitte*. You are not permitted to cross that line.'

'I am on a mission of the cloth.'

'With respect, direct orders from Obersturmbannführer Hauptmann are that no one is to come over the border today. There may be an opportunity tomorrow, or later in the week.'

'For God's sake, "border". It is a line on the ground.'

'I apologise, Father. Strictly no exceptions today. Come back tomorrow, around noon.'

'May I speak with your superior?'

'There would be no point, I assure you.'

Now he notices that she has called for her bill, is paying the waiter, who peers after her with a glower of mournful lustfulness as she tosses a banknote onto the saucer and heads away. A corner boy gives a wolf-whistle, she doesn't even glance. Black pillbox hat, black pearled mantilla around her face, grey overcoat open, stylish black oxfords negotiating the glassy cobbles, umbrella under her arm like a swagger stick.

Don't approach me, he thinks, they're watching.

She approaches.

To be still? Or back away? Pretend not to know her? Suddenly it is too late, she's only metres from him, nodding.

'*Signora*,' says the trooper, 'I warn you, remain in Rome. Do not cross the borderline into Vatican City. If you do, you will need a formal permit to return.'

'I am *Contessa*,' she says. 'Not *Signora*.'

'*Contessa*, then. Excuse me. The instruction still applies.'

Shaking her head without looking at the trooper, she lights a fresh cigarette, exhales a ring of smoke that wreaths itself around her, the same colour as her scarf and eyes. A breeze raises an ivy leaf against the collar of her polo coat.

'*Buongiorno, Monsignore*,' she says, in a formal tone, for the trooper's benefit. 'You won't remember me but we have met once, at a function with my late husband, the Count. It was some years ago, I think at the San Giovanni Hospital.'

'Good day, Contessa Landini.'

'What a pleasant surprise to run into you so unexpectedly. How have you been keeping of late?'

She stands on the Rome side; he stands in the Vatican, like people looking over a tennis net.

'Don't you have anything to do, yob?' she snaps at the trooper. 'If you don't, go and wash your filthy face.'

A century passes. The soldier nods, turns his back, trudges away.

'What is it?' she asks.

'Did you hear about Derry?'

'Perhaps he'll recover.'

'Is there a way of finding out?'

'I'll see what may be done. Leave it with me a day.'

'We need to find Enzo.'

'Didn't you receive my message?'

'No.'

'I telephoned the Collegio and left a message for you yesterday morning. I found him near his house. He agrees.'

'To what?'

'The Rendimento, of course.'

'But, what else did he say?'

76

' "Don't worry." '

'How in hell am I not to worry, I haven't heard a single word from him?'

'He'll be in touch today.'

'What time?'

'I don't know.'

'Do you know where the devil he is? He hasn't been around the square all week.'

'I'll go by his house again in an hour.'

'Careful not to get tailed. They're watching.'

'I won't get tailed.'

'How can you know?'

'I hid a change of clothing behind the cistern in the ladies' lavatory of an *osteria*. I'll slip in for a moment. You look ill.'

'I had fever.'

'Get better. I have a thousand dollars here in my handbag, is there a way you can take them?'

'That soldier's watching, I tell you. Better go.'

Lightning crackles over the Basilica, a bellowing groan of thunder. Waiters outside the cafés retreat beneath awnings. A mounted Fascist policeman emerges from the gloom of a side street, black horse steaming as it ponderously clops. Behind the centaur a ragged parade of barefooted children, high-stepping, cartwheeling, invisible rifles over shoulders. Handing him the umbrella for a moment, she pulls over her hat a capacious hood he didn't notice her raincoat having, and, without another word, she is walking away, past streetcars and dustcarts, through the parade of goose-stepping urchins, towards Via dei Penitenzieri.

Minutes later, returned to his room, he opens the umbrella. Inside is an envelope containing ten hundred-dollar bills, which he hides beneath the floorboards of his wardrobe.

Leaving the room, he hurries to the Vatican hostel where the British Ambassador and his servant are in refuge, but the Ambassador is not available, the servant, John May, insists. Sir D'Arcy is writing his December report, which is late. He is not to be interrupted.

From there, to the Lecture Hall, an hour on St Catherine of Siena with the Fourth Years but answering the seminarians' questions is like juggling with

77

mud. His mind keeps ratcheting back to the square. Something not quite right; he's not sure what it was. Did the sentry notice anything? Was the waiter a tout? The Fascist on horseback, why was he there, and that object he pulled from his greatcoat pocket as the rain began to surge, was it a radio mouthpiece or a camera?

Ending the seminar, he wishes the students a peaceful Christmas and returns to the square.

Mirrors of grey rainfall.

The same trooper on duty.

Still no sign of Angelucci.

'You've returned,' says the trooper. 'I was hoping you would.'

'Why so?'

Reaching into a pocket, the trooper produces a fountain pen.

'You dropped this. Earlier. I called after you, but you'd gone.'

Gulls swoop.

'Mightier than the sword,' says the trooper, eyes cold. 'Don't let me see you here again.'

10

SIR D'ARCY OSBORNE
Christmas Eve 1943
12.32 p.m.
Coded communiqué sent by diplomatic courier

From: Sir Francis D'Arcy Godolphin Osborne, His Majesty's Ambassador
to the Holy See, now in refuge in Vatican City.

To: The War Office, Italian Section, Whitehall, London

On: 24th December 1943, 10.32 hours, GMT; 32 minutes past noon,
Rome time

I should like to commence by apologising for the delay with this report. Winter has been uncommonly harsh here in Rome this year, and I succumbed to a most debilitating dose of bronchitis. The lack of fresh or adequate food has made life difficult from time to time, as of course has the fact that, following the German invasion of the city on 10th September, I and my staff had no other recourse but to move into the Vatican, where we are now living at close quarters.

We share a four-floored former hospice (in the Roman sense a house for pilgrims), with multitudinous mice and flying fleas, also with the diplomats of Portugal, Bolivia, Uruguay and Cuba, and so, as will be imagined, we have a certain amount of noisiness to contend with.

There is something wrong with the water. We all have eczema.

Not to dwell on misfortune but it does need to be added that we possess no means of heating any part of this building or of heating the water. Nearby is a bakery where, daily at dawn, the dough for bread is steamed. Every morning a good Sister goes there to collect the hot water that is a by-product of the process. It is only by dint of this that we are able to wash or shave. A litre of this water costs about the same as a bottle of Veuve Clicquot 1929.

A fortnight ago, as I was watched from my window, I saw that the Nazis had ordered a work detail of prisoners to paint a two-foot-wide white line around the edge of St Peter's Square, indicating the borderline between Vatican City and Rome as established by the Patti Lateranensi or Lateran Treaty, 7th June 1929. Notices on wooden posts have since been erected, to the effect that the citizens of one city must not enter the other city without applying for a written permit, which must be triple stamped by the military authorities and accompanied by a hefty payment. The Swiss Ambassador went down with several witnesses and asked the SS Officer Commanding what was the meaning of this outrage, were we all to be kept in?

'*Nein*,' the Hauptsturmführer replied. 'Kept out.'

But what about pilgrims?

Arrangements would be made.

'Of what nature, these arrangements?'

'You will know when you know.'

'I am a credential-bearing diplomat of the Corpo Diplomatico.'

'I don't care if you are Jesus Christ Almighty. Cross that line and you're in a concentration camp.'

An Associated Press newsreel crew had assembled their camera not far from where this exchange was taking place. They were commanded in plain terms to be gone. When they offered resistance, the Hauptsturmführer smashed their lens with the butt of his pistol, his subordinates chuckling as they watched. 'You show *lies*,' he screamed. 'Back to Hollywood.'

Since then, German patrols have been guarding the line, standing along it making louts of themselves or having their photographs taken with, or by, priests and other passers-by. Many of the representatives of the Master Race that end up here in Rome are generally of the stupider, box-headed sort, a clottish assemblage of conscripts pining for lederhosen and lager. Alas, some are more than that.

One week ago today, at 15.00 hours, I and my factotum, John May, went to the obelisk in St Peter's Square to meet with Golf, as had been arranged by coded message that morning. Golf had expressed himself reluctant to meet at the two rooms doing duty as Legation and Official Residence, feeling certain that they have been planted with transmitting microphones by undercover Gestapo. I am of the view that this is fanciful, that he attends the cinema too often. But after all, one can't be too careful.

Golf was late, as he too frequently is. As May and I conversed, we smoked several of the American PX cigarettes of which he seems to have a bottomless supply despite severe rationing. I did not like them but, as many of us will recall from when we schooled, it is good to smoke with another fellow, it fills in the time and gives him a reason to like you.

I should like to place on record that May, an inscrutable native of Whitechapel, has proven a veritable genius of on-the-quiet, resourceful scrounging, a filcher the like of whom has not been seen since the Artful Dodger. He is, after a fashion, quite the classicist, and is wont to quote or at least paraphrase the old saying one had caned into one at Haileybury College: *Dii facientes adiuvant.* The gods help those who help themselves.

Items procured by the great May to date include: drum of petrol, drum of grease, drills, metalworking tools, Benzedrine tablets, boots, shirts, magnetised razor blades capable of being used as compasses, underclothing, penicillin, ration books, running total of thirty-two thousand cigarettes, Andorran and Swiss identity cards, maps and ordnance charts printed on silk (of the type issued to Bomber Command to meet the eventuality of having to parachute over open water), lady's bicycle, Fascist police uniform (one), German uniforms (three), Swiss Guard uniform (one), Dominican friar's habit (one), box of N82 Gammon-bomb grenades. I will add that His Majesty's Legation on retreat in Vatican City has an uncommonly well-stocked drinks cabinet since May's arrival here, including a quite exceptionally fine Strathisla 1937 Scotch, aged in 34-year-old sherry casks, fifty guineas the bottle, not a libation encountered frequently these days outside the finest Whitehall clubs. One doesn't ask questions of a talented man.

What is more, May has the most likeable quality in a servant, in that he always goes one better. Lost in the jungles of Amazonia following an aeroplane crash, if you asked him to go away and come back with a guide, he would return with Rita Hayworth.

When at length Golf turned up, he was in a strange, quiet mood. I asked if he was well and what he had been doing. He looked exhausted, a little dishevelled and had in fact not shaved, the first time I ever saw such a slip in a man of the cloth. He fidgeted as we conversed, clearly is under strain. We went over the ground of a problem.

The number of Books in the Library was increasing by the day, he told me, and it appeared that we were approaching capacity. Two Books had arrived that very morning (both British), thus Golf's unpunctuality, and had asked to be shelved in the Vatican.

United States Books had been flooding in of late. The Library was running now to more than seventy, perhaps eighty. Even keeping an accurate tally was by no means without difficulty and would become impossible following the sharp and irreversible increase he predicted, which presently would see thousands of Books entering Rome. At that point we would be counting the loops in the Gordian Knot. No more could be accommodated within the Vatican itself, which, being neutral, is not supposed to harbour any Books at all. The solution was for all Books shelved currently throughout wider Rome to be moved out into the countryside in order to make space. This achieved, we would re-shelve those at present lodged in the Vatican in the vacated Roman billets.

A sum of money would be required to bring this about.

Ah, I quipped. The root of all evil.

Eighty thousand American dollars.

At this, I gave a chortle and asked if there was anything further Golf would like, perhaps a pixie or a couple of gryphons?

One's attempted witticism was met with a scowl.

I pointed out that such a sum was not to be encountered down the sofa cushions at the Legation and that the matter would have to be sent Upstairs.

There would need to be committees, I insisted, oversight, paperwork, carbon copies, a system, a way of doing things, or Whitehall would send for the smelling salts. These days one could not purchase a mousetrap without a receipt. I reminded him that I am a Civil Servant not some lonesome Man of Action in a Western. Nor was May my Tonto.

May now uttered a sort of barking, uneasy chuckle like a dog having a dream of cats.

At this, Golf became a bit schoolmasterly, which I did not like, now hectoring, now vengefully mimicking, now wagging his finger and scolding. There was a good deal of Might I Bring To Your Attention and I'll Have You Know, like a housewife returning something defective to a shop and wanting to be noticed by the queue. Golf is a reasoning and calm sort, usually, the finest company one could imagine for a round on the links (which is how I met him), but he does have this tendency, not unknown among one-time schoolteachers, who sometimes mistake uninterruptable blather for persuasiveness. He is one of those men possessed of the ability to deploy the word 'sir' as an insult, by a sort of wheedling, half-ironic inflection of voice accompanied by a low-lidded, unblinking, slightly deranged stare. One sees it in his countrymen frequently.

A volley of frightened shouts from just beyond the Piazza now drew my attention. Golf fell silent at the sight that had inflamed them.

Through the colonnade, on the corner of Largo del Colonnato and Via di Porta Angelica, I saw perhaps a dozen Hun motorcycles roar up, with two Sturmgeschütz armoured cannon, known as 'Stugs' by the Romans, and I should say thirty machine-gun-bearing, helmeted troops, some with Dobermann dogs (what a ghastly 'yike yike' bark those brutes have), and a large consignment of the Questura, the Fascist police. Also, several truckloads of the GNR, the National Guard, and a dozen shipped-in German Polizei. Out of his armour-plated black Mercedes stepped Hauptmann, the Gestapo chief of Rome, in mufti for some reason, and wearing dark spectacles. But I am certain that it was he.

Not a career police officer but a professional Nazi who joined the Party a little later than most Gestapo men, he evinces the zeal of the convert in intimate proportion to the arc of his personal advancement. Formerly a technical draughtsman with the Berlin electricity authority, he is of slim, athletic build, slightly shorter than he at first seems, high-cheek-boned, alert-looking, threw the javelin at school. Widely known in Rome to be a black-market king, he controls large warehouses of goods, foodstuffs, tobacco, spirits and medicines, and has access to considerable amounts in forged currencies, chiefly sterling. His speaking voice is quiet. His favoured interrogation tool is the blow-torch. He sends the occasional Renaissance altarpiece or Etruscan statuette to Hitler. One of Hauptmann's two children, an adopted daughter, on whom he is said to dote, is the product of the Lebensborn, the Nazi breeding programme. His wife, formerly a Berlin fashion model, is known to drink. (Despite the Reich's avowed disapproval of 'non-Aryan' modes, her cosmetician of choice is Elizabeth Arden and her favourite couturiers, Kuhnen, Goetz and Grünfeld, are Jewish.) On Hauptmann's left hand he wears a death's-head ring given to him in appreciation of his role in the release from captivity of the dictator Mussolini. It is said to bear the inscription, 'To Hauptmann, from Himmler' and an assortment of allegedly Viking runes.

Hauptmann is a regular visitor to Regina Coeli prison where one entire wing of the four has been commandeered by the SS. Here he takes time to peer through every individual spyhole systematically, one landing per night, making notes on the prisoners' appearances, in a shorthand of his own devising. He is said to have a photographic memory and is known to drive about Rome in the early hours by himself, observing curfew-breakers to see if they match the faces in his files. Petty criminals and the sexually compromised are lifted, beaten and brought by his henchmen out to the cave system close to the Domitilla catacombs, where they are offered the choice of being shot or becoming his tout, as a result of which he is reputed to have a tout on every block in Rome. Suspected Partisans and collaborators are interrogated at Gestapo Headquarters on Via Tasso, Hauptmann sometimes delegating the vilest tortures to a German-Italian, one Dollman, the obscenely depraved Chief of Police.

Both ends of Via di Porta Angelica were barricaded quickly, making access or egress impossible. Jerry riflemen appeared on balconies and rooftops. *'Alzate le mani'* rang out. It was clear that we were witnessing what the Italians call a *rastrellamento*, a dreaded blitz-raid or round-up. A systematic search began, conducted at gunpoint; men without identity cards were dragged away. A boy of perhaps fifteen years who was working on a miserably provisioned fruit stall cried out for his father not to be taken; he was pistol-whipped. A woman, protesting copiously, approached Hauptmann in remonstration. With his gloves, he slapped her face. At that thuggish affront, Golf bowed his head and cursed the Nazi.

I noticed that Hauptmann appeared to be looking at us, now. That is not an agreeable thing to notice.

'Steady, old man,' I whispered to Golf.

From the corner of my eye, I saw a trooper pass a pair of binoculars to Hauptmann, who raised them to his eyes, regarding us. I indicated to my two colleagues that we should turn our backs.

May began speaking as though in a light way, gesturing and laughing about his team, Tottenham Hotspur, the Spurs, and I joined in the effort, but it was hard. By these means and by his sparrow-like persistence, he persuaded Golf back down towards terra firma.

And I was glad of May's presence for a more personal reason; had I a revolver on my person I would have walked the fifty yards to the Vatican border and given Hauptmann a faceful of lead.

I asked Golf how many Books are shelved in our Library at the present time. He answered that he did not know for certain since some had been moved out and others were always coming in, but he would make enquiries. I suggested he do that expeditiously.

I feel something is up. It might be a most opportune moment to re-accommodate these Books, I added, for if the Gestapo were to discover their whereabouts, their fate would be sealed; so too would be that of many others.

Furthermore, the day was fast approaching when the Nazis might invade the Vatican itself. Anything we had by way of papers must be burned without delay. Here there is a difficulty, for in the Pilgrim House where we are living there is only one fireplace and the chimney is blocked. Golf said he would see what might be done about burying them in the Vatican gardens.

At that moment, a Sister in a navy-blue habit approached and asked with discreet decorum if I was I and if Golf was Golf. We said that we were. Indicating in unconventional language that she was glad to make our acquaintance, the holy lady proffered a hand. 'She' was in fact Joseph Thomas Coleman, a Shrewsbury-born Private of the Queen's First Infantry, captured at Tobruk, escaped from the prison camp at Bussolengo near Verona, now presenting for refuge in the Vatican.

The words uttered by Golf as he led our new friend away were unusual for a man of the cloth.

Life, May remarked, is getting odder.

Quod scripsi, scripsi, as Pontius Pilate is said to have remarked. What I have written, I have written.

11

Christmas Eve 1943

2.06 p.m.

8 hours and 54 minutes before the Rendimento

The needle is rusty and warped. His eyesight is poor. Difficult to find good spectacles since rationing worsened. As he bends to darn the frayed vest, he pierces a fingertip, utters a curse.

Blood beads. It won't stop.

Downstairs, there is no one in the refectory. Its fourteen tables have been reset after the lunch he now realises he forgot to come down for. Ghost-priests were seated in the room until the moment he switched on the light.

Hungry, holy ghosts. Meals don't take long anymore. Almost nothing to eat. Not for weeks.

He enters the cold-smelling kitchen, finds the First Aid box in its cupboard, unspools a sticking plaster, notices his face in the kettle's bloated reflection. Filling the kettle from the pump, he sets it on the burner; a sharp, yellow odour of gas moistens his eyes. From his pockets he takes the envelope of tea he's been saving for a month, a gift from his parents back in Ireland.

The odour, perhaps the blood, raises a realisation.

He goes to the swing door to check that no one is coming, returns to the greasy sink, the unruly cupboards, begins searching the drawers. Fingers clattering greasy cutlery.

A short, thick knife with a shellac handle and serrated edge.

Elena, a half-lame orphan, was kitchen maid here for a while. Three months since she stopped coming to work. He used to like watching her sharpen implements with that brick-shaped granite strop, her skill in the act, the nearly musical fluency; she could natter away to the other servants while sharpening, not even look at what she was doing. He goes to the brick-heavy strop, commences rasping the butcher's knife, sideways, but the knack of the motion eludes him and the act feels weirdly inhuman even though it must be old as the apes. The *rasp* draws the elderly cat, the College ratter, from the wine crate that serves as her basket, and she regards him with the green-gold-green assessing eyes that, years ago, made a young priest from Ruanda-Urundi give her a new name.

Cleopatra.

Approaching, she utters a purr, tendrilling her tail around his lowered hand before the shrilling of the kettle unsettles those eyes and she slinks for whatever Nile is contained in the pantry.

Slipping the knife into his breast pocket he goes to the bread press, finds a length of staling focaccia from two days ago.

Tea and bread. Could be worse. Probably will be.

Alone in the long, thin room, he eats, the heft of the butcher's knife close to his heart, the scald of tea dislodges an icefloe of childhood. That gypsy who'd return to the village every year in December, a black-haired, mauve-eyed, elderly man home from England, unable to read but gifted with the curing of horses, the ability by magic to help women in childbirth. He worked on the canal in Manchester. In Exeter, they jailed him. His hands had been blessed by the seventh son of a seventh son. He claimed to be able to make cider by looking at a barrel of apples, or the Cornish drink, perry, by looking at pears. For a shilling, if you gave him a knife, he would sleep with it beneath his pillow, and it would never again dull, the blade would slit diamonds. But greatest of his wonders was the tale he had in twelve parts, one for every night of the Christmas season: how the magi met a wren on their way through a forest and she led them to the clearing from where the Bethlehem star was sighted.

On the way, the Eastern Kings christened the nameless lesser stars and the wildflowers that sprouted in the forest track before them: calamint, celandine, aubrieta, bedstraw, the words perfumed as the flowers themselves. Their names in the gypsy's accent, tinctured by Manchester and Munster, made music. Juniper, arrowglass, purslane.

The people would crowd into the cottage where he stayed every homecoming, a bothy inherited by his widowed sister once married to a settled man, a miner from Cornwall. Others clustered to the lamplit windows like a murmuration of moths, no matter the weather or the lateness of the hour, many clutching bottles for him, or pipes of tobacco, or handfuls of ivy leaves, said to be lucky. He started when he started, he finished when he finished.

Some years, the whole townland arrived, there'd be throngs in the lanes, but if no one came it was the same to him, the story would be told anyway. 'I'd tell it to the hearth if I had to. Many's the time I did. I was in the Queen's navy one time, been up to the Arctic where it's blackdark half the year, Chicago, Guatemala, Australia, America. I been all over England and back ninety times, Coventry, Birmingham, Hull, pick your card, I seen things in Jakarta would grow a corpse's toenails, and there's no place like home, boy, I'd know for I was there and told my story in every kip and hive along the way.' It was always the same story. Everyone had heard it. But there was something in the telling made it sacred.

One year, a professor came all the way from Sweden to write the tale down, but the travelling man would have none of it, the scholar's pen must be broken and put in the fire, his notebook thrown in the river. The story of the stars and wildflowers must never be written. If it were, he'd forget how to say it.

Tea drunk, he rinses his cup, peers out the broken-shuttered window, through the hurtful winter daylight. In the distance, the grey expanse of the Vatican gardens, silver-blue lawns, gravelled pathways. Eleven escaped prisoners are hiding in those gardens, in outhouses, potters' sheds, the greenhouse, the empty icehouse. He wonders how long it can last.

A gruff purr from behind. He turns, to an offering.

Cleopatra, in her maw the veiny mangled mess that used to be a rat.

Making his way through the corridors, he hears laughter and coughing above him, the slam of a door. Not wishing to encounter anyone, he detours towards the back staircase, but the new Rector, an elderly, ostrich-eyed South German Jesuit, is descending in pyjamas and dressing gown.

'Ah, Hugh,' the Rector says. 'You have been busy in these past days.'

'Yes, Rector.'

'Very good. You are an example. What plans?'

'Catching up on the filing that needs attention before the Christmas recess. I have letters that must be in the post by this evening.'

'Again, very good. Was there something you wished to say?'

'Rector?'

'You appear, what is the word. Expectant?'

88

'No.'

'Did you sleep well last night? My own sleep is disturbed of late. Since the bombings commenced, I find that I have most vivid dreams.'

'I have heard that said by many.'

'Most vivid. Disturbing. But this is not your own experience?'

'No.'

'Very good. Go along.'

As he leaves, the Rector calls him back.

'Forgive me, Hugh. A possibility occurs. Might one ask?'

'Of course.'

'I am scheduled to celebrate a wedding this afternoon but a difficulty has arisen. I feel unwell, as no doubt you have inferred from my clothing. This sleeplessness, as I mentioned. And headaches. Also diarrhoea. Might you be able to stand in? Half-past three in the Chapel of the Relics. I am sorry it is such short notice. It is not too sudden?'

'No, Rector.'

'*Vielen Dank.*'

As the bells toll for three, he crosses the College cemetery, blessing himself hurriedly, then through the side gate that leads to the white expanse of the square, where pilgrims are already gathering at the vast doors of the Basilica. The queue spreading around the colonnade and beginning to double back on itself. Hawkers assailing them with medals and prayer books.

A hundred and fifty metres away, just over the boundary line, three open-backed trucks, spewing spectres of exhaust, flanks boasting the red-and-black swastika.

A trio of German soldiers with their backs to him, slouch-hipped, smoking, arms about each other, having their photograph taken by a fourth. St Peter's as backdrop to the comradely mirth. A tannoy in one of the trucks playing 'Lili Marlene'.

He circles the Piazza quickly, head up, breathing hard, is approached by a woman selling bottles of holy water shaped like the Virgin Mary.

'*Grazie, no.*'

'Do you wish me to give you holy water for nothing, Father?'

'I don't,' he replies. 'But I haven't any money.'

'Ten lire,' she says.

'Really. I have nothing.'

'Five.'

'I can't.'

'*Madonna mia.*'

With a roll of the eyes, she leaves, swishing at the non-existent flies, her sandalled feet dusty, tiny bells tinkling on her heavy velvet skirts, clutch-sack of plaster Colosseum paperweights banging her thigh. Pigeons rise around her as she goes.

At three-fifteen, the huge, heavy doors are pulled open. The maw of the Basilica yawns. He has his pass, but he waits in line with the pilgrims. There is solace in hearing the clamorous orchestra of languages, hopeful, excited, as people entering a theatre, or moved to silent tears by the immensity.

Women in front of him grasp hands, stifle sobs. An old man is murmuring the paternoster. Girl Guides praying in French, in every dialect of Italian, children dark-eyed with frightened awe, clutching their fathers' cuffs. A solemn priest in gemmed vestments stands sentry in the doorway, ensuring the rules concerning dress are observed with full propriety – no short sleeves for women, no men with hatted heads – and he nods like a metronome as they enter the cavernous space, its lungs breathing incense and age.

An unseen choir is singing plainchant and it echoes around the apse. Pilgrims gape up at the vaulted ceiling; the faraway frescoes shimmer, the air so very cold, so stern. In less than a minute, fifty candles are lighted, soon a hundred, then a thousand, a salt-shake of light in that lake of shadows and gilded murk. Weeping, a young woman kneels, kisses the feet of a statue. The susurration of seven thousand whispers.

He joins the line at a confession box near the *Pietà* side-chapel, for a priest about to celebrate a sacrament must always have confessed. His confessor listens in silence, gives five decades as penance – 'offer them for the conversion of Russia, my son' – and utters the final blessing and absolution hurriedly, as one trying to get through them before the shops close.

Leaving the confessional, he notices, in a pew near the candle table, the seated figure of D'Arcy Osborne, half-nodding, removing his spectacles. Taking a navy handkerchief from the breast pocket of his Savile Row suit, the Ambassador polishes the glasses lightly, holds them up to the stained glass.

The move is a signal. All is in place.

The Rendimento may proceed tonight.

Clusters of cooing pilgrims before the life-size manger, the chipped wise men, the camels. The young woman he saw kissing the statue – she looks like an art student – walks away from the railing, leaving a satchel by the marble steps. Crossing to the Madonna, she makes the sign of the cross.

The plainsong soars. He leans, picks up the satchel.

When he turns, the Ambassador has gone.

12

THE VOICE OF JOHN MAY
20th September 1963
From transcript of BBC research interview, Coldharbour, Poplar, East London

But people take a liberty. Making assumptions, all that. Down the years it's been presumed I only joined the Choir seeing I had to. Me working for Sir D'Arcy at the time.

Not so.

It don't go with no job that you do what you're told outside hours. What happened was, he's asked me. Sir D'Arcy, I mean. Tell a lie, that ain't fully true neither.

Before the war, I worked nightclubs in Soho, up west. I was trying to make it as a musician – saxophonist – but there wasn't no wedge in it. So I've done security to make ends meet. The Shim-Sham, the Windmill. Valentino's Nude Review. I was hospitality steward and doorman, which is a nice way of putting it. Chief knuckleduster more like.

One particular place, Billie's on Denmark Street, things could get a bit tasty. Particular sort of clientele if you know what I mean. Actors, jazzmen, queers, mad poets, villains, bent coppers, nervous wrecks. Nothing very wicked, the odd magic cigarette. You didn't shine your torch in the corners.

Mainly blokes, but you'd get the odd stripper or tart come in. Never met a nicer bunch, as it goes. But sometimes you'd have aggravation off drunks on the door. Some dummy has a skinful, wants to give you the great benefit of his views. Bam. Out of order. Couple of dry slaps. Sleep tight. Most punters are on the level but you'll always get one where it's lights, camera, arsehole. That's when you bang your clapperboard.

No queer's never done me no bother, I say live and let live. Leave them people alone, mind your business. Old music-hall song was popular here in the East End when I was a nipper. 'A Little of What You Fancy Does You Good.'

Sir D'Arcy Osborne's a regular. Big tipper. Nice man. Respectful, good-humoured. Very civil to the staff. Which I've noticed. If you're looking for a sign that a bloke is a chuntering tosspot, it's the way he treats the people who can't answer back, like waiters or cigarette girls. Sir D'Arcy treated them civil, always time for a smile or a kind word. Sort of thing gets appreciated. Manners don't cost. Some of the punters was married, others wasn't. Obviously. Sir D'Arcy used to say he never met the right girl. Or was 'married to his career'. You didn't push.

Blokes dancing with blokes in a nightclub don't bother me none. If you're bothered yourself, don't go, mate. Have a dance with your bloody wardrobe as far as I'm concerned, and take it to bed with you after, if it's willing to go. Best of luck to the pair of you. Free country.

So, Sir D'Arcy's in one midnight with a couple of his old school muckers and they're larking about with the drag boys. It's coming on a bit fairyland and hark-at-her, Gladys, and they're calling Sir D'Arcy 'Francesca', just good clean fun, but there's trouble outside as they're leaving. Gang of Blackshirts wants to give them a talking-to. With a brick. I've dealt with the difficulty efficaciously, as Sir D'Arcy puts it later. I wasn't what you'd call the most elegant pugilist, but let's just say they wouldn't have been doing the foxtrot for a while.

The surprise was Sir D'Arcy, he's gone off like a ten-bob rocket. During the ruckus, I've looked up, he's battered one of the tosspots half-stupid, stuffing his face through the hole in a letterbox. Roundhoused him. The other, he's give him an unmerciful bunch of fives up the bollocks. Queensbury rules? Not tonight. After they've scarpered, he's doing his cufflinks, straightening the dickey bow in a barber's shop window, cleaning blood and snot off his wingtips with his cravat. Tell you, I'm impressed. 'Boxed at school,' he's explained. 'Never cared for a bullyboy.'

Well, we've needed a couple of stitches, nothing major, just a graze, so it's cab down the hospital, long wait. Porter asks him, 'Is that your son, sir?' Sir D'Arcy goes, 'No, but I should be proud if he were. Might I introduce to you my associate, John May Esquire of Whitechapel, a goodly knight and true.' Sign on the wall says 'Silence', but Sir D'Arcy won't stop talking; he's either burbling away in Latin or he's making me laugh. 'Those ruffians, all they want's a good shagging. Why don't they just *ask*? One might *like* a bit of rough. Ah, nice to see you, Matron, good evening, *enchanté*.'

Couple of nights later, he's asked me to come and work for him, been posted to Italy, do I fancy it? As it happened, I'd a spot of bother going on over a matter of missing gelt from a certain enterprise, mate of mine's happened to accidentally wander into a spirits-and-fags warehouse down Deptford with a crowbar, wandered out with a truckload of Scotch. Fortnight later give us the loot to mind, Old Bill's sniffing around, then there's a concatenation of misunderstandings. Also, I'd be overdoing it a bit on the giggle-smoke of late. Also, a woman I was involved with told me she's stopped loving her husband. I stopped loving her, right then, if ever I had. Be handy to get out of Soho.

'Tiny matter – my handle's a bit of a mouthful, John. I am Sir Francis D'Arcy Godolphin Osborne. Ordinarily, as you know, I am addressed as "Sir D'Arcy", but I prefer to be called "Frank" by my friends.'

I said I shouldn't think it quite proper to address a Sir as a friend.

'I do wish you would, John.'

'Thank you, no, sir.'

'What about "Sir Frank", then? As a workable compromise?'

I've thought about that. Felt acceptable. Had a ring to it.

'Sound,' I've told him.

'Excellent.'

We shook hands on Sir Frank and a week later off to Italy. But things didn't turn out simple. Never do.

What's occurred, we was there in Rome when Fritz come rolling in and we've had to scarper into Vatican City a bit lively. Fairly cramped, I'll be honest. But needs must. That's that. I've kipped in worse places than the Vatican. I've even kipped in Chislehurst. Spent forty years there one evening. Long story.

You might think the Vatican would be boring. You'd be sodding well right. Bugger all to do at night if you ain't a bat or a bellringer. That's what got on my wick, the monotony. Do your head in something proper. Another thing, I'm Jewish, not that I'm religious, never was. So there wasn't even Catholicism to get the horn about.

Young gun at large in Rome, the evenings tend to be full, if you know what I'm getting at. Presentable-looking fella with a few pound in his pocket? You'll have a good time in Rome, never fear, and a story to tell after. Suddenly, all that's gone.

It's me and Sir Frank and his horrible little dog, Sirius, cross between a Jack Russell and a gnome. Most kickable living thing I ever had the misfortune to know. The sheer amount of shit come out of this dog? Had to be seen to be believed. Go out for a stroll, it's priests and nuns everywhere. Nothing against them, like I said, but we ain't having no bottle party. Knees-up with a nun? Ain't fun.

Sir Frank, see he's lucky, able to go into his own imagination. Talking to you about the Riviera, the nightlife in Cannes, skiing with the sodding Kaiser in Switzerland, all that. One morning I've come in and he says to me, 'John, I'm off to Locarno tonight for the spa and the baths, going to have a lovely time, come back slim, fit and handsome.' I've said, 'It's Locarno you're going to, not sodding Lourdes.'

At least I had the sax, so I'd practise, do my scales. Chromatic, octatonic, pentatonic, the lot. Two, three hours straight. I'd blow till my lips hurt. Flaming sax would be speaking. Or squeaking. But you can't practise all night on your tod like a pranny. You're missing the drummer, a pianist, the double bass. Belting out a blues in the Vatican felt dodge. Also, you've come over a bit sad. Blow an F-sharp, you're seeing Greek Street, punters in the clubs, some killer-diller brunette giving you a smile through a sandwich-bar window across Dean Street. A sax can get into you that way.

So it's me and Sir F, staring up at the walls. There's a gramophone record of some Scottish bird wailing about the glens, the way they do, but we ain't got no gramophone to play it on. Only one solitary book any normal person would read, history of the Vatican down the ages. Tell you what. Cassocks up. *Buongiorno*, darling, I'm a Cardinal. There was Popes got banged more times than an anvil. Well, it's power I suppose. And they're sharp dressers, Popes. A bloke in a frock can do well.

Apart from that, a load of books on theology and eschatology and epistemology and bollocksology, tripe no one would read except at gunpoint. Pneumatology, ecclesiology. Right page-turners. We've smuggled in a radio but the crystals ain't working. One night he's come in, all smiles, silly berk. 'You'll never guess what I've found at the back of the sideboard, John. A special treat once you've finished sweeping the chimneys.'

This was his little joke. We'd had a row about the way he was overworking me.

'Our entertainment difficulties are a thing of the past, John, dear boy.'

Five-thousand-piece jigsaw.

Of the Vatican.

Do what?

I've said thank you very much, leave it out.

Soon after, I've noticed this particular Padre's started hanging about like cheap aftershave. This big Paddy, dropping in now and again on Sir Frank for a cuppa. Bit funny, my pal. Bit odd.

Or Sir Frank's having a natter with him down in the courtyard late at night when no one's still up, just him and the Padre, rabbiting away in Latin, playing *darts*, and the cats in a circle staring up at them. Or Ancient Greek. Couple of nights, the same, then he don't come near or by. Then he's back. Now he's gone. Bit curious. I think they'd met before, on the golf course, it was. Seemed an all right sort of bloke. Fairly nondescript, I'll be honest. Bit serious for a Paddy. That worried me.

Paddy's all right when he's cracking jokes. When he's serious, it's a worry. When Paddy's quiet, watch out, he's doing one of two things. Resenting you, or scheming. Or priming his bomb. Not being funny. Watch your Paddy.

In the pictures, a Paddy priest, he'll be played by Bing Crosby. This one was more your George Raft. Tough. Quiet. Wouldn't want to mess him about. Touch of the Robert Mitchums. Not a talker.

Soon after, I've started noticing something odd in Sir Frank. His requests and that. Seem unusual. One morning he's asked me on a sudden if I can lay hands on a couple of shirts. Course I can, sir, how many would you like?

He's looked at me in a funny way and said, fifteen.

Five small, five large, five medium.

Kind of thing makes you think. You've time on your hands. Fifteen shirts, what's he at? Forming a rugby team?

But if the boss wants fifteen shirts, then fifteen shirts he gets. That's part of being a manservant. You don't ask no questions. I know this second-hand clothes geezer down the market, the Mercato Rionale, and he's fixed me up handy. Fifteen shirts. In a bag. *Grazie, Luigi*. Here's a tenner, have a good drink. There's always a Man to Know in Italy.

'For the poor of Rome,' Sir Frank's told me, later. 'Even in adversity, we must think of those less fortunate than ourselves, John.'

As a manservant, you come to expect things. It's part of the job. Discretion. You saw nothing. Keep shtum.

You'll find bosses might ask you to lay hands on a case of vodka. Packet of

French letters, a particular cigar. Stockings for his bit of frippet, sleeping tablets, a girlie film and projector. Or if he's the other way inclined, what used to be called a weightlifting magazine. It ain't Jeeves and Wooster no more, if ever it was.

Done a spell in the army as a batman for a titled gentleman, you'd have heard of him. One day he's sent me down to the chemist in the village.

For what, sir?

Nothing.

Beg pardon, sir?

Nothing. Simply ask for the chemist in person, explain you're from the Manor, you'd like the usual nothing, and wait for the package.

The package, sir?

Yes.

Of what, sir?

Nothing.

Nothing, sir?

Stop complicating matters, are you deaf?

But it's come to the point with Sir Frank where I can't go on remark-less. Thirty pairs of trousers. Forty sets of underwear. Train tickets to Zurich in the name of everyone on this list, memorise the list, then burn it. Forty overcoats, all different. Forty cardigans. Forty hats.

I'm to bag the stuff up and cart it over to the Padre's rooms in the Collegio. Leave it outside his door. Knock twice. Disappear. All a bit secretive and mysterious, that Paddy. I've give him the nickname 'Hughdini'.

Suits. Jackets. Train driver's overalls. It's coming obvious by now, they're running one of two things. An Amateur Dramatic Society or an Escape Line.

I've tried dropping the hint, I know what's going on, but Sir Frank won't give me no gen. I mean, nothing.

I ain't stupid. Course I knew. Impossible not to. So, one morning I've said to him, pouring the nettle tea for his breakfast, because you couldn't get coffee in Rome for love nor cash money, 'I've a surprise for you, sir. Here you go.'

What I've put on the table is a shopping bag from Barbiconi, a posh shop for priests near the Trevi Fountain. A priesty boutique, if you will. The clobber in Barbiconi, it's none of your muck. Silk soutanes. Hand-stitched shoes. Black cashmere gloves. Velvet slippers. The Pope gets his socks and drawers off Barbiconi, so they say. Upscale clerical schmatta, no fannying about. You want the

Mae West? Look no further. Only, it's come to my attention from Luigi down the market that stuff can be arranged to fall off a lorry now and again. What I've got in the bag is two dozen priesty shirts, nice texture, charcoal grey, assorted sizes.

I've said, 'I should like to assist more fully in the endeavours of your good self and the Padre, sir.'

That's how I've put it. Nice and discreet. You didn't want to startle him, dear me, no. Sir Frank wasn't a man for startling early in the morning. He felt things heavily then.

Well, his newspaper's twitched – a copy of last week's *Times* – and slowly he's lowered it, dramatic like, *tense*, and the eyes behind the specs are giving it large.

'To which endeavours in particular do you allude, John, may one enquire?'

Public school is marvellous, though, isn't it?

'The work you and the Padre are up to for the poor of Rome, sir. If you take my meaning.'

'Ah.'

'Yes, sir.'

'I had rather formed the impression that our work was a secret, John, old thing.'

'Any secret's quite safe with me, sir. As you know.'

'John, dearest, one's been waiting so long to hear those words from your lips. How deliciously you flirt.'

'I'm serious.'

Well, he's looked at me a while. I can hear his brain turning.

Because it's a crossroads, when you think. A moment like that. You'll remember it the rest of your life, depending on how you chose. There's a swamp between you and the right thing; how far out are you going to wade? It matters, what you did. Always will.

'Fetch another cup, would you, John?'

'We expecting a guest, sir?'

'I should like you to have a cup of this ghastly brew with me, John. Be seated.'

'What are we going to talk about?'

'Nothing.'

— 13 —

Christmas Eve 1943
3.29 p.m.
7 hours and 31 minutes before the Rendimento

In the sacristy, he dons the heavy vestments, begins preparation for the wedding. The ledger must be completed in Latin, and, since Fascism came, in Italian. As he turns through the ancient book, a scrap of hand-drawn manuscript that someone folded into the pages is revealed, a fake signature half-obscuring the watermark.

He recognises the script as John May's. A couple of minutes to decode the message.

Sam Derry is back but weak and in pain. These addresses are to be avoided. Angelucci's on his way.

Taking an empty shampoo bottle from his pocket, he quarter-fills it with altar wine, screws it tight, slides it into his soutane.

A knock, and the best man returns, now accompanied by the mother of the bride, expensive hat in hand, her hair a sprayed-on grey helmet.

'I understand we have a difficulty,' she says.

'Not a very important one. The position is as I explained to this man.'

'What did you mean, "ill", Father?'

'My title is Monsignor.'

'Monsignor, this is my daughter's nuptial Mass. His eminence, the Rector, was asked a month ago to perform the ceremony.'

'I understand, *Signora*, but illnesses do happen.'

'My guests have been informed that the priest will be a Rector.'

'That won't be the case, I'm afraid.'

'What am I to tell them?'

'Whatever you wish.'

'Fetch the Rector quickly, Monsignor, he won't be needed longer than one hour.'

'That is not possible.'

'My husband is high up in the Party, I warn you. We are friends of Obersturmbannführer Hauptmann.'

'The Party has no authority here.'

'I – beg your pardon?'

'You are in the house of the Almighty, *Signora*, not a Meeting Hall.'

'The Party has laboured endlessly for the betterment of Italy.'

'God has no country.'

Shock lights her.

'Where are the altar boys? I ordered six.'

'One does not "order" altar boys, *Signora*, they are not frittata sandwiches.'

'I shall have to cancel the ceremony. The Party shall hear of this affront.'

'As you wish.'

She turns to the best man. 'Guido, take that idiot's look off your face and wait outside for them as they arrive. Don't "but" me, do as I say. My good God, the shame. Get going, don't stand there like a lamp post.'

'Monsignor, what shall I do?'

'I warn you, son, *Tra moglie e marito non mettere il dito*. Woe to those coming between husband and wife. *Signora*, if you wish to cancel the ceremony, I insist that you discuss the matter with the couple. Stop wasting my time. Out you go.'

'You dare to speak to me like what, an old mongrel?'

'I will not permit you to send a proxy to do your bidding. If the bride or groom come to me in person with word that we are not to proceed, their request is granted and the subject is closed. But if they prayerfully aspire to be husband and wife, they are already married in the eyes of Almighty God and the Church. All the celebrant does is bear witness. Be he Curate, Rector, Cardinal or Pope.'

At the deployment of the final word, she gasps as though spat at.

'Perhaps,' the best man ventures, 'the *Signora* and I might step outside for a moment.'

'There's the door. Don't let me detain you.'

As they leave, he resumes work on the parchment, filling in the date, the place, the names of the couple, then his own. It is one of those moments when writing your name feels strange and you wonder how it belongs to you, if it does. John May's radiant frown seems to flicker at him from the flame of a candle. 'Chin up, Monsignor Mitchum. There's my boy.' His Londoner's courage. The music of his English. Even his way of lighting a cigarette has a sort of correctness and suavity, a physical grace, an ease. 'Monsignor Mitchum, you're a jazzman only you don't know it yet. We'll go down Soho when this is over. Never fear.'

Guido returns with a message. The wedding is to proceed.

An unsmiling, frock-coated Don who can only be the bride's father is ushering guests to seats in the side chapel, accepting their kisses to his hands. The Man Whose Daughter Was Married in St Peter's. Lengths of white ribbon have been draped through the ironwork of the gates. Almond sweets are being placed on dishes, for luck. The groom, a moustachioed Private, is missing a leg and is leaning on a crutch. A bridesmaid offers to fetch a chair but he insists on standing. Peaked cap beneath his elbow, hair black and lustrous as his epaulets. Dress sword glinting on his hip. Behind him, six comrades, polished as new plums, at red-faced, high-necked attention.

The bridesmaid and maids of honour in a line by the altar rail, rosary beads dangling from gloved, slender wrists. Old uncles suited like disappointed bank managers beside their disappointed wives, glaring sullenly from the benches or staring hard at their prayer books as though apparitions are happening in the margins. It is a way of not noticing the unannounced guest. Despite the best efforts of the couturier, it is evident that the bride is pregnant.

Shining with hurt handsomeness, the soldier's face is that of a Raphael archangel, but his accent is southern, *Siciliano*. His voice quivers with feeling as he utters the vows, and the bride clutches his hand in a lover's reassurance.

Drawn by the bride's beauty and the magnetism of weddings, pilgrims stop to watch, to the evident irritation of her parents. The first marital kiss raises cheers from the aisle. *Viva gli sposi!* Long live the newlyweds.

The couple sign the register and ask him to stand with them for a photograph. The soldier's arm about his shoulder, the warm, sweet strawberry scent of the bride's perfume.

As the show of politeness required in Italy, he at first declines the offering made by the bride's father, and the Don in turn insists, handing over the envelope.

'A discreet word, *Signore*? Step into the corner with me a moment?'

'*Monsignore?*'

'A minor difficulty.'

'How?'

'That amount is not sufficient.'

'*Mi scusi?*'

'The offering to a priest for a marriage carried out in St Peter's is customarily three times that sum. Naturally I do not wish to embarrass you in front of your guests.'

'That is all the money I have with me.'

'Then you shall have to ask your friends.'

'Can you be serious?'

'The labourer is worthy of his hire.'

'You think yourself clever to quote scripture? Even Jews can do that.'

'That is hardly surprising since they wrote a great deal of it.'

Muttering, the Don turns his back, rummages in his wallet, hands over a wad of bills the thickness of a roof slate.

Not the worst feeling to know that a Fascist's money will be given to a Jewish escapee.

Hollow victories are not quite defeats.

———

Changing out of the stiff vestments, he hangs them in the sacristy garderobe, locks it and leaves the room, re-entering the transept, satchel in hand.

The Basilica heaves, pilgrims crowding into every nook, surrounding the vastness of the altar to take photographs of the statues and monstrance. Swiss Guards hissing them to cease. A souk in Palestine comes to mind, where he once got lost. Far above, the bells toll four.

A German naval officer in black uniform leads a woman from chapel to chapel, gesturing up at foreshortened, hair-lined frescoes, the fine lace of an altar cloth, his black-gloved hands pointing out the numerous intricacies no guidebook is able to show. From time to time, she leans her head back in almost convincing imitation of hanging on his every word.

An African Sister in a white habit kneels alone on the stone of the aisle as the choirboys loft a harmony towards the dome. Old vowels lengthening, *In Excélsis Deo*, the 'o' echoing back like a recollection. A party of bored-looking schoolchildren tolerate the remonstrations of their teacher, who had to bribe someone to get to the top of the Christmas Eve queue but now feels her money was wasted.

Laudámus te,
benedícimus te,
adorámus te,
glorificámus te,
Dómine Deus, Rex caeléstis,
Deus Pater omnípotens.

Outside, he stands a moment on the steps, in the smoky minor chord of a Roman winter. Larks rise from the colonnade, circling the Piazza, or swooping over the gypsies selling chestnuts at braziers. A band of pilgrims brandishing a tricolour he doesn't recognise are trying to get a communal hymn going, howling it at the vast and roiling crowd, but not many are taking it up and after a minute, it dies, replaced by the mass murmur of prayer.

With a start he sees Angelucci, a hundred metres away.

Slouched against the rim of the fountain, hawking candles and Mass cards at the foldable card table he brings to the square. The red hunting cap means he's received the message, knows what to do. The pilgrims try again with the hymn.

Emerging, the German officer and his lady notice a Monsignor descending the steps hurriedly, now pushing through the people and the smoke of the chestnuts, towards the fountain, where he turns his back on a candle-seller and makes the sign of the cross towards the Basilica before heading on, in the direction of the Holy Office.

The huge, studded door of the sombre fortress is hard to push open, heavy as it groans closed behind him to sepulchral silence. The city vanishes. Like being inside a pyramid. After four on a Christmas Eve, no one will be here.

Caged light bulbs hum as he flicks the switch. An elephant's-foot umbrella stand containing a single umbrella and a cluster of canes. The concierge's desk is draped, the porter's counter untended. He enters the lodge, checks his pigeonhole.

A Christmas card from his Fourth Years, a Waugh novel from the Book Club, a circular from *Newsweek*, a late-delivered essay on St Theresa, a loaned-out volume of Housman's poetry that a seminarian is returning after almost a year. A scrawl in the Rector's handwriting, on the back of a reused envelope, 'Hugh, I have a favour to ask. Come and see me.'

Six months ago, a lift was installed in what some of the older priests don't like calling the foyer, but he distrusts it, finds the mercilessly efficient turn of its wheel and greased cables threatening, like a machine encountered in a Breughel purgatory. Anyhow, it often breaks down.

He climbs the steep, granite staircase through the many-roomed emptiness, the walls around him substantial, four hundred years of silence. Well-connected Cardinals used to live at the Holy Office. Since the invasion, they've all moved away.

On the fourth floor, breathless, he unlocks the scriptorium and enters. The vast shutters of his workplace half-closed.

Bowed bookshelves. Onyx inkwells. Stacks of mouldering files. Mouse-gnawed dissertations on Christology.

Quills and their sharpeners. Letter-openers. Ledgers. Spiderwebbed portraits of virginal martyrs. A knot of tangled scapulars dangling from a doorknob, near a trinity of rickety candlesticks. Relics and rat traps. A skull doing duty as *memento mori*. Tomes. Bones. Combed texts of encyclicals. Leaded windows left unwashed for as long as anyone can remember. Only the heavy shellac telephones and the red metal fire-bucket announce the twentieth century as fact.

A young priest from Melbourne used to refer to the room as 'The Old Girls' Dormitory'. He didn't last long in the Vatican.

An empty ashtray on a windowsill.

A copy of the Catechism.

A teacup with something growing in its depths.

The old painting of St Cecilia that always reminds him of Marianna de Vries, his Dutch comrade from the Choir. When he told her, she laughed, 'I am no saint, my dear friend.' And yet, the woman in the picture has the same stoicism and strength, the jaw of a survivor, someone not to be fooled. Not exactly matter-of-factness but a high cognisance of realities, an absence of hate, a sort of reasonableness in the place where prejudice should be. If the world were governed by women like Marianna, he often thinks, famine would long ago have vanished. 'That is nonsense,' she tells him. 'But you tell charming untruths. Since I irritate myself so much, I will try to believe.'

On his Dickensian accountant's desk, a head-high stack of parchments, petitions for the granting of annulment. His task and that of the twenty other functionaries who work in the scriptorium is to read and reflect, to evaluate and categorise, most petitions to be dismissed, others considered by canon law scholars, a small few to be adjudicated by the Papal advisors.

It is work he loathes, as anyone would. Doing it feels the burden it is.

A woman in Toulouse wants her marriage ended because her husband is a violent drunkard. A man in Guatemala 'has become separate' from his wife. Sexual relations have 'long ceased' between a couple in Ottawa, never took place between a couple in Chicago.

He checks his watch. Already four-forty. The telephone will ring at five. Important to fill the time, to settle.

He pictures Angelucci in the square. Hopes he's ready for the danger. That lofty-browed, umber-eyed, unimpressible Roman, face made to be stamped in profile on an imperial coin, his nosebone the length of Italy.

Give me a shot, Monsignore. I despise these bastards.

That's why you're a risk.

One chance.

There is a last task to be faced before the Rendimento is able to be launched, but he'll wait until after the telephone call before taking that on, so he faces into a clutch of subpoenas from a woman in Paterson, New Jersey, but can't settle or think, mind flitting like a wasp. The couple's children, a boy of seven and a nine-year-old girl, seem to knock on the windows of what their mother is saying, frightened, pleading, contriving bad bargains, not wanting the marriage that gave them life to be ended, no matter its imperfections. He considers the Bishop's letter carefully, weighing, sifting. There are no grounds; the application for annulment will be refused. But after a moment of nagging conscience, he changes his mind. For pity's sake, let the poor woman be free.

Five o'clock comes rowdily with the Basilica's bells. He crosses to the telephone, ready to snatch it and respond to the code word with his own.

A minute past.

Nothing.

Five past.

Silence.

Dread creams in his stomach. He swallows it down.

On seven minutes, he lifts the receiver, taps the cradle, hears the purr. Quickly he dials the exchange to confirm the line is working this evening. The operator assures him that it is.

Quarter past. Twenty past. Twenty minutes to six.

The task must be done now, while the building is empty.

Approaching the ancient bookshelves behind the oaken screen in the darkest corner of the scriptorium, he pulls over the sliding library ladder, climbs. A powdery reek of mildew cracks open his headache and he sneezes so hard that the ladder rocks and creaks and he grasps it like a mast in a storm. On the penultimate rung, he steadies, reaches for the hefty book shoved in hard at the back, a folio of a medieval codex.

106

The cover, faded calfskin, is shredded and mottled, the heavy, atlas-sized lectionary is hard to manoeuvre down the ladder.

Still no call.

Hefting the book onto a table, he opens the cover, turns carefully. Illuminated grinning evangelists, scarlet dragons, silver gryphons, the rook-black of the text, the black of burned coal. Then a carnival of ornamented capitals wound in eagles and serpents, the haloes of archangels forming ivory O's, to the hollow where the middle quires have been patiently razored out, in which eleven folded pieces of architectural paper are hidden.

Each piece, the size of a tablecloth, covered in his minuscule handwriting.

Names, contacts, hiding places, dates. Regiments, ranks, camps from where each man escaped. Amounts bunged as hush money, bribes, rents, payments for forgeries of passports. Monies In as donations, Monies Out and to whom. When, which currency, what for. The code he uses is complex, mirror-writing and musical notation, but Hauptmann at the Gestapo has opened a sub-office in Via Tasso dedicated to the breaking of codes. The papers must be destroyed before tonight's Rendimento. Too late to bury them in the Vatican gardens with the rest.

Each sheet is too large to be burned in one piece. From his pocket he takes the carving knife filched from the kitchen, begins hacking the papers into halves, quarters, then eighths and sixteenths, slow, tedious work but the fragments can be placed one at a time in a candle flame, then the ashes in the wastepaper basket, which he can empty every few minutes out the window.

The stench of ashen scorch in the room is heavy, more lingering than he expected, and he wishes there were something he could do to disguise it. But on Christmas Eve, no one will come, not the cleaning ladies, not the guards; anyway, he will leave the window open. He works his way through the first sheet's tatters in just under seven minutes, sweat stippling his brow, slickening his upper lip; finds a rhythm as he moves to the second. But the paper is now damp from his perspiration and won't light. Cursing his ungainly fingers, he tears it into the tiniest pieces he can contrive, a confetti he flings from the mullioned oriel window, now drying his hands on his soutane.

The telephone trills.

Crossing, he grasps the receiver.

'Good evening, Monsignor, just to confirm, the piece is in G-sharp,' the voice says.

Blon Kiernan, Delia's daughter.

'Understood,' he replies.

'Happy Christmas, Monsignor.'

The line goes dead.

Important to hurry on.

Slashing the remaining sheets into rough eighths, he balls them, scrunching tightly, forces them into the red metal fire-bucket. Unwise, he knows, but time is running down.

Angelucci is now in place. Derry is briefing him.

As his match yellows the paper, an unmistakable *clank* floats its way up from the lobby, magnified by the soundbox of the lift shaft.

He stalls.

A mishearing?

The cables grind and buzz.

Iron gears whingeing with exertion.

Rain pelting the windows.

He hurries to the scriptorium door and locks it.

The dull metallic *thunk* as the lift bumps to its stop at the end of the corridor. The clank of the caged door yanked open. Slammed shut.

Footsteps, then.

A middleweight.

Booted.

Slowly along the landing, as a jailer on his rounds. Opening and entering the rooms in turn as he goes, the clank and rattle of a great chain of keys. Now pausing outside the scriptorium door.

Nothing is said.

A cuckoo-clock chirps.

The pages in the fire-bucket smoulder but don't light.

Smoke whirls.

The handle turns.

Quickly sits to his desk, spreads a parchment before him, black words and accusations seeming to spin, a miasma of recriminations. Fingers trembling, he pares a quill, rearranges a jug, pours himself a tumbler but the water slops on his wrists and tastes old and rancid and glassy and greasy, and the children of the unhappy couple in New Jersey pulse with him, somehow, like the after-image of something dark seen in light.

The handle is tried again.

Twice.

Three times.

A rattle in the lock. The door is pushed but doesn't budge.

The intruder utters a sigh, now clomps away down the corridor, slowly, with eerie stateliness, hobnails clicking on the mosaic.

The *huff* as breath is sucked in, the quickening, running boot-steps, and the pummel of the body charging the door like a stabbed ox and the metre-high plaster statue of St Anthony of Padua topples from an alcove overhead and smashes on the desk and again the body withdraws, again bull-slams the door, now grunting, moaning, seething, screaming, but the studded oak, the door of an imperial bastion, refuses to give, and the architrave is granite and the frame is heavy marble and the volley of hard, sharp kicks rattle the vehement lock in its cast-iron moorings but nothing more and the ox-man retreats.

The lift gate whangs open, and, after a moment, closes, and the cage whines its descent to the foyer.

He creeps out to the stairhead. Two cats in a doorway. He can hear the intruder downstairs, going about in the foyer, rummagings and burrowings, opening and slamming drawers in the concierge's desk, going in and out of the porter's lodge, wrenching open the filing cabinet, then the cannon-boom slam of the closing front door.

From the scriptorium window, he peers down but the rainfall is heavy and his spectacles fog. The figure, beneath the umbrella from the hallstand, is making its way across the Piazza, with odd daintiness, avoiding puddles and dogs, like a murderer pretending to be a lady, in the direction of Largo degli Alicorni.

Sleet hisses hard on the ivy-choked skylight.

He empties the fire-bucket of the smouldering, stinking pages, stamps them out on the floor, bundles them as best he can, places the mess under his arm as he leaves the scriptorium, now hastening, half-tripping down the stair-case. Best to dispose of them later, get out of the Holy Office while he can. The intruder might return with a Luger or a crowbar. Any sort of incident must be avoided.

Several times tonight, he will wonder what force drew him back to the porter's lodge, to glance a last time into the pigeonhole he emptied only an hour beforehand.

In it now, a brown paper bag, plump as a pouch. The handwritten name and address are very slightly inaccurate.

Hugo Flaherty

Personal

The Holy College

Roma

Inside is a small envelope, which he doesn't open immediately, containing what he thinks, from the scrunch beneath his fingertips through the paper, must be rosary beads.

The sheet of white airmail flimsy is folded into careful quarters, feels delicate as a page torn from a Bible. Three words, in the same hand, underlined in red ink.

YOUR

LAST

CHRISTMAS

The smaller envelope contains thirty-two still-bloodied human teeth.

Hail beats the stained-glass windows.

ACT II

The Solo

14

MARIANNA DE VRIES
November 1962
Written statement in lieu of an interview

During the war I was a freelance journalist based in Rome. I was introduced to Hugh O'Flaherty at the opera. *Tosca* was the piece. I do not recall the singers' names.

I attended as the guest of a Swiss diplomat who had been invited by Mrs Delia Kiernan, wife of the Irish Diplomatic Consul. There were some other Ambassadors and Envoys there. I don't remember now.

Sometime afterwards, I was commissioned to write a series of articles for an American newsmagazine on the artistic treasures of the city's lesser-known churches. 'Hidden Rome' was to be the title. Monsignor O'Flaherty did not of course carry a business card but had obligingly, at my request, that evening scribbled instructions as to how to get to Ostia Antica, on a scrap of the Holy Office headed notepaper that had been doing duty as bookmark in the Louis MacNeice book he was reading, *Autumn Journal*. The telephone number was visible on the scrap, so I called.

That morning he was on the way to a doctoral student's viva voce at the Angelicum, therefore was too busy to converse, but in the coming days he dropped me a note, advising me to undertake the Walk of Seven Churches, a pilgrimage established in the sixteenth century by St Philip Neri, but even though the walk included such beauties as San Sebastiano Fuori le Mura and San Giovanni in Laterano, there was nothing I wanted to write about. There were too many visitors. Nothing here was 'Hidden Rome'. I telephoned the Monsignor again.

We met in a café near Piazza Venezia. When he regarded you through those horn-rimmed spectacles, the effect was a little forbidding, like a torch being shone on you at a midnight roadblock. We spoke of Auden and MacNeice. In the Monsignor's leisure hours, which I gathered were few, for interest he had been working on a translation, *Diario d'autunno*. He felt that 'we don't really know a language until we can translate a poem into it'. Like every priest I have met, he was not without oddities, but I found him warm, genial company, a thoughtful man in both senses of the word. He said that I should feel free to address him by his first name, 'if you are comfortable doing so'. I wasn't, fully. 'Ugo' was the compromise.

At the time I was having an unwise love affair with a married contact, in fact the diplomat with whom I had attended the opera on the night that Ugo and I met. The matter ended when the man was summoned back to the bureau in Zurich. I had suddenly more freedom and time.

I am myself Swiss by birth, which meant that my passport had to be respected by all sides in Rome; I could go about the city, not exactly as I pleased, but with a good deal more latitude than others. Over a couple of weeks and two or three meetings, Ugo assembled for me a list of what he thought the most interesting if less frequently visited churches – there might be a Caravaggio Virgin and Child, say a fresco by Raphael, or a neglected but imposing piece of pre-Renaissance statuary – and I commenced a rigorous process of visiting them. The English church on Via del Babuino was a great favourite of his, for example. I had never heard of it but found its simplicity beautiful. He knew every Abbot and Reverend Mother, wrote letters of introduction or placed somewhat furtive preludial telephone calls requesting that I be assisted.

'Ask for Brother Such-and-Such. Avoid Sister So-and-So.'

One felt he rather enjoyed the skulduggery.

I and the roster of commissioned photographers were shown turrets and secret chambers, hidden crypts, disguised vaults, cupolas where medieval lovers were whispered to have trysted, bookshelves that, when a concealed lever was pulled, creaked open into cobbled passageways that led to Rome's sewer system, from there to the banks of the Tiber. Some disclosures were made on condition that precise locations were not revealed; others, custodians insisted, were only for our eyes 'as friends of the Monsignor' and must never be published or hinted at. In one chapel we were permitted to see, set in a wall behind a candle table, a grating no larger than a woman's headscarf. The person squeezing through would find himself in a marble bedchamber which, delightfully, had a skylight and its own tiny fountain. In my mind, Rome turned itself inside out, if one can put it like that. Europe's most majestic city is wearing a face. Behind it, she has numerous secrets. One biblical text, John 14:2, came to have resonant meaning. 'In my Father's house are many rooms.'

Ignorant as to how remunerative matters should be raised with a priest, I suggested that I might pay him five per cent of my fee for the set of articles, a proposal he dismissed with a woof of shocked laughter before proposing that I would instead, if I wished, make a donation to charity.

'Which charity?' I asked.

'Buy yourself a hat. As my gift.'

I donated five per cent to the Blue Nuns for the hungry people of Rome but I did buy a hat, a fedora by Borsalino. As for Ugo, he continued to refuse any payment but once, perhaps twice, permitted me to buy him tickets for the Hospitals' Sweepstake, a sort of lottery involving horseracing. He never won, a fact he liked joking about. 'If I backed the tide, it wouldn't come in.'

My series on 'Hidden Rome' was well received by readers, therefore was popular with my editor. Quickly it threatened to become a book of the same name. The advance I accepted was generous, the work would be pleasant. Ignobly, I was pleased that my former lover, back in Switzerland with his wife, would hear of this success and have the smooth lawns of his life disturbed by it, since the more independent a woman is, the more a certain sort of man will resent her, and resentment, for such a man, is part of what sexually attracts him. But as every guilty-hearted author will know, there are afternoons when you are supposed to be writing when all you can face is a cup of tea and a walk. A book rather gets its hands around your throat and shakes you until your fillings fall out. Some writers are skilled with words, but all of us are skilled with procrastination. What I wanted was to postpone the inevitable.

I kept in touch with Ugo now and again, until we were lunching fortnightly at Rompoldi's bar in Piazza di Spagna or the Trattoria Il Fantino in the Jewish quarter, a down-to-earth place he liked. The quarrelsome waiters flicked beer-towels at the flies or sighed with magnificent and vengeful gloom into the nicotine-stained Coca-Cola mirror.

Having lived in a great many places, Ugo had what is sometimes called a well-stocked mind but his knowledge had not the prim tidiness the phrase connotes. I had never been west of Cape Finisterre but at school had been special friends with a girl raised in San Fernando in Trinidad, the daughter of diplomats, so I was fascinated by Ugo's recollections of the Caribbean. He spoke vividly of the purple-and-ochre sunsets of Port-au-Prince and sombrely of the Vodou priests. I was intrigued by his photographs, of which he had a great many, all monochromes. His was an old Brownie box camera he had picked up in a junk shop on London's Portobello Road. You held it at the waist and looked down into the lens. The click the shutter emitted when you pressed it would have wakened the dead. He was endearingly a little boastful of being rather a good amateur photographer.

Clearly the poor of Port-au-Prince had permitted him to go among them: there were studies of women carrying water jugs, boatmen on a rainy dock-side, ragged fisherfolk hauling and mending nets. His photographs of Czechoslovakia riveted me with a different sort of force, the farmwomen stonily stoic, their pebble-eyed children mirthless. He had many pictures of New York, iron skeletons of yet unfinished skyscrapers groping at the air, tenement fire-escapes on the Lower East Side, a whole album he had taken during a World Series baseball game contested by the Brooklyn Dodgers. I had little idea what the World Series or even the Brooklyn Dodgers might be, and, like all males, dear Ugo rather overenjoyed filling you in, not realising that I didn't know because I couldn't be bothered knowing and I not realising at the time that he had little interest, either; it was more that he liked having something to talk about. Pretending to love the Dodgers gave him that.

Ugo did not like silences; they made him uncomfortable. Soon, in Rome, they would become essential.

My favourites of his photographs were those of London, a city I always feel is most glamorously conjured in black-and-white: Soho doorways. Tower Bridge. A cinema queue in Leicester Square. Actors in a coffee shop. Spivs at a boxing match in Limehouse. He was able to gift you Chelsea, Tottenham Court Road or Primrose Hill as you sweltered in that workmen's café in Rome and the Nazi advance on the city commenced.

Before long they were only two kilometres from the walls. Still Ugo and I continued to meet. He would bring along a wallet of his photographs and we looked at them over coffee, even as we pretended not to hear the artillery in the distance, the shriek and burst of shells.

Indeed, on the afternoon before the Germans overran Rome, I remember

116

him disconcerting a barman. The fellow had joked with him in the manner of the typical Roman male who believes he has invented flirtation and for some reason would like you to think him oversexed: 'Is this beautiful lady your girl-friend, Monsignor?'

Ugo answered, 'Her twin sister.'

The friendship was comfortable but was not close if I can put it like that. One was always aware that Ugo was an ordained Roman Catholic cleric, with the outlooks and boundaries of his calling. These he did not push but, as with all unseen foundations, one assumed they were implacable, no matter the grace of the edifice they supported. He was in many ways a rather conservative person.

Another important element was that I had no religion myself, had been raised contentedly atheist. My view of the universe was, as it remains, that there is nothing to hope for and nothing to fear; to live just once is miracle enough. So, we came up to one another's walls but did not go through the gates. In some ways, it was what made our friendship a happy one.

My father, from Rotterdam, and my mother, born in Harlingen, in Fries-land, were research physicists at the university in Zurich. My parents were both born deaf, and so I knew sign language, a mode of communication that fascinated Ugo. He and I spent a number of enjoyable but profitless hours in Piazza Navona, me attempting to teach him the rudiments over cappuccino, to the waiters' bewilderment, but, like most languages, sign language takes from the start or not at all. After the Choir was formed, John May and Delia Kiernan proved good, sensitive learners. As May liked pointing out, the Italians have vivid hand signals of their own. 'You see them when you step in front of a car.'

Ugo's Italian was the most perfect I have heard spoken by a non-Italian, zestful, performative, alive to the juiciness of Roman common speech (although Roman friends we were to have in common would tease him for speaking the language dully). It gave me great pleasure to hear him speak in the clear, grace-ful English of rural Ireland, full of timbre, subtle expressiveness, friendly seriousness.

Part of the journalist's training is to notice what is unusual. Sometimes it occurred to me that Ugo, by his own account, had embarked on priestly for-mation at a relatively late age, in an era when most seminarians went immediately from school, a fact that explains much, but not all, about what is dismal in the Roman Catholic Church. One wondered about his early twenties, was tempted to think of them a bit melodramatically as the Missing Years. It was not that I was imagining a tour of duty with the French Foreign Legion, but his silence on the matter inflamed the nosiness it was presumably intended to dispel. I knew he had worked as a schoolteacher, but he volunteered little more. You wondered. That is all I can say.

It was understood between us, as perhaps between all friends, that there were questions not to be put until the time became right, which would either never happen or happen so far into the future that we would both be different people, so the questions would not matter anymore. On one of the only two occasions when I transgressed the unwritten law – a glass of wine with lunch was perhaps the instigator – I worked my impertinent schoolgirl curiosity up into a query of hideous clumsiness, on the matter of priestly celibacy. Had he known, as a young man, a physically intimate relationship?

He stared coolly in response. 'A policeman wouldn't ask me that.'

When Ugo changed the subject, it stayed changed.

I remember to this day the one moment on which his guard slipped, also how thrown I was by the remark in question because it was so unexpected, by him (I feel sure) as well as me. We were exiting St Peter's Square on a bright, cold afternoon, the time of early evening when schools have just finished. Ugo had been asked to give the sermon at a funeral Mass in St Monica's, had requested moral support from the Contessa Landini and me. His apprehensiveness was justified, the sermon had been poor. Not long after Mass concluded, the Contessa left for an appointment and Ugo set out to walk me to the tram. Many Roman mothers and one or two slightly embarrassed fathers were waiting at the gate of the schoolyard for the emergence of their little darlings, who were biting and fighting and insulting each other, as their misfortunate teachers scuttled about like shepherds attempting to corral them. Traffic lights stopped our path for a moment.

Noticing his priestly attire, some of the parents nodded in courteous respectfulness or blessed themselves at his presence, a well-meant Italian custom I think he always found a little discomfiting. A certain amount of anti-clericalism has long been known in Italy; as a result, its mirror has existed, too, an unhealthy over-reverencing of clergy. As we waited for a green light, we watched the bellicose goings-on in the playground, and he asked me if I wished to be a mother.

Rather, he assumed that I did, and enquired as to when I might marry. It was not wise to wait too long, he added, in a meaning way. I was then aged thirty-four, a fact that seemed to dangle in the air for him, somehow. I replied that I was not the marrying sort, was adequately content single and intended to remain so all my life.

'Then, you would not like to have a child?'

I did not tell him that, in fact, a year previously, I had had an abortion.

'No,' I said. 'I would not.'

He attempted what I suppose must have been a diversionary nod but clearly was unsettled by my words or my certitude. The unsettlement, I think, brought his next remark. 'I would have loved to be a husband and father.'

It took me aback. He rarely spoke about himself without veils, evasions, ironies, the easier modes of concealment. I would say that it changed how I saw him. Until that moment he had seemed to me maddeningly rocklike, bulletproof in his self-certainties, impregnable as to his choices, especially the main one of his life. If Ugo had a fault, and who does not, it was perhaps this slight air of the loftily seigneurial, the superiority of the hermit. We like haloes in old pictures, rarely in our friends.

But suddenly, that afternoon, he was a person without a family. What I had seen as solidity came from a depth where there was something bereft. In a way, he *had* married. It was the first time I saw it. With another, one might have taken him by the arm or spoken a gentle word. The fact that he was a priest would have made that feel improper, would have embarrassed him, I felt, or given him the script to rebuff consolation, which perhaps was what he wanted. But often I wish I had. I would, now.

We continued our walk. I was going to the tram. At my flat, I knew, was the draft of an article for which the deadline was pressing. Time seemed to scrunch into a ball. As ever he doffed his trilby as he bade me farewell and we made conversational nothings for a final minute or two, I think attempting to find a bridge back to what he had told me. But the bridge, once noticed, was burned by the noticing. I think we both knew we would never speak of the matter again.

On the tram, I thought of him walking back to his room, alone. He was going to listen to the radio. I pictured him doing so with the lights off.

My parents worked hard to become scientists. I do not believe in ghosts.

119

But at the end of my journey, I went into the church near my flat, where I lit a candle for Ugo, knelt, and said an unbeliever's prayer. My story was late. But another had revealed itself. In as much as it ever would.

That was in the autumn of 1943. Soon, the Nazis – he pronounced the word 'Nazee', without the 't' – swarmed in. I became aware that Ugo and a number of associates intended doing something small to stand against the plague, and I resolved that, whatever it was, I would help. In this, I was motivated by the thought of my parents, whom the Nazis would have thought nothing of murdering.

I was motivated, too, by a certain Rubicon I had crossed in relation to my private life, central to which was a reality I now found myself wanting to articulate. Certain friends knew of it; most of course did not. My mother I think had long known but persuaded herself otherwise. Perhaps the resolve had been in part sparked by Ugo's and my conversation about marriage, perhaps by the proximity to death that war brings about. In any case, I wished to be truthful. On the morning of the Nazi invasion, we met at my request. I told him I had something to say, to which I wanted him to listen; I had known and loved men and could see their special beauty but had long preferred the companionship of women.

Who in their right mind would not, he remarked.

It took a moment for what the English call the penny to drop. One almost heard the clunk.

'Oh,' Ugo said.

That monosyllable, in its glorious rotundity, was that. The matter, being raised, was not mentioned by him again.

Ugo lived at the time in the Collegio Teutonico, under the right arm of St Peter's Basilica. The Choir, soon established, would meet for 'rehearsal' in a tumbledown, long-abandoned annex of the College, not a wing but a separate building, a fortlike block that had at one time been a hospice for fever victims, in another era a lodging house for pilgrims. It was whispered by many in Rome, a city of ghost stories, that the stark Gothic edifice was haunted by a sixteen-year-old girl who had fallen pregnant by a Cardinal and been banished to the nunnery that once stood on the site. Poor Emerenzia, as she was known, had starved herself to death and been interred in a cobbled wall.

I used to imagine what she saw as we rehearsed.

Three flights of cracked marble steps like a dinosaur's spine climbed up through the torso of rotting landings. You ascended to a long, gloomy corridor, five metres wide, like a passageway in a gallery but with smashed or crumbling tilework and many of the oak floorboards missing. Vast tapestries of queer toadstools spread themselves along the wainscot. Glassed arrow-slits admitted something that had once been light but was now an oyster-coloured, smoky, oppressive miasma, by which one could see, through astonishingly thick drapes of spiderweb, that the passageway had long ago been pressed into service as a storehouse for unwanted church statues, too broken or ugly for anyone to want them. Yet no one could throw them away.

Decapitated Madonnas, Christs with one hand. Wingless, chipped angels. Toppled, lurching prophets. Disciples and evangelists with sockets for eyes, a Sacred Heart missing its halo. Crooked, plaster martyrs. St Sebastians with snapped arrows. A John the Baptist with the face of a lavatory attendant. St Peter writhingly raving in chains long rusted away. A rat-gnawed Mary Magdalene, nest of wasps in her bosom.

Lazarus stolen from Mexico, throttled by woodworm, in a shifting bib of paint flakes explored by seeping ants. A lacerated donkey from a mahogany crib. A Christ-child's murderous eyes.

At the end of the passageway, you encountered an oddly modern door, like the flimsy timber door of a 1930s Mussolini schoolhouse, but whitewashed, badly, and, like the wainscots, mushroomed. This opened to an old Symposium Room that contained a long wooden table and a wheezy harmonium carved with owls and angels.

If she watched us, Emerenzia saw an odd, lamplit coterie.

The Choir comprised eight including our *Kapellmeister*, Ugo, whose custom was to sit facing the doorway. Delia Kiernan, Enzo Angelucci and I tended to place ourselves on his right, D'Arcy Osborne and John May to his left. May, a gifted musician, sang in his cello-like bass voice or trilled and weaved on his saxophone. Sam Derry toiled at the harmonium, perhaps the only person in history to have done so with a stolen German army 7.63-millimetre Mauser semi-automatic pistol in his belt. The eighth person, her back to the door, was always my dear friend the Contessa Giovanna Landini ('Jo', she preferred, for Jo March in *Little Women*, one of the only titles ever improved upon by its Italian translation, the lovely *Piccole Donne*) whose bleak joke was that if she was going to be shot by the Gestapo, she would rather it came from the back so that she might have an open coffin at her funeral.

Strange, the family we made.

The long, oak tabletop had an archipelago of antique ink-stains and scratchings, some in what I supposed must be Ancient Greek. That broken-down, yellow-keyed harmonium gasped beneath a skylight which had not been cleaned since Garibaldi was a baby. When a strong wind rattled the attic, as happens in a Rome winter, the harmonium uttered a lugubrious groan of complaint like a walrus prodded with a stick. One October evening, into a corner Sam Derry lugged up a potbellied stove, where it pretended with great valour but little effectiveness to heat the room. If anything, whenever that grate was lit, our eyrie seemed colder. Mostly, you wore your overcoat.

It was understood between all eight Choristers that questions about matters other than the weather were forbidden. The Nazi occupation, the war itself, the atrocities of the Gestapo, the controlled starvation that was the food ration, must never be discussed at all. The atmosphere before the music commenced was one of restrained geniality, like a bridge party or a dinner engagement between people who do not know each other very well and are on that sort of questing start-of-the-evening best behaviour. If talk threatened to drift in a direction that Ugo thought unhelpful, he would shoot you a look or draw his fingers across his throat. J. S. Bach and the weather were the permitted topics. If you didn't know anything about them, you had better learn quickly. Few of us being musicologists, we became meteorologists. Anyone can be one of those.

At the time, coffee in Rome was as desert sand in Antarctica, a matter of agony to the Romans, a most caffeinated people, but now and again John May or Delia would have somehow managed to get their hands on some, and Jo Landini might bring a plate of cannoli she had made. Sir D'Arcy often brought wine, but I remember nobody drinking it. Ugo would stand at the head of the table, handing out sheet music, explaining the background to the pieces or giving potted biographies of the composer. As though it truly *was* a rehearsal. Which, in a way, it was.

What was being rehearsed would have got us tortured to death by Hauptmann.

Presently Ugo would call the group to order and play the keynote on a harmonica. As the singing began, which usually happened ten or fifteen minutes after the last of us had arrived, sometimes white-faced and breathless, up the haunted steps, his practice was to systematically make his way around the table, from one of us to another, talking in whispers or showing scribbled notes on lavatory paper, which he would tear up and burn in the stove when we had memorised them. Rome was of course a nest of spies in those months; Hauptmann's Gestapo had planted microphones widely. It was common knowledge that they had taken over the telephone exchange, that every operator was now an SS agent, every call monitored, every meeting of more than six people covertly photographed. A secured radio-transmitter at Nazi Headquarters in the fashionable hotel neighbourhood had a direct channel to Hitler's lair, the Berghof at Obersalzberg. In the streets and markets near the Vatican it was whispered that Himmler himself eavesdropped on Rome every night, moving around the dial at random. Here, in the forgotten loft, we could be reasonably certain that nobody but Emerenzia was listening. In case we were mistaken, we sang.

Allegri's *Miserere*, Dowland, bits of plainsong. Early Elizabethan madrigals and Alleluias. The usual repertoire of an amateur chamber choir or singing society such as you might find in a small town in England, but sometimes we stretched to an attempt at that glory of glories, Palestrina's *Stabat Mater*. The occasional *Tantum Ergo*. A motet of Josquin or a Gregorian chant, some weeks a medieval carol. The Cornish anthem 'Trelawny'. That enchanting Welsh song, '*Ar Hyd y Nos*'. 'The Braes of Balquhither', a beautiful love ballad of Scotland, though Ugo insisted it had Irish cousins. As a piece of insurance, if I can put it that way, we did a German song, '*Hupf, mein Mädel*', but then one evening on my way to rehearsal I heard a Nazi column sing it as they goosestepped down Via Flaminia. We didn't do that one again.

Not entirely jocularly, John May objected to Bach on the basis that he had been 'a Jerry'. Dear John. But when he heard '*Wenn ich einmal soll scheiden*' from the Matthäus-Passion, the most austerely magnificent two minutes of music ever created, he lowered his gaze in awed reverence and hummed solemnly along, as anyone who has ever heard it must. I do not believe in God. But when I hear that piece, I do.

We were no Coro della Sistina but we brought heart to the effort. Lotti's '*Crucifixus*', Byrd's '*Haec Dies*'. Ugo would conduct, lilting along, a competent tenor, but mostly his approach was stern. We took the music seriously, in our

123

way. If the hymn included harmonies, we practised them assiduously at home. He made clear that our rehearsals were not occasions for learning or pleasure; our time together was precious; it must be used to form plans. So, you came to rehearsal 'on book', as professional singers put it, knowing your part so well that you could sing without thinking about it at all, could sing it while thinking about something else.

But, even if the singing was a camouflage and not at all the true purpose, I must say that I adored it, even came to depend on it. And I believe I was not alone. In those dark, violent times, I longed for our weekly rehearsal. I would burn for the night to come.

Some consolation of the spirit, some release happens when human beings sing in a group, wherever and however that occurs. In a place of worship, on the terraces of a football stadium, in a cramped and draughty attic, bombers droning overhead. Nearly all music has beauty, but when it includes the marriage of baritone and soprano, of bass and alto, chorus and soloist, it becomes something more than merely the upliftingly beautiful. Harmony is an everyday, achievable miracle. Imagine having been the first person to think of it, to attempt it with another. *I* shall sing this. *You* sing that. Something greater than I or you will result. And, as everyone who has ever heard singing in a classroom knows well, when we are not wonderful singers, are in fact not musically gifted, singing has a special sort of sacredness that is impossibly moving. When we sing, we cease to be scum.

We sang, Delia Kiernan leading, in her pure, strong, soprano. I loved watching at such moments, her eyes closed, hands clenching and unclenching, the light, coltish gentleness of how she swayed her shoulders. The serenity of her smile between lines. I swear that when she sang, any wrinkles left her face, she was twenty years younger, somehow became her own daughter (who herself sometimes attended our gatherings). Delia was no longer someone's wife, a troubled woman in wartime, but a person in the radiance she believed she had been given. Little wonder we refer to music as 'a gift'. My make-up was often ruined as I listened to my wonderful Delia. I don't know how I held back from applauding her.

One night, D'Arcy Osborne did so. Ugo shot him a terrible glower. 'Couldn't help myself, old man.' Dabbing his eyes with a handkerchief. 'Reminds one why one's alive.'

'*Bravissima*,' the Contessa whispered, also moved to tears. Angelucci and Johnny May stared hard at the floor. Derry shook his head in awed, stunned reverence. The harmonium wheezed its low-toned whistle.

Ugo would move between us under cover of the music, explaining plans, routes, false names, contacts, addresses we were to memorise but never to write down. This escaped Sergeant had emphysema and, by nightfall tomorrow, must be moved from the damp garage in which he was lodged; that American Corporal had gone 'doll dizzy', sexually obsessed, and must be warned to stay in the safehouse on Via di San Marcello and not venture out to visit either of the girlfriends he had mystifyingly acquired since going into hiding. A South African Private had a septic gum infection and needed a dentist. Another had syphilis and would die without penicillin. All of us knew *some*thing, one element of that week's plan. Ugo was the one who knew everything.

At the start, numbers varied, swelling occasionally to sixteen or seventeen, sometimes other priests but mostly everyday Romans. Then, things would get too hot for a particular Chorister; perhaps the Gestapo had been observed watching her apartment from the upper windows opposite or had been asking questions at her husband's workplace or child's school. In such cases, retirement came early, as Ugo put it. Sometimes he met objections, but the Choir was not a democracy. No matter the asset, he wouldn't take the risk. The core remained the same, the octet mentioned above.

It was Angelucci's task to scrutinise the newspaper classifieds that offered lodgings or to walk about Rome identifying flats that might be rented in a false name. Sir D'Arcy and Jo Landini were assigned the duty of fundraising among sympathetic donors; Sam Derry collected the money in secret, commonly going under disguise, and delivered it to the safehouse's owner or landlord, whom we called in code 'the Benoit', the name of the landlord in *La Bohème*. Whenever the Benoit was a woman, it seemed easier, for some reason. Not that it was ever easy. The penalty for 'false renting', as it was termed by the Nazis, was death. So, the rent money would need to be substantial.

Then – this was work I frequently did myself – a dossier of abandoned houses and other possible hiding places had to be compiled. I must have walked a thousand kilometres about Rome that autumn, protected by my Swiss passport and my international Press Card, noting bombsites, manholes, follies in public gardens, rusted cisterns, gullies, storm drains behind apartment blocks, stables, henhouses, viaducts, storerooms, disused barges on the Tiber, a crashed train carriage, derelict factories, the abandoned traffic-tunnel on Via del Traforo. The parks were a sorrowful sight: all the benches had been ransacked for firewood; there might be a potting shed or dilapidated conservatory where prisoners could hide. Rome is built on a warren of volcanic rock, in which are scores of age-old subterranean quarries; asking around, I learned of several ways in. Beneath the Basilica dei Santi Giovanni e Paolo is a network of preserved ancient Roman streets; these, too, went on my list. The hidden aqueduct behind the Spanish Steps. The marble sewer-tunnel that, long ago, served a bathhouse. I made it my business to befriend the Fascist structural engineer commissioned to blueprint Rome's metro system, and to – shall I say – borrow his drawings.

Forgery was another important element of the repertoire. Often, while the Lord was being glorified in plainchant, Ugo would quietly make his way around the table – you slightly dreaded his approach – and whisper that this week we needed a Vatican City Employee card, two Swiss passports in the name of Franz and Heinrich So-and-So, ten hundred-franc notes and a set of Fascist Party membership documents with an early serial number. Had you any ideas?

It was expected that you would have. He became surly if you hadn't.

John May knew a crooked printer in Trastevere who, as he put it, 'would knock you up a Gutenberg Bible for three quid'. May was a good-looking man but, oddly, that was not what made him attractive; rather, it was his gloomily humorous manner, the sort of confidence that, in men, masks itself as self-deprecation. Seldom short of female companionship, for a time he knocked about with a *signorina* who worked as a typist in the Mayor's office. The Mayor liked a good lunch and was one of those gentlemen who do not attend too closely to the paperwork placed before them for signature during the afternoon session, particularly when an embodiment of Roman pulchritude is doing the placing. A number of our passes were signed by that Mayor, I regret to say, without his knowledge.

There was the exhausting, unending demand for clothing, and for it to be distributed without anyone noticing. Ugo instituted the practice that every Chorister turned up for rehearsal bearing at least a man's shirt or jacket. You found them in the second-hand markets or wherever you pleased. The booty was conveyed by May to a laundry where dyers and seamstresses got to work.

Indeed, a seamstress would play a central role in the Christmas Eve Rendimento. But here I get ahead of myself.

Rome, for obvious reasons, has a good deal of male prostitution. Several of these men, at appalling risk, were helpful to the Escape Line, and some met terrible deaths as a result. As for the women of that profession, I think it no exaggeration to say that their courage and tenacity, and the invariable accuracy of their information, saved hundreds of lives.

During every rehearsal, Ugo and I would find a few moments to go through the latest scheme. Rome contains thousands of religious institutions – monasteries, convents, pilgrim houses, seminaries, generalates, colleges, abbeys, individual churches – some of which had made it known they would be willing to assist our endeavours but were anxious to limit the danger. Ugo, Derry and the Contessa contrived a sort of timetable, a traffic-light system, by which a premises would be brought into play.

First, we would anonymously report the convent or church to the Gestapo as a place where late-night arrivals had been noticed. The ensuing German raid found no fugitives. A week or ten days later, the denunciation was repeated more ardently: a poison-pen letter reporting the monks as harbourers and black marketeers, possessors of an illegal radio or a hand-operated printing press. A detailed map of the building's floorplan and hiding places was provided; the abbey's doors would be kicked in by Hauptmann's search squad. This time, in addition to there being no escapees, there would be found on the Abbot's desk a well-thumbed copy of *Mein Kampf*, with warm annotations in the Abbot's own hand. Our forger ran us up six dozen autographed photographs of the Führer; we ensured that these were displayed in many of the nunneries where prisoners were reported to be hiding. War brings strange sights, but one does not expect to encounter a framed portrait of Hitler outstaring you over Reverend Mother's bed. We arranged for that treat to befall quite a number of German soldiers.

The fake report might be repeated four times, until we felt certain that the Germans had lost interest. At that point, the monastery would be flooded with escapees from crypt to belfry, and the fictive denunciations continued elsewhere.

There was another silent legion of brave Romans, often the poor, those who lacked space at home to hide a fugitive, but who wished to assist us all the same. Derry and Ugo came up with a means by which anyone living in the city could help. If you were willing to endure the unpleasantness of a Gestapo raid on your apartment, we asked that you anonymously denounce yourself or get a family member or neighbour to do it. The raiding party would arrive, smash down the door, empty out the wardrobes, clamber into the building's loft or descend to its cellars, but it could take them half an hour to discover that you were hiding nobody, that the denouncement had been groundless. To waste the enemy's time was to deplete his resources. Into the night with the Germans, but Angelucci would by then have made certain every urchin in the neighbourhood had sprinkled the street with caltrops – cross-pronged nails and bent screws – so that the tyres of their jeeps and motorcycles would be punctured. The caltrops were an idea of Sir D'Arcy's, adaptation of an ancient Roman sabotage weapon he had first read about as a boy at his mortifyingly expensive school and then seen in the Musei Vaticani.

There were bad days, many of them, when plans went wrong. Mistranslations. Slips. A misremembered sequence. A terrified Book in hiding – we termed the escapees 'Books' – might lurch towards losing his mind and have to be moved at short notice, or spoken to harshly, even threatened with court martial and execution, but his fellows in the same attic must be protected. Books under lockdown bickered and often enough came to blows. No privacy, little space, stale air, perhaps nowhere to wash. The natural desires of young people, given no outlet. One's face heats a little as one recollects the moment when Derry brought us the grave complaint that an escapee had been seen by his cohabitors indulging in a not unknown practice, one Derry refused to name except to say the man had been 'doing as a schoolboy does'. It was Osborne who, without deciphering, at least broke the tension. 'Darling, if everyone guilty of *that* were to suffer eviction, every room in bloody Europe would be empty.'

No news; rotten food, weeks of silence, warring rumours. Ten or a dozen palliasses crammed into a room. These were not professional soldiers but enlistees or the drafted: tradesmen, schoolteachers, postmen, farmers' sons. Their training for an existence in hiding was scant; their eyes had seen the horrors of battle or the *Stalag*. In stories for little children who know nothing of the world, the suggestion is often made that adversity stirs the best in the human person, but in war this is not always so. Envy and resentment sprout when men are shut in together, bullying, boredom, anger, restless fear, the exhaustion of literally never sleeping a full night, the famishment of sharing rations among eight that were intended for one. There is unease about status; who is in charge? Rank is exposed as a fiction.

Men of numerous nations and colonies served in the Allied forces. If colour prejudice began its hideous writhing, we crushed it. Ugo was vehement on the point; no excuse was given ear. Any man voicing such bigotries would be evicted. An Alabaman once made the error of exculpating away a filthy remark he had uttered, on the basis that in Alabama it was 'how folks do'. Ugo told him in blunt terms understandable anywhere in the English-speaking world that he was not in Alabama now.

There were other forms of behaviour that drove Ugo and the rest of us to rage. Often, they were explained as playfulness. Escapees who were sworn to maintain the secrecy of their hideouts, tossing a baseball back and forth, across from balcony to balcony, or firing golf balls in catapults to crack the windows opposite. Donning the landlady's wig and underclothes to pirouette on a rooftop. Dancing galliards with one another. Kissing brooms. Emptying chamber pots or armfuls of homemade tickertape into the street. Did they *want* to be caught? Was the boredom that poisonous? In prison, might these men feel freer?

As for the Choir, we lived with the never-ending dread that an escapee might die, which, given that some were wounded, seemed grimly inevitable, and would need to be buried covertly in some equivalent of a potter's field. These possibilities loomed, always. My nightmares were terrifying. I grew addicted to the barbiturate methaqualone, which made them worse.

There was also, it must be admitted, the constant fear that we were compromised, that an apparent supporter, perhaps even one of us in the Choir, might be a Judas. Stranger things have happened and always will. Often, as we met, among the ghosts and dead statues, Mistrust sat down with us at that long oaken table. A hard guest to banish. He convinces you he's a friend.

A good day occurred when the Contessa received word from a hawk-eyed informant of a certain large apartment house near the casern in Prati, in which sixty German conscripts were billeted. It was their habit to shine their boots last thing at night with a polish that was quite wickedly malodorous – human urine was rumoured to be one of its ingredients. So vile was the stench that the men would leave the boots out in the rear courtyard until reveille at dawn. One morning, they and their *Oberstleutnant* received a surprise. A crack squad of layabouts had been paid by Angelucci to scale the moonlit wall, each mountaineer bearing a pillowcase that was empty when he commenced his climb but clumpy and full when he came back. 'Booty is truth,' Sir D'Arcy remarked. 'Truth, booty.' The ghost of John Keats gave a groan.

Some will aver that far worse should have been done to those German soldiers. If you have murdered a man in cold blood, I will listen. If not, I suggest you admire yourself in the mirror of your certainties – but know where the light is coming from.

We were not paramilitaries. Our purpose was to hide fugitives from the tyranny. Doubtless, we had members that were also supporters of the Roman Partigiani, the largely Communist armed resistance, a body from which the Choir turned its gaze. Rightly, wrongly, that was not our business, nor was the matter debated at rehearsal.

What I see is a group of slightly odd people singing in an attic, Ugo O'Flaherty circling the table, looking stern.

I can picture that room to the tiniest detail. Moonlight silvering the ancient, dented table. Stove-light yellowing the keys of the decrepit old harmonium and purpling Jo Landini's eyes. Sometimes, as we sang, I would reach out to clasp her hand, for I knew that her departed husband felt close to her then. Dead statues, broken crucifixes on the landing outside. A ring on Angelucci's finger. The glint of D'Arcy Osborne's spectacles. Some nights, the certainty that Emerenzia was watching.

For always I felt watched.

Recorded.

Observed.

Lamplight on seven faces.

The Choir.

Together, but, in the end, one was out on one's own.

Always there would need to be a solo.

15

Christmas Eve 1943
5.47 p.m.
5 hours and 13 minutes before the Rendimento

Dusk is descending as he takes a glass of hot water and cloves, alone at a rusting garden table in the refectory's allotment. Ravens strut and squawk. Smoke on cold air.

Seeing him through the windows, the other priests look away, sup a snout-and-lung stew in silence, play draughts. It is not unknown for those of their calling to turn introspective at Christmastime. When your only home is a linoleum-clad room up a landing, festivities can be trials of endurance.

At six o'clock he is seen walking in the Papal gardens. Soon afterwards he calls into the Montessori School for the children of Vatican employees, where the usual seasonal play is being subjected to production. He makes conversation about A.S. Roma with the father of St Joseph, a driver, blesses rosary beads for the shepherd's twin brothers, both sick from sweets, permits himself to be photographed with the innkeeper's aunt, a Sister home from Africa, a trainee radiographer in a Nairobi hospital, at whose mother's funeral Mass he assisted last April.

A cadaverous, broom-waving Befana, the bountiful witch of Christmas-time, is borne in on an ecclesiastical sedan chair, brandishing the school's heavy handbell. Bambino Gesù is a little girl's doll and is missing a leg. As the nuns announce the *limonata*, they call for '*nostro amico, il Monsignore*' to say a few words, give a blessing. It takes a few moments for people to realise he has left.

At quarter to seven, he is covertly filmed crossing the gardens in the direction of the infirmary. Rain is falling but he is wearing no coat.

In the lobby, he is approached by a Polish Nursing Matron whom he's known a long time. She tells him he's looking terrible, insists he sit a moment, examines him. His blood pressure is 160 over 90, his heart is 'banging drums'. She advises him to return to his room, 'avoid all anxieties', otherwise a coronary might be his Christmas present.

In the ward, he prays the rosary by the deathbed of an elderly gardener, assuring him from time to time that there is no need to utter the responses: 'I can do it for both of us, Gino, rest your spirit.'

An applewood bowl of winter laurels on the bedside locker, beside a stone jug of water from the spring the man unearthed behind the Basilica with his sons some thirty years ago, on a morning when a sinkhole opened, the dawn after a thunderstorm, and they dug into the sandy, rasping schist, joyous as Texan oilmen.

Nurses come and go amid the reek of disinfectant. The gardener accepts the Communion host, strange roses in his eyes, touches a napkin dipped in the chalice to his parched, pale lips.

'*Grazie*,' he wheezes. 'Now my bag is packed.'

'The Lord doesn't want you yet, Gino. Bad manners to arrive early.'

'I'm on my way, anyhow.'

'We shall walk to your spring again, my friend.'

'Remember the newspaperman, *Monsignore?* Who sold papers in the square?'

'Angelucci?'

'Came to me in a dream last night. Guy liked boxing.'

'Still does.'

'Liked boxing. Can't remember his name. I never did, myself.'

'Why not?'

'*Bontà mia*, life is full of fights already. Why invent them?'

'For sport.'

'Liked boxing, that guy in the square. Newspaperman. Can't remember his name.'

'This beautiful nurse is telling me you must rest yourself, Gino. You don't want to disappoint her.'

'Think I'll have a little siesta.'

'Do, my friend. Rest.'

'Thanks for coming, *Monsignore*. *Buon Natale*. Goodbye.'

'I'll come again soon.'

'You won't,' mutters the gardener. '*Paisano*, you're betrayed.' As he slips into morphined sleep.

At the College, the furnace has chugged on. Pipes crossing the ceiling of his room give their clicketting hum; the aroma of roasted dust arises. In the swelter, he strips to his underwear and socks, lies on the narrow bed.

Just ten minutes.
Rest his eyes.
Try to calm.
Long night coming.

A whirl of propellers
chop crisp London air
The engines cough
a scutter of smoke
and weep an oily tear.

Knowing he is dreaming, he turns, attempting to surface. The gardener is here, in groves of winter laurels. The children from the nativity play, toy Nazis in their hands.

Far below, the river
winding like a sentence
etched by the jeweller
in spirals of mind
a ribbon of silver
on a ballgown of rushes
laid on a springtime featherbed

Out, over townlands
football fields, estates
manses, cattle marts

brickfields, farmlands
the miracle irregular of new forest fields
grown glorious now in a lamb-bleat of March
as the farmer looks up,
scythe in hand, from his bees
at the fall and the all of the SCREEEEEEE—

Shuddering, wrists thrusting, handcuffs of damp sheets. The vast bells of the Basilica tolling for eight, answered by every other chime in the city.

A certainty, like the memory of a broken bone in midwinter, that he does not belong here, has never belonged.

B'long, say the bells. Rolling, tolling, with clappers the size of a battleship's anchor or the tinkling of a porcelain thimble. *B'lung*. *B'lang*. Orchestra of bell-song. Lambastes of blowsy gong-song, the jangle of Rome. Pealing. Clanging. Booming and bawling, spangling from steeples, dovecots, turrets, the billow of bell-song so you feel it in your coccyx, the shock, the mockery, in dour orato-rios, knells, dirges, tolling, rolling, piping *soprani* or piccolo jingle, rolling the *doloroso* of orotund bass, over martyr's bones, immemorial stones, pulsing out spheres of iron unseen, Atlantics of sound every second.

The bells roar for eight.

The dream roils again.

In the clouds, a dead gardener, howling, *pointing*. But his words can't be heard for the bells.

———

Across the city, a man enters an improvised office that used to be the kitchen-ette of the German Cultural Centre. Removing his cap, he crosses to the sink.

Evocative, the bells.

He counts them down.

Eight.

Christmassy, of course, like cinnamon turned to sound. Berlin will be lovely tonight but cold, damp, foggy. Mother and Father having the neighbours in for a little glass of schnapps. Sad time for some, Christmas Eve.

The gramophone plays Grieg's A minor Piano Concerto, Op. 16, the

Schnabel recording, a little old-fashioned, but muscular and finessed. The blurt of water against metal is pleasing, a comfort to the senses, blanking, as it does, the screams from the cells downstairs. He washes the butcher's-shop smell from his hands. But now it occurs to him that he has forgotten to buy a Christmas present for Elise. He curses his stupidity and forgetfulness.

What would she like? Shoes? A piece of jewellery? A pet, perhaps? An antique? If he could summon from memory her dress size, perhaps a gown? Or stockings. It is only eight o'clock, some of the merchants will still be on their premises.

A fortnight ago, while leading a kidnap squad to Trastevere, he happened to notice, on a mannequin in a couturier's window, a tight-fitting, ruched ivory silk ballgown, slit to the thigh. A woman of Elise's figure would appear a goddess in such a garment. And it would be a way of asserting that he still found her physically attractive, which she sometimes says he doesn't, 'since pregnancy destroyed my body'. At such moments, he embraces her, covers her hands with kisses, thanks her for the strength and affection she shows their children, thanks her for coming to Rome to be with him at this trying time. The gown would be a sort of lovemaking.

But where would she wear it? It is not as though they go out. The opera is far too dangerous, too public, he has been advised. A Partisan sniper in the wings, a bomber in the box above. The Communists are getting reckless; they no longer fear reprisals.

Perhaps at a ball in the Villa Farnesina for the Führer's visit in the spring? Humming along with Grieg, he rinses the iron-smelling blood from his knuckles, bundles the reddened tissues, drops them out the window, before noticing, on the carving table now doing duty as what he calls 'the Urgent Desk', a document needing his attention, the now-completed dossier on the priest.

Damn that wretched typist, why couldn't she go home early for Christmas as ordered?

Now he will need to read it, Elise's gift will have to wait. An idea occurs to him. Is the typist still here? She is the same sort of height and build as his wife, perhaps she would accompany him to the couturier's, try on the gown for him? He sees her standing very straight, graceful hands on her hips, dark Italian smile in the long slim mirror.

For God's sake, man, that would be disrespectful. Improper to ask a woman to do any such thing. Get a grip on yourself and grow up, you are not sixteen.

Strange, the background thought that haunts his reading of the dossier. Bells and the blood taste the same.

———

INTELLIGENCE REPORT
CONFIDENTIAL ON PAIN OF DEATH

File commenced: P. Hauptmann, date redacted. Information added: E. Dollman, 24th December 1943.

Subject: Hugh O'Flaherty (surname on certificate of birth is 'Flaherty'; has been checked in person by agent of the Reich, Public Records Office, Dublin).

Date of birth: 28th February 1898; i.e. subject is aged forty-five.

Place of birth: Kishkeam, County of Cork, Ireland/Éire, but was raised in County of Kerry.

Address: Collegio Teutonico del Campo Santo, Via della Sacrestia, Rome. Informant confirms the subject's room is on third landing, eleven paces from stairhead, door numbered '15'; two small windows. Subject eats (often alone) in communal refectory, ground floor, five large windows. Often walks unaccompanied in cemetery garden. Wall is two metres in height; one gate leading to passageway. Gate often locked, soap copy of key to be investigated. See sketched map and floor plan supplied by informant. (Building is an extraterritorial property of Vatican City, i.e., not legally part of Rome or Italy.)

Subject's Occupation: Roman Catholic priest, ordained 1925, now '*Scrittore*', clerk / lecturer / diplomat of the Curia, rank of Monsignor. Has worked previously in Haiti, San Domingo, Palestine, Czechoslovakia, London. Summoned to Rome 1934.

Place of Work: Office of Marital Nullity, Supreme Sacred Congregation of the Holy Office and Propagation of the Faith, Piazza del Sant'Uffizio, Rome, known as 'The Propaganda'. Building is extraterritorial property of Vatican

City. Calls to and from telephone on subject's desk are monitored (commenced seven weeks ago), transcripts available within thirty-six hours.

Passport: Ireland /Éire. Is thought may possess counterfeit Swiss papers and Vatican Secretariat *carta di identità* in false name but with own photograph. (Subject speaks Italian, Spanish, French, Czech. No German. Is conversant in Latin and Ancient Greek.)

Height: 1.88 metres.

Weight: 90 Kilos approximately.

Eyes: Blue. (Subject is short-sighted, wears spectacles. Photograph of recent prescription attached.)

Complexion: Ruddy.

Medical Condition: Doctor's records (photographs attached) indicate tendency to high blood pressure, varicose vein in left thigh, bronchitis in wintertime, otherwise reasonable health. Capable of withstanding very severe interrogation.

Pursuits: Reads, goes to art galleries (holds three doctorates), conducts a choir. Rides a motorcycle in countryside around Rome. Known to attend boxing. Does not consume alcohol, does not smoke. Opera, bridge, golf, through which he has met and fraternised with Rome-based enemy sympathisers including Sir Francis D'Arcy Godolphin Osborne (British Envoy Extraordinary and Minister Plenipotentiary to the Holy See), Mrs Delia Kiernan, née Murphy (professional singer, wife of diplomatic 'Minister' of Ireland, formal term for de facto Ambassador), the Contessa Giovanna Landini and her circle (Communist apologists).

Political beliefs: Pro-American. Frequent attender at American motion pictures. Was official Vatican visitor to Allied prisoners of war in Stalag 369, Trieste, and many other concentration camps, but raised morale of prisoners, distributed books, cigarettes, sheet music of songs, accepted letters for posting, in disobedience of Papal policy of strict neutrality, attempted to demoralise guards. Was disciplined by Vatican late '42, removed from role as visitor and has been confined to Vatican City since but is rumoured to disobey under darkness. Informants have heard him deride Mussolini. Has been seen not to stand in the Cinema Clodio while Fascist anthem 'Giovinezza' is played. Claims to have visited British Navy submarine docked at Ostia in 1934. Has been observed in possession of *Avanti*, socialist degenerate newspaper. For some time has been suspected of being complicit in the hiding of escaped enemy prisoners and Jews, in disobedience to martial law decree section IV, paragraph X, punishable by death.

In recent months, complicity has intensified.

On foot of recent intelligence gathered by surveillance and other methods, subject now thought to be centrally involved with well-funded Escape Line, operational methods and precise source of monies as yet unknown. Co-conspirators refer to escapees collectively as 'The Library', to individual fugitives as 'Books', to hiding places as 'Shelves'. Chief mission-runner thought to be escaped British officer, surname possibly 'Kerry', 'Terry' or 'Bury' (as in the English place name). Several substitutes in training, all Italian.

Subject's Vulnerabilities: Yet to be uncovered. Investigations continuing. Is not thought to be homosexual, molester of children, or womaniser. Evinces no interest in money.

Suggested Action: Subject received shock-visit at his workplace this evening with purpose of inducing fear / disorientation. Advise close surveillance of subject, three weeks, commencing immediately on receipt of this now-completed dossier, followed by covert night arrest of subject and intensive Gestapo interrogation.

To be shot while trying to escape.

— 16 —

On the roof of the hotel across Via di Porta Cavalleggeri the German sentries switch on the arc light.

Through the gaps in his shutters the beam comes glaring, grids of chemical whiteness along the marble floor and up the wainscots. Over the face of the Sacred Heart, the sad eyes of St Bernadette Soubirous. A tin-framed wedding photograph of his parents.

It started in mid-September. Every night since. That unblinking, unkillable stare. They stole the lamp when they ransacked the Cinecittà film studios, trucked it through the streets like a hostage, roped on the back of a flatbed, a deity of glass, the thousand-watt tungsten bulb of a lighthouse. The brightness confuses the birds, makes them croak and whistle all night, illuminates the facade of the Collegio, its entrance gate and garden, the graveyard.

At one time, until not long ago, the hotel was a *pensione* for pilgrims, now it is a brothel and drinking den. ('The wine list is said to have improved,' Jo Landini bleakly joked.) From his room, he sees the Fascist police arrive and depart, hears the maudlin, lurid singing about *Vaterland* and thunder, the drunken braying of folk songs.

The Steinway thieved from a Professor of Music, a Jew, was pulleyed in one midnight by prisoners at gunpoint, pawed at and mauled by some hammer-handed Klaus before being doused in gasoline and set on fire as a prank. Across the street, in his window, he watched the brave piano burn, smoke belching into the dawn amid the smash of shattering bottles. Every night since. The singing, the roaring. The Reich is cried up, the Communists cried down. Prostitutes are manhandled in.

On such nights, it brings ease to picture the five-hundred-year-old buildings around him. The empty churches and palazzos. The tens of thousands of empty rooms. He counts the cracks in the tin ceiling as he listens to Algiers Italian News or the BBC. Possession of a wireless has been made punishable by ten years in prison but the thought of life without it is unbearable. He pretends not to know that several of the younger seminarians have smuggled in their own radios or built them. Jazz is being quietly listened to in the darkened Collegio, sometimes with a cigarette or a shamefaced beer. It isn't his job to know.

Through the hissing weep of the airwaves, newsreaders talk of firepower and battleships. Pincer movements, fighter planes, pontoons. The crackle wefts and warps; strange interplanetary whoops. To hear the words 'London calling' consoles him, as a full moon at sea, or the boom of a friendly cannon. The wet streets of Piccadilly arise through the sibilance, in sepia, molasses-tinted, a watercolour of themselves, or Kerry sometimes comes to him, the coconut aroma of gorse on the bog road.

His father, putter in hand, on the fourteenth green at Killarney, dark glasses and spats, sunburned with August laughter.

A December evening when someone had been to Glasgow for a cousin's wedding and brought back a clockwork racing car that chuntered round the chair legs all St Stephen's Day, bumping into grown-ups' shoes. After the tea, a troop of mummers bumbled in, all straw masks and sackcloth tunics, to perform their charade of hunting the wren – as a boy, he had always found it more disturbing than it was meant to be – but they'd been stilled into marvel by the buzzing, insistent toy, as it nosed at the dozy cat and headbutted the fire irons. One by one they queued to take their own turn winding it, until a man named Mulvey whom people said was simple-minded had overwound the ratchet, wrenching the mechanism, and the car never raced again. He had wanted to strike Mulvey, to scream in his strange face. His mother warned him not to cry, it would make 'poor Michael' feel awful.

Across the street, the Nazis slobber, brangle, murder folk songs. Sometimes he hears them blamming their pistols and he wonders what they're shooting at – each other? the night? the paintings on the walls? – for the curfew has emptied the streets. Only the most desperate of the women appear beneath the lamp posts, skeletal, empty-eyed, offering themselves for a quarter loaf of bread, but they are beaten away by the Fascist Youth corner boys, the *squadre d'azione*, who burn to impress the Germans.

At nine o'clock, the Basilica bells roar like a vengeful immortal, raising jeers and choruses of mockery in the hotel. He finishes a letter to an old friend, Moss Trant, a man who left the priesthood to marry, became a dentist, is now living in Detroit. Then he reads over a single page of notes, commits to memory the three locations at which Angelucci must make drop-offs of money to buy safe passage for the escapees – a dustbin in Prati, a coalhole in Parioli, an address not yet known, over the river in Campo Marzio – tears the page to shreds, which he swallows. Along the way there'll be a stop to take on board more cash. Like the drop-offs, that will be a dangerous moment.

He looks at his watch, pictures Angelucci with Derry.

The Basilica is closing.

What will happen, will happen.

Remember me to your parents, Moss, when you are next in touch. Sending you thoughts of happier days, and the blessings of the Prince of Peace on Yvette and you and the children. I don't know when you'll get this but may the new year of 1944 bring you and yours all you'd wish. Pray for me, dear friend, and I'll pray for you.

Your old pal,

Hugh O'F

PS : I mean it about the request, Moss. Say a rosary for me one evening. I feel certain I am in imminent trouble or danger this weather. If anything does happen, I want you to know I'll be thinking of our friendship at the end, and all the good times we shared, and that I loved you dearly as my brother.

17

Christmas Eve 1943
9.17 p.m.
1 hour and 43 minutes before the Rendimento

He bolts closed the shutters, extinguishes the candle. In the slatted beam of the arc light, he disassembles his makeshift wireless, hides the coil in a bedspring, the valve behind a book, Dostoevsky's *Notes from the Underground*.

Forming a sphere of the knotted escape rope he keeps hidden beneath the wardrobe, he arranges it on the pillow and covers it with a sheet. The bolster forms a body; he drapes blankets, a bedcover. The result would not fool anyone coming into the room but a watcher glancing from the doorway might think the bed's occupant were asleep.

He unscrews the shampoo bottle, sprinkles altar wine about; a sudden silence and he hears the droplets splashing on the floor. This won't be the first room in a seminary to know that aroma. Good for any observer to think the sleeper is drunk. Raising the two floorboards, he retrieves the canvas knapsack.

Makes the sign of the cross.

Leaves the room.

At every point of what is coming, he will need luck to go undetected. Just walking down the stairs, he'll need luck. Long practised, he is careful to avoid the floorboards that groan or chirr, to zigzag where he needs to, not to cough.

In the hall, he slides the letter to Trant into the residents' post box, which is stuffed with Christmas cards and slim parcels. The casement clock bongs soberly for half past nine. Everyone in the house will be at evening private prayer.

Entering the cubbyhole beneath the old staircase, where the telephone for the use of residents is mounted to the wall, he pulls closed the flimsy curtain behind him. If the telephone should ring now, all is lost. Somehow, on these nights, it never has, but luck can be ridden too long. Sweating, he takes the penknife from his pocket. Three raincoats are hanging on the wall behind the seat. He parts them. It will take two and a half minutes to remove the eight screws in the panel.

He starts working.

Pipes clank in the wall. Somewhere above him in the house, a man is laughing. He fumbles, drops the third screw, bends to feel for it beneath the bench, and as he does, is ripped into by stomach cramp.

The telephone shrills.

Like a glass bowl smashing in the stilled, dark hall.

He lifts the receiver.

'*Pronto?*' he murmurs.

'*Mi chiamo Silvia,*' the young woman says. '*Posso parlare con Maria Elena?*'

'*Non è qui.*'

'*Ma . . .*'

'*Mi dispiace, Lei ha sbagliato numero.*'

Her voice takes on a tearful urgency, she must speak with Maria Elena. Through a chink in the curtain, he watches as the cat pads haughtily along the corridor, yellow-eyed, imperious, reigning. The caller disconnects. Wind buffets the house. He replaces the receiver but slightly off its cradle, so the telephone cannot sound again.

Removing the last of the screws, he lifts out the panel, climbs into the crawlspace behind it, to the odour of old plaster and damp. So quiet, he can hear the tippet of fleeing squirrels. Raising the panel behind him, he pulls it back into place, and, with a match, lights the stub of candle from his pocket.

Four metres take him to a junction where the crawlspace enters a downsloping cobbled passageway echoing of dripping water. In a cleft in the brickwork, his electric torch. He switches it on – the battery is weakening – and continues into the murk.

Descending into the shaft by the iron ladder on its wall, he enters a cellar system that has not seen light in seven hundred years. Long ago, Vatican servants lived here among the pantries and wine vaults, the ice rooms, vats and ship-sized casks; there is no plan of this warren, at least none he has ever seen. Not even the fleets of Roman workmen who came in to shore it up following a collapse thirty years ago were able to count these passageways.

Passing a grotto, he glances in. Three men in ragged RAF uniforms are playing cards by candlelight. The Sergeant salutes him wordlessly; he motions back for the man to keep silent, and the Sergeant nods gravely, returning to the game as though the intruder was only a shadow.

Eyes behind gratings.

Thumbs-ups from alcoves.

Hammocks and blanket-rolls.

A chalked Stars and Stripes on a cavern wall.

Nooks where a whisper is heard.

Soon he is under the cobbled yard separating the College from the Basilica. Above him, the Swiss Guardsmen will be on duty, he knows, the arc light on the roof of the conquered hotel picking out the blue, red and orange of their uniforms. Tiredness washes over him, and again the pulse of stomach cramp through the sharply sluicing fear; it is still not too late to turn back. A moment. He goes on.

Lichen on wet slabs. Rugs of hairy white weeds. There must be rats here, but in all these months he hasn't seen one; perhaps never having known light they are afraid of his torch. The beam yellows plasterwork, ancient crests, skulls-and-crossbones, a carving of Romulus and Remus on an ancient man-hole cover. He approaches the oaken door into which someone centuries ago carved an obscene cartoon: Gluttony Forced by the Devil to Drink. The hinges are rusted to powder; he wrangles the door ajar. Behind it, as in a mine, a vented crawl-way extends into the stark, cold crypt of unremembered Popes, their strange names graven into the marble coffins.

Through the sepulchre, torch struggling, his gasps are orbs of steam, and he slides behind the sarcophagus of Pius II, a tight, painful fit that can only be accomplished by inhaling as hard as he can. Through the squeeze, into an opening like the burial chamber of a passage grave, from there through the culvert and into a smaller, lower crypt where a pirate crew of disgraced Cardinals sleep their last. The fourth marble casket has a fake lid of painted plywood; he removes it, climbs inside, drops down slowly on the knotted rope through the false floor and into a bat-flickering passageway beneath.

Thirty-two metres brings him to an X-junction. Then eleven metres west.

He knocks four times on a length of broken pipe.

Three knocks come back.

He knocks again, once.

'Beethoven,' he says.

'Evening, Padre,' comes the echo.

Behind him, the black curtain is parted.

The ancient Romans believed ghosts looked like living people, only wearier. The figure parting the curtain has that hauntedness. In the candlelight, Sam Derry is old-porcelain grey, looks exhausted and breakable, like the flawed hero in the final scene of a tragedy done in military dress. Shirtless but wearing his officer's khaki jacket, bandages around his abdomen, long-john underpants, stolen Wehrmacht boots.

Five months ago, he jumped from the moving prisoner-train into a ravine; his limp has never healed. He gives a shuddering wince, like a man nodding away a mosquito. His Shelley-like hair in wet straggles, spectacles repaired with wire. He is not religious ('part-time Church of England') but is wearing a St Christopher medal about his muscle-roped throat, gift of the Genovese medical student who four nights ago performed his appendectomy herself, no surgeon being obtainable, and who, early this morning, helped smuggle him into the hidden floor of the laundry truck that returned him over the Vatican line.

'Major Derry. How are you keeping?'

'Mustn't grumble, Padre. Yourself?'

'Right as the mail.'

'You don't look it.'

'Never did.'

They shake hands, then embrace. 'You had us up the walls with worry, Sam, I thought you were a goner.'

'The things I have to do to get noticed around here.'

He is fond of Derry's turn of phrase and glum humour, his seriousness. Easy to see why he was appointed OC by the men in the prison camp. The guards would have found his solidity unnerving.

'How's the pain, Sam?'

'Worse at bloody night for some reason, so sleeping is hard. But they gave me a bucketload of sedatives to bring home. There's also gin. So, I'm keeping sedate. Speaking of which, could you or the excellent May lay your hands on a bottle of disinfectant, even a floor cleaner, and bit of gauze and a needle? Need to keep the wound clean. For when I take out the stitches.'

'Of course.'

'Soon as you can, Padre, bout of sepsis could complicate matters.'

'Sorry I'm late, by the way.'

'Oh, my social diary isn't too busy these evenings, Padre, don't worry.'

'I wasn't.'

'*Molto bene*. Stands the Eternal City as it stood?'

'Bread and oil are gone invisible. We heard there might be rice. A bold butcher in the Mercato Rionale fairly got himself lynched for admitting he'd a kilo of guanciale hidden behind the counter. Oh, I forgot. A Christmas banquet.'

From his pockets, he takes a bread roll, a hunk of cheese wrapped in a page of yesterday's *Corriere della Sera*, a pack of Woodbines and a pint of Scotch.

'Riches,' says the Englishman. '*Grazie mille*, Padre. You won't object if I don't stand on ceremony?'

'Tuck in.'

'Onward, Christian Soldiers.' Uncorking the Scotch, downing a glug.

'Get a bit of air yet, Sam?'

The Englishman shakes his head. 'Tried this morning around eleven but the gardeners were about. Saw them through the grille, didn't like the look of their slash hooks. Thought it might be best to spend a few hours with the thoughts and my Eye-tie grammar.'

'How did that go?'

'Entertainingly enough.'

'Introduce yourself to me, so. If you dare.'

'*Mi chiamo Samuele Derry e sono inglese. Buona sera.*'

'You have to put a bit of bodily *feeling* into it, Sam. It's why Italians talk with their hands, they're conducting themselves.'

Derry gives a gruff chuckle, gnawing on the bread. 'Afraid I shall never conduct. Well, perhaps on a bus. Oh, this afternoon I finished the Marcus Aurelius you brought the other week, rum stuff, a lot of it. But food for thought, too.'

'I'm fond of old Marcus.'

'You would be.'

'Why's that?'

'One assumes he was a Mick. With a name like O'Relius.'

'After the war, don't attempt a career as a comedian, Sam, will you?'

'One of his sayings rather struck me as worth putting on a poster in the Underground or somewhere. "Think of yourself as dead. Now, return and live your life."'

'We'll natter about that again. There isn't much time. How's your student getting along?'

'Come and see.'

Derry leads him into the rock-lined passageway, now through a high-roofed, flooded, taper-lit cavern over which a bridge of roped-together pallets has been slung. Up a shingled, slippy embankment, into the cell-sized alcove.

Angelucci is seated on the narrow outcropping ledge, chain-smoking. The glow of the cigarette reddens his glittering eyes as he mutters at his shadow, an actor learning lines.

Behind him, on the wall of the cave, a tin Peroni sign and a pin-up of a tight-sweatered Jane Russell. Somehow an electric bulb has been wired from a length of flex. The battered ice-bucket pressganged as ashtray is overflowing. Damp items of malodorous clothing have been draped on the rocks to dry by a nest of whitened, sighing coals. A kettle gives an incongruous hoot.

'Enzo.'

'*Monsignore.*'

'Ready?'

'Sure thing.'

'Know your stuff?'

'Back to front.'

'You look anxious.'

He drags on a cigarette, eyes widening. 'I'm not.'

'You should be.'

He shrugs. 'Then I am.'

'Did you tell anyone?'

'No.'

'Your wife?'

'Are you nuts?

'So where does she think you are?'

'Drinking with the boys, playing cards.'

'She doesn't mind?'

'I didn't ask her.'

'Enzo—'

'When I need advice on the Immaculate Conception, I'll ring your doorbell, *Monsignore*. On my girl, you leave it to me, good idea?'

Derry utters a chuckle, cups his hands, lights a Woodbine, with a click of his chin expels smoke rings. Some trick of the breeze brings the gurgle of running water into the cavern and the candle flames gutter, casting lambent purple light over the crevices. Angelucci's wearing a look that even his friends don't like to see, a sharply defiant smile that could change at any moment.

'You look worried, *Monsignore*. For a guy with God on his side. What's rattling your cage over there? You having doubts?'

'Tell the itinerary, Enzo. Don't pause.'

With heavy, pantomimed patience, Angelucci shuts his eyes, raises his face to the dripping roof, begins intoning the route as though a litany, his drawl studiously colourless, rote-learned, unexcited. Counting off the street names and back alleys on his fingers, as though if he ran out of fingers he'd run out of alleyways, now staring at the icon of half-reclined Jane Russell as though the list is being addressed to her as a homage. The circuit is so detailed, it takes four minutes to recite. He never falters or stammers. It's perfect.

'Then home.' He grins defiantly. 'To the wife.'

'Via Orsini is blocked,' Derry counters. 'What's your alternative? Quick.'

'So I take Farnese, then left. Nothing simpler.'

'The Jerries have barricaded the Ponte Cavour.'

'They'd never do that.'

'Say they do.'

'I take the quay. Figure it out. What's this, a competition?'

'That won't work.'

'Madonna mia, *I'm a Roman*, I know *my own city*. Give me a chance to damn well *breathe* here, why can't you? Hand to Jesus Christ Almighty, you two are worse than the Gestapo. The way you *look* at me, *Monsignore*. Calm down.'

'Three hours from now, I'm Hauptmann walking into you on Lungotevere Michelangelo. Show me your card. State your name.'

'We've been over this a hundred *times*, Derry, what's the matter, you deaf?'

'State your name this minute, Enzo. Or the Rendimento is off.'

'Francesco Lynch.'

'That's it?'

148

'That's what?'

'I'm Paul Hauptmann, you ignorant bastard, your life and the lives of your comrades are in my hands. You address me as sir or I'll take three days to bleed you to death.'

'Lynch, *sir*. Francesco.'

'Occupation?'

'Technical Operative, sir, Vatican Radio, sir.'

'The man on this identity card is older than you.'

'*Con rispetto*, that is me, sir.'

'I don't think so.'

'Yes, it is.'

'What keeps you looking so young?'

'Your wife riding my face.'

'Enzo—'

'I've grown out my beard, sir, since that photograph was taken. People say it makes me look younger.'

'That seems strange.'

'Strange that I look younger, sir? Or that I grew out my beard, sir?'

'Both.'

'Razor blades are hard to come by since rationing, as sir knows.'

'Date of birth?'

'Seventh December '22.'

'Where?'

'Bologna, sir.'

'I know Bologna well, I was stationed there for a time. What street?'

'Milazzo.'

'There is no Via Milazzo in Bologna,' the Monsignor says. 'You are lying to us. Why?'

'With respect, sir, there is, it's off Via dei Mille.'

'Current address?'

'My apartment block was destroyed in an air raid, so I'm living in a storage room at the radio station, until I get back on my feet. Sir will see a telephone number there for my manager, Father Rainaldi. He's well connected in the Party.'

'Married?'

'Sir, yes.'

'Your wife also lives in this storage room, as you call it?'

'Sir, she went back to her parents.'

'I have heard your wife is a whore,' Derry says. 'How much does she charge for an hour?'

'Sir's joke is amusing, sir. Thank you.'

'I daresay she'd like a proper German who could satisfy her, not a puffed-up Italian queer.'

'I daresay you're right, sir. Who wouldn't?'

'Where is Vatican Radio located in relation to St Peter's Cathedral?'

'St Peter's is not a cathedral, but a basilica, sir. The radio station is a five-minute walk from there. In the Vatican gardens.'

'Your citizenship?'

'Vatican City passport, sir. I am legally a neutral.'

'Why are you breaking curfew? You are unaware of the rules? *Stand up straight when you are addressed by an officer of the Reich, you Italian son-of-a-bitch.*'

'With respect, sir, there is an exemption under article nine, "technological necessity". We have an equipment failure at the station and it is my responsibility to get it fixed.'

'At two in the morning? Do you think me a fool?'

'All I need is a metre of electrical cable, sir, and a length of copper wiring. I can find them on any construction site or in a builders' yard, sir. The matter is urgent.'

'Surely the construction sites and builders' yards are locked up for Christmas.'

'Perhaps not all, sir, it is my duty to look.'

'How is it so urgent that you presume to ignore the curfew?'

'We at the radio station will broadcast the Christmas message of the Holy Father at noon tomorrow, as I'm sure sir is aware. The Duce mentioned the fact in his article in Wednesday morning's *Regime Fascista*, as sir will have seen. There will be a worldwide audience of forty million listeners. It would be a mortifying embarrassment to Italy and the Duce were the broadcast to be cancelled.'

'I glanced through the *Regime Fascista* on Wednesday and there was no such article.'

'Sir, a copy of it is here in my pocket. Should sir wish to see it?'

From his jacket Angelucci produces the scissored-out sheet of newsprint, handing it across with the inscrutability of the poker player presenting a royal flush.

'Think that's clever, Enzo?'

'Who are you now, sir? Hauptmann or yourself?'

'Hauptmann would have put a bullet in your guts the moment you reached for your jacket, Thickhead. Stick to the script. *Don't improvise.*'

'I knew you'd say that. Turn over the paper.'

Scrawled on the back, in Angelucci's handwriting: 'GIVE ME MY CHANCE.'

'It's the smart lads get people killed, Enzo. I told you that before.'

'Then you don't need to worry, *Monsignore.*'

'Sam, what do you reckon?'

'Above my paygrade, Padre. Your decision.'

'What's your instinct as lead mission-runner? Is he ready?'

'We've gone through it two dozen times. I say put him in.'

'Cargo here, is it?'

'Last consignment arrived this afternoon. I sent it up top as agreed. Francesco, tell the holy gentleman where you'll find it.'

'In the fourteenth nook along, in the cloakroom near the exit door of the Musei, a postman's sack, canvas, the notes are wrapped in stacks of five thousand each, I could recite this whole thing *in my sleep.*'

'Thirty thousand American dollars,' Derry says. 'Believe me, Padre, I had time to count them. He collects the remaining fifty along the way.'

'My feeling is to postpone, Sam. It feels ludicrously risky.'

'It's not ideal,' Derry concedes. 'But Jerry might storm the Vatican any day, any hour. Then it's curtains to our little Glee Club and we're probably dead. With every escaped prisoner in Rome.'

'We *can't* postpone,' Angelucci says. 'Let's stick to the plan.'

'A plan should never be stuck to just because it's a plan,' Derry says. 'That's the Catholic in you talking.'

'Go to hell.'

Something stirs in the shadows. The three men snap silent, Derry's hand goes to his inside holster, pulls out his Webley.

151

A starling, lost, butts its way through the crypt, trilling in panic, and enters a grating.

Derry lights a Woodbine on the one he's already smoking, the glow illuminating the isobars of his face, the scars and broken teeth he received from his captors in Camp 21. On the train, they threatened to give him a death that would turn his children's hair white when they heard of it. Not that anyone would hear of it, the chief torturer assured him. 'What's left of you will be poured down a sink.'

Angelucci regards him. Water gurgles on rock.

'I'll go with him,' Derry says. 'Down a couple of painkillers.'

'Sam, you can barely walk. That's the worst idea of all.'

'Why?'

'If one of you got lifted by the Gestapo, he might just about stand a chance of not breaking. Not two.'

'We'd be halving their chances.'

'We'd be doubling them.'

'I'm granite,' says Angelucci quietly. 'I despise these whores' bastards. The chisel to crack me has never been made. If you think I'll let these nobodies catch me, in my own city, you know nothing. They're scum. They're zero. I'll go through their locks. Like smoke.'

'Take this,' says Derry, offering his pistol.

'I won't need that peashooter.'

'You might.'

Angelucci shakes his head.

'*Buona fortuna*, Enzo,' says the Englishman. 'Whatever else happens.'

'My name isn't Enzo. I'm Francesco Lynch.' He stares. 'Thought you'd catch me out, *inglese*? Try harder.'

'Good luck, Francesco Lynch. Hope to see you tomorrow.'

'Not if I see you first. *Andiamo*.'

18

THE VOICE OF ENZO ANGELUCCI
8th November 1962
From transcript of BBC research interview, tape 3,
conducted Bensonhurst, New York City

That night, I'm in condition.

Best shape of my life.

I been training two months, flat out.

In the apartment block, we got a stairwell right outside our front door, I hung a twenty-metre knotted rope from the eighth storey, down into the lobby. Seventeen seconds, whole climb. My neighbour Mike Festa used to time me, friend of my old man. By Christmas week, I could do it in eleven.

Squats. Sit-ups. Lost four kilos. Got strong. If my time slipped? I wouldn't be intimate with my wife for three nights. We were young. That time ain't slipping.

Ran barefoot up the staircase without waking a soul. I could run up them steps like a *bat* wouldn't hear. Guy name Crivella lived on the block, good long jumper, this guy. Starts giving me lessons, chalking out lengths right there on the street. He don't know it's the distance between two rooftops.

Fast? I could catch a fly between my fingertips, not kill it.

This means everything to me, the chance I might get my shot.

I can stand forty minutes holding two saucepans of water parallel to the floor. Think that's easy? Go ahead. Try five.

We say *arrivederci* to Derry. It's quarter to eleven, something. I can see he don't got full confidence, wishes he's running the Rendimento himself. But what's he going to do? No choice. Got a hole in his belly the size of a sundial, and a head full of black-market morphine.

Heart whomping against my ribcage as the Monsignor and me climbs into the tunnel. He's going like a train, you want to see this guy move, in front, and he's urging me all the time, hissing over his shoulder, 'faster, Enzo, faster, *Più veloce, andiamo'* and we come to this stretch where we got to crawl along through a grid of old sewer pipes, like snakes. I'm thinking of my wife, picturing her at home with the baby. The Gestapo don't kill me? She will.

Here and there, they got them guide-ropes, like below deck on a ship. But other places, nothing. Just the darkness. How in hell he knows where he's heading, I got no faintest idea. Like a mole, this guy. Like a sandhog. Guess he'd studied it all out, saw the map in his mind. Him and Derry knew the necropolis every which way and then backwards. Like you'd know your own reflection. Like they *created* that damn warren.

Before long I see an elevator shaft, old-fashioned cagework, black. We go in and climb up the bars one storey. Now we're in some type of basement, wooden boxes and crates. Electric light bulbs in muzzles. Is that the right word?

Fire Exit signs on the walls, dust-buckets, janitors' carts. Like an industrial type of feeling in the way it's been painted, this green-blue porridge-gloss everywhere, and fire extinguishers and fire buckets. The place smells of cats' piss and lonely old men. An axe in a glass case on the pillar.

I always thought it would be like I'm Sugar Ray walking into Madison Square Garden. Name in silver on my back, tricolour on my gloves, double-shuffling down the tunnel, punching air. The crowds, the flashbulbs, the cheers, the applause, here comes the hero. Stupid fool. There wasn't no flash-bulbs, there wasn't no ring girls. No one's clapping my shoulders, massaging me with towels. Only second I got in my corner is the *Monsignore*. I'm scared. It ain't no night at the Garden.

He hands me an envelope and I ask him to bless me. Communist as I was. Who cares? There's free insurance going? Brother, I'll take it.

I thought it would make him feel better, if you want to know the truth. So he says the stuff in Latin and does whatever he does. I don't feel no different. But that ain't the point. Someone wants to give you something, accept it, let them give. Sometimes that's all they got.

What he's giving, it's his conscience, he wants to feel he done his best. That's the difference between us and the animals, you want to do more than the least you can get away with.

Says, 'Enzo, stay where you are for *exactly* twenty minutes. Then, open that envelope. Couple of last-minute instructions. And be brave.'

He gives me this big bear hug. And I hug him back. Sure.

154

Because I loved the guy to pieces. Though he'd drive you batshit nuts.

In a Dick Powell movie I seen one time, this cop says about the gangster's wife, 'She'd make a Bishop kick a hole through a stained-glass window.' Guy wrote that must have met the *Monsignore*.

After he's gone, I stay where I am for ten minutes, fifteen, like he told me. You never saw time go so slow. There's this clock on the basement wall – I can still see it, clear as day. Man, the second hand on that clock is moving like it's glued.

I slide over to look at the fire-axe in the glass case on the wall. Thinking, maybe I'll take it, break the glass, could be useful. They got words stamped on the shaft, so now at least I know where I am. 'Property of the Musei Vaticani'. So I'm under the Museum, right next door to the Basilica. All kinds of crazy things, I'm thinking about, in a tumble, up and down. My parents, my babies. Of course my wife. *Her* parents. They ain't never liked me none. Feeling's mutual.

And I'm thinking, could you take that axe and smash a human being in the face? Angelucci, or Francesco, whatever in hell you're called, could you murder a fellow creature, even a Nazi, with a hatchet? Tough guy, you could? Who you kidding? One time your grandmother told you, wring the neck of that chicken. Remember the shake in your fingers? What in hell do you think you're doing, about to run a Rendimento like this? You couldn't run water. You're weak. This Hauptmann, he catches you? He got ways of making you die take a long, slow time. You'll beg to be dead. He won't let you till he's done. Empty you out like a suitcase.

What I do, I'm scared, so I picture the whole world. It's a thing my old man used to do when he had worries. Starting out right here in Rome, then up to the north, then all around Europe, Norway, England, then up to the Arctic, then over to Canada. Through the States, Chicago, the Great Lakes you seen on the globe in school, across the oceans, then Australia, China, Burma, huge seas full of islands, all these other places I'll never see and the people there won't see me neither. And, who cares? You got people live in igloos, tepees, caves, mansions in Los Angeles, mud huts on islands. They ain't thinking about you, *stronzo*, you ain't thinking about them. They all got their problems, you got yours. They fight, they fool around, they figure it out. I'm saying, Angelucci, you ain't nothing, you're a speck on the ass of the world, you're zilch. And in some ways, you know? That's fine. The world been here a long time, got no plan to go nowhere, *vaffanculo* to the Nazis, so they catch you and kill you. At least you died fighting. Let's go.

Ring the bell. Round One, come out swinging, drop your jaw.

See, I'm young and dumb, too. Wanted in. Be the tough guy. Made it to nineteen and a half minutes before I opened that envelope. There it was, in his writing. Man, I'll never forget it.

I cried. Like a baby. Guy broke my heart in ten pieces.

'Enzo, you're a hero. But you're not ready. Another time.

Go home a different way.

Respects,

GOLF'

19

Christmas Eve 1943
11 p.m.
The Rendimento

In monk's cowl, he opens the air hatch, admits himself to the vast, cold, resonant silence, screws closed the grille behind him.

Ninety metres away, on a pillar near the steps to the altar, the scarlet lamp
glows in its high, silver bowl.

His torch beam illuminates smoke-grey marble sconces as he crosses the
Basilica, hurries along the nave. Past the rosewood murk of side chapels, the
confession boxes and stacked collection plates, the squat, iron tables of extinguished candles.

Past the wild eyes of martyrs, the crossed hands of virgins. Raised swords,
crushed snakes, burning pyres. A hundred graves are stared down on by the
ceiling-high organ, its flues whisperingly hissing at his trespass. Candle stands
and candle racks throw shadow as he goes. The marble-stern Madonna cra-
dling her broken son.

Over flagstones worn smooth by pilgrims' sandals. Tombstones whose
names have long been ground away. Moonlight glows the indigoes and ochres
of stained glass, the purples, the fiery gold of the pulpit. So quiet that he can
hear the swish of the cowl. Ghosts look down on the beforelife.

An affront to some immensity to be the only creature drawing breath in a
fortress the size of a stadium. Long benches have been placed for High Mass
tomorrow; the tall, black cross, the long, empty benches, the glaring, pointing
Pharisees, the nailed-through hands. Something about the candlesticks and the
frescoed Roman spears gives the aura of an execution chamber.

Wind squalls outside. Mammoth organ pipes groan. Pages of ten thousand
prayer books riffle on their pews. He sees himself as from above, a grain of sand
in a Colosseum, Angelucci's insulted rage, Derry pacing and smoking in the

depths, the Contessa at silent prayer. Delia Kiernan drinking. Marianna typing words. D'Arcy Osborne and May saying nothing.

Through the linger of incense and candlewax, the colder smell of rain, like a secret refusing avoidance. He genuflects before the red lamp, hurriedly, shivering, now making a way up the steps and into the shadows of the sacristy, where heavy silken vestments draped from railings dangle in a draught and the sherryish odour of altar wine thickens the air. Dark sideboards return the moonlight. An alarm clock ticks.

The tabernacle's studded doors. A medieval hassock. Two wardrobes like upended coffins.

Opening the first, he finds nothing but an accusation of chattering clothes-hangers, in the second the working man's grey suit, homburg and overcoat. Quickly he changes garb. In the fourth Bible down, on the eleventh shelf, near the monstrance, a key is hidden, which he retrieves and uses, opening the door to the stairwell.

At the top of the stairwell, the gate to the Sistine Chapel is bolted; from the breast pocket of the jacket he takes a copied wooden key for the padlock. The key is long and gaunt and must be turned with great care or it will snap. 'Imagine it is made of water,' the lockpick told May.

He prays as the key turns, feels the action's heavy click; hurries into the vestry of the chapel. Above him in the darkness, the Creation of Man, the fingertip of God outstretched to awakening Adam. Hell behind the altar, reddened tridents, flayed pelts, the torture house shadowed by age and night.

Two kilometres above that ceiling, the heavy bombers droning. He pauses, uncertain, listening.

Luftwaffe returning to base? RAF? The Americans?

The drone brings his room to mind, the coil of rope on the pillow, the arc lamp gridding the shutters. But vital to hurry, the plan must be followed. The security guards' round will bring them through the Basilica in seven minutes. Then will come the octet of silent, elderly monks whose duty is to prepare the altar for Christmas Mass.

He takes the staircase that leads into the Musei Vaticani, the long, narrow corridors, through the Sala di Mappa, charts of all the oceans and known lands of the world, cartouches, sea monsters, legends, mottoes, then he's moving through the dust of the Sala Rotonda, by manuscripts in glass cases, rubied reliquaries, chalices.

Roped-off masterpieces, 'FORBIDDEN TO TOUCH' signs. A tapestry in which Christ's eyes follow him along the passageway. Alcoves of crewel and lace.

Past the nook where it is said Michelangelo lived seven years, past twisting marble torsos, castrated Grecian huntsmen, armless naked goddesses, lapis lazuli urns the size of tramcars, a swan raping the Spartan queen.

His meek torch flickers, threatening to die. Switching off, he goes by the moonlight that pearls the long windows from the fairyland of the Vatican gardens.

Men speaking.

The murmur and low laughter of the security guards on their rounds, and he slides behind an alabaster pillar as they pass. Two minutes have been wasted. He opts for a shortcut.

Through the side door, into the boudoir of the old Papal apartments and out into the ceremonial corridor. Approaching slowly, heads down, hands in their cowl sleeves, the octet of blindfolded, barefoot monks, before them, three candlelit nuns, chanting an Ave Maria, and an Abbess carrying a plaster Christ-child half her own height.

Stepping backwards into the darkness, he waits.

Et benedictus fructus ventris
Ventris tuae, Jesus . . .
Ora pro nobis
Ora pro nobis . . .

Hurrying through the Museo Gregoriano Egizio. Past mummies and death masks of dog-headed pharaohs. Nobodaddies, ibises, a leering, bald sphinx, jagged panels of cracked hieroglyphics. Into the marble entrance hall, past the ticket booths and coat shelves. Entering the women's public lavatories, he checks each stall before opening the mop room at the back.

Brooms in metal buckets.

Overalls hung on hooks.

The words *'Uscita di Emergenza'* in fluorescent green on a door.

Which he pushes.

The door clicks open.

Night tries to come in, cold and foreign.

Taking a matchstick from the box in his pocket he places it in such a way that the dead-weighted door will remain infinitesimally ajar. Steps out into the street.

But the money!

Hastens back through the lavatories, gapes for the alcove Derry mentioned. Again, he hears the security guards talking, again he retreats, into a long, narrow anteroom that has no windows.

Through the darkness come strange sounds – gasping, a moaning. A young woman, dress opened, leaning back against a sarcophagus, a security guard kneeling before her, their urgings and whisperings, her fingers in his hair as she shakes.

What shocks him is not the sight alone, but the word they are passing to one another.

Sì.

Sì

Dio.

Sì.

Hurrying from the anteroom to the lobby.

Dazed, among the shelves where pilgrims stow jackets and hats, he sees the folded canvas sack.

Minutes later, the moment of maximum danger returns, for there is no way of seeing outside to the street, no means of knowing what awaits.

A patrolman. A Nazi. A rainstorm of bullets.

He steps through the door.

The night smells bitter.

A tram's bell clangs.

Sparrows mimic a machine.

From somewhere in the middle distance, the bawling of youths.

A rat scuttles out from the foot of a municipal tree trunk and into a broken manhole beneath a house-sized mural of the Duce.

The street falls silent, as though obeying a command.

Weak legs carry him across the Via dei Bastioni di Michelangelo. He enters a butcher's doorway, tries to calm. Counting backwards lowers the heart rate, Derry once told him.

Backwards from a hundred, blinking hard, he counts. Through the windows, he sees the aprons, the hooks and glinting cleavers, the massy bronze hulk of the till. On a blackboard at the back of the shop, on which the butcher chalks his prices, someone has scrawled a lewd cartoon.

The couple in the Museo shimmer and writhe, their trembling, the fire of that *sì*.

A street-cleaning truck trundles past, spraying hoses over the kerb, the stink of disinfectant assaulting his eyes and throat, raising his gorge, and he swallows, retches, coughs into his gloves, hoping the men in the truck haven't heard him above the cacophonous engine.

It slows to a shaking stop, black windows rolling open, and it shudders as though digesting the rubbish in the back, crimson winkers in the mirrors behind the butcher's counter. The daubed names of meats, a statue of the Infant Jesus of Prague.

The black-masked driver climbs down from the cab, his apprentice, in balaclava, from the footplate at the rear. They swish at the pavestones with long, filthy brooms, the older man whistling a folk song, the other muttering blasphemies. Dabbing at the telegraph poles with a rag on a stick, kneeling to scrape gum from a grating. The truck's engine grumbles. Scarlet lamps click. An old garbageman sings of the sea:

Andiamo a vedere la spiaggia
mentre splende la luna piena

He watches as the dustmen edge nearer to his doorway. Now so close he can hear their banter.

People are animals. Look at this filth. Mother of Christ, the stench off this trashcan is worse than your breath. Shut your beak and get mopping, you donkey.

Above the butcher's, on the third floor of the apartment block, a window is tugged open and a woman caterwauls down at the disruptors.

'*Deficienti*, it's Christmas Eve, must you make so much racket, go home to your slum and leave good people in peace.'

The older dustman, disguising his hurt as amusement, shouts back.

'Why don't you have a husband? Oh, I think I got the answer. I'm doing you a service, lady. Shut your mouth.'

Soon his decrial becomes a performance intended for the entertainment of his trainee. *Get your backside to Mass tomorrow, missus, and pray for a new face. The one you got there would crack a bell.* He enjoys this self-awarded role, the Man Who Speaks his Mind. But after a burble of dutiful laughter, the lad isn't interested. On the pavement, he's found a broken cigarette, pulls askew his balaclava, lights up with a Zippo, smokes hard, deep and long, stares up at the moon, crushes out the butt, back to work.

Sweeping lazily, steadily, outside the trattoria, the grocer's, the tobacconist's that had its windows smashed because the proprietor was a Jew, outside the hardware store where sweepstake tickets are sold beneath the counter, then the bar, the boarded-up travel agency, the office of American Express. Steadily, lazily, lazily, steadily, the steadiness feeding the laziness. He pauses with the broom, as a crooner into his microphone, whispers a phrase from a Hollywood love song, clawing at the air.

Sinatra of the sidewalk, star of a mind's-eye Manhattan. Lazily towards the butcher's doorway, lazily, steadily, a drummer using brushes, doobie-dooing, la-la-la-ing, now spitting on the pavement he's just pretended to sweep. Closer every second, until he has entered the doorway.

Cold, curious eyes through the holes in the mask.

Unblinking.

Expressionless.

Two search-lamps.

A century passes.

'Antonello,' yells the youth.

'What's happening?' the old garbageman calls.

'Nothing,' shouts the younger, gaze not leaving the man in the doorway. 'For God's sake, let's get on. We've wasted enough time here already.'

'Lazy bastards, you kids. If there was work in the bed, you'd sleep on the floor.'

'We need to get back to the depot.'

He turns, leaves the doorway, cricket-bats a pebble across the street with his broom, climbs up into the cab and waits for his galumphing captain to join him, which he does in a fanfare of valedictory denunciations of the woman in the apartment above.

'*Puttana*,' he yells.

'*Cornuto*,' she shouts down.

'Get yourself a husband. *Shut your mouth.*'

The truck judders awake with a storm of racking coughs. For badness the driver tugs hard on the claxon as they inch away. He doesn't know there's a third rider on board, a man on the rear footplate, holding fast to the handgrips, vibration through his torso, face a concealment of dirt.

The reek of fetid rubbish Sometimes the rider half-turns, gulps the night. Past churches and empty piazzas, by Swastika banners and machine-gun posts.

At the roadblock, the truck is waved through, the German sentries chuckling at the stink. Pinching their noses, miming vomiting. Middle-aged men, the weird excitability in their eyes. Six of the seven will die in March, blown to pieces by a Partisan bomb in the Via Rasella. The seventh will lose his hearing and sight.

Past palaces, monasteries, a closed-down nightclub. Fountains that have sparkled for three thousand years. Past a nunnery from which four hundred eyes are watching. Down a laneway off Via Segundo.

A left turn into a barbed-wired, filthy, gull-assailed yard where a dozen similar trucks are parked in an unruly line, the green-blue stench almost visible. The two dustmen alight, pull their sodden mops and buckets from the cab, trudge towards the corrugated-iron hut near the crooked back gates.

The yard falls silent.

Pulling up his coat collar, he goes.

Through the reeking fetor, the zizz of a million flies, along a passageway to Via Agazzari.

Again, the moan of bombers, heading out or returning.

He crosses the street, turns onto a tiny laneway behind Via Alessandri, through the bullet-strewn yard of a derelict hotel. Up the crumbling wooden steps, through the devastated kitchens, their sinks, taps and refrigerators crowbarred out by looters, the pantry used as a latrine by people of the street, past weird, scarlet lichens sprouting on scorched tiles, through the vandalised circular lobby and the shattered, reeking ballroom, a burned-out double bass and smashed chandeliers, glass tables upended, stacks of rotting velvet chairs, past a line of bedroom doorways, paint shorn by the fire, doors with withered spats and melted stilettoes still outside for the bootblack, along a corridor

163

where larks have nested and some predator has clawed tatters of mouldering silk off the wainscots, emerges down the shuddering fire-escape onto Via Vittoria Aleotti.

A black Mercedes passes.

Then an empty tram.

Fifty metres south before squeezing through the gap between two tenements, then across the Z-shaped patch of filthy wasteland behind them, where old bicycles and lengths of chain and beer kegs and pram wheels are strewn. Spools of rancid wiring, sheaves of radiator pipe, the skeleton of a Fiat cannibalised for parts. A tramp asleep in a hammock between cadaverous trees.

Back lanes and alleyways, across a vacant lot.

Wind gusts up as he makes for the passageway called Vicolo Cozzolani, so narrow that it appears on no maps. Crossing now by the entrance to the Cavalry Academy, slowing his pace as he approaches every streetlamp, quickening as he passes, recollecting Derry's words after a Rendimento that had to be aborted. *Light is the enemy, it must always be avoided. Every time you see your shadow, you're in trouble.*

Now, as he hurries, the shadow starts whispering.

You're condemned by your own vanity. What did you think you were at, playing God? Derry's a hero; you're a pretender, a clown. When they catch you, as they will, that stupid collar won't save you. Every one of those prisoners will be tortured to death. So will you. As an offering to your pride.

Via Stolto. Via Tonto. Via Balordo. Via Morte.

You're stumbling down Death Street. You blindman.

The Contessa had an idea but you shot it from the skies. Didn't like someone bringing something useful to the table? Beggars to be paid ten lire for every street bulb smashed, that way a completely dark route across the city could be cut. But Monsignor didn't listen. Monsignor knows best. Monsignor's the conductor. Bow your heads.

The shadow-voice flames, refusing to let him alone. He turns towards the gust from the river.

A deadly stretch now, the long, broad thoroughfare. Elegant couturiers, jewellers, shirtmakers, fine hotels. A German machine-gun turret on high black stilts at the northerly junction sixty metres away. He can see the three soldiers in the watchtower.

Silhouettes against the moon.

Night-binoculars glinting.

Around the corner, onto a side street of high-bourgeois apartment blocks. Gleaming motorcars beneath elms. Rampant stone lions above mullions.

Brass panels of doorbells shining. On a manhole cover, the letters 'SPQR'.

A baby is yawling but quietens as he passes.

The mewl of cold cats, the swishing of restless leaves. Something boils in his stomach. He looks at his watch. One-seventeen. Hurry on.

In Kerry, they've the three miles from the chapel walked by now, will be coming in from Midnight Mass. Frost on sacks of caustic by the half-door to the stable. Your mother making tea in the aluminium pot got from Limerick. The maple smell of the lake by the water fields in wintertime. A glaze of frost on the yew berries but your father's warning that they're poisonous.

See the pictures? Stop walking. Give in.

You remember it, don't you, that night you couldn't sleep and you stole down for the sup of milk.

Heads bowed, murmured words, Daddy and Mam praying. The votive lamp before the picture of the Sacred Heart making the wireless dials glow red. Bread had been baked; the air over the kneading-board was like gauze. The kitchen smelt floury like a cakeshop.

The sweetness of that milk, your father's mild admonishment, the low of the calves made nervous by starlight. Your mother fetching milk to the pair of you.

You and Daddy out the back yard, him smoking a Players, Mammy accepting the odd puff like a girl outside a dance hall. He was tracing you the stories of the stars, the Hunter, the Plough. Beards of cloud and they rolling past the gleaming coin of the moon. Birdsong and horses nickering. The three of you there a good hour, so you thought, but Mam's watch said only ten minutes. In the India-blue darkness, the silky-blue blackness, and you marvelling at the whistle of a pair of stubborn blackbirds that refused to return to the nest.

The Christmas you turned fourteen.

'You'll have lovely nights like this with your own children, please God,' Daddy said. You didn't want to tell him, but already you felt you'd be a priest. There wouldn't be children or wife or home. It frightened you, didn't it? You couldn't tell anyone.

In the same kitchen now. Two old people praying.

Our son, a priest in the Vatican.
Stop this madness.
Turn around.
Go home.
Grow up.
It can yet be yours again, that night of the milk.
I'm your shadow.
You'll never lose me.
Stop walking.

20

THE VOICE OF JOHN MAY
20th September 1963
From transcript of BBC research interview, conducted Coldharbour,
Poplar, East London

There's an exam you need to pass if you want to be a London cabbie. Sorts the sheep from the goats. Called 'The Knowledge'.

Takes three years of graft and practice. Moves in like a lodger. You're *dreaming* the streets, the railway stations, the terraces. Five hundred hotels in London, you've got to know the address of every one of them. Cinemas, football grounds, theatres. Whole lot. Twenty thousand streets in London. Ain't easy.

Your missus is demented because you've roped her in and all. You've told her, ask me surprise questions. Catch me out.

Then the morning comes around when you show what you're made of. You're washed, scrubbed, combed, polished, best bib and tucker. Game on.

You're sitting there in front of the examiner and he's got a map of London the size of a tabletop. Every laneway, back street, alley, crescent, streets you ain't never seen, where no one's ever going. Streets that don't bleeding *exist*. It's formal, no chit-chat, he's an experienced, senior cabbie, a professional. He's asked you what's the route from Piccadilly Circus to Brickfields Terrace in Maida Vale. Nice, simple start. Draws you in.

You tell him left, then right, then round by the park, then right, then left, then north, then west, then straight along Whatever You're Having Yourself — only you can't go by Queensway being it's one-way at the moment — so you turn down Westbourne Gardens and you're there.

You ain't got no map yourself but the one in your head. You do it from memory or you're stuffed. Fastest way from Rupert Street to Craven Hill Mews. Simple? Only, now he's throwing googlies. Watch out.

I'm at Royal Oak station, need to get to the tailor's in Duke Street, St James, then Caulfield Gardens, Earls Court, look lively, I'm picking up the wife, then Cropley Street, Shoreditch. In rush hour.

'The Knowledge', like I said. Sorts out your contenders.

That's the way the Padre knew Rome.

Avenues, alleyways, parks, tram routes. Near on a thousand churches. I swear he knew all of them. In Dublin – anywhere in Ireland – they give you directions by the pubs. 'Turn left at John Grogan's, take a right by the Palace.' The Padre was like that with the churches in Rome. 'Go straight at Santa Maria, cross the lane behind Sant'Ivo alla Sapienza.'

Don't ask me how he learned it. But he did. Had the nous. You didn't fanny about with Hughdini.

Also, a walker. Shanks's Pony, all that. Wasn't a cobblestone in Rome he didn't know. People *born* there would be stopping him in the Piazza to ask the best way from Trastevere to Prati. I used to tell him, 'If you wasn't a man of the cloth, you'd have made a pukka cabbie.' He'd be tickled. 'Maybe it ain't too late, John.'

When he was bored or couldn't sleep – this is what he told me -- he'd lie awake driving his taxi from Buckingham Palace down to Deptford and back. 'That usually does the trick.' We was fishing when he told me that, it was one day in the country, Sir Frank, the Contessa, the Padre and me. Miss de Vries and Delia come later. At Ostia, near the seaside. String quintet on the bandstand. Wurlitzer horses, a roundabout. Kiddies running around. Almost normal. Delia sang 'Danny Boy' and the girls all cried. The Monsignor sang 'Take Me Back to Blighty' in a terrible cockney accent. *Take me over there, Drop me anywhere, Put me on the train for London town.* I'm giving him stick. Calling him 'Aitch' for a laugh. He's calling me 'Johnjoe' like they do in Ireland. Happy day.

Funny, it was always London, not Rome, when he couldn't sleep. I think he found London a comfort, a mother. You'll get that with the Irish. They're free here.

Another thing, he was on the level. Down-to-earth bloke. And it don't show in photos but the Padre was tough. Like they say where I'm from, he had bottle. I was thinking before about Shackleton, the poor sods in the Antarctic, their whaleship was hulled with this Guyanese wood, greenheart, so hard you can't hammer a nail in it. That was the Padre. Proper greenheart. An old-fashioned, stand-up, don't-take-liberties sort. Dressed like it, too. Yes, he did. All the photos, he's in priest's clobber naturally enough, but a different story when he was off duty, in mufti. Camelhair coat and black trilby. All that. Shoes you could shave in. Sharp dresser. The moxie.

Short-back-and-sides once a fortnight, hot comb, touch of Brylcreem. Maltese I knew as a nipper done a seven-stretch in Pentonville for a bank job in Mayfair, when he's come out, he's like royalty, cock of the walk. The Padre had shades of same. A good front.

Seen him down Whitechapel, you'd say, that's a Face. And you wouldn't want to cross him, he'd have a razor up his cuff. Funny thing to say about a man of his profession but he walked like what the Italians call *il capo dei capi*, the godfather.

That's the way he'd come over, 'I ain't scared of bugger all.'

But that night, I'm telling you, he must have been scared. I don't like to think of it.

Can we stop?

Let the bridge be open, let the bridge be open, let the bridge be open, he prays.

The identity card was forged with skill and its photograph is real but that won't be enough. If he's stopped, there'll be questions.

Who is your father? In what city was he born? What is your brother's birthdate? Are you married? To whom? How is that spelled? What age is your mother? Which soccer team do you support? Who's their captain?

Every non-Italian in the Choir has been given an alias in case it's ever needed. Delia Kiernan's is Mary Lavelle, Sir D'Arcy's is Robert Melmoth. May becomes Kenneth Oliver, valet to a difficult Cardinal. ('It ain't far enough off the truth,' he says.) Marianna is Ann Brunner, an actress and dramatist, whom she says she prefers to herself.

In the mornings he and Derry ('John Atkinson', Vatican librarian) work an hour on the aliases alone. Fine-sanding their stories to smoothness takes detail. The date of the first Fascist rally I attended, the city, the friend I went with, the length of the Duce's speech. The number of bodyguards, the reasons why I joined the Party, the names of the businesses I've burned, their addresses.

169

One night at rehearsal, he made the Choristers imagine their aliases meeting in a room, told them to sing as their Others, in character. Each alias was then subjected to a public questioning from Derry in the meticulous briskness of his own. The Contessa left the rehearsal. There was a bitter, loud argument, 'We are not staging *an operetta*, Hugh, what time-wasting idiocy is this?'

'For God's sake, Jo, would you calm yourself, we've *work*.'

'Stop "Godding" me! You talk as though you *invented* God.'

Out spilled their exhaustion, the terror they carried, a closeness turned inside out.

'Must you always be the diva?'

'You know *nothing* about me, Hugh, you never have.'

'How can you speak in this manner to someone who cares for you?'

'Cares? How, *cares*? I am to be a puppet in your drama, robbed of even my name, my meaning, because you deem it better?'

'It's your name could get you *killed*. Don't you *see*?'

'Then *let it*.'

'What?'

'I am Giovanna Landini and I bear my husband's name.' Her quiet, cold words seemed to cut the dusty air. 'I will bear it until I die, come Nazi, thug or priest. The name I freely took, that is mine. *Do you hear me*?'

'There's someone ninety miles away can't hear you, woman, why don't you *shout a bit louder*.'

'People call you "Father", Hugh. You are *not* my father.'

'Thank God.'

'You will not dare to baptise me. Get it into your brain.'

'*At least I've a brain to get it into.*'

'Would you like the last word? You can have it, *Monsignor*. Do not tell me what I am, or who I am, ever again. *I* shall decide who I am.'

'I can see who you are, never fear.'

'Hugh.' This was Delia, gently. 'Let's ease down the gears. We're tired. There's no harm meant. Come on. Back to work. Jo, love, I've water in a flask out beyond. Dry your eyes, there's my girl. *Andiamo*.'

For an hour after the mutual apology and the continuing of rehearsal, the quarrel had remained between them, a stranger in the room. At midnight, they shook hands, then embraced, swallowing tears.

Let the bridge be open, let the bridge be open.

Turning right onto Piazza Corelli, he puts on his Other and feels it envelop him like a cloak.

Marco Mancuso, translator, Vatican secretariat, born Glasgow, Scotland, of Italian immigrant family, came to Milano '33, parents Gianluca (meaning 'gift of God') and Elisabetta. One brother, Giancarlo, deceased, two sisters, Catalina and Elena. No registered political affiliation but strong admirer of Fascism. Unmarried, former seminarian, left a month before ordination, brother-in-law a minor Party official in Brindisi. Manager of the Italy team in the 1934 World Cup was Pozzo; midfielder was Bertolini.

Illegally open, the last cafés are closing. From an upper room comes the blared bay of a mediocre tenor mangling '*E lucevan le stelle*', counterpointing the bayed blare of groaners asking him to stop. Two drunkards plod the footpath like men treading water. No licensed premises anywhere in Rome may be open after the curfew, but in Italy, as in most places, there are always exceptions. The manager is connected. The magnate brings his mistress. The bribe has been generous. We'll dynamite you if you refuse.

Crossing the tramlines, he falters, happens to raise his glance.

A woman in a window is watching.

The glow of her cigarette, reddening, fading.

She bites her thumb, a gesture of contempt, at someone in the *strada* behind him.

The unease is so sharp, it's like encountering a stench. When he glances over his shoulder, no one's there.

Wind billows, blowing folds of old newspaper across the Piazza like weird birds.

In the distance the Musei, the scowling dome of St Peter's.

A Stug truckles past, leaking oil.

Marco Mancuso walks on.

On the quay, facing into the slab of a growing storm, he tosses a Lucky Strike packet stuffed with hundred-dollar bills into a dustbin daubed with a treble clef – first drop-off accomplished, almost on time – as he passes the padlocked gates of an Augustinian chapterhouse where seven escaped paratroopers have been hiding out for a month.

Across the street, over the bakery, two Iowan rear-gunners and a B-26

Marauder pilot from New Orleans whose ulcerated wisdom tooth is giving him agony. Something will need to be done for him. Not tonight.

In the wine cellar beneath a trattoria on Via Geminiani, three; in the stock-loft above a shop selling priestly vestments and fine chalices, nine; behind a false partition in an art gallery on Via Bellini, one, in the coal bunker of a tobacconist's, two.

Seventeen in the pilgrims' dormitory of the Capuchin Monastery on Borgo Scarlatti; nine in the monks' quarters, four beneath the kitchens. Two in a tailor's back room amid the mannequins and spools, seven in a fruiterer's warehouse. Nine in the grounds of the Palazzo Leoncavallo, two in a mechanic's workshop behind Via Palestrina, three on a half-sunken old sightseeing boat moored on the Tiber. Fifteen in the three-bedroom apartment of a Maltese widow and her children, who every day go without food so to feed them.

Men disguised as friars, sleeping on granite shelves in belltowers. In bivouacs on rooftops, among the chimney stacks and pigeon lofts. Bayonet blades in their cassocks, or billhooks beneath pillows. Men with hidden pistols and one remaining bullet. Making garrottes from piano wire, shanks from chisels. Men dossing under bridges, on park benches, in sewer-shafts, on rusted trams, in burned-out ticket offices and ivy-swathed graveyards, on crashed buses in side streets. The army of the attics.

It feels to him as though every last one of them is parading behind him now, down Corso Paganini, roaring to be noticed.

A torch-flash in the highest window of an apartment block on the corner is answered from a rooftop several houses down the street. Three glints, four. Four glints, three.

Derry has sent urgent messages warning them to stop; this behaviour is endangering every escapee in Rome. But the men it's endangering never stop for long.

High windows flicking Morse messages over a deserted piazza, across the wide banks of the river, all night. If one Nazi clocks your whereabouts, a hundred of your comrades will die. A thousand could die. So could you.

A couple of nights, then, when the signalling fades. But soon it returns like the tide.

Injunctions to keep up the spirits. Obscene jokes. Requests for news. Sports results. Ribaldries. Mock insults.

How do they find each other? He hasn't an inkling. Some nights it's worse – 'Christ's sake,' John May sighs, 'it's like Times Square on New Year's Eve' – but every night you'll notice it if your eyes are halfway open, the shooting stars sent by the frightened.

It's the only thing he has ever seen to make Derry lose his temper. How strange to hear the Englishman curse. 'Don't the bastards realise what they're *doing*? Don't they *know*? Fucking *idiots*. They want shooting, the selfish pricks. Why bother?'

What he knows is that if you confiscated their flashlights, they would signal with matches. They'd set bonfires on the rooftops that protect them. He has come to accept it, wishes Derry would, too; opposing it is like countermanding gravity. A vow of silence, like most vows, is not workable all the time. He hurries on beneath the bantering beams.

A streetwalker is watching as he passes on Via Boito, through the shadow of broken bottle-ends on walls. Moving quickly, head down, as though that posture will take up less space, he looks, she will say later, 'like a man with a target on his back'.

Where are the Allies?

When will they come?

They're not coming, says his shadow. *You know it.*

Who do you think you're fooling? Your feeble, murdered God? Derry is at least a man, you're not even a footnote. Afraid to live life. Snivelling behind vows. Your fool's errand means nothing. Too late.

He reaches into an Ave Maria, blindly, afraid.

A foxhole *prayer, my favourite, go ahead, deluded fool. I'll say the words* with *you, they're mimicry, an idiot's cackle. Your gruntings mean nothing, they're* noise, *they're bad music. A chimp hurling shit at the bars of its cage.*

I was here long before you. I'll be here when you're gone.

Shapeshifter, they call me.

Changeling.

Turncoat.

I am not your shadow. You are mine.

His reflection passing the windows of a knife-grinder's premises. Spits of rain on the dust-smeared glass.

Left onto Via Martucci.

Blood in his stomach congeals.

The roadblock has been set up from pavement to pavement. The belch of a brazier spluttering into ashen, wintry gloom. A golden-sepia flicker across the sky-high brickwork and the flanks of an open-backed truck.

Smoke pulses from the exhaust. A Stug's engine grovelling.

He can see, in the lorry, a dozen cowed prisoners, cuffed wrists, hands up, lowered heads. A gnarled, chained Rottweiler snarling before its handler as the man lights a cigarette at the brazier. An order is screamed for the captives to kneel – *knien!* – but some don't understand or are too petrified to move, so the handler and his comrades truncheon them down and the dog lifts its leg to a tyre.

Too late to step into a doorway. If he fled?

No time.

A dark-featured welterweight with the blunt head of a bull shark sees him first and beckons coolly, in no hurry.

The dog tugs on its restraint, now turns its dripping maw, trying to gnaw through the rope-thick chain.

The trooper's breath reeks of rancid cheese, of old, stale coffee.

'Name?'

'Mancuso.'

'First name.'

'Marco.'

'Identity card?'

He presents it.

The trooper glances down through the fiery shadows at the photograph, muttering to himself in what must be some obscure dialect of German, now regarding the nightwalker assessingly and repeating the name 'Mancuso' as though doing so might weigh it on a scale. With a yelp he summons over a younger comrade, who examines the document. A long look is shared between them. They hold the card up to moonlight.

'You are aware there is a curfew,' the welterweight says.

'I have an exemption. As you see.'

'Where are you going?'

'To collect an item of medicine.'

'Excuse me?'

174

'Sir will have seen that Cardinal Hinsley of Westminster is on a private courtesy visit to the Vatican with the Papal Envoy to Nairobi and his sister and father. The Cardinal became ill this evening with suspected malaria. No physician was available but a well-wisher in the city has quinine. His Eminence's valet requested me to collect it.'

When lying, as Derry says, you have two options that might work. Keep it simple or make it complicated. Then stick to it.

'How long will you be out, Mancuso?'

'Two hours at most.'

'Make sure it's no more. Move along.'

'Who are those prisoners?'

'Curfew-breakers. Undesirables.'

'What will happen to them now?'

'A little sightseeing trip.'

'Where?'

'Somewhere that doesn't concern you. Get going.'

As he passes the rear of the truck, he hears the whispered word in Italian.

'*Salvami.*'

Nothing he can do.

If he pauses, all is lost.

'Save me.'

Stars glint.

He keeps walking.

Let the bridge be open, let the bridge be open, let the bridge be open, he prays.

21

THE VOICE OF SAM DERRY
27th September 1963
From transcript of BBC research interview,
conducted Newark-on-Trent, Nottinghamshire

Seven weeks beforehand, an informant had passed us the word, through Miss de Vries I think it was, that on the night of Christmas Eve, between midnight and two in the morning, certain strategic points around Rome would remain unguarded by Jerry or be only sporadically patrolled.

She was a typist at Nazi headquarters, the young woman I'm speaking of. She couldn't be certain fully, didn't overhear every word of the order Hauptmann gave, but over cigarettes in the courtyard one of the junior Gestapo officers seemed to confirm it. The important bridges would be roadblocked but not the Ponte Sant'Angelo.

This had formed part of our thinking.

An unbarricaded bridge can of course be a significant opportunity. It is also, in classical warfare, a trap.

Previous information from this young woman had sometimes proven unreliable. Sir D'Arcy had in fact wondered if she was a double dealer, a Fascist. I never liked trusting an informer I hadn't personally met but obviously it wasn't possible to waltz her into the Vatican for a chinwag over tea and it could have fatally imperilled her to meet anywhere else. All you had in the end was your instincts, I suppose.

I do remember the Padre insisting, 'She's a risk, Sam. A very real risk.'

I said, 'Who bloody isn't, when you think?'

'We can't trust her,' he repeated. Back and forth it went, like a slugfest. The disagreement in fact threatened to become quarrelsome, accusatory. In the end, time pressed, we agreed to the pull of a playing card. The Monsignor drew a three, I drew the Queen of Spades. The plan would be retooled in line with the young woman's information.

'And if the Tiber can't be crossed, Sam?'

'We abort.'

'That's that?'

'A gamble, I admit.'

'Much more than a gamble.'

'My lookout, I suppose. Since, my life on the line.'

'It isn't only yours.'

'No, I don't suppose it is.'

'She's not to be trusted.'

'We'll see.'

In the end, all you know for certain about an informer is one thing: they're an informer. It's like falling for a proven liar, don't be surprised that they lie. It's something they do well, they've had practice. And it's easier the next time to break what's left of their word. They know what it feels like and it isn't that bad. Leopard and spots. Old story.

So, there you have a bridge. And here, you have a story.

———

Quietly along Vicolo Sgambati.

Let the bridge be open.

Adrenaline boiling in his stomach as he steadies himself in the bus shelter, gathers, counts to five, turns the corner.

Ahead of him, the searchlights, the trio of armoured cars with their red-and-black swastikas. Magnified silhouettes of police horses on the far riverbank's wall.

The informer got it wrong. Or was lying.

Away to his right, the course of the Tiber takes a sudden, wrenching turn, and he can see that the Ponte Vittorio Emanuele II, too, is barricaded, by a Panzer, as is the Ponte Umberto a few hundred metres to his left.

Down the slick, crooked steps to the riverside path, the rank stench of damp and wet rotting moss. A line of bollards in the gurgling darkness, the stilted croak of ducks.

Could you swim it? A hundred metres? Two hundred? More?

Try, the shadow snickers. *I'd like to see you drown.*

In the seethe of black water before him, a nest of punts and chained rafts, bow-seats improvised from lengths of plank and sawn-apart fish crates. A trio of low-floored dinghies, clumping together in the wavelets.

The ropes, thick and wet, in his cold, ignorant fingers. The harder he twists, the harder they entangle. The old boats rock with mockery.

Now he sees, far to his right, two soldiers descend the staircase beneath the bridge, rifles shouldered, black helmet rims low. Behind him, between slabs of ancient embankment wall, a crevice the height and width of a man; he backs into it, waits.

The murmur of conversation as they approach.

He tries not to breathe.

They can't be more than twenty paces from him; he hears the word '*Huren-haus*', answered by a bark of spluttered, coughing laughter. A cigarette is lit; he can smell the match's sulphur. They come to a pause with their backs to him.

Begin to kiss.

Moving against each other, groping, pretending to moan, and they resume their patrol and an empty bus passes, above on the windswept quay.

Thirty metres away from him now, receding into darkness. He steps into a filthy dinghy, the nearest one, black, 'Santa Maria' painted on its prow by an amateur. It bobs in a sickening sway that makes him throw out his arms and flail.

Kneeling, he goes at the rope again; it refuses to loosen. From his pocket he pulls his torch, smashes the glass, starts sawing at the knot, but it's the thickness of an oak root, refuses to fray.

Down the path, the soldiers reappear, rifles shouldered, walking slowly. He lurches, sags forward, arms by his side, face an inch from the briny slops. A long two minutes later, the thunk of boots as they pass, and the clank of a buckle, and the scraping of a rifle as it grazes the riverside wall.

Peering, he sees them ascend the crooked, stone stairs to the bridge. How long before the next patrol?

A plash. Hard and cold. As though someone has flung a stone into the Tiber.

Again, comes a splush, then a volley of spatters. A pebble strikes the boat. Another lands behind him. The moon sails from behind a cupola.

Looking out through a knothole in the side of the smack, he sees a steady rain of pebbles being thrown from the bank.

Now, a battery-torch signal. Three dots and a dash. The opening notes of Beethoven's Fifth.

The password employed by members of the Choir at the door of the rehearsal room. Derry chose it because everyone knew it, the signal was unforgettable.

Again come the glimmers. Three shorts and a long. The sharp, yellow pin-prick through the murk across the bank, where a row of shacks or crumbling warehouses is too vague to be made out.

Kneeling up, he sees now, emerging from the shadow, the black prow of a skiff being rowed with firm, strong steadiness in his direction, the rower bent low, straining, back to him. An eerie skreeking grind as the rowlocks give and swivel. The skiff enters an eddy, turns in a sudden, wild circle. The rower pulls down a balaclava before continuing, oaring hard, coughing breathy grunts at the Tiber as it is fought and overcome.

A trick? A trap?

The shadow gives a chuckle.

Who put that three of diamonds in your hand? I hold all the cards.

He glances towards the bridge, where a *Panzerkampfwagen* is nuzzling into position.

'Padre,' hisses the voice from the boat. 'Look lively. Step aboard.'

A volley of mumbles as the figure rows closer.

'Top o' the morning, Aitch,' he whispers.

22

THE VOICE OF JOHN MAY
20th September 1963
From transcript of BBC research interview, conducted Coldharbour,
Poplar, East London

See, the Tiber ain't no river you want to go swimming in. You could develop film in the Tiber. But not swim in it.

I don't want to dwell on this particular episode. Had my sources, that's all. Move along.

Well, it ain't nothing mysterious, just a personal matter. Let's just say there was a certain young lady in Rome and we'll leave it at that.

She was a cashier in the bank where the Embassy had our accounts. They had to be in fake names, which she must have known well – the Escape Line account was Vincento Bianchi and Company – but she never asked no questions, just a firework display of a smile. That's how we met. No, I won't give her name. Rather not. I believe she's still alive.

Burn you down to the floor, that smile.

I'd say she was maybe thirty. Not that I've asked. Her husband was indisposed, being as he happened to be in a prison camp at the time. Needs must, as they say. War is war.

I wasn't no matinee idol to look at. Whereas she was a proper dinger. Like the actress Laura Nucci, with the brown eyes you could drown in. Lovely lady, she was. I like the Italian people. You know where you stand with them. Got a natural love of life. They don't mess about. They're exuberant.

So the afternoon of Christmas Eve, I've arranged to make my way over to see her, quiet like, and we'll have a discreet little celebration, is the plan. I've ways of getting about the city in the daytime. False card. Fake name. Don't matter. I've a bottle of bubbles, a nice box of chocs and the natural instincts of the season. Well, we've had a little dance, and we've had a little drink, and one thing's led to The Other. As it does.

Only afterwards, we're laying in bed and we're listening to a record, and she mentions she's heard the Teds are closing the bridge tonight.

'Teds' was what the Romans called the Jerries.

Chiedo scusa? Do what, love?

Barricading the bridge. She's had it off her mate, bird works down the hairdresser's dyeing wigs. Apparently, it's all over the quarter. So, I'm welcome to kip over with her, and we'll have a bowl of grub and play an Ella side she likes, once I've scarpered before the sister and the nasty brother-in-law and the army of nasty kids trundles over in the morning to fetch her off to church, then the mother's.

I've gone, are you certain?

About kipping over?

No, about the effing bridge.

Sì, sì, this bird down the hairdresser's heard it off her brother and her brother's heard it off Pierluigi and Pierluigi off Massimo. Ted is barricading that bridge tonight, sure as eggs.

Well, now it's on my mind, see. I've a fair inkling of the plan. After Derry got sick, it was obvious the runner would have to be Angelucci, who I liked. You didn't need to be no supernatural medium or nothing; it's plain as your face he's going to need to cross the river at some point and it's plain he ain't sprouted wings.

So what I done, I went down there, and waited, that's all. Wasn't expecting trouble. Just go down for a butcher's.

That quiet, you'd hear a mouse piss on cotton.

It's got darker and darker. Sky black as your boot. Ticker's doing the tun and I'm frozen to buggery. It's that cold, I can't even feel my fingers no more. I'm thinking of my hero Shackleton and the poor sods in the Antarctic. I've seen a snap of their ship, in a book Sir Frank was reading. Their ship in the ice. Stuck there. Break your heart. 'Beset', the chapter was called.

And I'm thinking of *la mia lei* a few streets away in the flat, in a nice big feather bed with more pillows than you ever seen. In the green silk pyjamas I've give her. Dear me. *Madonna mia.* Wouldn't mind getting beset over there.

We've had plans for the evening. Ain't going to be happening. I'm starving, too, nothing to eat since a bit of heated-up bucatini and spam at lunchtime, which I've had to pretend to like if I know what's good for me. So, the picture ain't good. Not at all.

I'm waiting and waiting.

Suddenly, what's this?

I've recognised the gait. Think I'm losing my reason. Christ on a bike. It's the Padre.

There he is, across the Tiber, prancing up and down on the walkway like a tit. And the Teds not a spit away on the bridge.

What's happened to Angelucci? Where we going now?

I fling over a few stones but he don't see me, the blind sod. Now what do I do? I can't shout. Giving it large with the torch but he ain't seen that either. Waving my arms. Leaping about. *Willing* him to clock me. I'm dancing the bleeding fandango the other side of the Tiber but he won't look my direction. Blind sod.

Now there's action up on the bridge, I've seen the lights moving. I've scarpered up the embankment behind me.

What do I see then? Pair of Jerries coming down the steps, that's all. His goose is bleeding cooked, it's curtains, *arrivederci*, but they've passed him and headed away, and he gets in a boat.

Don't be a tit, Aitch. The current's too strong.

Big bloke, the Padre, but he ain't got the strength for rowing. Where I'm from, you build your arms as a kid coming up. You don't win no fights with weak hands.

I've seen this little skiff there, ten yards down from me, and managed to get open the ropes. But now, there's no sodding oars.

So, what does Muggins do? I've rowed across the bleeding Tiber using the bench of the boat. True as you're sat there. What happened.

They was having problems with their tank, the turret wouldn't stop revolving. Snag with the gears. You get that with the Panzer, a lot of them had been in the desert, gummed up with sand. So, all eyes was on that, Jerries coming and going. And I've weaselled across the Tiber. Loaded up the Padre. Crossed him over.

He was shook something awful. But he insisted on going on. I asked him

182

where he's headed but he won't give us no gen, 'need-to-know only', all that. He'd cut his hand on broken glass, I asked him if it was okay, he said he'd get a bandage later on the night 'from Lonnie' if he needed one. I didn't have a monkey's who that was, and in the Choir you didn't ask. He shouldn't have mentioned no name, it was a slip.

No, I didn't offer to go with him, I won't lie. I didn't. And he wouldn't have let me if I had. He must have thanked me a dozen times, then off he heads on his tod. He's insisted. I've begged him not to go, but he wasn't a bloke for persuading. And I've took myself back to the flat.

No, I didn't see it as no heroism. Nothing like that. Mate of yours is in trouble, you front up.

See, people had their different reasons for being in the Choir. Some reasons was religious – not being funny but you're going to get that in Rome – and some was whatever they was. Political. Patriotic. Bleeding-heart do-gooders. Me, I was none of the above.

I daresay some was Communist, others was Labour, some Tory. Sir Francis D'Arcy Godolphin Osborne? Ain't from the Old Kent Road. But I never ask your politics, they're all the bloody same in the close. To me, there ain't no reason people has to like each other's countries. Look at the Welsh. Don't even like their own. What's the first thing they done when they got to Australia? Call part of it 'New *South* Wales'.

Don't give a monkey's what church you go to, or don't go at all. Synagogue, Chapel, Methodist, what you fancy. As for me, I was in the Choir for one reason and one reason only.

Won't lie to you, darling. Fritz ain't my cup of tea.

We ain't supposed to say it but at my age you do.

Funny thing, I felt different way back as a youngster. After I got the jazz trio going, we'd get the odd gig in Germany, string a night or two together, make a tour. The money was fair, they paid you same night, they listened, applauded, all handsome. Very polite people, never no bother. The other lads would scarper home just as soon as they could, I was footloose, no ties, hang about a day or two, go mooching. One day – we'd been supporting Nat Gonella and the Georgians – I'm in Düsseldorf, lovely old part of town, wander into a fish restaurant on my tod. Lovely piece of *Seezunge mit Mandeln*, sauerkraut, pickles, bit of slaw, nice capers, black rye. Done with a bit of care. You respect it.

Half-bottle of Weissburgunder, pack of smokes, article on Coleman Hawkins I've been saving. Wintry day outside, plan is to settle in until the train. But then there's this noise, out the window.

Gang of numpties in lederhosen, shouting at everyone. Singing '*Die Fahne hoch*', big Swastika flag. I thought they was funny, like Morris dancers back home. Blockheads. Bit pathetic. Half-extinct. But soon it gets angrier. Spitting on old men passing by. I didn't know German. But I know what '*Juden*' means.

I turn to the waiter, ancient geezer in a suit, and ask what's occurring, is this some kind of sodding joke? He says, 'That's the future, *mein Herr*.'

I'm an East End Londoner. Tell me Hermann's on the level? I got two words in reply. With three effs.

It wasn't the Quakers firebombed Whitechapel. We all know who it was.

Oh, I'm sure there must be good ones. Well, there was. Before they murdered them all.

That's Jerry; only following orders.

Forgive the enemy, turn the other cheek? Off you pop, love. Not John. Once bitten, twice bite, that's my motto.

I ain't British, not first. Ain't English. I'm London. Come at me and mine and I'll forgive you with a machine gun. Take a knife to my mother's throat? You'd better hope you're struck by lightning. Bet the rent I'll catch up on you one night.

Jerry's good with the smile these days. Giving it all that about peace and starting again. Flannel. Stroll along. Not buying.

My grandkids sometimes ask me what I done in the war. I tell them, every single day I could balls up a German, I did.

And I tell them, so should they.

That's my politics.

Wouldn't give you half an inch of Whitechapel for the whole of sodding Germany. Welcome to it, Ted. Get fucked.

So, that's the way it was. I'm back at the flat with *mia bella amore*. Only, soon it starts nagging me, he's out there on his own with the Teds, the Fascisti, God knows who else. Nagging like a bastard. He's alone. And, who's this 'Lonnie' he was on about?

When you think, might be the last time I'm ever going to see him. Should have gone with him, or stopped him. And I didn't.

It was all so quick. I wasn't thinking rational. Now it's nagging me something awful. A torment.

I've no way to contact Derry. And Angelucci don't have no telephone. I could go after the Padre but I ain't got the foggiest where he's gone, who's his marks. I kick myself for not going. But I know he wouldn't let me. And I kick myself for not making him call the whole Rendimento off, come back to the flat, lie low.

But that's cobblers, too. He's stubborn, the Padre. Wouldn't never see reason, drove us all flaming scats. Typical bloody Paddy. World of his own. Ask Pat to do the sensible, obvious thing? May as well dig a hole in the sea.

Now it comes to me, on a sudden, the neighbourhood he's heading for. It ain't 'Lonnie' he's mentioned earlier, it's 'Blonnie'. 'I'll get a bandage from Blonnie.' Tell you plain, I've sat up in that bed like a vampire on Methedrine. 'Blonnie' is Delia's daughter.

I've asked *carissima* for a map of Rome but she ain't got one in the flat so we've found a fountain pen and notepaper in a drawer. Funny thing to remember, she can't find no ink, so she gives me an eyebrow pencil, all she's got. I can still see the two of us, sat there, stark bloody naked, sketching out the districts, and she's telling me the names of the streets.

Now I'm certain I know where he's headed.

What I've done, I've asked her to place a call. If it's a woman's voice, an Italian, Jerry won't be so suspicious. I've told her speak quick as you can, love, Italian's hard to follow when it's quick. Which was lunacy, an impulse. The whole idea was lunacy from start to finish, as it goes. But there wasn't no choice. Needs must.

I tell her the code words. She puts through the call. And I'm watching her fingers as she turns that dial, it's like seeing in slow motion, and waiting for the answer, and thinking this could be the biggest mistake of my life.

Place that call and two hundred prisoners might be dead by tomorrow.

Half of me was hoping there wouldn't be no answer.

But there was.

And I swear I didn't sleep one second the rest of that night.

The not knowing was the torment.

Always is.

185

Clambering from the rowboat, he gestures wordless thanks to May and mimes for him to get going, which after a moment or two of remonstration May does, sidling away from him, hands in pockets, down the path, into the smuts of cold, as the Panzer on the bridge judders a metre forward, gears clanking.

Sleeves soaked, he ascends the steps, crosses the quayside, takes the laneway beside the fishmonger's a winding, narrow *passaggio* lined with warehouse doors.

Nineteen minutes behind schedule.

He breaks into a run.

A person running at night is always suspect, Derry says. No Chorister on a Rendimento is ever to run unless under fire.

Twenty minutes behind schedule is fire.

His feet sound to him like whip-cracks as he trots across the Piazza, head low. Past the hulks of shuttered souvenir stalls and tarp-wrapped news-stands, the statue of a forgotten General, plinth bespattered with hammer-and-sickles, the fountain giggling at the swear word daubed across its cherub's abdomen.

Skidding, he steadies.

Ghiaccio.

Ice.

Gashing into his cheekbone.

Head fills with asterisks.

A moment, and the pain comes. Shocking, dredger-like thirst, and the bounced-around echo of his howl.

The rim of the fountain smashed him in the chin as he fell. Pain again, blazing, like a truncheon to the spine. Pain roaring through his jawbone, through the bones of his cranium. Tiny, incendiary lights, the audible *slosh* of his eyeballs, the fading, blackening Piazza, the *cut* of that swear word. The shimmer of the General on his shimmering horse.

Don't let me pass out.

You're passing out, goads the shadow.

Thirst battling nausea. Blood in his throat.

Elbowing up, he vomits, right trouser leg ripped from ankle to knee, livid handprint-sized graze down his calf. Manages to stand. Rinses his mouth in the bitter water of the fountain that floored him. Pain grasps him by the ribcage, monkey-wrenching his spine, but he's able to limp onward through the

186

sleet-slick Piazza, past a church whose name he knows but the fall has banged it out of his head, into the dark, narrow mouth that is the rendezvous street, high dwelling-houses on both sides, crossed clotheslines.

Three seconds, four.

He knows he's been clocked.

A boy on the fire-escape whistles, chucks a pebble across the blackness and it lands with a clatter by the finial on the opposite rooftop.

There, a girl peers over the edge, now whistling back.

The shadow gives a scoff.

Night swims. The smell of coal.

— 23 —

MARIANNA DE VRIES
November 1962
Statement in lieu of an interview

The first drop was in Prati. I lived on the edge of Parioli and had volunteered to receive the second. Added to the danger and anxiety was the fact that the Choir never met for a week before a Rendimento. So, you were going on trust and whatever instincts you had. And the plan you'd dinned into yourself.

At the appointed time I went from my apartment, leaving the front door slightly ajar, as agreed, and made my way down the maid's back stairs to the communal coal cellar next to the boiler room.

To pass the hours beforehand, I had been reading *Romeo and Juliet*. 'Afore me,' says Lord Capulet. 'It is so very, very late that we may call it early by and by.' That line was lodged in my head.

It was by now a quarter to one on Christmas morning, but some of my neighbours were playing radios, others quarrelling. My plan, if I was discovered, which I thought unlikely, was to say that my room had become unbearably cold, that I thought the house's furnace must have gone out. For that reason, I had left the radiator off all that day and night, in fact broken its valves with a screwdriver. The apartment was indeed so cold that ice was forming on the insides of the windows, something I had never seen in five Roman winters.

Down I stole, teeth knocking, blanketed, to the darkness. I found the key to the coal cellar, on the frame over the door, where I knew the janitor kept it – he did not live in the building. I unlocked the cellar, entered and waited.

It was dusty, hard to breathe, appallingly cold. On the street, a few curfew-breakers passed but no sign or sound of Angelucci. I could tell from their footsteps that all the passers-by were women or slighter men than Enzo. A Stug trundled by, slowing as it passed our building. Its terrible gurgling whine and the crew shouting in German made me sick with fear. Where was Enzo?

The plan had been worked out to the tiniest detail, and yet Angelucci, after Derry the most dependable man in the Choir, was not here. A sometime hothead, yes, but that was a mask. If Angelucci told you he would do something, it was done, no question. What had gone wrong? I began to dread the worst. Despite being in a coal cellar, I had to smoke a couple of cigarettes, but I was careful as to where I extinguished them.

At length, some thirty minutes late, I heard the pipe in the ceiling give a rattle. This meant the girl watching from the rooftop had seen Angelucci turn our corner. With some difficulty I crawled across the crunching mound of anthracite, to the coalman's hatch in the wall, and pushed it a couple of centimetres open.

I heard a man draw closer. It was unmistakably not Enzo. Foreboding seized me like a monster, should I follow the plan or not? Were we betrayed, was this limper a Nazi, a tout? On the point of fleeing the cellar, I heard one short, barked word.

'*Sol.*'

My Chorister's code name.

I could not make out who the barker was, I knew only that it was not Angelucci. The queerest feeling possessed me, that it was, of all people, Ugo, but my assaulted rationality told me this could not be the case, he was in the Vatican, no doubt pacing his room. All of this happened in seconds. I must make the most dangerous decision of my life.

When I guessed that the man was two metres away, I took the chance and pushed the hatch open further, as far as it would go. Without a word, he dropped the satchel through, and I bundled it into a pillowcase I had brought in the pocket of my dressing robe. I left the cellar, locked the door, restored the key to its dwelling place over the frame, and crept back up through the night-sounds of the house, to my apartment.

Luigina, the girl from the roof, was now in my bedroom, with a good-looking boy I had seen in our neighbourhood but did not know by name. They waited while I quickly showered (in cold water) and put on clean clothes, then, at my signal, followed me into the bathroom.

The boy, whom I should say was seventeen, was dressed in a workman's blue overalls. The girl addressed him as 'Eugenio' but another time as 'Beppe', so at least one of these must have been a *nom de guerre*. Without speaking, we put the grimy satchel in the empty bathtub and spilled out its contents, bundling the dollars into careful stacks, which we sealed with rubber bands. I helped the girl conceal three of the stacks in her underclothes; the boy took four, placing them in the large, loose pockets sewn into the thighs and calves of his trousers. Producing a switchblade, he deftly hacked the satchel to shreds, some of which he flung in twos and threes out the window, handing a bundle of others to the girl, then off they went via the roof they had come from. I hid the remaining stacks in the lavatory cistern and dumped my coal-dirtied clothes.

In the coming days, I distributed the dollars, one or two hundred at a time, in small bills, around the contacts I had learned by heart over many a night from Derry and Ugo's list. It was a matter of leaving an envelope addressed to a false name with the barman at such-and-such a café near the Fontana di Trevi, of folding a couple of fifties into a copy of Dante's *Inferno* and replacing it on the shelf in the back of an antiquarian bookshop in a side street by the Scala Santa. An elderly Carmelite Sister visiting the Colosseum stood close to me as our impromptu group listened to the guide conjure the well-worn marvels: eighty thousand hooting Romans, brandishing fists, eating still-warm entrails, the flooding of the arena for naval spectaculars. The Sister returned to the convent with three hundred dollars she hadn't had when she arrived and an escaped Canadian tail-gunner disguised as a monk.

On the Sunday I went to Mass six times, five in the morning, once that evening, an unusual practice for an atheist. As had been arranged, I gave plump envelopes when the collection plates were passed around, the sacristans in each case being friends of the Choir who had instructions on where to further dispense the money: ultimately almost all of it would be used for bribes and forged papers, to get the escapees out of Rome and hidden in the countryside.

It was an interesting Sunday. Well, that is not quite true. The shattering level of its boredom was interesting. It put me off plainchant for life. Also, each of the six priests preached a sermon on that day's appointed reading from the Gospel and all differed in their elucidations, in some cases markedly, as in the various lengths it took to loft them, one good man needing five minutes, another, half an hour. It made me wonder what would happen if a sinner attended confession ten different times to as many different confessors, uttering the same set of sins each time. Would the penance be different depending on the listener, on his mood, his age, the quality of his breakfast? But I believe we know the answer. Wittgenstein (I think it was) once put it rather tartly: on subjects about which there is nothing to say, it is wisest to say that.

One morning as I went to meet a source for an article I was preparing, I noticed the boy from the roof, now outside a bar in my neighbourhood, but he looked through me, as though I were weather. What was odd was that he was in the company of a group of youths singing the Fascist anthem while banging down dominoes in a desultory fashion. I was alarmed and for a day or two wondered whether we had been compromised.

Every footstep on the stairs of my apartment house had me swim-headed with fear. If a woman glanced at me in the Piazza, I was seized by the impulse to run. A counter assistant at the American Express office asked me, somewhat briskly, to repeat the spelling of my surname and then appeared to check it against some list she had in a file; I broke into a heavy, headachy sweat that came and went all day. Panic blooms during wartime, particularly, some would say, when one lives alone. But perhaps it is worse for the married.

I came in from a walk one night and convinced myself that the typewriter had been moved during my absence, that the sheets of carbon paper on my desk had been shifted and examined, that a cupboard containing medicines and personal items in the bathroom had been opened and interfered with. It seemed to me that there were fingerprints all over its mirrored door, that the whole apartment stank of stale sweat and cigar smoke. The pillow beneath which I kept my nightdress had been moved, I was certain. Maybe I was watched even now.

Was there a hidden camera, a microphone? A minuscule spyhole drilled through the wall? There is no paranoia like the one that festers when we fear that our privacy is stolen. The Gestapo were well capable of that, as Ugo had long warned. 'Walls Have Ears' was his watchword.

When I tried to sleep, the intelligence photographs I feared had been made flashed at me, wrenched me awake. Strange whispers, mocking leers haunted my insomnia. Soon I had in mind to go *myself* into hiding, or get out of Rome altogether, so chilly my certainty that we were duped and betrayed. Indeed, I would have done so were it not for the fact that we in the Choir were sworn not to contact each other for a full fortnight after that night, and I did not want to imperil my friends or disappear without them knowing, for that would inflame suspicion.

All that unending week, the boy stalked my nightmares. I even went looking for him about the neighbourhood, intent on some sort of insane confrontation. A grown woman drifting the streets, peering in through slatted windows like some lunatic in a Gothic novel, or a peeping nuisance. I don't know what I should have said to him, perhaps did not know even then. In any case, my walks did not find him.

On New Year's Eve, it was made known to me – I do not wish to say how – that the boy was secretly a Communist, a plant in the Fascist ranks. We had given him eight thousand dollars. I hoped my informant was correct.

The coalhole was the second of the three drop-offs poor Ugo would attempt that night, a night when I feared the dawn would never come. When I think of it, I remember the girl, who would one day become a renowned actress, and the boy, who would be tortured and murdered by the Gestapo in the first month of the new year, his body dumped near the back of the Stadio dei Cipressi, which was later named the Stadio Olimpico. So long as there is air in the sky, the five rings of the Olympic symbol will for me always have private meaning: that boy, his defiance, his calm, his courage, his love for his magnificent country.

I do not think I shall ever forget the cold of my flat that late December. And the dread of not knowing what would happen.

It was a few days that changed my life. I did a great deal of thinking.

If I survived the war, I resolved, new roads would be taken. I would return to the university, complete the studies I had abandoned in my early twenties. I would end what I privately knew to be my dependence on barbiturates. I would write in a different way. I would live as myself.

Dawns could be imagined, but it was still the night.

I heard nothing from any member of the Choir.

The fear came, then, that all my friends were dead.

Was Ugo alive?

Was anyone?

———

He crouches behind a line of dustbins as a quintet of armoured Nazi bulldozers roars past, along the quayside.

Up ahead, like a battlement, a cluster of darkened lockups. Behind him, the stinking breeze off the Tiber.

He enters the Campo di Giuliani, uncertain, eyes pounding.

High on a stone loggia off a long, ivied rooftop, a flautist, an elderly, white-bearded Moses from a Raphael, in moth-eaten dinner jacket and cloak. Beside him a lop-shouldered tenor singing 'Una furtiva lagrima', outstretched hands squeezing teardrops from the air. Far across the Piazza, in a candlelit upper window, a young woman in harlequin mask is accompanying them on piano. The spangling, clear chords and dulcet arpeggios echo on old, cold stone.

Every other window in the Piazza is shuttered. The residents must be able to hear, yet no one is listening, unless listening beneath blankets, in the land of counterpane. Perhaps they don't mind being kept awake.

> Un solo istante i palpiti
> Del suo bel cor sentir.
> I miei sospir, confondere
> Per poco a' suoi sospir!

Stilled by the fragility, he looks up from beneath an awning as the aria starts to soar, every vowel blade-clear, the coo of the flute like a dove's call at dawn through the dewfall of the tenor's *esses*. It shimmers, unwinds towards the sob of its climax, and the pianist and the flautist and the tenor bow stiffly, first to one another, then to the empty Piazza, before withdrawing to the darkness they came from.

The clack of shutters closing. Then birdsong. Then silence.

Did it happen?

It must have.

The windows are empty.

The music has opened something he wants closed, postponed.

Slithering on greasy cobbles, stumbling, he steadies.

A boy shinning across a washing line five storeys up in an alley.

Two brothers in a courtyard, cutting each other's hair by candlelight.

A rat staring up at a steeple from inside a gnawed melon.

Moonlight on tombstones.

Stone wolves over a doorway.

A woman on a balcony, being murmured to by her lover, an eternal eight feet away, in the opposite window.

— 24 —

THE VOICE OF SIR D'ARCY OSBORNE
14th December 1962
Interview with BBC researcher, recorded 66 Via Giulia, Rome

It is not, with respect, a matter of my being evasive. When one signs the Official Secrets Act, one signs it for life. You will appreciate, therefore, that there is a limit to what one wishes to say – or would be permitted to say, even now, after a not inconsiderable time has passed – on the question of how monies were put in place for the mission undertaken by the Monsignor on the night of Christmas Eve, 1943. Secrecy exists between countries for good reasons.

I daresay people will come to their own conclusions on the matter. Some realities will be so obvious as to hardly be worth denying. For example, it would not be ten million miles wide of the mark to assert that most of the monies were shall we say brought into Italy through the offices of various neutral or friendly Ambassadors, in small enough amounts at first.

It will be evident, too, that individuals were involved. That part of the thing was coordinated by me. As an Englishman, I am free to speak with whomsoever I wish once no law of my kingdom is broken.

Owing to currency fluctuations and what shall we call it, the light-fingeredness one can encounter in my beloved Italy, there proved to be a shortfall, which arose at the last minute. The Contessa will not mind me placing on the formal record that it was she who, as it were, rode to the rescue. I believe the selling of jewellery given that good lady by the late Count was part of it, but one was never quite told, for good reason. I should like to add that this was an exceedingly dangerous thing for my friend the Contessa to have done. The SS watched the bank accounts of all non-Fascists assiduously. The consequence for Allied collaboration was death.

Around that time, I became aware, I do not wish to say precisely how – and again, I will ask you to forgive my tergiversation – it will be obvious that the intelligence services and counter-espionage were involved – that Hauptmann, the SS commandant in Rome, was being telephoned with notable regularity by Himmler himself. This fact disconcerted me considerably.

On a nightly basis, sometimes twice nightly, the Reichsführer – after all the second-most powerful man in the Nazi empire – was raging at Hauptmann and his odious deputy, Dollman, about the Führer's perception that Allied escapees were waltzing about Rome at will – 'like whores in a *Bierkeller*' I seem to recollect was one haunting phrase. He threatened Hauptmann that, were the situation not resolved expeditiously, the Führer's displeasure might narrow down to a rather tight focus, in effect, that Hitler had Hauptmann in his crosshairs.

One had known for some time that Hauptmann was developing what the renowned Professor Freud might have termed 'a complex' about the Monsignor. We had a plant in Gestapo headquarters, a courageous young woman, indeed a heroine, whom I do not wish to name or otherwise identify. I neither confirm nor deny that she was herself German. I will say nothing whatsoever of her, except that she had informed us that, among other things, the Nazi would stride about the office ranting about 'that bastard priest' and glaring at surveillance photographs of him like a druid trying to set them on fire. I apprised the Monsignor of the facts, but, perhaps like others of his country-men, if I may say so, he was not always the sort to take facts in.

There it is.

The Celtic peoples – and one admires them – excel as exponents of bard craft. But as rationalists? *Satis dictum*.

I wish to state for the record that the Monsignor had an eminently clear picture of the peril he was facing on Christmas Eve 1943. Any suggestion that he did not is, frankly, horse-feathers. What I mean is that such an insinuation would be totally unfounded. I warned him, and he knew the danger.

That is my solemn word. After that, cleverer people than I must believe what they wish. As Mr Orwell is supposed to have said (though I have never found the reference), 'There are some ideas so stupid that only an intellectual could believe them'. Mr Orwell attended Eton, thus must always be trusted.

Not long after the series of angry telephone calls from Himmler com-menced, the unfortunate Jews of the ghetto, most of whom were very poor, hard-working Romans, were ordered by Hauptmann to collect up a preposter-ous amount of gold so as to avoid deportation to the camps. With a great deal of trouble, this total was raised. Again, the Contessa was involved, at least peripherally, or so I have reason to believe. It was obvious that matters were now spinning very fast.

I have never stated previously – none but the Monsignor and Derry knew at the time –that an approach had been made by the Nazis to compromise me. This took place one afternoon some months before that Christmas, I should say in mid-October, perhaps later. I was noodling through *The Times* over a gin and French in a little café I liked under the colonnade of St Peter's Square, a fortnight-old copy my man May had somehow got his hands on, but one had to make do. A crossword need not be up to date.

It was one's custom, at the café, to spend a little time simply looking about and doing one's best to enjoy the fact that one was there. The Italians are an eminently social, embracing, demonstrative people. Part of their culture, their identity, is to be communal. Eating together is important to them. They kiss, they embrace. Men, women, the young and the elderly. They display their feelings, their emotions, in a way we in England generally do not. For me it makes Italian life most attractive and uplifting. So, that is what I was doing. Taking in the scene. Suddenly, an interruption arrived.

This louche-looking Johnny with something of the pimp about him strolled up and asked if *mein Herr* would mind him sharing the table. Since he was already doing so, indeed had his elbows on the place mat, there wasn't all that much one could say. He did not introduce himself but I was aware of who he was. Dollman, Hauptmann's deputy.

The cigarette was slim and black with a gold-coloured tip. The cufflinks were miniature theatrical masks, a downcast Tragedy and its smirking cousin. Presently he ordered a cappuccino, a further lapse of taste. Italians, correctly, regard that beverage as suitable with breakfast only. No cultured Roman would order it after eleven o'clock. In any event, as the waiter told him, coffee was not to be had anywhere in the city, owing to rationing. Dollman took from his pocket a pill bottle and handed it to the man.

'Inside you will find three teaspoons of hundred-per-cent Costa Rican Arabica. Make me a cappuccino. Do it quickly.'

Pretending that a thought had just this moment occurred to him, he turned his sluggish eyes in my direction. Might he have the honour of buying me a cup of coffee as his neighbour?

'*Nein danke,*' I replied.

'Later, then,' he said, placing a second pill bottle by my saucer. 'That is a little gift for *mein Herr.*'

He spoke with a cultivated Kraut accent that was at odds with his spiv appearance and deportment. The nails of his many-ringed fingers were untended, I noticed, and his expensive-looking spats had not been polished since the fall of the Weimar Republic. Aptly named, he had curiously puppet-like movements, frequently nodding his head, as though his strings were being jerked. A sulphurous reek of what I suppose must have been cologne or after-shave wafted across, battling with another, less mentionable odour. He was at least wearing a tie, if overly vivid, like a shred torn from an artiste's bodice during a striptease. Apart from the sad, tawny eyes, somewhat syphilitic but thoughtful, he was as one of those types hanging about the back door of a nightclub in Berlin being buzzed at by gnats and jazz.

Would I care for a cigarette? Was *The Times* of London interesting today?

At this point I beckoned for my bill.

'You find your new life in the Vatican amenable, *mein Herr*?'

A revealing question. He knew precisely who I was.

I said that living in the Vatican suited me adequately for the moment.

'Yes, you Englishmen like a monarchy,' he replied.

'Sir, you are inside the boundaries of an independent, neutral state,' I reminded him. 'If you are a combatant in the present hostilities or any sort of Axis operative, your presence here without advance written permission from the Vatican authorities is forbidden under international law. I must bid you return to Rome. Over there. Good day. If you don't, I shall have you arrested.'

'An understanding between men of the world, Sir D'Arcy,' he replied. 'That is all I seek. Perhaps you will indulge me one moment.'

A fat, weary bluebottle happened to be inching across the red-checked tablecloth, and as my intruder waited for my reply, he pointed to it, now hold-ing up his nicotine-stained fingertip and grinning at me with disturbingly porcelain-like teeth.

'"Mark but this flea and mark in this, how little that which thou deniest me is." That is a couplet of your English clergyman and poet, Donne, I believe. From a poem of seduction. Is it so?'

I told him I was not in the habit of indulging in literary disquisition with strangers (although, in fact, I am, when the opportunity arises), he must say what he wished, then cut along. A diplomat must sometimes tolerate persons one would rather slap across the face. That is why we have diplomacy, after all. One felt a certain degree of apprehensiveness, naturally enough, but would not give him the satisfaction of showing it. Most probably he had a Luger in his armpit; all Gestapo men had. But even a Hun would be on balance unlikely to shoot me in St Peter's Square. Not during daylight, at any rate.

'I would like to speak with you concerning the matter of another clergyman,' he said.

'There are many of those in Rome,' I replied, kicking for touch like a springbok, if I say so myself.

'Not all of them so troublesome, *mein Herr*.'

I said I hadn't the foggiest inkling as to the advertence of my unwanted visitor. He nodded in an overly mild manner, like a bad actor nodding mildly, and muttered, 'Of course.' Then he took from his inside pocket what I thought was a piece of card, which he pushed across the table, now fingering the tips of the toothpicks in a sherry glass and squinting hard at the menu a waiter was attempting to give him, as though being offered a menu in a café was an event of inexplicable strangeness.

The piece of card turned out to be a reasonably well-defined photograph of the Monsignor, the Contessa Landini and me, on the putting green of the eighteenth hole at Viterbo. It had been taken from a distance through a window of what I knew must be the clubhouse. The Monsignor had a putter over his shoulder, rifle-style; he'd been heavier at that time. Rationing thinned him considerably. The Contessa's head was leaning back and she was laughing with abandon, a sight I couldn't remember having seen. Odd, the things that strike one under stress.

'We are in what I believe is termed a "pretty pickle",' the Kraut said, pleased with himself for knowing the expression. 'A spot of bother, don't you know, old sport.'

'How so?'

'There are laws, after all. International conventions. Germany does not assist German prisoners of war in your country to escape.'

'I shouldn't think they'd want to.'

'It is a question of mathematics. Also of perceptions. One man's happy situation is another's little difficulty. Much depends on the vantage point from where one is observing. Thus the common ground must be sought in all things, must it not.'

'Go on.'

'It is quite evident that an Escape Line is being operated, illegally, from within Vatican City. Do you agree?'

'Do I agree that that is evident?'

'Do you agree that it is being operated?'

'I have never heard of a body called anything as vulgar as an Escape Line being operated in the Vatican. Elucidate a little if you wish?'

'We believe that this is a photograph of three of its leaders. The Holy Trinity, one might call it.'

'I would call it a trio of casual acquaintances playing golf.'

'Dear sir, I do not think so.'

'I don't give a fish's tit what you think.'

'Admirable,' he said with a facial movement that I think was intended to be a smile. 'The British independence of mind, what? The refusal of convention. This extends to other areas, other *aspects* of your life, I think, *mein Herr*. Your nightlife in particular. Does it not?'

'You're the expert.'

'No crime to like the gentlemen, *mein Herr*. Well, strictly speaking, yes. To be "cut from the different cloth", as the Englishman says. You have homosexual friends and associates, who does not, after all?' He chuckled. 'Here we are in the Vatican, are we not? Boys' Town.'

'You can tell all that from a photograph of three people playing golf, can you? Wondrous. Ever think of taking up clairvoyance in a bunko booth?'

'Yes, the evidence is circumstantial. But more shall be found. The proposition I now put to you, and, if you wish, to your comrades, is that a certain number of Allied escapees shall be permitted by us to go their way. "Nod as good as a wink", as it were. On the strict proviso that fifty or sixty a week will be handed back to us for immediate return to the camps. In this manner, honour is satisfied.'

'What would happen to those returned?'

'Exegution.'

'Your pronunciation is lamentable,' I said. 'Do you mean "execution"?'

'I mean being shot. Or hanged.'

'You would term such a bargain honourable?'

'War is war, *mein Herr*.'

'Is it?'

'We must all swim in the same sea. Come, let us take a coffee and discuss.'

I picked up and unscrewed the pill bottle, poured the ground Arabica into my cupped palm, inhaled. It was rich, cherry-ish, sumptuous, finely roasted, with notes of chocolatey sandalwood, a truly exquisite blend. *Puff* – I blew it in his face.

'Run along, darling,' I said. 'You're smudging your lipstick.'

He responded with a volley of filth I shan't repeat.

At that, I stood up and called out affectionately to a duo of the Swiss Guard who happened to be patrolling nearby, picturesque gentlemen in their quaint medieval livery but well known in Rome for carrying Thompson sub-machine guns sequestered in their cloaks and not being afraid to use them if told the Pope or his State is being assailed. As they approached, giving me a cautious version of their fist-to-forehead salute, the Kraut slipped from the table and hurried across the boundary line, where he stood for a moment, grinning his puppety grin in my direction, before slouching away through the construction site of the Via della Conciliazione.

The guardsmen asked if I wished to report him but I told them not to bother with his ilk. One day a slighted Roman would deal with him face to face, I felt. Not the most diplomatic of thoughts. There we are.

Returning to my quarters in the Vatican, for a time I paced and smoked, in a condition of some anger and vengefulness. Again, these are not good traits to be allowed to seed themselves in an Envoy of His Majesty. But they sank in deep that day.

Nonetheless, in one respect, the vile upstart had done me a favour. I would go so far as to say that, without his attempt to corrupt me, I am not sure that I would have permitted myself to become too involved in the Escape Line. But then I thought: ruddy nerve. Ruddy *nerve* of the bastard. It ate at me all afternoon. It enraged me.

They would murder every Jew, every gypsy, every artist. If ever they got to London, they would go directly to Soho and murder a number of my closest friends. And then, they would murder me.

I think you know what I am referring to.

I seemed to see them, one by one, old classmates, colleagues, companions. Decent, good men, witty, loyal, brave. Some had fought for their country, for the decency of many of her values, our system of parliamentary government, our non-hatred of our opponents. Our very-far-from-perfection but our wish to do much better.

The laughter and late nights we had shared in better times.

I said 'no'. You fucking thug.

Not without a fight.

So I went to the Monsignor and told him to count me in, as it were. I had of course known of the Escape Line, had, I dare say, assisted it in small matters, but had officially looked the other way so as to preserve a certain, shall we say, deniability. But no more. He was praying in the garden of the Collegio, at least I assumed it was prayer. Seated on a bench with a Bible on his knees.

We talked for a while about missions that had already been run, the hiding of prisoners in such and such a convent, the moving of escapees or medical supplies at night. Then we spoke of a mission that was coming. A Rendimento.

After an hour or so, a man in gardener's overalls happened along the path and was introduced to me as Major Sam Derry of the Royal Artillery, 'the Gunners', my own former regiment, an escapee hiding in the Vatican *scavi*, the excavations.

What took me aback was how quickly he and the Monsignor told me everything. They and a helpmate in the city had been putting together monies for some time. There were too many prisoners in hiding, they would need to be moved out of Rome into the countryside, before an expected large influx of Nazi reinforcements early in the New Year. The cash facilitating this would be dropped on Christmas Eve night.

There would be three drops, the smallest in Prati, the medium in Parioli, the largest in a location as yet undecided. The round trip would be a walk of fourteen and a half miles. Arrest would result in prolonged torture and death. Derry had volunteered for the mission.

A grisly part of the business was what we did next. It turned out that, in the Bible on the Monsignor's knees, he had underlined many names in red ink, which Derry was committing to memory, in their Italian versions. Luca. Paolo. Marco. Matteo. Giuseppe, Elisabetta. Pietro, Stefano.

Why was he doing this? I asked.

'In case I find myself in Club Hauptmann, sir.'

'Beg pardon?'

'Slang some of the boys use for Gestapo headquarters, sir,' Derry said, in a matter-of-fact manner that floored me. 'Club Hauptmann, they call it, or Dollman's Basement. If I get tortured, I want to have actual names to give up. So that I don't betray my friends. I meet the Monsignor here every day for my homework. Bloody tough taskmaster, too.'

We sat beneath the cypresses, the Monsignor, Sam Derry and I, as the nightingales came and went, and the Roman sun gleamed, Derry reciting the names, I testing him on their fictional addresses. At one point, I was unmanned, gave in to my emotions. With gentleness the Monsignor took my hand and murmured, 'Courage, old man.' Derry said, 'Chin up, sir. We're Gunners.'

And I told them something which was true, that I missed my brother back in England. But that I loved them as my brothers and always would. To the end of my days. Beyond, if possible.

They indicated to me that that was a comfort, and on we went. Speaking names and addresses, by birdsong.

25

A left off Via Boccherini, through a gap in the barbed wire, now picking his way across the bombsite. Notices say the ruined schoolhouse could collapse at any moment; loitering and 'immoral behaviour' are punishable by death.

The rocket crater overflowing with oily, littered water, islands of mould-covered plasterboard, broken boxes. The bomb shattered the building into diagonal halves, the corkscrewed central staircase now exposed, half-collapsed, the shattered sinks and exploded lavatory cisterns blackening with rust. Obscenely, a child's tennis racket dangles from a window sash.

Graffiti splatters every millimetre of the shrapnel-scarred walls – '*Viva l'Italia!*' '*Morte al fascismo*' '*Roma '27*' '*Libertà, sempre!*' – Six of the seven oaken buttresses brought in to shore up the gable have had their cast-iron brackets stolen by looters; the seventh has been attacked with a chainsaw. Discarded French letters lie in profusions of broken glass like jellyfish torpedoed ashore.

A spectral nun intoning the alphabet arises from the rubble but he blinks away the memory, if that's what it is.

'*Hände hoch!*' snaps the voice behind him. 'Hands high. Do not turn.'

His arms anvil-heavy as he raises them. Mind ticking. Stomach boiling. In the ruins, a starling chirrups and a mongrel gives a scuttle. Boot-steps crunch through the rubble.

'Keep your back to me,' now in Italian. 'Spread your feet.'

The voice is brisk, local, sickening in its confidence. A careful, probing hand pats the rear pockets of his trousers. A pistol presses his back. Fingers grope his jacket.

'Take three steps forward and kneel.'

Prickles tingle his jaw. Bracing for the bullet, he speaks.

'I am content to step forward, not to kneel.'

'You'll do as commanded.'

'In that respect, no.'

'*Mi scusi?*'

'Have respect for a man twice your age, you ignorant lout. Or I'll do what your father should have done.'

A mangy, three-legged vixen trots out from the rubble, whining with hunger or pain.

With a roar, she explodes, blood slops across brickwork. The pistol shot echoes. The voice gives a sigh.

'*Allora*. Remain standing. Now, turn to me, *slowly*. Try to run and you'll get the same treatment.'

What he sees when he turns is a moustachioed, pig-eyed, twenty-year-old bruiser, in the drabs of the Fascist police. Stocky, long-reached, adept in a brawl, a human hammer in search of a nail. Some emptiness of the eyes is like the bombsite's broken windows.

'Grandad,' the youth sneers, 'why are you not wearing the Party insignia?'

'I dressed hurriedly. If it's any of your business.'

'How is your trouser leg torn?'

'I slipped on the ice.'

'You slipped?'

'That's right.'

'You are aware of the penalty for disobeying the curfew.'

'My profession is such that I am exempt.'

'You speak stiltedly. You are not an Italian. Where are you from?'

'That information is on my identity card, which you will find on a string around my neck, inside my shirt.'

The Fascist reaches and finds it, reads the lying words by torchlight.

'Mancuso,' he says. 'Kind of name is that?'

'You tell me.'

'We have reports of Communist activity in the city tonight. Partisans, terrorists, they attack us like cowards from the darkness. Know anything about it? Signor so-called Mancuso?'

'Forgive me, what does a Communist look like?'

'Got a mirror? You'll see.'

'I pay no attention to such matters. I only do my work.'

'It says here you grew up in Milano. Is that right?'

'That's what it says.'

'Which is your football team?'

'Inter.'

'What's the name of the church in Milano where *The Last Supper* is?'

'Santa Maria delle Grazie.'

'Bullshit. This card is a forgery.'

'Why would you say such a thing?'

'You are not an Italian. I can tell by your accent.'

'I didn't say I'm Italian. Can't you read?'

'You shall come with me to the police headquarters. *Andiamo*.'

'Mother of God, degenerate criminals are walking the street. Not ten minutes ago, on Via Peri, I passed a prostitute openly revealing her body. Half-naked in a doorway. On Christmas Eve. You tell me there are Communist insurrectionists and murderers at large. And you wish to arrest an innocent man at his work? *È bene*, I have tolerated enough, let us go to the station. We shall see what your superiors say to this time-wasting.'

'Think you're cleverer than me?'

'I think a sack of stones would be that.'

'Quite the stuck-up, aren't you. *Professore Partigiano*.'

'Let me tell you something, son, before you embarrass yourself further. Today I was one of a small group invited to a wedding in Saint Peter's—'

'Big deal.'

'The bride was the daughter of Traetta, yes, the Fascist official. A close, personal friend of mine, since before you were born. Take me to the police station, I will telephone him from there.'

'I don't believe you. What's she called?'

'My goddaughter's name is Alicia.'

'You're Traetta's girl's godfather?'

'Her husband is Luca.'

'Anyone could know that. You're trying to trick me. Stay *back*.'

'In my breast pocket, you will find a copy of the Order of Service. Signed and dated by the happy couple. And Traetta.'

'Take it out. *Slowly*.'

He does. Hands it across.

'There. You see the words. You have made a mistake. Tomorrow I shall telephone Traetta to commend your dedication and hard work.'

'Say "Damn the Jews".'

'Why would I say that?'

'Because I told you to.'

'That is no reason to say anything. Another man might tell me to say "Damn the Duce".'

'What?'

'You heard me.'

'Withdraw that remark.'

'What remark?'

'"Damn the Duce".'

'Now you've said it yourself. Do you think that is wise? Someone could be eavesdropping and denounce you.'

The Fascist reaches out a fingertip, touches the top button of his prisoner's jacket.

'Big-Brains Mancuso. Big men fall hard.'

'Touch me again, son, you'll know all about it.'

'You're threatening me, Professor?'

'Not threatening. Warning.'

He touches him again.

Mancuso lunges.

Grabs the index finger, bends it, *hard* back against the wrist, and the youth utters a scream of shocked, gulping pain, falls sideways, arms flailing, somehow regains his balance, manages to haul out his pistol from its underarm holster but he can't get the safety catch off. Eyes rolling, he totters, spews blasphemies and avowals, Mancuso hits him again, a battering parry at the temples, but the Fascist ducks, swinging, they're into a bad wrestlers' clinch amid the stench of unlaundered linen and dirty pomaded hair, as he gropes at the pistol butt, bites at Mancuso's ear, fingertips clawing towards eyes.

A masked figure looms from the schoolhouse, length of scaffolding in gloved hands. As the Fascist turns toward the footsteps, he's struck hard across the chest, staggering backwards into a pile of toppled bricks and slates and the assailant seizes him by the windpipe, kneeing him hard between the legs, and the Fascist sinks, retching, in agonised gasps as the figure unleashes a kick at his head.

A roar in German from the laneway, *Hands up or we shoot!* and the figure hurtles into a run, clambering over the broken wall.

From the street, three German soldiers, a storm-lantern, rifles jutting.

'What is going on here? Do not move. Raise your hands.'

'My name is Mancuso, this officer was being beaten as I passed and I came to his aid. He needs an ambulance, he's concussed, have you a radio-set at hand? His attacker fled away in that direction.'

Two soldiers hurry towards the wall. The third utters a long sigh.

'Your identity card, *bitte*?' he says.

26

THE VOICE OF DELIA KIERNAN
7th January 1963
BBC research interview, recorded White City, London

A Roman winter, you see, throws a lot at a building. The Embassy, an old villa with no heating system and clanky piping the age of your granny, was receiving a sorely needed renovation at the time. Buckets up and down the corridors, we'd that many leaks in the roof. A burst water-main in the cellar. Rats you could saddle. The swimming pool froze solid and became a right, effing nuisance, pardon my French, because the mosaic in the floor cracked and the *caementicium* was destroyed.

My husband felt he should remain onsite, in the servants' flat, which in truth was little more than a boxroom; you'd fit a camp bed, nothing more. Our daughter Blon and I had taken an apartment in the city for the ten weeks. That's where I was on Christmas Eve.

It was a night you wouldn't put a milk bottle out. Sleet. Bitter cold. Pulverising furies of wind. My father used to joke that the rain is liquid sunshine. That Christmas Eve it was liquid depression.

Half past two in the morning comes a battering on the front door like an army of angry devils. When I open it, there stands Hugh, by his lonesome own, and he blinking at me like a lighthouse, eight to the bar, as though trying to signal me something urgent.

'Good evening, Signor Mancuso,' says I, with any calm I can muster, though the fear is making me unsteady. 'I assume you are here for the bottle of quinine, as arranged?'

The look on his puss.

'Thanks indeed, Mrs Kiernan,' says he.

'Won't you mosey in for a moment?' says I. 'It's a chilly night, so it is. You'd take a little nightcap for the road?'

That's when the three Nazis step into the porch. Well, maybe not Nazis, three German soldiers, conscripts, I'd say.

One from the right, the other pair from the left. They were after waiting, hidden, the way I wouldn't be able to see them but they could hear anything I was saying to Hugh, or he to me.

Pistols in hand.

Not saying a word.

Two of them were unattractive lads, may God and Mary love them, but the third, their superior, was an absolute fright. A haddock-faced, lumpen-shouldered, *Wurst*-fingered corner boy, that ugly the tide wouldn't take him out. He'd a face like a Lurgan shovel.

'Good evening, gentlemen,' says I. 'Or an early *Guten Morgen*, I suppose. And how may I assist your excellencies?'

They said nothing.

'You are associates of my husband's friend, Signor Mancuso, I assume?' says I. 'Well, thank you for escorting him to my door, very considerate of you altogether. There's a horrid lot of thievery and crime these nights in Rome, so there is. A body would be afraid to go out.'

They're gawping at yours truly, then at Hugh, then at each other. Fine examples of the super-race. Three wise men. But you want to be good and careful when you're dealing with the stupid. Stupidity has cunning, otherwise it would have disappeared a long time ago. Stupidity is a shark. It outlasts.

The problem was to get Hugh into the house without making them more suspicious, which wouldn't be easy, for by now he was beside himself with anxiety. Also, I was needing to think on my feet. Christmas isn't an easy time for me, I was after having a few brandies to try and help me get to sleep. I wished I hadn't, for now my thoughts were all in a hames. At that moment, it started to snow.

It was a dirty, bitter night, the snow was the wet sort that soaks through your clothes, and the soldiers were white with the misery. There was that awful smell you get off filthy socks once the wetness gets through boots. One of them now asked me in very broken and embarrassed English if he might step in for a moment and avail himself of the lavatory. That was when the solution occurred to me.

'Sure wouldn't you *all* come in?' says I, and I sobering fast as a cat. 'I've coffee got for Christmas, you'll take a cup just in your hand.'

'I don't think that would be proper, Delia.' This was Hugh talking now. 'These men are on patrol. They've their duty to attend to.'

'Arra, Marco, don't be so dry, sure it's Christmas Eve night,' says I. 'Let them come in and stand by the fire ten minutes itself and get a thaw in their bones, the poor dotes.'

Well, the murderous look he gave me. But I knew what I was at. Or I thought I did, anyhow. Either way, the bolt was shot.

The three start colloguing together in German a minute, then in with all four to the hall. The fellow in need takes himself off to the closet below the landing. Blon, who that moment came down the stairs, helped me take the soaked overcoats of the other pair and put them below in the cloakroom. I winked her to be calm.

'There's a German gentleman in the lav, dear,' I said, for we hadn't a lock on it. 'And may I introduce you to Mr Mancuso,' meaning Hugh, whom she knew well enough to regard as an uncle. She nodded as she shook his hand.

Blonnie had turned nineteen that October and was what used to be known as a knockout. The Italians have a phrase, *fare bella figura*, which means looking your absolute utmost all the time. That's how she was: confident, in control. She'd sell a double bed to a Reverend Mother. Blon had every bit of her father's handsomeness, and something of the defiant spirit of the women in my family but was lovelier than anyone I had ever seen. Her father used to say she had the sort of beauty that machine-guns a room, a quip that always drove her batty, but you knew what he meant, for you'd seen it. Hearts had been broken from Bundoran to Bologna. Brown eyes you'd drown in and a heads-up-straight walk and a figure like Veronica Lake's. Fluent in three languages, halfway through her science degree. As for charm? She'd talk rain out of wetting her.

Introductions were made and the visitors bowed and clicked their heels. You could tell the poor looders were machine-gunned. Trotting after her, the creatures, bumping into each other, into the living room, where the hearth was angel-bright and the Christmas tree lit and the Waterford crystal plates of candies and apples, and Blon's harp under its cover by the window. I did up a plate of proper sandwiches you'd need a weightlifter's fist to hold, and put a mutton soup on the boil, and got the trifle out of the refrigerator.

'*Freunde*,' says I. 'Fill your boots.'

Appetite?

Man dear, you'd want to have seen them. They'd ate the leg off the lamb of God.

Like most in Rome that time, they were half-starved alive. Hunger was rampant, you'd see people faint in the street, even die. Worse was coming, too, it would be a famine by March, and, like many a famine before and since, the people did the starving were the poor. It was well known the Nazi officers stole any decent food for themselves and their families, the conscripts in the lower ranks could hang, they lived on the dregs. These three, shall we say, were not officer class.

By the time I got the gramophone going, there was scarcely a crumb on a plate. I thought they'd eat the cushions. It was pitiful. I saw hungry people when I was a girl, they eat calmly and quickly, not stopping to talk, not wanting to waste. As though someone will take it away from them. Like automatons.

Blon, wonderful Blon now pushed in the drinks trolley, which I may add was plentifully supplied. Scotch, vodka, schnapps, grappa, whatever you fancied and more besides, port, chartreuse, Bourbon, Dutch gin, and the pride of the bundling, three naggins of Powers White Whiskey, the most exquisite occasion of sin you ever savoured. It was Johnny May got them for me, on the Roman black market, where they cost a sultan's ransom, ninety-five dollars the bottle. But they earned their keep that night.

'You'll take a drop of this, boys. It's very rare,' says I. 'Indeed and you will. Don't be girls. *Prost!* The traditional way is down in one. Do it fast.'

A grand hole was soon made in the first naggin, the lads nearly lowing in pleasure. Before long we were punishing the second. The daggers Hugh was shooting me would have cut through a safe. Blon brought more scoff, dishes of tiramisu and panna cotta, and had by now been prevailed upon with beckons and leery smiles to give us a tune on the harp.

Blon is classically trained and had played in the university orchestra; her end of the forest being that dreadful modern stuff, what do you call it, atonal, like a bag of blind cats mating, but she obliged with a few gobbets of misty-eyed Celtic bilge, which foreigners, especially Germans, seem to like. And when you've never seen a harp played, it's really and truly remarkable, especially if you're a bit scundered at the time. You sort of think, that's impossible.

It's like watching a unicycling juggler. I didn't sing myself that night – I'd a touch of laryngitis – but Blon rose to the occasion, lots of *mavourneen acushla*, and her voice was light and lovely. Soon the lads were humming along, pearly tears in the peepers, as though the gentle grey-haired mammy in the songs Blon was singing was their own little *Mutter* back in Nuremberg.

Second bottle down, we uncapped the third. They started appearing a little, shall we say, woozy. Powers White Whiskey is not for the faintheart. It's what they use to eke the rust off old coins.

An aunt of mine used to say so-and-so was 'drunk as a boiled owl'. I never knew what it meant before that night. I was able to take Hugh aside and put him in the picture. Ten minutes before himself and the Teds appeared at the door, Jo Landini knocked on my bedroom windows, which were at the back of the house, having come in through the garden and crossed the courtyard. Johnny May was after telephoning her, she'd slipped straight out to Angelucci's apartment, then the pair of them went searching my neighbourhood with the hope of finding Hugh, when the sound of a pistol-shot a few streets away drew them to the ruined school.

Angelucci was at a safehouse, was after escaping the pursuers, was delighted to have cold-cocked a Fascist policeman before taking flight. As a travelling man that used to camp on my daddy's land used to put it, 'he left him for priest and doctor'. It would be a consolation for not being permitted to run the mission. He intended to lie low for a fortnight, get out of the city, would be in touch when the coast was clear.

I gave Jo a hug, the dear mite; she was cold and gone quiet. She said, 'Delia, your arms are springtime,' and we laughed a little moment. 'When all of this is over, invite me to Ireland?' she said, and I promised I would, never doubt it.

'What shall we see there, Delia?'

'Muddy lakes. Scrawny cows.'

'Will you find me an Irishman to marry?'

'I'd never inflict that on you.'

'Have you a cigarette, *carissima*? I'm gasping for a smoke.'

It was an Irishism I'd taught her, well, hadn't *meant* to teach her, but I suppose she picked it up, she was always listening out. I gave her a Woodbine, and she coughed as she lit it. It was a moment I saw the girl in her, and also – this was strange – the old lady. I was so fond of her, somewhere along the way we were after becoming great pals. Tough, she was. Witty. Never back down. It's hard when you're beautiful, I saw that with my own daughter, because a beautiful-looking person will always attract trouble. But Jo had more sense in one fingernail than anyone I ever met. I loved the bones of that woman. Never more than that night.

She was now upstairs, I told Hugh, hiding in a crawlspace behind the ceilings and attic. I said I'd send Blon up to tell her to either stay hidden or make her getaway, for there was by now no way that our visitors would be able to see a staircase, never mind climb one, let alone conduct a proper search when they got there. They had been with us less than an hour but were scuttered.

But when Blonnie went up, she was gone.

Hugh said he was leaving, too. Blon brought in an old overcoat of her father's, a heavy frieze ulster patched up here and here.

'This is for yourself, Uncle.'

'I'm grand,' he told her.

'I'm not asking. I'm telling, put it on.'

I nodded for him to do as commanded.

Too large, it wasn't a great fit, but it was adequate for purpose, if I can put it like that. I could see him start to twig what was happening.

'Is it altered?' he asked us.

I told him it was.

'Nice bit of tailoring,' he said.

'We work cheap.'

Presently, he slipped away, through the pantry at the back and into the laneway at the rear of the house. By now it was gone three in the morning. Soon our other visitors departed, too, by the more orthodox exit. Off into the night, with a fanfare of confused and confusing salutes and rebuffed attempts at embraces. I regret to say that they would receive an unpleasant little surprise when they got back to barracks, for their ration books, German currency and military identity cards would somehow be missing from the greatcoats Blon and I had put in the downstairs cloakroom to dry.

Opportunity must be availed of, especially in wartime. The Powers had been expensive, after all.

Which would have been fine, in its way. But you know what happened next.

It turned out that one of the boyos had not been quite as drunk as I thought, or the cold night sobered him fast.

At the Carabinieri headquarters on Via Busoni, he radioed the Gestapo.

It was Christmas, so most of the regular goons were off. The message went direct to the SS commandant at his villa.

The most dreaded man in Rome.

Paul Hauptmann.

ACT III

The Huntsman

27

On Saturday 6th March 1475, two peasant boys were swimming in a lake seven leagues south of Rome when they observed what they described as 'a scarlet light' in the depths and tried to swim downwards to investigate.

The distance was too far.

They were idiots, their parents said.

In the coming spring and summer, the boys trained themselves to dive a little further each day, to fill their lungs like swollen wineskins and keep open their stinging eyes in the murk, until the afternoon arrived, near the start of that autumn, when the younger made it down to the sandy, silty bed, and, gasping, trembling, slick with weird weeds, brought back a ruby the size of a grapefruit.

Even the wisest of the village could not explain the find.

Rubies in a lake?

Impossible.

No ruby mine existed in all the lands of Lazio. Some Caesar long gone to dust must have dropped it while charioting or hunting, or flung it away, a sacrifice, perhaps, to Diana, goddess of love, who lowered the moon into the water on the nights of her unhappiness. As with all inexplicable finds and all facts resisting reason, the ruby of the lake inflamed stories. Children of that lakefront were lulled to wondrous dreams by legends of the red dragon's eyeball.

Ninety years later, on the morning after a bad storm, the net of a weary fisherman pulled out no fish but an object that turned out to be, when he wiped off the mud, an opal-encrusted, golden goblet. Rowing out to the middle of the lake, he looked down into the depths, and saw, far below him, a presence that had not been visible before, 'the dragon's long black shadow'.

Terrified, he fled, through the splashes of his oars. 'I heard it roar behind me,' he testified. 'I was too frightened to turn and look.' Breathless, he hurried to the elders. Warriors were given harpoons, ordered to dive down to the dragon, measure and observe it, come back with sketchable details. A scribe would be sent to consult the bestiaries at the ancient library in the Vatican to see if the lake's beast had precedent or name. But the divers, when they surfaced, nets heavy with gemstones, said the dragon was not a dragon but a ship.

For days afterward, the townspeople crowded into the lake, returning with crystals, jade goblets, terracotta tiles, plump diamonds and opals, silver statuettes of leering pagan deities, jewelled daggers, golden platters depicting copulations. One morning, a thirteen-year-old farmgirl, the deepest diver yet, reported seeing the vast hulk tilt. It turned appallingly onto its starboard side and broke into three, an immense billowing cloud of black, rotting splinters, half-sunken into the muck it must have come from. A hunk of iron that had belonged to the anchor was dragged to the shallows by the girl and her father. The oxen that pulled it from the mud all died within a week. On its length was stamped the name 'Caligula'.

In 1927, the Duce, avid for the past, commanded his archaeologists to drain the dragon's lake. Through a radius of ten kilometres, the fields were dammed or flooded. Two pleasure-ships were found, the larger the size of an Olympic soccer pitch, the smaller not much smaller, a barge. There was also an ancient rowboat filled to her oarlocks with stones. A museum was built on the lakeshore; the three vessels pulleyed out of their long, dignified slumber, the restful sleep of antediluvian secrets, and placed on display like captured princesses, in the bleak, cold stare of touristry.

It was at Nemi that Obergruppenführer Hauptmann established his weekend home, in the pleasantly appointed cut-stone villa constructed in 1929 for the Museo's Chief Curator and his family. The master bedroom and reception rooms overlooked the lake; the little kitchen faced south and was sunny and dappled, perfumed by a herb garden and lemon groves. The house was cool and shaded, had an electricity generator, efficient plumbing, its own well. Importantly, it was three kilometres from its nearest neighbour. Hauptmann did not like to be observed.

Here he could be himself, could loll about in a dressing gown, playing his beloved gramophone records as loudly as he pleased. From hidden loudspeakers, Mozart and Beethoven boomed through the forest, frightening the nightingales and water rats. It was not done in Party circles to admit anything non-Aryan as having merit, but here, by the lake, his guilty secret, Verdi, could be indulged in private, a peccadillo no one would uncover. A great pity that Verdi had been Italian, member of an inferior race. But no one is perfect, Hauptmann told his children.

Only one person in the history of this world has ever been perfect. That person suffered unimaginably but has risen again, and we must follow him without the slightest question for he is leading his people into the future-

'Daddy means Jesus,' his wife interrupted. 'Don't you, dear?'

'What? Oh, yes. Our Lord.'

He loved his retreat, half an hour's drive from hot, filthy Rome with its battalions of tireless beggars, the reek of shit and olive oil. The crumbling, dusty piles of mediocre, popish rubble. Machicolations and murder holes, the never-ending bells and processions. An apparition here. Some saint's liver there. Touch that statue with your forehead, you'll suffer a thousand years fewer in purgatory. Talking crucifixes, bleeding friezes, barred windows, mouthy gargoyles. And always, *give us money*, at every turn, money. The incessant, donkeyish bray and hand-waving inanity that passed for talk. The only city on Earth founded on superstition and fleecing credulous old women. Rome was a capital of stupidity and childishness. Nemi was a world made for men.

Swimming naked in the lake, the whiff of blood would clear, the tang of the cell and the torture room. The gape of a prisoner as you attached electrodes to him would be rinsed away. The rasp of the file as you worked his teeth to pulp. Cold water was so replenishing that your whole head felt new.

He began to spend more time at Nemi, reduced the size of his establishment in the city to a single, small room on the top floor of Gestapo headquarters to be used in case of absolute necessity, if an interrogation, say, were running on late, or a captive was close to breaking. It was understood among his men that he was living at his retreat. Summoning his wife and children from Berlin, he installed them at the villa. They arrived on the morning that the telephone was installed, a symmetry he often quipped about, for it pleased him.

'Now, I have everything I need.'

'Thank you, Daddy.'

Often as he strolled in the cypress woods with his wife, one of those odd tricks of water would bring them the children's echo-splashed laughter as they played tennis or dress-up or tag with their governess, a local girl, and the world seemed sanctified, restored. At great cost, his official Mercedes was armour-plated, fitted with bullet-resistant windows, a lead floor, bolt-on cage

work tyre-protectors of his own design; the mouth of the fuel tank was moved to the dashboard so no one could push a burning rag down it. Now the car was too heavy to manage the pine-needled country tracks or the fragile wooden bridge leading over the streamlet, so it had to be garaged in the city. But, as Elise pointed out, this meant a healthier, more wholesome life. At the weekends and in the evenings, he walked.

Since boyhood he had loved a book by an American author, Strauss, entitled *The Huntsman and the Lake*. A presentation copy had been sent to him by an aunt in Plainfield, New Jersey, for his fourteenth birthday; perhaps one day he would come for a visit, she wrote. She directed the *Turn- und Gesangverein*, the gymnastics and singing club, in Plainfield; her young people would love to meet him, New Jersey was a welcoming place for the Germans. The excitement of seeing the American postage stamps, the franked words 'Liberty and Prosperity', the blue scrawlings of the customs official across the packet. Often, he thought the book's title the loveliest in all of literature. Simple and clean like its subject.

The huntsman as an orphan had been adopted by the Iroquois but now lived in the Great North Woods on his own. His longing was to return to the Southwest Miramichi River, where his parents had lived on a houseboat near Push and Be Damned Rapids, but the thaw required for the trek never came. You wanted it never to come because then the book would end. It was possible for you and the hero to want different things even though the side you were on was the same. By day he fought bears and rattlesnakes, by night, mountain lions and coyotes. His truer enemy was 'the do-gooder', a schoolteacher from the town twenty miles away who was always trying to tempt the huntsman back to the falsehood called civilisation. The lie of bank managers, conformity, medicines you didn't need, cages called houses, opium dens called saloons. It was a novel of fishing and trapping, of landscape and water, but could be read in another way, too. Indeed, that was part of its magnetism to the lonely, fatherless, privately troubled, teenaged boy. This was the first time he realised that a book *can* be read in more than one way, is often about a secret at which the title does not even hint. A story was a bottle, a way of storing something valuable; what was printed on the label was only part of the preciousness, if that. The discovery was so thrilling as to feel almost sexual, like coming to understand the new things your body was doing. It was not a book about a lake but about how to be a man. Life was an accommodation with vast, roiling systems, most of which wanted you dead. Now he had his own lake, and the lake had its stories. It was not unlike owning a world.

Prisoners were brought from the camps to construct a sauna cabin of pine logs, and an elaborate treehouse he designed for his son and daughter, with staircase, heart-shaped portholes, battlements, retractable ladders. In the garden, he lifted barbells, bammed at a punchbag. He picnicked on the shore with his wife, their children and the nanny, beneath wild-grown figs and olives. Salami, fine cheeses, succulent San Marzano tomatoes, glinting aubergines, grapes, *pepperoncino, arrosticini*. The cook made a *sgroppino* that would coax sighs of bliss from a rock. Truffles from Piedmont. Basil pesto from Liguria. The glory of a hunk of ciabatta dipped in olive oil and salt, eaten in ecstatic sunshine, with a glass of something crisp. A corrupt race, the Italians, but by God they knew how to live.

After lunch, he and the children would kayak in the cool shallows beneath the willows or swim near the lemon-wood dock. Elise smoked, or wrote letters home, and read on the shore, sometimes played cards or talked clothes with the nanny, gave the girl fashion magazines. On warm autumn afternoons Hauptmann taught the children to fish. His daughter was better than his son, who lost patience, grew petulant. She was clear-eyed, persistent, watched the surface like a gull. He saw a great future in the Party for his daughter.

Perch, roach, bream, squalius. He loved saying the Italian names of the lake fish to his children, how his son and daughter ran to their mother with a wriggling bream in their hands, calling, '*Mutti, Mutti, wir haben einen Fisch gefangen!*' Since coming to Rome, she had been drinking too much; sometimes he noticed her stumble, slur her words. One night, they'd had a disagreement, he had asked her to stop reading the Grimm brothers' stories to the children: 'They need something more modern, Elise, something of the *now*.' He gave her a young people's book he had sent to Berlin for, Hiemer's *Der Giftpilz, The Poisonous Toadstool*. 'As it is difficult to distinguish the deadly mushroom from the good one,' he read aloud, at random, 'it can at first be difficult to tell the murderous outsider from the friend.' She had countered that the Grimms' stories taught the most important lesson any child, especially any girl, would ever need.

'What is that, Elise?'

'Men are beasts.'

She had the cook gut the catch, the children would roast it on a campfire. A motorcycle outrider would be sent into the city for *cioccolato* ice cream and cannoli, to the Piazza Navona, where the children's favourite gelateria was, across from the Fontana del Nettuno. Often the rider made a stop at Gestapo headquarters in Via Tasso on the way back, where he collected that day's file of intelligence reports and bloodstained confessions, fetching them out to Nemi by nightfall.

Night fishing was a particular pleasure, the velvet of the forest in darkness, water moving the rushes; the fireflies. You didn't have the assistance of a cloud of bubbles on the surface. If a breeze came, you couldn't see the lapping wavelets because you couldn't use a torch; the fish would be watching through the water. Light made them scatter. You needed to learn how to listen.

He had a feel for it. *Einen Instinkt.* His son would never have it, Hauptmann knew, but he hoped that his daughter would. Often, he sensed he could angle without bait, a true master. He *knew* where the fish were, how they moved, at what times, which pools they liked, which currents, what sort of moonlight. It was simply a matter of waiting.

He could sense in his daughter the same knowledge.

She was thirteen now, and, as Elise phrased it to him one morning, had recently 'become a woman'. Her bedroom door was to be knocked upon before entering; she must have a small allowance of her own. Important to afford a little independence, a space into which she could grow. There were times when she mentioned that she would like to be either a structural engineer or a Luftwaffe pilot. It unsettled her mother. The latter was no job for a girl, Elise would say. Hauptmann disagreed, why not?

At night he walked the museum with her, explaining the glass cases of swords and cracked oars, the helmets, the battered platters, the ancient ships themselves, their black, broad beams and long hulls. Nineteen hundred years beneath the water, but they had held out, not disappeared. He would smoke and talk, she would listen and nod. The future would knock on the windows. Many visits concluded with him showing her the exhibit he valued most. A cracked terracotta tile the size of her lovely face, but graven with a line from the Roman poet, Accius.

Oderint dum metuant.

Let them hate once they fear.

'Say it for Daddy.'

She did.

A dozen of his most trusted plainclothesmen patrolled the barbed-wire perimeter, with Rottweilers kept perpetually half-starved. In concentric circles reaching outwards, a squadron of elite Panzergrenadiers guarded lanes and old roads, approaches through the forest, the warren of cart-tracks. The instruction was 'shoot to kill, presume guilt'. Pictogram signs of the death's head were nailed to the larches. Poachers in the woods were horsewhipped.

Trenches were dug, the surrounding meadowlands mined. *Chevaux de frise* barricaded the laneways where the vines sprouted so uncontrollably that they wound themselves about the spikes like garlands. Prisoners from Regina Coeli were trucked in and forced to build a breastworks and moat.

The Museo, of course, he closed to the public. You didn't want the conquered getting ideas. Sometimes, late at night, he walked its moonlit aisles, alone, enjoying a last cigarette before bedtime or a glass of fine Amaretto with the ghosts of Caligula's ships.

The artefacts thrilled him: broken daggers, little axes made for use by children. A parallelogram of jagged terracotta, somehow still intact after its centuries sunk in sediment, depicting the sloe-black 'O' of a goddess's eye or part of a peacock's wing. Elise found the Museo intolerably eerie at night, the writhe of looming shadows in its windows made strange by some effect of lake water, the faint but unkillable odour of rot, the lecherous grins of the figureheads. Hauptmann found the place arousing to the imagination, the faculty his wife called the soul.

In some night-lake of his mind, the ships still plunged, vast, Herculean, unearthly in their awe, powered by the oars of a thousand snorting slaves, manacles carved from queens' bones. Little wonder the peasants had glimpsed a dragon. Sometimes even Italians were right.

One day soon, the Führer would return to Rome. Hauptmann would give him a conqueror's welcome. Here at Nemi a grandstand would be constructed, there would be fireworks, a procession, a naval rally filmed by that Riefenstahl woman. *Why not?* 'Elise, that is my motto, why not?'

The ships would be re-floated. The impossible would be done. It must happen at night. The drama.

Piped march tunes and Bach. Handel's 'Zadok the Priest'. The Führer will glimpse what could be forged for the Reich here in Italy. Arc-lit on the stage he will scream paternal thankfulness to *our greatest of Germany's sons, Paul*

223

Hauptmann. Elise by Hitler's side, with her husband and the children, all standing to attention, saluting the Führer. An example to the whole Fatherland. The Hauptmanns.

His career will be strengthened; the family will prosper; the only roadblock is the matter of those accursed escapees. After Christmas, he will refocus, bear down harder on the problem. What he's planning is a January that Rome will never forget: hourly raids, a thousand interrogations, total war on the Escape Line's leaders. Kill the snake by cutting off its head.

Soon will come the turn of that interfering Irish priest. Like all troublemakers, a self-important little gnat. There is enough in the dossier alone to have him in front of a firing squad; that's before an interrogation extracts the full story of his involvement. Which it will. One of these nights, he'll flit out of the Vatican; the vain are unable to stay long in a room. He'll never see daylight again.

Perhaps, after the war, a Ministry in the government – he had discreetly let it be known in the sections of the Party that mattered that he was interested in the Education portfolio, had been reading up on pedagogy – or an Ambassadorship somewhere. *Why not?* Elise had often told him he was a man of charm and force, attractive to women, envied by men, no mere soldier to do the dirty work required of the present but a superior who should be raising his eyes to the future, when this terrible war would end, and there would be no one left to butcher, and strong, clever leaders would be needed by Germany. Times would be happier. No more awful duties. Their children would fondle the Führer's dogs.

In the early hours of Christmas morning, he is working at the drawing board in his study, small glass of whisky at hand. His pencils moving carefully, cross-hatching, filling in. A slide-rule measuring out the distances and scales, a compass tracing circles that will be artificial islands for the cameramen. The larger of the ships will be launched down a gangway, the smaller, the more fragile, lowered into place by three vast cranes, the whole spectacle enthrallingly torchlit from a diagonal line of pontoons moored across the surface of the lake.

Lately he has been suffering a recurring irrational dread, that an air raid is unleashed as the Führer takes his seat in the grandstand. Those prows and poop-decks and figureheads burning. Turrets of sparks gushing into the sky over Nemi. Yellow-black flames, Elise's silhouette weeping. The stench of ancient pitch. It is hard to sleep. So he draws, pyjama sleeves up, measures the angles, sips whisky. It helps to kill the time.

At noon yesterday, the scheduled telephone call came from the Duty Officer in Rome. The city was unusually quiet. No burglaries for two nights, little of the usual seasonal drunkenness or curfew-breaking, no women reporting molestation, no petty thefts or public disorders.

'It would almost make one wonder, sir.'

'I know what you mean.'

'I feel something might be afoot, sir. We have a prisoner here, a Communist, he might be close to talking. What are your orders?'

'Cancel all leave, will you, and shut the main highway. And close all the bridges. I'll be with you in half an hour.'

He had led the interrogation personally, but the student did not break. The body was taken away in a mailbag, so the neighbours wouldn't notice. One doesn't want to discomfit people at Christmastime.

It is to the Nemi house that the second telephone call comes from the Gestapo sergeant-on-duty through the cold, sleety hours after midnight on Christmas Eve. A patrol trooper has reported an unusual nightwalker, a man bearing a false identity card. Through a misunderstanding he has not been arrested, is at large in the city. At present thought to be heading for Trastevere.

Hauptmann doodles on the drawing board, scrawls a triple spiral while he listens. Call completed, he enters the living room. Three-thirty in the morning – far too late for the children to be awake – but they've been unable to sleep, Christmas has taken hold. He blames himself for overexciting them earlier by his talk of the astonishing gifts they'd be receiving: chocolate money, clockwork soldiers, a doll with real hair, a fort, a toy aeroplane that flies. By firelight, Elise is reading them a story, 'Hansel and Gretel', and sharing their daughter's mug of hot chocolate. He does a thing that always makes them laugh – *Oh, Daddy's making a moustache of the whipped cream!* Part of being a father is to clown for them, don't pitch yourself too high above the weak. Children must never fear Daddy.

The aromas of cinnamon and cloves, an incense of burned brown sugar. Foil stars and scarlet candles have been placed in the living room windows, a line of lemonade bottles on the sill. He hears the telephone buzz briskly again, down the corridor, in his study. Elise stumbles away to answer it.

'Are you and Mummy friends again?' his daughter asks.

'We are always friends.'

'Are you going to fight again?'

225

'No, we're not.'

'I hate it when you fight.'

'Even friends have fights sometimes.'

'Are you getting a divorce?'

'Don't be silly.'

As he ruffles his daughter's yellow hair, she yawns and curls up. Her brother gives a chuckle, bulge-eyed with tiredness, and squeezes his father's hand. Their hair smells of the carbolic shampoo Elise makes them use. How miraculous, these children, with their mother's charm and witty serenity. If only she would not drink so much. He wonders what the matter is.

To hear their breathing lengthen as they approach sleep is one of the great and healing pleasures, often raises tears of raw protectiveness. Elise enters the living room, haughtily beautiful, in a powder-blue dressing robe and pyjamas and a mismatched pair of slippers. 'Paul,' she murmurs. 'They say it's an emergency.'

'Damn them,' he replies, unpeeling himself from the sofa.

'I'll make coffee,' she says. 'In case you need to go in.'

'I shan't be going anywhere.'

The Duty Officer apologises. A further report has arrived. The curfew-breaker observed earlier would seem to match the appearance of the priest whose photograph is on the office noticeboard.

'The priest? You're certain?'

'Reasonably certain, sir.'

'Where is he now?'

'Not quite sure, sir. We're looking.'

'I'll be there in thirty minutes.'

He hurries up the stairs to his bedroom, takes off his pyjamas, hands shaking. From the clothes-rail near the window he pulls his pressed uniform, dons it quickly. Wind rattles the windowpane. Mice tippet in the walls. In the pier glass, he adjusts the death's-head epaulettes, shines the peak of the black cap with a spat-on handkerchief.

'What has happened, Paul,' she says, slurring. 'To make you smile so?'

'It seems Christmas has come. Kiss the children goodnight.'

28

The moon creeps behind a drumlin of smoky cloud.

Blon Kiernan leads him by flashlight through the darkness of the rear garden, the munch and champ of icy gravel underfoot, marram grass through stones, the croaks of woken birds, to the rusted old gate that opens onto the coach alley.

As the gate clunks behind him, he hears the heavy working of the lock, the thunk of old bolts being pulled, her receding footsteps.

Solitude clutches like a jailer.

The alley is narrow and furrowed. Ruts filled with filthy ice. He makes his way past the stable doors and along to the street, which he reckons must be Via Cimarosa, and edges around the corner, heading north.

Stops.

That sound?

Over there, from the doorway.

The click of a pistol's safety catch.

Or the whirr of an insect?

The broad street is empty, traffic lights clacking from green to orange.

He waits thirty seconds.

No one there.

Mind playing tricks. He hastens onward, coughing. The fabric of the unfamiliar coat smells of pipe smoke and sweat, of hedgerows and mothballs and mildew. Tired, you sense the fairies, an old saying of his grandparents. He gulped a bowl of rigatoni before leaving the Kiernans, now regrets the onsetting heaviness, the longing for sleep.

Again comes the *snick*. He turns.

The heat of his breath mists his spectacles to fog. Cleaning them on his handkerchief, he hears a *cha* that might be a suppressed sneeze. Fifty metres behind him, near that news-stand outside the side entrance to the chapel.

Should he run? Stay silent? Could he make it back to the Kiernans if he bolted?

A skeletal fox hobbles out from behind the news-stand, gull in maw, urinates on a fire hydrant, gives a dull, rasping bark.

Now, the moan of the bombers, high above Rome. Goggled, starey men in their cramped glass cockpits, ten miles up, beyond the range of the ack-acks, fingertips poised on release buttons. In the bowels of every death machine, sixteen tonnes of dynamite. Enough to obliterate half a town.

Seventeen years ago, that night flight from Orly. Not long ordained, he spent a winter ministering at St Gabriel's in Archway, standing in for a curate who was ill. He and two confrères, a Glaswegian and a South African, had gone to Paris for a rugby international, had stayed at the Collège des Irlandais. En route back to Beaconsfield, a storm raged up out of the Channel without warning; the little Airco 16 had been battered. The dizziness, the nausea. The wrench of timber splintering, the screams of the passengers. He had prayed, had pleaded. Felt certain he would die. Somehow, inside the terror was a bead of certainty that he was redeemed, the afterlife was real as that storm. But the other priests had not felt that; the Glaswegian left the ministry a year later and married. The South African had taken to drinking.

Turning, he faces into the blackness of the side street, crossing quickly to the shadows by the chapel's high wall, past the railings of the Franciscan cemetery. Bleak statues of the martyrs adorning the mausoleums. Broken, marble fingers groping at the boughs.

So cold now, and silent, as the moon reappears. Its shadowed, unblinking eye.

Across a piazza where every shutter is dark.

A strange fluttering above him.

At first, he thinks they're moths.

In spiralling, dreamlike, downward glide, white swallows in a murmuration, or a flock of youngling doves, silver in creaming moonlight.

Dozens become scores, hundreds, thousands, swooping, coasting, dipping, rustling. As the first of them float within reach of his grasp, he sees they are pieces of paper.

Falling, they flutter around him, drifting, dancing, a snowfall of black-smudged white.

Flapping against the windows of apartment blocks and cars, into dustbins and prattling fountains, over park benches, steeples, the domes of old Rome, the ghetto, the empty tables, the parks and palazzi, the slopping, gurgling Tiber, the barracks and pillars, the highway towards Nemi, to the cobblestones in waterlogged silence.

A moth dances before his eyes, floating on the breeze, backing and forthing, upping and downing, as though animated by his desire to clutch it. When, finally, he grasps it, the paper is damp; ink blackens his fingers as he reads.

PROUD ROMANS!
TAKE COURAGE
THIS IS YOUR FINAL CHRISTMAS UNDER TRYANNY
LIBERATION IS COMING
SABOTAGE THE ENEMY IN EVERY WAY YOU CAN
THE DAYS OF THE NAZIFASCIST OCCUPATION ARE DYING
HAPPY CHRISTMAS TO YOU AND YOUR FAMILY
DESTROY THE INVADER
LONG LIVE ITALY
LONG LIVE THE ROMANS
GENERAL CLARK
UNITED STATES ARMY

The memory comes back to him through the sleet and the fall of wet leaflets. That dark October afternoon, two months ago, the week the Jews were deported. The young Ethiopian seminarian had found him in the Library to say there was a visitor in the Reception Room, a lady that appeared distressed. The rain was atrocious, had emptied the streets. Choir rehearsal had been postponed. Danger felt close. By now, the patrols were passing the gates of the Collegio three times hourly. Fascist police had been seen photographing the building.

In the large room downstairs, she was seated by the window, which someone had forgotten to close. The rain brought in the aromas of earth and the garden. Her hair was wet, in string-like straggles, and the shoulders of her raincoat, which was too large for her, were dark. He asked if she wanted a towel.

'*Bitte*,' she replied quietly. He rang for the servant.

Nothing was said while they waited. He knew who she was. She smoked, stared into the ashtray. He wondered what she would say. The servant came in, listened, hurried from the room, came back a minute later with the towel, went again.

He turned toward the empty fireplace while the visitor dried her hair. The act seemed too intimate to be watched.

When she had finished, she asked with her eyes if she might light another cigarette. He nodded, pushing the onyx ashtray across the table towards her.

'Thank you,' she said, 'for agreeing to see me at such short notice.'

He offered no reply. It was probably a trap.

'You are wondering, I think, why I am here,' she continued, her clipped, formal English plain and elegant.

'I have not had the time to wonder that.'

'I am most anxious. Forgive me.'

'Frau Hauptmann—'

'Might I ask a glass of water?'

He filled a tumbler from the stone jug on the table and she drank it in three swallows. It occurred to him that he should have requested the servant to remain, or that he should send for the Rector; that this conversation should be witnessed. Her wedding ring was unusually slender, like a piece of bronze twine. It brought the presence of who had placed it there into the room.

'There is a matter I would like to discuss with you,' she said. 'A private, family matter. If I might ask your assistance.'

'Are you a Catholic?'

'A bad one.'

'Is it a spiritual question?'

'In its way.'

'Does he know you are here, Frau Hauptmann?'

'No, he doesn't. Not yet.'

'There is nothing that I wish to say to you, Frau Hauptmann, but I am willing to listen. For ten minutes, no more. By that clock on the mantelpiece. After that, if you wish I will send for another priest, a confrère. You may speak with him in full confidence, of course.'

'It is you and only you that I wish to speak with, Monsignor.'

'Why is that?'

230

'Because I am lost and do not happen to know another priest in Rome.'

'You don't know me either.'

'I have heard my husband mention you.'

'Charmingly, I'm sure.'

'Violently. Angrily. But not always. There are moments.'

'Are there indeed.'

'He sometimes says that in different circumstances you and he might have been friends.'

'Rubbish.'

'In another life.'

'This is this life.'

'Unfortunately.'

'Frau Hauptmann—'

'I have come to ask your protection.'

'In what sense?'

'I wish to enter the Vatican City as a political refugee from Germany. To repudiate National Socialism. With my family.'

A door slammed in the room above. The heavy clock placked.

'I have considered the matter thoroughly,' she said, 'and am ready.'

'You expect me to believe this?'

'It is true.'

'With your family, including your husband? The commander of Rome's Gestapo?'

'I believe his wish is the same as mine but that he is afraid to face it.'

'What is the basis of this belief?'

'A wife's instincts.'

'Have you discussed this matter with your husband or not?'

'The fact that you have never been married is clear. If one may say so with respect.'

'What does that mean?'

'Merely that sometimes in a marriage there are understandings. Silences. The couple are moving towards a moment that has not been articulated in words. But they know it, all the same. What was once believed is over. Sometimes not discussing a subject is a way of discussing it.'

'I ask you a last time. Have you discussed it with your husband or not?'

'I intend to do so this afternoon.'

'Frau Hauptmann, you'll forgive me for not seeing you out. I have pressing matters to attend to. Good evening.'

'He is a caring, considerate husband. A most utterly devoted father. That is his essence, his true nature. He supports his parents financially, also mine, from a salary that is not large.'

'Don't talk rot, would you, Frau Hauptmann. Now I insist that you leave. Take your farrago of untruths and self-deceptions with you.'

'I did not marry a Nazi.'

'This conversation is over.'

'We shall be in St Peter's Square at five to midnight tonight. All I ask is a chance. Do not close the door on us. I beg you. Mercy for my children, if not me.'

'Go now, Frau Hauptmann. Never come here again.'

Angry, he left the room and returned to his work but at quarter to midnight had entered the square, pretending to take photographs of the full moon.

He drifted between the hissing fountains, the obelisk and the steps, aiming his camera at the ocean of the sky. Rain and the curfew meant nobody was in the vast space but for a trio of street sweepers who worked a slow way around the colonnade, occasionally calling out instructions to one another or crossing to their arch-backed truck to empty out a bag of rubbish. By midnight, they too were gone.

The October moon in his lens was a yellow-tinged coin. The great bells tolled. No one came.

The fountains slowed to a dribble. Then, silence.

Had she been fishing for intelligence? He tried to remember what he had said to her in the Reception Room. He wouldn't put it past Hauptmann to use his own wife as a tout. Perhaps he should go to the Rector this minute.

Ten past. Quarter past. A lone cormorant squawked.

A vision assailed him of the obelisk toppling into the square, bombs exploding around it, hails of shrapnel. Augustus's armies had brought it from Egypt on a vast silver barge, the largest vessel the world had ever seen. For twenty centuries the pillar had been tortured by the weather of Rome. Any night, it might fall. Would he see it?

Twenty past.

Half past.

Photographs of the moon.

At quarter to one a gust blew around the square, raising cold and grit. As he pocketed his camera to leave, and lifted his collar to the night, the black, bulletproof Mercedes purred into view, halting at the Vatican line.

Steam rose from its hood. Headlamps darkened.

The two children emerged abruptly, as though someone had pushed them, each bearing a cardboard suitcase. The girl had with her a doll, the boy a teddy bear. Then came their mother, then Hauptmann in civilian clothing.

All four walked to the perimeter, Elise Hauptmann fighting tears, the children bumping their cases along the cobbles. On her back was a hiker's rucksack, under her arm an umbrella. Hauptmann did not wave as they walked away. Tugging a bottle from his pocket, he took a long, spilling swig, hurled it through the air in the direction of the obelisk but it smashed on the wall of the fountain.

'*Are you happy, Priest?*' he roared. 'To have stolen my family? Planting stupidities in my wife's head in order to trap me? I see you there in the darkness, you skulking, sly bastard. Come out, you filthy thief. Here's your loot.'

Elise Hauptmann bowed her head, sobbing hard, as she kept walking, children beside her.

'I told her, *go if you wish*,' her husband howled, 'only *never come back*. Never contact me again. Desert me and you're dead. *You think you can bait me, O'Flaherty?* Take them. Do your worst. *I'm still here.* You have murdered me, Priest. But look hard, *I'm still here.* Be afraid, there is nothing else you can do to me now. *You have shot your last arrow.* You cur.'

Returning to the Mercedes, Hauptmann entered. The engine chugged on. The headlamps glowed large as he began the very slow three-point turn, their yellow beams sweeping the square.

Imploding into tears, the little boy turned and ran for the car, hurtling, spilling his suitcase, crying out '*Vati, bitte geh' nicht*,' followed by his weeping sister, and now, by their mother, whose left shoe came off as she ran through the billow of her children's spilled clothes.

The boy pounded on the back window as the Mercedes continued inching away. He followed, begging his father to let him in, not to go, and his sister wailed, too, in a terrible rending scream, '*Verlasse uns nicht, Vati. Es tut uns leid!*'

Daddy, don't leave us, we're sorry.

The Mercedes paused for a moment before permitting them to enter.

Then heavily, slowly drove away.

October. Two months ago. Taillights in the mist.

The crossroads, rejected.

The last chance, declined.

Now, in the small hours of Christmas morning, he seems to remember a sight he never saw, Hauptmann at that wheel. Driving in silence.

Cigarette smoke. Gear-grind. His children's sobs.

Why didn't you stop him? mocks the shadow.

There was more you could have done.

He walks on, towards the backstreet, feeling followed.

The sidecar in which Hauptmann is being carried feels frail as an egg. On the ride down from Nemi, through the dark, wet meadows, away from the lake and the cinnamon-scented children, he loads his Luger with seven high-pressure cartridges, checks there are more in his tunic pocket, calculates the hour to come.

He has given his orders. No arrest, nothing hasty.

The priest is to be tracked; a list of his movements compiled. The message is going out over the radio now. Commander Hauptmann will take charge of the surveillance when he arrives in the city in twenty-seven minutes. Wake his driver. Prepare the Mercedes for collection at Gestapo headquarters. Be sure Interrogation Cell Zero is free.

The forest track wends down towards the highway for Rome and the pillion car bounces with every jounce and sharp swerve, bolts and rockers creaking, engine razzing like a hornet, but the rider, a heavy man, stands hard on the accelerator and soon they are gunning towards the amber glint of the *autostrada* lights, up ahead, through the winter-thinned trees.

'Faster,' calls Hauptmann. 'Get your foot off the brake.'

The box of ammunition in his pocket gives a glum little rattle as though wanting to assent to the urging.

Over the speed-mounds leading to the barricade at the edge of the clearing, the troopers Hitler-saluting as the red rail is lifted, the orange-purple glow of a brazier on their helmets. He greets their raised arms with a wave. Brave lads, so far from their parents at Christmastime. Tomorrow he will get the cook to bring them a turkey, plum cake, a bottle of schnapps. But better – *why not?* – to serve them himself. He and Elise will visit the barrack-house, perhaps bring the children. An old military nobleness, to swap roles on Christmas Day. All officers should remember they were once common soldiers. They'll sing '*Stille Nacht*' together. He hopes Elise won't slur.

As the compound's exit gates are approached, the dirt track becomes gravelled, and the floodlight blazes on a young woman pinned to a pine trunk by two troopers. She fights back with such vigour, landing punches and head-butts, that a third trooper, a veteran old enough to be her grandfather, approaches with a truncheon, smashing her into a hedge.

Hauptmann barks for his rider to stop, steps out of the pillion car. The air smells of cold and petrol.

'What is going on here?'

'Sir, we came upon this trespasser twenty minutes ago, in the woods. This man was with her.' He nods towards a handcuffed, face-beaten youth. 'Courting couple, they said. He was armed with a shotgun. And making his way towards your house.'

'That's a lie,' the youth insists.

'Shut your mouth.'

As Hauptmann approaches the young woman, she goes to speak but lowers her head. The children are so fond of her, it will be hard to administer punishment. But perhaps there is an innocent explanation.

'Maria?' he asks the nanny. 'What were you doing in the forbidden zone? And who is this man?'

She says nothing.

'Shall I ask him?' Hauptmann says. 'Is that what you suggest?'

The youth displays no fear but stands straighter, taller, his lean torso visible through the ripped shreds of shirt. It is hard to dislike him. Something admirable about a streetfighter.

'Explain yourself,' Hauptmann says quietly. 'And tell me the truth.'

'I was out setting traps. I am a hunter. As I told them.'

'A poacher?'

'I strayed into these woods by accident. My torch stopped working and anyway, there is no fence.'

'Sir, there is,' a trooper snaps.

'It was cut.'

'Because *you* cut it.'

'Every farmer for ten kilometres around knows the extent of this property,' Hauptmann says. 'It is clear you have been lying to my men.'

'I am not a farmer. Until recently I worked at the cement factory in Velletri. Before it was bombed. My livelihood is gone. And this has nothing to do with Maria, she's just a girl I know from the village.'

'What was she doing here with you?'

'Walking.'

'You are aware of course that poaching is a capital offence.'

'What is a man to do when his children are hungry?'

'Hold out your hands.'

The youth does as commanded.

'I do not think you work in a cement factory. You look soft. Like a city girl.' Hauptmann's men laugh, a sound he enjoys hearing. A good officer should always be admired by his soldiers. 'You are a Partisan. A Communist. You know the fate that awaits you.'

'I am no Partisan, no Communist, I cannot afford politics. I am nothing but a father desperate to feed his children on Christmas Day. You have children yourself. For pity's sake, let me go.'

'How do you know I have children?'

'Someone told me.'

'Who?'

'Sir, I – can't remember, it's well known, people talk.'

'Try a little harder. *What concern of yours are my children?*'

'I was speaking in a general way; they are none of my concern.'

'What is your name?'

'Luca Ricci.'

'You swear to me on your eternal soul that you are not a Partisan, Luca Ricci?'

'I swear it.'

'On your children's souls, too?'

'Of course.'

'Very good. You may leave. Just this once. Happy Christmas. Never again make the mistake of trespassing onto this compound. Understand me?'

As Luca Ricca turns to go, Hauptmann steps forward and fires through the back of the neck. Crossing to Maria Esposito, he shoots her in the forehead.

'They tried to escape,' he orders the sentries. 'Now, quickly. To the city.'

29

Crossing the tram tracks, breathless, he hastens through the passageway and into the Via Ventinovesimo.

Two figures are huddled near the advertising sign for the *Corriere della Sera*. Seeing him, one drops a lighted cigarette to the pavement; the other picks it up, tosses it into a stone trough by the garage.

The signal.

A heron gives a shriek. Wind blusters up. Approaching, he now sees that the figures are both in priestly clothing.

Without acknowledging him, they start northward, quickly, almost lurching, in the direction of the widening, statue-adorned end of the piazza. A dozen paces behind, he follows.

Ahead of him, they bolt into an unseen laneway. When he catches up, rounding the corner, one figure has vanished. The other is revealed to be a young woman.

'*Andiamo*,' she says, nodding briskly towards the half-opened shutters of the abandoned theatre.

Through the glass-strewn foyer surveyed by a vast, shattered mirror, the moon in a hundred shards on the floor. Down the aisle through the burst-apart, burned velvet seats, scorched putti capering on opera boxes. Up the carpeted steps to the stage, the slink of a dozen meagre cats around a papier-mâché shipwreck. Pools of fallen plush.

Now into the wings, her torch-beam on bare, knotted boards. A stench of mould, of blue-rotting oranges. Past hulking, draped shapes, plaster heads still bewigged, the haggish ghoul of an upturned mop in a bucket. Down a flight of trembling wooden stairs, through the fire-escape doors, into a yard giving out on an alley.

Turning, she asks, 'Are you ready? It will be difficult.'

'I understand.'

Nodding, she pulls a hessian hood from inside her jacket, places it over his head, tightens the fasten-cord.

'Take my arm,' she whispers. 'Two steps down. Then left.'

In blackness, he feels himself led, but he falters, stumbles, hot mist in his eyes, the tutting impatience of the young woman. Then someone else has joined, is clutching him by the left elbow, and they're flurrying him through what feels like a garden or a terrace, through a smell of wet vegetation and oversweet winter lilac. He asks them to slow, but the woman says they can't. Time has run on, they are late.

Ropes of pain in his thighs. A firestorm in his lungs.

He's aware of being helped across streets, the change from tarmacadam to cobbles. For a minute, the river feels close.

Not water, but sopping sedge and the tinkle of halyards. The thought looms that Mark Antony knew the stench of that sedge, that it pinkened the nightmares of Nero.

He does not want to get into the motorcar, feels a hand pressing down on his head. *We're lying you on the back seat, be quiet.* As he obeys, a heavy blanket stinking of wet dog is flung over him. The car jolts away; a bad driver, young? The woman whispers in staccato; the driver hisses back, coughing. After ten or a dozen minutes, the rear door is opened. He's hauled out, legs unsteady. She checks the hood is still tight.

'Careful,' she murmurs, 'do not be afraid,' as he's led into a building he can tell by the reek of smoke is a bombsite, and now up spiralling stone stairs as in a medieval castle's turret. He feels his spectacles slip loose, gropes through the hood of sacking to get them back on, begs the duo leading him to pause even a moment but they don't. The smell of their perspiration, the aroma of washed hair. Wooden doors roll open. A chain is clanked free.

Down what might be a concrete ramp, the stench of gasoline and auto grease; bolts being unshot, the heavy *skreek* of metal gates. A blinding wash of thirst. Cold air. He's outside.

'All right,' says a man's voice. 'You're here. Count to twenty. Then take off the hood, not before.'

'Where do I go, then?'

'Count to twenty. *Buona fortuna.*'

By the time he has unhooded, there is no one on the long street of apartment blocks. Its thousand shuttered windows are dark.

From somewhere in the middle distance, the bleat of a police siren. He blinks,

239

after-images of hydrants and doorways on his retinae. Behind him, the locked gates of a mechanic's workshop, the '*O*' in the '*AUTO*' sign a cartoon archery target.

Wiping runnels of sweat from his forehead and arms with the hood, he pushes it into a dustbin.

On the corner, a scallop-shelled fountain in a little archway set into a cobbled wall. The coldness of the water. He bathes his wrists and throbbing face. Wheezing, sneezing, he looks at his watch. Twenty minutes to five. The stillness of Rome before dawn.

Across a wall, a stencilled notice in German exclaims:

'*Strassen gesperrt. Bandengebiet.*'

Streets closed. Gang Area.

Their code for the Partisans.

The thrown pebble turns him.

Fifty metres away, between the tramlines, a bin lid is rolling.

Slow as a rowboat, he approaches.

He halts at a gateway, through which he can see a Fiat up on bricks, a relic from the twenties, cracked windscreen, gull-ripped soft-top.

After a moment, the signal.

So quiet; hardly audible.

A scratchy gramophone record playing the *Moonlight Sonata*.

He enters the arched portico, past the mailboxes and dustbins, crosses a tidy, pave-slabbed courtyard, the glazed pots shining.

Behind him, he hears the heavy gate being shut but he doesn't turn. Ahead, the door opens, a bulb blinks on in the narrow hallway. He enters, walks through the corridor, out the back door, across a laneway, into the courtyard of a much older house.

In a window, a middle-aged woman in an indigo dressing gown and hairnet is smoking, avoiding his glance, looking up at the dawn. They don't know each other's names, never will.

Pushing open the door, she crushes the cigarette out beneath her slipper, steps backwards.

Entering the living room, he crosses to the fireplace.

The curtain to the courtyard has been pulled closed by a barefoot teenaged girl in boy's trousers and work shirt. It is clear she and the middle-aged woman are mother and daughter.

The gramophone plays. Framed tintypes on the walls. Old men in military uniform, children in First Communion clothes by a lake. A poster for a performance of *Tosca*, 'Beniamino Gigli' in bold red. A dog-basket under a rococo mahogany table. A twelve-armed candelabrum.

A lidless, pewter teapot bristling with pencils and pens. In the corner, an eerie, firelit, cast-iron-wheeled apparatus that it takes him a moment to recognise as a sewing machine.

She asks with her eyes if he is ready. He nods that he is.

Pulling a scissors from her pocket, the seamstress approaches. He takes off the old overcoat, hands it to her, she lays it on the workbench, parts its pleats, begins cutting, from its depths. She retrieves the taped packets of banknotes, working carefully, methodically, in wordless concentration, now circling steadily around the laid-out coat. The deft, slick snip of the scissor-blades. Frayed lengths of fabric fall to the rug. The girl kneels, brushes them into a large metal dustpan, empties it into the seething hearth.

Through a door towards a candlelit pantry, he sees that a third woman, far older, in housecoat and pince-nez spectacles, is standing over a table, slicing open the stacks of banknotes with a steak knife. Distributing them between envelopes, which she places in a shoebox. Glancing up, she wordlessly offers a glass from the bottle of wine at her side and seems unsurprised when he shakes his head.

Nearby, on marble platters, three fruitcakes cut into hollowed-out halves. She wraps bundles in foil, wedging them into the cakes, pushing the halves back together, now sheeting them with wraps of yellow marzipan. The girl enters the pantry, fetches a bowl of unset icing from a cupboard; starts into icing the cakes as the old woman nods approbation, sometimes guiding her, now taking her wrist, showing her to move the spatula smoothly, deftly.

The Beethoven skips, returns to its beginning.

A new old coat is brought for him, and he dons it.

Not one word is uttered during the drop, which takes less than a hundred seconds. As he goes, the seamstress dips her fingertips into a Holy Water font by the door and touches them briskly to his forehead.

Two masked youths are waiting in the street, he permits them to blindfold him; he is walked for a time, then driven in a car, then walked again until he hears the river. 'Count to ten,' they whisper, 'good luck,' as they go, and he waits for the receding footsteps to be no longer audible before he uncovers his pulsing eyes.

Ahead of him, the Tiber. Over rooftops, the dome of St Peter's.

Quickly along the quay, into strong slabs of wind, past the high, rusted gates of the prison. Up the steep steps of the passageway, through a sloping street so narrow that the front rooms of the apartments look into one another, and the washing lines strung between them are hard to tell apart with their buntings of grey chemises and socks.

Some brave Roman has draped a tattered tricolour over a half-collapsed balcony, the red, white and green faded by laundering and quarterlight. Across the flag, the patchwork words '*Viva l'Italia!*'

The clank of a shutter. He stops.

Birds churring faintly.

So quiet.

He can hear the river moving, the shush-and-lapping on old, cold stone, the swaying of sedge in the shallows near the banks, water rats nuzzling beneath the bridges.

Twenty past five. Vital to make haste.

He turns. Via Segundo. Rain starts to fall.

The back streets that lead to the Basilica.

Ambling towards him out of the shadows, at an easy, measured pace, two men in grey raincoats, homburgs low. He knows they have seen him; too late to turn back. They pause beneath the only lamp left unbroken on the street, light cigarettes, begin to talk, gesturing, nodding, as though explaining something contended, but their voices are so low that he can make nothing out.

They're standing sidelong, half-facing away from him, but he knows that doesn't matter. Gestapo men can see out of the backs of their skulls. Don't pause, walk steadily. If you bolt, they will catch you. They're armed and half your age. You are Marco Mancuso.

'*Buongiorno,*' one of them murmurs.

'*Buon Natale,*' he replies.

They're not SS, he sees now. Too relaxed, conversational. An older woman with a suitcase approaches from the end of the street, they greet her with filial embraces and stroll away together in the direction of town.

He hastens around the corner.

Into Hauptmann's jutting Luger.

Everything is quiet. The Nazi's eyes shining.

242

The shock is like a punch. A pummel to the stomach. A thousand times, a million, he has anticipated this moment, but the scald of it shocks him, the physical closeness of the other, the veins in his eyelids, the pallor of his lips, the throbbing worm in his temple, the whiff of his steadying breath.

Far above, the drone of bombers, grey light in the sky.

From the gun battery dug into the peak of the Palatine Hill, the searchlights spring on, white beams criss-crossing the clouds, and the ack-acks begin to rattle. Hauptmann half-turns, oddly childlike, as though magnetised by the music.

'Walk,' he says. 'Ahead of me. Hands high.'

Down an alleyway reeking of bins. The Mercedes waiting at the end.

Hauptmann opens the rear door, kicks him into the seat, climbs quickly in beside him.

'Proceed,' Hauptmann commands the driver. 'Gestapo Headquarters.'

The car moves off, at first slowly, then climbing sighingly through the gears, Hauptmann lighting a cigarette, now seeming to frown at the match before blowing it out. For a time, he says nothing, as though comforted by the soothe of the engine. The car stops at amber lights, allowing an early tram to truckle past.

'I can answer the question that is upmost in your mind,' Hauptmann says. 'Your friends are as good as dead. By tonight or tomorrow morning I shall have extracted from you their names and whereabouts. Their final knowledge will be that you betrayed them.'

The walkie-talkie receiver crackles on the Nazi's left lapel, then a softer sound, murmurous, like a waterfall heard from a distance.

'Perhaps it is even yet not too late, Monsignor. Are you prepared to be reasonable? I am a believer in mercy.'

'Go to hell.'

'Ah, here is Via Tasso, Monsignor. Your final address on this Earth.'

The driver gets out, ascends the three steps into the building. Lamps go on in windows. Now Hauptmann steps out, yawning, walks around the back of the Mercedes.

'Exit slowly, Monsignor. With your hands on your head.'

He does as commanded, Hauptmann regarding him.

'The high-and-mighty Monsignor. Where is your Choir now?'

'You poor man,' O'Flaherty says.

'Why so?'

'Have you truly not realised what this entire charade was about?'

'Enlighten me.'

'What time is it, Hauptmann?'

'Thirteen minutes past six.'

'Just so.'

'Meaning?'

'Thirteen minutes ago, your wife entered Vatican City with your children and sought asylum. All we needed was a decoy you'd bite at, to get you out of the way. Elise swore you'd fall for it. I didn't believe you'd be so gullible.'

Hauptmann smiles bleakly. 'This is the best you can do?'

'News of their defection will be announced on the BBC World Service in seventeen minutes. The Vatican photographer is with your wife and children now at the British Ambassador's apartment. A sea plane is waiting at Ostia to take them to Dover. Your wife intends to seek British citizenship.'

'Monsignor, don't you know that it is a sin to lie?'

'Telephone your villa. No one will answer.'

'You think me so weak-minded that I would actually test this nonsense?'

'A photograph of your family with the British Ambassador has just now been cabled to Berlin. To every newspaper in Europe and to the Führer's personal office. Your wife's statement condemns National Socialism and predicts its imminent defeat by the Allies, a defeat she now pledges to do all in her power to support. She adds that you yourself know the war to be lost by Germany. That you plan the assassination of Hitler.'

'Rubbish.'

'I have a signed copy of her statement, here in my breast pocket. Would you like to see it?

'DON'T MOVE.'

'Calm down.'

'Do not tell me what to do.'

'Step closer, take it out of my pocket. Or I'll do it? As you wish.'

'Be silent, I warn you. *No more of your lies.*'

'I realise this is a dreadful blow to you. The loss of your family. Never to see them again is a terrible fate, I know. She asked me to say that she left a goodbye letter for you. On her dressing table at your villa. With her wedding ring.'

Hauptmann makes for his radio mouthpiece, O'Flaherty uppercuts the

Luger from the Nazi's right fist, not a heavy punch, but fast and accurate, an ice-hard, driven drub, the gunmetal slicing open his own knuckles so he cries out in pain, the pistol somersaults into a wall before clattering to the gutter, and he dummies, as though making a snatch for it, as Hauptmann dips, grasping, but the slimy handle is slippery and the pistol spins in gutter water and the priest is *in the car, at the steering wheel,* revving, spots of blood on the bullet-proof windscreen and now the Mercedes is moving.

Hauptmann grabs at the door handle. The jolt rips his left shoulder from its socket.

Is the screech out of his own mouth? Is it tyre-rubber shrieking? The choke of black smoke as the car jounces away from him, sheering like a colt unleashed. That stench of burned Firestones. The bawl of the engine. Smoke spewing from the wheel-wells. Vomit of exhaust in his face. The *blam* of his Luger, stink of cordite, wet lead.

Now he's running after the Mercedes, swim-headed with pain, but running, *running,* shooting into the blackness, the car strikes a news-stand, graunches, reverses, he kneels, like a marksman, one accurate shot is all he needs, bullets crunching off its armour, sparking away in silver flakes, and the Mercedes squeals and rasps around the corner whose name he doesn't know and his Luger screams its fury but the Mercedes is gone, roaring down the blitzkrieg where his shoulder socket should be, in the direction of the rain-boosted Tiber.

He bellows for help, the SS driver runs from the building, stupefied, cursing, the priest has escaped, Hauptmann staggers from door to door along Via Tasso, but nobody answers.

Pounding, threatening.

'*I need help.*'

Somehow, in the agony, he sees the Mercedes speeding through Rome, saluted by sentries, barricades lifting. Tottering after it, he's lost on a filthy back street, a hail of bricks and chimneypots raining on him from the rooftops. Minutes later, delirious with pain, he is encountered by German patrolmen to whom he manages to stammer what has happened, but when the Sergeant radios for the Mercedes to be stopped at any cost, the troopers guarding the bridge are discomfited, sensing trickery.

Fire on Hauptmann's car? The Gestapo commander? Sign your own death warrant first.

Now the Mercedes has crossed the Ponte Cavour, has been logged approaching the Interior Ministry at speed. A sentry in a third-floor window radios an emergency. 'Hauptmann is running amok.'

Over the bridge, the Contessa is waiting in the rendezvous place, the porch of an abandoned bakery. Right hand bleeding, he jumps from the Mercedes. Reaching into it, she plunges her lighted cigarette down the maw of the fuel tank, leads him through the maze of passageways and cloistered footpaths where the stolen motorcycle is waiting, climbs onto the bike, he behind her; she kicks the starter, swerves, curses over her shoulder, 'Head down, Hugh, head down,' gunning along the passageways, the labyrinth of dark lanes, as behind them the explosion roars, smoke roiling and dense, blown down through the narrow back streets into the Piazza del Risorgimento, where it stains the awnings black.

In the shadowed doorway of the Musei Vaticani, Derry and Osborne are waiting, beckoning, waving, faces etched with anxious joy, summoning their friends in from out of the rain that is pouring its coldness on Rome. He staggers, slammed by breathlessness, the Contessa's shoulder supporting him. 'Gentlemen,' she says, 'may I present the doer of the impossible.' Embraces and back-slaps, towels, flasks of tea – well, not exactly tea, as Sam Derry puts it, not the tea they deserve, but cloves in hot milk – well, not exactly milk, as Osborne remarks, but sock-flavoured toothpaste, dissolved. Through the corridors of the museums, keeping quiet, moving quickly, stumbling, gasping, a deep diver surfacing, half-carried by his companions, in serious, efficient silence, for the security guards are on duty and not all to be trusted, down the landings, up the staircase, through the Cappella Sistina, where he pauses a moment in the numb, white blaze that is the prayerfulness of a survivor, a joy that includes grief and loss. For his parents on Chrismas morning, for every friendship not made, for the escapees who will now live and the thousands who need them, for the numberless, nameless, suffering fallen for whom no one but their comrades ever fought. For Derry, Angelucci, Delia and May, for Osborne, Marianna and Giovanna Landini, praying beside him now, hand in his hand, who, often, when she recollects their dash to the Vatican that dawn, the Roman sky purpling the silhouetted statues, hears him singing a Puccini aria behind her, though she knows that can't have happened. For his sister and brothers, for everyone a prisoner, for all starved of mercy or force-fed on lies. But it's time to hurry along now, Derry says, quietly, arm around his shoulders, 'Lean here, Padre.'

'I do think you might address him as "Hugh" at this stage,' Osborne chuckles.

'I've a better idea,' says Derry. 'Been practising my Italian. Give me your arm, *mio fratello*.'

At Lake Nemi, Frau Hauptmann and her children sleep late on Christmas morning. Daddy won't be home for a while.

Near five o'clock that evening, Hugh O'Flaherty climbs to the roof of St Peter's, alone.

Domes and high dovecots. Campaniles. Seven hills. Stately, grey seabirds whirling in the mist. Chimneypots and steeples. The glister of early stars. Dusk is coaxing lamps on, all over the city. Torches glint from attic windows, carving lines through the smokefall. From Flaminio to Ponte, from Prati to Campo Marzio. Bridges. Palaces. Tenements. Fallen temples. He waits for the great bells to salute the close of day.

Afterwards, such silence.

Almost music.

————

Dear Mam and Dad,

Just a note from snowbound Rome.

I said Mass for you this morning, the feast of St Stephen.

In case I never told you: No one ever had more loving parents.

Thank you for my life.

Happy 1944.

Your Hugh

30

MARIANNA DE VRIES
November 1962
Statement in lieu of an interview

More die coming down Everest than perish on the way up. A fact known by soldiers and bank robbers everywhere. Every raid needs its getaway driver.

From the outset it had been agreed that Jo Landini would rendezvous with the mission-runner two kilometres from home and that a motorcycle was the best option, or at any rate the least-bad. One would never plan a Rendimento without plotting with fanatical assiduousness the safest way back to base. That was at Derry's insistence, fruit of his Sandhurst training. A mission-runner can get sloppy at the very end of the run; he's exhausted, falsely elated; it's the most dangerous few minutes. He needs help getting over the line.

Jo, as I have said, was a woman of immense personal courage. She insisted that she would be what we termed 'the guidelight' for the Christmas Eve Rendimento, a role she had fulfilled on seven previous missions and would reprise on a further five in early '44. Usually, we stole the motorcycle from the German army. A certain Londoner whom I need not name assisted in that respect. 'All's fair in love and war,' was his watchword.

I lay low for ten days, then fled into the Vatican. Delia Kiernan and her daughter had done the same. Apart from the further Rendimenti with which she was centrally involved, Jo did not leave Vatican City for the remainder of the German occupation. She and I lodged in May and Sir D'Arcy's quarters, to the amusement (perhaps the envy, she used to say) of certain ordained observers. An eminent Cardinal was once seen not quite kneeling to the keyhole but hanging about in the corridor as though awaiting an invitation to join the non-existent orgy. 'Perhaps we'll make it existent one evening when we're bored,' Sir D'Arcy said.

'One would need to be *quite* bored,' Jo rejoindered.

The flat, which had three rooms, was cramped enough but comfortable. Its little circular windows gave out on a garden. We played backgammon and parlour games. There were books. Sometimes we gazed in companionable silence at the mint-and-cherry Roman sunset, an event for which Sir D'Arcy always donned his Black Watch tartan smoking jacket. The peak of nightly excitement was choosing which pair of his carpet slippers to borrow and enduring his eye-watering tales of the corns that made his frequent recourse to such footwear inevitable. ('Good ladies, I have had bunions one could place a hat on and put up for election.') Food was in short supply and what passed for coffee tasted like sludge. But we had plenty of Piper-Heidsieck '33, thanks to May. The King was toasted respectfully by our British hosts at six every evening. People had worse early 1944s.

We became a quintet when Angelucci, too, took refuge with us, having got his wife and their children out to the relative safety of the countryside beyond Viterbo. She would die in a bombing raid in March, having briefly returned to Rome to visit a family member who was ill – this tragedy was some months ahead of us, as were many more.

For now, Angelucci proved an excellent cook – the art of eating well is to the Italians one of the highest arts. He was able to do a lot with very little ('like all Marxists,' Sir D'Arcy used to quip). Enzo could make a pasta of wheat and water, without eggs, a luxury we didn't possess, that, with a little pepper and Parmigiano, if we had it, would make one sing. Sir D'Arcy would wickedly tease him by saying, 'Dear boy, *all* the finest people in England are Communist these days, why, one can't throw a stick in the Magdalen dining hall without hitting a comrade or whatever they are. Pass the Nero d'Avola, there's a love.'

Angelucci was a magnificent person whose contribution was beyond measure. Even his habit of going about shirtless was forgivable. There are unfortunate people one meets who see food as merely bodily fuel. The Italians know that it is a very great deal more than that. When asked if he believed in God, Enzo used to answer that he believed in *risotto al radicchio e Gorgonzola* with a glass of something fragrant and one's friends. For him, there was no holier word in any language than '*mangiamo*'.

'Best answered with a silent Amen,' Jo Landini answered once, serving out the food.

'Contessa, we'll make a Communist of you yet,' Enzo responded.

'My dearest chef, you wouldn't have terribly far to go. Now for pity's sake, put on a shirt, we're eating.'

'Come the revolution,' remarked Sir D'Arcy, 'everyone shall travel First Class.'

'Count me out,' said Johnny May. 'I ain't toiling for the masses.'

'*Toiling*,' mocked Sir D'Arcy. 'You think being handsome is work.'

'If it is,' said Jo, 'he works hard.'

'Don't be talking of Communism in front of my daughter,' Delia said, both Kiernan ladies being our guests that night. 'She'll assassinate me in my sleep.'

'Mother, for God's sake.'

'Is there e'er a drop of wine? I've a thirst would sink ships.'

'Mother, you've had *enough*.'

'If I'm not given a drink this minute, it's my *own* shirt I'll take off.'

'Jesus Christ Almighty.'

'More pasta?'

There was not much room. People could become irritable. But if some of us jumped our trolleys, the others were forgiving.

In truth I remember it as a not unhappy time. Major Derry would often surface from his lair in the excavations, Ugo might pay us a visit for a hand or two of poker or lansquenet, games he played with unpriestly vehemence. In the end, at our insistence, he joined our household at the lodgings, a place to which he referred as 'the digs'. It was evident from intelligence reports that he was in very grave danger anywhere else. Indeed, it had been brought home to us rather sharply.

One February afternoon in St Peter's, two Nazi operatives in plainclothes arrived, with the intention of hustling him out of the Basilica and over the boundary. Thankfully, Enzo had by then assumed responsibility for Ugo's protection. A squad of fourteen escapees dressed as cowled monks – Enzo favoured Glaswegian dockworkers and Yugoslav miners – formed a covert diamond-pattern around the Monsignor whenever he entered a public area. The two plainclothesmen were shall we say assisted out of St Peter's that afternoon, unfortunately tripping on the steps. Several times. Nasty men, in a most unsporting manner they kept attacking Enzo's fist with their faces. I would imagine they recall the occasion now and again, even yet, for example whenever they need to move their jaws.

The bunks and hammocks in the flat – indeed, the little round windows, too – gave the place something pleasing, the feeling of a ship. In the evenings, to sustain the spirits or to tire ourselves towards sleep, we often sang an old Scottish song from those nights of rehearsal, gentlemen taking the verses, ladies the chorus.

> *Let us go, lassie, go*
> *To the braes of Balquhither,*
> *Where the blueberries grow*
> *'Mong the bonnie Highland heather;*
> *Where flie the deer and rae*
> *Lightly bounding altogether,*
> *Sport the lovelorn summer day*
> *On the braes of Balquhither.*
> *Let us go, lassie, go.*
> *Lassie, go.*

Funny thing, none of us had ever been to the Scottish Highlands, a place I never think about without hearing that song, near the end of the war in Italy, among backgammon pieces and glasses of Chianti, in our little *ménage à huit*.

The Christmas Eve mission succeeded. Hundreds of Books were safely moved from Rome into the countryside. We ran many further Rendimenti, perhaps fifteen or two dozen, between that Christmastime and late spring, 1944 – including one mission to steal or destroy Hauptmann's hoard of forged currency, another to smuggle a surgeon into a safehouse not two minutes from Gestapo headquarters, to attempt a lifesaving procedure on an escapee. But this is not the time to speak of those terrifying nights. Doubtless there will be other occasions. It became an era of great personal pain.

I suppose that what must be called tensions came to exist in the Choir, as the Allied advance on the city progressed. Ugo wished to aid deserting German conscripts, every one of whom was in peril of being beaten to death. Sir D'Arcy saw matters differently. The Monsignor and he quarrelled.

Cracks worsened. Foundations shifted. Harsh words buckled pillars. Things were said in the heat of argument that would have been better left unspoken.

Over the subsequent months, the Choir fell apart, as all good things will. Ugo and Sir D'Arcy stopped speaking. Ugo departed the flat.

There was innocence on both sides rather than guilt on either. Poor Sir D'Arcy, I believe, had misunderstood, had all along not quite seen the point. One can persuade oneself for a moment that the same song is being sung. But that is rarely the case, alas. What is happening is little more than the concretisation of a Venn diagram. Which isn't nothing, by the way. But there is more to life than geometry. My enemy need not of necessity be the enemy of my friend. But it helps, I suppose. There it is.

Attempts were made by the redoubtable Delia to mend burning bridges – I seem to remember a luncheon or something of that nature being mooted – but for some reason it never happened. I became so distressed by the implosion that, in the end, on an early June morning, I left, returning to my old apartment through the cold, scarlet dawn. On the way, I saw the spectral and astonishing sight of a lone American Army jeep heading towards St Peter's Square. Liberation had come to Rome.

Enzo and Jo would be awarded high honours by the Italian government, as was Ugo.

Dollman was lynched while trying to get out of the country. It was widely felt in Rome that he was in as much danger from Hauptmann as he was from the Romans, the two having fallen out badly when Hauptmann began suspecting his second-in-command of touting on him to Himmler. Sometimes I have seen it written that the National Socialist movement was a brotherhood. In fact, it was a hate-gang, led by inadequates and psychopaths, loyal as that species of poisonous frog that eats its own siblings after it has devoured everything else it can find. What is chilling is how many people permitted themselves to be led. 'Permitted', in fact, is not quite an active enough verb. Agreed in warm enthusiasm to be led.

Hauptmann was tried in 1948 for the murder of three hundred and thirty-five Romans in one night, retaliation for a Partisan bombing that killed thirty-three German soldiers. In the court it was detailed how he spent hours in his office that day, among his beloved files, compiling the death list, including Jews, old men, children, prisoners from Regina Coeli, several helpers of the Escape Line. Ten for every German. Plus five, to make certain. Taken to the Ardeatine Caves and gunned down.

He was tie-less in the dock, spoke quietly, often blinking hard or glancing about the courtroom in an odd, intense manner as though startled by something nobody else could see.

During the lunch break in the proceedings, I filed my report. The act of writing out what had happened made me vomit.

When the hearing resumed, it returned quickly to events at the caves. Photographs were displayed but it was difficult to look at them. A Nazi officer had waited at the entrance, Hauptmann's list in hand, on a clipboard. Most methodical. The prisoners were beaten from trucks, roped together in groups of five, led into the darkness, shot, bodies dumped where they fell. Hauptmann led the shootings in person, to give an example of leadership to his men.

Even working with such efficiency, the killings took all night – sometimes a prisoner did not die immediately and had to be finished off – but yes, Hauptmann said, probably some were buried still alive. The task was so arduous that, in order to complete it, he and his gunmen had to get out of their minds on brandy. At dawn, the mouth of the caves was dynamited and blocked with cement, and the Germans drove back to the city. Thousands of copies of a poster were already being plastered on the walls of Rome, warning that further reprisals would follow any Partisan attack.

There was an intense silence in the courtroom as sentence was handed down, apart from the faint sound of a stenographer trying not to weep. Hauptmann in the dock displayed no emotion whatever but turned the winder on his wristwatch as though correcting the time.

Life imprisonment without parole, to be served in Modena prison. Other Nazis involved in that night's horror escaped to Argentina.

Following painstaking work at the Ardeatine Caves, many belongings of those murdered there were recovered and identified. Pocket books, crucifixes, combs, gloves, love letters, paperbacks, pens. Some were placed in the Museum of the Occupation, the former Gestapo headquarters on Via Tasso, a place I have never been able to visit.

During the nine-month occupation of Rome, eighteen hundred Roman Jews were deported to the death camps. Fewer than twenty returned.

CODA

This is Your Life

31

THE CONTESSA GIOVANNA LANDINI

From an unpublished, undated memoir written after the war

There are cities where we feel part of the streetscape, not visitors but returned exiles. We are at home so completely yet inexplicably that fond thoughts are permitted: we must have lived here in a previous life or were conjured into being by one of the metropolis's pantheon of artists or poets, sculpted from its ancient stone.

When I was younger, London was that, for me.

In my twenties, newly a wife, I went four times with Paolo. We had visited during our courtship, too. The grey of the stately terraces was restful after Rome. The hymn of London rainfall on a gallery roof stirs recognitions, is somehow the music of the sublime. If there is a peace that passes all understanding, it is to awaken from lovers' bliss in London during murmurous rain, to stir in bed and hear it.

We spoke often of purchasing a town house, perhaps in Chelsea or South Kensington, but our marriage was to prove so brief that we never began the quest, and, for a time after he died, I was too broken to go there anymore, for always I felt he would come walking around the corner of Sloane Square, or wave to me from Claridge's window. Or step down into fog from one of those wonderful buses whose reds are always redder in memory.

But in the years after the war, I Londoned again. I felt I was returning to faith.

Old friends were looked up, concerts attended. Two brief love affairs (the phrase is not quite correct but things have to be called something) were had and were gently unregretted when they came to a courteous close. I was not free to fall in love. I never would be again. London gifted me that realisation, among others.

The last time I went there was early in 1963. The circumstances were unusual and memorable. I had by then taken a permanent apartment in the penthouse at the Savoy, with views over the Strand and the Thames. On the day I wish to tell about, a wintry Thursday in late February, my London chauffeur's wife had recently given birth and I did not want to bother with arranging a replacement so I rose early and started out for London airport on the Underground.

On that morning, the beeches and elms were just commencing to put on their spring finery: yellow chiffons, white buds that would be blossoms. But I was anxious. There was a question I needed to ask Hugh, a question I suspected he would not welcome. But I had made up my mind: it would be asked.

As I waited with my magazines and newspaper in a corner of the arrivals hall, my heart bumped like an ingenue's in a novel. I had not seen my friend in two years. Ill-health had assailed him, as I knew from his increasingly rare but increasingly amusing letters. His handwriting had deteriorated badly but he was still able to type.

Retirement, back in Ireland, was not suiting him well. He was living over a hardware store with his widowed sister, of whom he wrote in affectionate, slightly tolerant tones, as though she were a creature from a distant galaxy. (As no doubt she would have written of him!) But he missed his Roman life.

When he came through the gates, he looked irritable and alert, ruddy of face as ever, but was of course in the wheelchair to which his most recent stroke had consigned him, a vehicle he insisted on referring to as *la biga Romana*, the Italian word for a chariot. He had lost a little weight. In all my life I have never seen whiteness akin to the merino-wool-white his thick hair had turned to. The airport had provided a porter to push the chair, but Hugh would not hear of the possibility and kept flapping him away, insisting on 'going by my own steam'. As we embraced, tears overcame me. He gave the exasperated sigh I had long adored.

'Sweet Mother of James's Street, is this the way it's going to be?'

As we made our way through arrivals, the porter and Hugh conversed of something that I realised after a while must be the West Indies cricket team. I tried not to reveal that even the most rudimentary rules of cricket were as a long-dead language to me, a tongue I had no interest in acquiring.

Outside, the man fetched us one of those magnificent London taxis. My old friend and I climbed aboard into that ecstasy of blackness and leather-polish. The wheelchair was placed in the boot.

It was obvious that his speech had been affected quite severely by aphasia. He had told me of this in letters, but hearing it was another matter. I would not say that he was slurring; that would be inaccurate. It was more that he seemed uncommonly reluctant to speak, spoke with slowness, over-enunciation, not-quite-necessary deliberation, like a man who has taken too much wine but must converse with his wife's awful family. He permitted me to hold his hand as we rode into London.

He had not seen the city in a good many years. I was touched to hear him greet it again. 'Ah, there you are, Hammersmith. Ahoy, Shepherd's Bush.' The poet best-loved by Hugh was always Louis MacNeice, whom he more-than-slightly misquoted as we approached Hyde Park, 'her eyes saw all my waterfalls'. It enthralled him to notice, near Paddington, an Indian restaurant; such wonders were not to be encountered back at home in Cahersiveen, County Kerry, where a bottle of tomato ketchup would be considered exotic and possession of a clove of garlic would have you burned as a witch. This led him into a reverie on the food of beloved Italy: fat figs and *baccalà mantecato*, the fish in lamplit markets.

How was such and such a street in Prati? Were there fireworks in Piazza Navona for a festival these nights? He had been told by a Kerry neighbour recently returned from pilgrimage that the Trevi Fountain was fenced off for renovations; when would it reopen? He spoke of the city with such affection and everyday knowledge, as though he had departed it only yesterday and would be returning tonight, although in truth he would never again see Rome, except in dreams, a fact I felt he was coming to final terms with.

But Ireland was beautiful, too. He had been thinking of his childhood, the people in the town, the February light on the lakes. To awaken on a summer morning to the chaffinches in his sister's garden, her roses.

'At the back of it, the old motto is true, there's no place like home,' he said.

I asked if there was a particular part of Kerry for which he felt this home-comer's affection.

'Oh, I didn't mean Kerry. I meant Rome.'

As he said this, our taxi was passing St Francis House, a hostel for men on hard times. He mentioned that, as a young Deacon, he had once spent a winter in ministry there, living alongside the guests in a bleak plywood-partitioned cell off their dormitory, which rang nightly with threats and uncorkings.

'What was that like?' I asked.

'Bloody awful.'

One November evening, a stern Redemptorist Abbot from Belfast had loomed in from the bleak and angry rain, to inflict upon the residents a soul-improving tirade of the blood-and-thunder variety then popular. My friend was a good storyteller, the scene soon swam into being. I saw the cadaverous, thin-lipped ogre as he ascended the rickety steps to the pulpit, his mirthless, glinting eyes on the upturned unshaven; his ghastly little knuckles clutching the lectern.

'Look at yourselves,' he commenced. 'A nice pack of Fancy Dans.'

Alcohol was evil. The pub was 'Satan's waiting room'. Whiskey was 'the sweat of the devil'. There were more Fancy Dans in hell because of drunkenness than there were stars in the sky. It led to fornication, disobedience of the authorities, marital disharmony, impurities of thought, unhealthful association between the races and creeds, hair-raising sicknesses, early death. The ruination of women, the degradation of men, the starvation and orphaning of the infant. On the Final Day of Judgement, the drunken would be punished. Scripture had assured it. No escape would be possible. 'Lo, there shall be a weeping,' threatened the Redemptorist, 'and a gnashing of teeth.'

One of the older inmates, emboldened or bored, had the temerity to raise his hand. 'Saving your presence, Father,' he said, 'but I don't *have* any teeth.'

Hugh was poker-faced but corpsing a little as he delivered the sermoniser's punchline. 'Teeth shall be provided.'

At the apartment, he was tired and, after a sandwich lunch with me on the balcony, went in to take a siesta. His overnight bag containing clothes and shaving things had been mislaid by BOAC, a matter about which he was fretting, for his medicines were also lost, but while he rested I saw to matters. The Savoy had its own pharmacy and a collection of upscale shops, including a tailor's. Hugh's measurements were duly taken, and he was kitted out by Anderson & Sheppard of Savile Row, in a charcoal lounge suit and slightly racy polo neck, like a raffish uncle home from the theatrical tour of the provinces that ended in gossip. Dignified ties and fine-cut shirts were also provided. He delighted in the louche cravat.

Thus attired, he asked in a throwaway manner if I wished to say a rosary with him. I have always loved the rosary, finding its incantatory aspect transporting to the spirit, sometimes soothing, sometimes sad, always bringing the strange consolation of repetition but in truth I had never prayed it with Hugh, a fact he appeared to have forgotten. From his notebook he took a postcard depicting a Russian icon of Our Lady, which he placed against the carriage clock on the mantelpiece. Then he asked if I would help him to kneel down.

I ventured the view that Our Lady and Her Blessèd Son would find Hugh's prayer as acceptable if offered from the wheelchair but, in his quietly obstinate way, he insisted. It may have been the only time the holy rosary was prayed by two people in a bedroom at the Savoy, one in a fine lounge suit, the other in a dressing gown, hair still wet from her bath, while the traffic noises and police sirens arose from the Strand below, through the shining opened windows.

Years later, I saw that this was the moment I should have asked my difficult question of Hugh. Perhaps I knew this even then but was afraid. In any case, I did not ask it and on went the day. On go all the days. Alas.

At that era, there was on the English television a programme entitled *This is Your Life*, the premise of which involved a surprise being unleashed on some misfortunate personality of note, who would be whisked from the fake appointment at which he had innocently presented himself and conveyed to a studio where he would be confronted by the friends of his youth, as the Christians were confronted by the lions.

If anyone needed proof that no good deed ever goes unpunished, a conspiracy had been concocted to anoint Hugh the latest victim, in recognition of his leadership of the Escape Line. The researchers had done extensive preparatory work, tape-recorded the recollections of several of the Choir, sent us transcripts for correction, unearthed writings one or other of us had published (or not published) down the years. An assistant producer travelled to New York for a lengthy interview with Enzo Angelucci, and to what was by now West Berlin to meet Marianna de Vries, who, under a name changed by deed poll, had become a university lecturer, then a distinguished novelist and member of Parliament.

But, trove of research assembled, wiser counsel had prevailed. Vascular neurologists were consulted. Hugh was in no condition to endure the planned shock and the subsequent sixty minutes in the footlights. It was decided, instead, that Major Derry, our indomitable Choir colleague, would receive the BBC's laurels, if laurels they were, and that Hugh would be the surprise guest who always appeared through the curtains at the denouement, reducing everyone to lachrymose ecstasies as the credits began to roll. It really was a most vulgar programme. People adored it.

Hugh managed the experience admirably, as I knew he would, shyly passing around signed copies of *O Roma Felix*, a little guidebook he had written some years previously, and refusing to accept the compliments of his friends. (Its blunt subtitle, *'Practical Guide for Walks in Rome'*, was amusingly typical of him and, to we veterans of the Escape Line, not without ironies.) In addition to Sam Derry, who had grown ever more spectacularly handsome as he aged, a good number of our old Choir-mates were along. Delia Kiernan, her daughter Blon, Enzo Angelucci now of Brooklyn, John May of Whitechapel, dapper as a film star, and the inimitable but frequently imitated Sir Francis ('call me Frank') D'Arcy Godolphin Osborne, KCMG, soon to be named 12th Duke of Leeds. His Grace amused everyone, especially his most treasured audience, himself, by pretending never to have heard of the programme and insisting on addressing the presenter by surname. 'I say, Andrews. You're Irish? Ain't we all, what! Libations!'

Johnny May, in houndstooth mohair, was suntanned and splendid, although the years had not always been kind to my diamond. 'Evening, Treacle,' he twinkled, introducing me to his wife, Janine, whom he had met when she auditioned to sing with his bop quartet. Oesophageal cancer meant that he was no longer playing in public, had become a London cabbie, 'But I blow a bit at home.' Janine's parents had a sweetshop-and-tobacconist's in Loughton, a town in Essex, and Johnny did the weekly run to the wholesale. He and Enzo greeted each other with kisses and back-slaps, Enzo doing a lot of 'Willya take a look at this wiseguy,' Johnny affectionately telling him, 'Sod off.'

'Big occasion, Angelucci,' Delia said. 'You're wearing a shirt.'

'Don't look at me with those beautiful eyes or I'll drown,' Enzo countered. 'You remind me of a beauty I used to know but you're too young to be her.'

She pucked him, before they embraced, and afterwards too. And he lifted her, laughing, in his tender Roman arms, calling her *'bellissima* Delia'.

'God almighty,' she said, 'I'm glad my husband's not here to see this. Come over here, Jo, till we get a photo of the old gang. Stand in the middle, that's right.'

Delia, me, Enzo; behind us Johnny May and Frank Osborne, Johnny making the V-for-Victory sign, Frank raising a wine glass. In front of us, in his wheelchair, a blanketed, stone-faced Hugh, mug of tea in one hand, Lazio soccer pennant sent to him by dear, brave Marianna de Vries, who could not be with us, in the other. Hunkered beside him, Sam Derry, stern, mild and knightly, arm about Hugh's left shoulder.

Apart from a picture of Paolo and me, taken on the morning of our wedding, it is the only photograph I have ever had framed.

One of Johnny's subsequent remarks was excised from the programme as broadcasted but I have checked with my darling Delia, with whom I am still in monthly contact, and she is quite certain that my memory of it being made is accurate. He was recalling to the genial presenter a spirited quarrel he had had with Hugh on one occasion, because a promised couple of hundred dollars for the Choir had not been delivered on time.

'So, the Padre, he says to me, Johnny, we ain't got no money. Ain't you listening, Dobbin? It's a serious situation. And he spells it out for me, lively, in case I don't get the point. No M. O. N. E. F. Y.

' "Padre," I tell him, "there ain't no eff in money."

' "Exactly," he says. "Go and *get* some!" '

'I'm sure it didn't happen quite like that,' the presenter laughed, a little anxiously.

'It did,' Hugh replied. 'And worse.'

A little party had been arranged in a room above a local pub after the recording, the George in Portland Place, a premises haunted by BBC types and their forlorn-looking girls and radio scriptwriters in Aran sweaters wanting their multisyllabic bawlings to be commissioned. For some reason, it was almost empty that night. I seem to remember a severe rainstorm, or perhaps the forecast of one. It was thoughtful of whoever had organised things but Hugh was tired, a bit distracted, disconcerted I should imagine, by such a sudden re-exposure to the past and the gale of raw goodwill to which he had been subjected.

The room was up a flight of stairs once fallen down by Dylan Thomas, and they were difficult for Hugh to manage, even with the help of Blon Kiernan and Frank Osborne. A reporter from the *Standard* materialised, wanting to interview him, and had to be shown the door. Sandwiches failed to arrive.

After a time, Johnny May and the inexhaustible Delia got a sort of singsong going. Things cheered up a little, or pretended to. Somehow, perhaps through some influence or intervention of the programme's host, a relative back in Ireland was spoken to on the pub telephone. Enzo sang something from Verdi down the line. Later, I seem to remember dear Frank making a speech peppered with quotations from Demosthenes and the like. Usually he did. Easier to stop the sunrise. Unlike most men, Frank became more attractive as he drank, his auburn eyes glistening like demerara sugar, and his gestures more Italian, vowels voluptuous and rich, like a man doing an impersonation of himself, as he almost certainly was, almost all the time. After a distinguished Foreign Office career, he retired to Rome. Sam Derry's children thought him a sort of astonishment. The boy, a long-haired bohemian, the girl, a short-haired bohemian, appeared not to understand at all.

Towards the end of the night, Frank proposed that the Choir all stand together and sing one last hymn for the old days, 'Abide With Me'. ('You too, Andrews!') With mild firmness Hugh let it be known that he didn't want that, and Frank, a skilled backtracker like all his profession, with silken elegance retreated.

'Friends, Romans, countrymen,' he said. 'Memory Lane is a thoroughfare best visited fleetingly. But permit me, gentles all, one valediction of the heart. When I have been requested down the years to define the Rome Escape Line, I have always said the same thing. And I always shall. It was my dear friend Hugh O'Flaherty and a number of us who loved him.'

Hugh's head was bowed. When he raised it again, his whole face was wet with tears.

A taxi drive through the West End in the rain is not the worst way for a night out to conclude. I recall a forest of umbrellas, as in an impressionist painting, the silver and amber shadows of Oxford Street, young people going into nightclubs in Soho. The London of my salad days was changing.

I asked if he had enjoyed the evening and he conceded that it had been a pleasure, if a painful one, to see old friends again, but felt that too much limelight had been shone on him, not on the wider doings of the Choir. Quoting his favourite Shakespeare play, *Coriolanus*, he said he did not like to see his nothings monstered.

'Don't you think you did a lot?' I asked.

'Not enough,' he replied.

Again, my unasked question loomed. But by the time I had framed its words, he was pointing with delight. 'Oh, look, Berwick Street, will we get a fish supper, do you think the driver would mind? Lots of vinegar on mine, no salt.'

The following morning, I let him rest; in fact he slept until noon, emerging then from my bedroom with mole-like blinks, like one uncertain as to how he had arrived here. The fantastically expensive silk pyjamas he was wearing had been ordered but never paid for by a Socialist cabinet minister, now disgraced, a matter the tailor had slyly let slip to us. My own bed had been the couch in the sitting room, a fact that appeared to appal Hugh, but in truth I am rather fond of dozing off on a well-upholstered old couch in firelight, a ghost story or a book of poems I don't understand by my side and a small whisky and water on the ottoman. A certain amount of sleeplessness seems to suit me.

We breakfasted simply – one can breakfast at any time from sunrise to midnight at the Savoy – on the terrace overlooking the Thames. He told me he still suffered nightmares, dreams of Hauptmann and his thugs, the caves, the deportations, 'the more we should have done'.

Eichmann had been executed the previous summer, in Israel. Hugh followed the trial in the newspapers. One of the Israeli soldiers given the task of committing the Nazi's cremated remains to the sea, six miles beyond Jaffa and therefore outside the national waters, remarked in an interview that he had been struck by how minuscule is the handful of ashes left by a human being. Hugh had seen a news-magazine photograph of the vast mountain of ash at Auschwitz. 'Everyone should look at that picture,' he said. 'Is there someplace we could go and say a prayer?'

'We can pray here,' I said.

'I'd like to be in a congregation.'

At that time in St Paul's, Bedford Street, known affectionately among London's night-people as 'the actors' church', a service was held in the afternoons. Actors being actors, as the vicar once told me, there would be little point in holding it in the mornings. 'St P's', the place was termed by those in the know. The atmosphere was bohemian-thespian-diva-fallen-on-bad-times. Monogamy, one felt, was not the universal practice, nor perhaps was heterosexuality, though nobody called it that in those days.

It bothered Hugh that he had missed Mass and so we went together to St P's, I having warned that this would not be vespers in a nunnery.

The meagre congregation of shatter-eyed nightclub performers and jaded dancers delighted him, the bleary jazzmen and five-o'clock-shadowed blues shouters. In the porch arose a distinct aroma of something that may not have been frankincense. Hugh was the only gentleman in the church wearing a collar and tie, indeed one of the relatively few not wearing rouge.

Afterwards he got into a conversation with a sort of bedraggled busker, a former mathematics professor, or so the man said, about the accursed heavyweight boxing they both liked. During this ordeal, I looked at the stained-glass windows and the tombstones. Protestant tombstones are so touching, full of tenderness and anecdote, their euphemisms for death so hopeful. *My son who fell asleep. Returned to the Light. His beloved wife departed to that further shore. Gone away to glory. Called home.* It is one of my lasting postcards of Hugh. Chuckling about boxing, in stained-glass dapple, with a person many would have termed a tramp.

That evening I achieved a long-held ambition to take Hugh to Covent Garden. It was a magnificent production of *Tosca*, featuring Tito Gobbi and Callas, and he would have been enthralled by Act Two, his favourite forty minutes in the history of music, had he only not fallen asleep shortly before '*Vissi d'arte*'. I hadn't the heart to wake him.

After the performance, I recall a strange moment that I still think about from time to time. We were making our way along Wellington Street, Hugh blanketed in his wheelchair, I pushing, when, through a cracked dirty window on the ground floor of the old Lyceum, he thought he saw a white-faced adolescent girl staring out at us. That theatre had been derelict for many years by then. But he was convinced. She seemed to have shaken him.

I had asked the concierge to book Montinari's for supper, for Hugh, like all admirable and trustworthy people, liked his food – he once signed an antiquarian book of Artusi's recipes, a birthday gift to me, with a beloved quotation he translated from Wilde, '*Dopo una buona cena si può perdonare chiunque, persino i propri parenti*' – 'after a good dinner, one can forgive anybody, even one's own relations' – and I wanted him to see that great ocean liner of a restaurant that sailed so many years on the Strand. Signed photographs of unremembered actors bedecked every wall, often a troubling signal in a restaurant, like having photographs of the food, but Monty's whilst past its best was still by some distance the finest Italian in London in those days, meaning that it was almost

266

as good as the worst railway station café in Italy. Their famous *Penne all'arrabbiata* had been retired from the menu by the night of what would be our only visit, but the maître d, whom I knew of old, arranged its fleeting resurrection.

Hugh and he conversed in Italian, a delightful exchange to hear, Hugh telling him of the filming of *Quo Vadis* in Rome back in '50, the Metro-Goldwyn-Mayerification of the city, the suave limousines and swarms of helmeted extras, the ranked paparazzi, the stupefying sets, the terrifying detail that went into the gladiatorial fight scenes. 'The lions were brought from Germany, the bulls from Portugal, and the four white horses from Ireland.' Robert Taylor and Deborah Kerr had stayed not far from the Collegio; he had seen them walking with Nero, the actor Peter Ustinov, in the gardens of the Villa Pamphili. When the penne arrived at our table, he dutifully pronounced it unsurpassable, though in truth it was mediocre at best. As always, he refused even a half-glass of wine, and as always, insisted I have one. I had two while he sipped at rather dusty-looking orangeade, containing, marvel of marvels – again, unknown to the indigenes of rural Kerry, who seemed to be managing without it – crushed ice.

I recall his suspicious glower in the light of the crêpes Suzette that Luigi Montinari himself would do at your table. Monty's was the only 'Italian' restaurant I have known where the menu featured 'jelly', and even, if one asked carefully, that culinary abomination which young people were learning to call 'fries'. One was oneself learning, of course, to call these people 'teenagers', and to call their music 'music' through a tight smile of unfelt empathy. Born after the war, they knew literally nothing. There were times when one was glad to be childless.

Coffee was called for. The floor show began. A handsome big-eared lunkhead in a once-black dinner jacket sang Gershwin, in the finger-clicking, low-lidded, crooning style of his grandparents' remote youth, often smirking at his pianist, a cadaverous ghoul in a cummerbund, who *hulked* over the keys as though resenting them for some crime, or shooting what I suppose he must have thought were enticingly boyish winks at the vodka-soaked dowagers and one-time flappers and chain-smoking Henrys and hooting Wilfs who were among the last remaining denizens of Monty's in those days, exotics possessed of the strange, poignant beauty of creatures becoming extinct.

From time to time the singer attempted a Charleston or did that hands-criss-crossing-on-your-knees trick so beloved by very little children, and the old people chuckled dutifully, Hugh and I among them. The satirist David Frost came in, with his mother, as I recall. I had seen a photograph of him in the newspaper with several Beatles.

I do not know how it got about the restaurant that Hugh was who he was – some years previously he had written a regular column for the *Sunday Express*, 'Our Correspondent in Rome', his by-line including a rather flattering photograph he never liked – but drinks with fruit segments and tiny Japanese umbrellas and miniature plastic swords in them started to be conveyed to our table. There were collegial waves across the hors d'oeuvres and the odd cry of 'Well done, that man.' Thankfully, no one went so far as actually to approach; Hugh seemed to be emitting a force field. But it was wonderful to see him contend with his suddenly arrived celebrity by appearing to turn quite luminous with embarrassment, like an angry squid. The coffee bean in the Sambuca someone sent over burned less hotly than my friend.

'You should hold my hand,' I teased. 'We'd be in the *News of the World* on Sunday.'

'I don't want to hold your hand, thanks,' he confirmed.

With a final murdering of Cole Porter, the singer departed the dais, tripping on his shoelaces as he went. The conversations over which he had been performing intensified quickly. Candles glowed in Chianti bottles.

A young woman came through the kitchen's swing doors, wiping her wet hands on a cloth, crossing quickly to our table in a way that made clear she had been watching us for some time, and enquired in a reticent, apologetic way if she might speak a moment with Hugh.

She was already battling tears.

He asked if she wished to be seated.

Shaking her head, she indicated she didn't.

She wished to thank him, she said, for having saved the life of a nineteen-year-old Glaswegian, Private Michael Robert Connolly, First Battalion, King's Fusiliers, on 20th September 1943. Did Hugh by any chance remember him?

Hugh said that in plain honesty he did not – there had been so many prisoners – and she nodded as though having expected this answer.

He had escaped from Modena prison camp while on a forced labour detail, made his way towards Rome, barefoot, by night, exhausted and starving, snatching whatever rest he could in haggards and hedgerows, found the strength to stagger across the Vatican boundary and into St Peter's Square, from where the Monsignor had smuggled him into hiding at a convent near the Holy Office, St Monica's. He slept in the ruined dovecot that had once been a Roman *columbarium* and recovered from the scores of gangrenous wounds that his scramble through the barbed wire had wreaked on him. In a military hospital near Croydon aerodrome, en route home after the war, Michael Robert Connolly met a nurse a year older than him, a girl from the New Forest. They married after a month; their first child, a daughter, was standing before us now.

'I wouldn't be here,' the young woman said, through rivulets of tears, 'if you hadn't done what you did. Neither would my children. So, thank you.'

She was named Monica, after the convent. Her sixteen-year-old brother was Hugh, after Hugh.

Every year on 20th September, they prayed thanks for their father's deliverance, and for the man who saved his life.

'Dear child,' Hugh said.

'God bless you,' she whispered.

'Is your father in good health?'

'Yes, he is. He's very well.'

'Will you give him my best. And your mother. And your children.'

'Of course.'

A lovely thing happened, then. Hugh began to speak to her of his own time in the New Forest, the six months he had spent as a young priest in Brockenhurst. I had not known of this before, did not even know where it was.

He spoke of wild ponies, I remember, and the seasons of forest life, the customs of that part of England. Clearly it gave him pleasure to say the names of the local towns, as it always gives us pleasure to say the names of places where we encountered the fleeting ghost that is happiness. Lymington. Beaulieu. Lyndhurst. Hythe. Keyhaven. Barton on Sea.

I am bitterly sorry to say that, later that night, back at the penthouse, Hugh and I had a very serious quarrel. There was a question I had long wanted to ask him, I said; he raised his voice when I did. Nevertheless, I persisted.

I had heard certain whisperings, which I detailed; would he confirm they were false? He would not speak of the matter at all, he replied. 'It's nobody's damned business what I do.' The moon, if there was one, went down on our anger. Doors were slammed in the penthouse that night.

Next morning at London airport, I bade him farewell. A bundle of opera records, a gift for a neighbour back in Kerry, was wrapped in brown paper, there was also a present for his sister, a fine linen tablecloth we had bought in the hotel lobby. It was Hugh's manner, following a disagreement, to pretend it hadn't happened. So that's what we did. I was glad.

We spoke of the weather, as often we had done in the Rome days at rehearsal. Did I listen to Bach anymore? No, I didn't.

A fine, soft day. Yes, it was, I agreed.

But in England you'd never know, he said, it could be thundering by noon.

He was trembling when I embraced him. So was I. He kissed my hand.

I murmured, '*Grazie mille*.' So did he.

As he trundled down the departures corridor, and away from me, he raised a clenched fist in salute. The last time I would ever see him, we both knew.

In my head was an old ballad we used to sing at rehearsal.

It seemed a long time before his flight went, but I waited, every minute.

> *Now the summertime is come*
> *With the laurels richly blooming,*
> *And the wild mountain thyme*
> *All the moorlands all perfuming;*
> *To our own beloved bower, let us journey altogether,*
> *Where the wild lilies bloom*
> *'Mong the braes of Balquhither.*
> *Let us go, lassie, go.*
> *Lassie, go.*

Cathair Saidhbhín
County Kerry
October, 1963

Cara Giovanna, my Jo,

My dearest old friend,

I don't think there have been such lilacs since the year I met you.

By the time you receive these words, I shall have departed this weary body and gone wherever we go when evicted from it. I have left instructions that this letter be sent to you three days after my funeral. Forgive my sloppy typing. It is late.

Always, as you know, I have been a neurotic writer-down. Things didn't seem quite real unless written.

It has lately been at me a bit that those lovely few days in London may have been spoiled for you by our quarrel, by my adamant silence on the question you asked. For my stubbornness, I apologise, you know how pig-headed I always was. But there were other reasons why I was reluctant to speak.

The truth is that, yes, I did attend Hauptmann in Modena prison. Nine times in all – there was to be a tenth but I cancelled the arrangement. The visits were made at his request.

During the first, we scarcely spoke. In the second, he was self-piteous and vengeful, pacing the cage, smoking, ranting that he had done no more than obey orders, spewing obscenities I felt had been meticulously contrived to shock and hurt a celibate person in a particular way (but they didn't). Some men adjust to being in a cell. He hated it.

Did I understand that he was married, had responsibilities, onuses? He could no longer see his wife and children! How was this justice? My daughter who has done nothing is denied her own *father*? My parents are elderly! I am to excrete in a bucket, like an animal. For doing as legally ordered! There were many worse than I. Do you know what it is like, to exist in a cage?

I did not go again for two years.

He wrote asking for a third meeting, I discussed this with my Rector. It was decided that I would go, and I went. At that time, the burial places of many disappeared Romans were still unknown; there was talk that Hauptmann might supply details so the proper rites could be done. I knew he wouldn't, but hope is hard to kill.

Hauptmann greeted me as a beloved cousin returned from long abroad – an act, of course – 'Sit down, let's play chess.' Somehow, he had organised a cake, I seem to remember, and 'a pot of your English tea'. What he wanted, of course, was for me to tell him I wasn't English. I told him I wasn't thirsty. This defeated him. He claimed to know nothing of the disappeared. He knew nothing of anything. He asked would I shake hands. I would not.

At our fourth encounter the chessboard and pieces were again produced – he had fashioned them himself, during woodworking class – which gave him the opportunity to deploy the Italian proverb any psychopath would find meaning in: '*Alla fine della partita il re e il pedone vanno nella stessa scatola*' He then said it in English, as though I did not know Italian anymore. 'After the game, the king and pawn end up in the same sack.'

I told him his accent needed work.

He was able to pretend to be mentally troubled if he thought that might be useful, but was in many ways a rather humdrum, sane, mediocre individual, a manipulative narcissist with, like many such people, a remarkable capacity to attract. The guards would sometimes confide that there were moments when they found him hard to dislike; 'irresistible', I remember one warder saying. He had a way of exuding vulnerability, a babes-in-the-wood incognisance, and a particular mode of not-quite-apologising in which 'all of us' had been victims and of generalising outwards with deft, disingenuous cunning. 'Of course, always where there is violence everyone seeing it is maimed. This has been observed by psychiatry.' His magnetism made him a very frightening person to be near. You felt your edges blurring.

I suppose it should never begin to surprise us that the murderer wears a mask. Yet it does. We all of us wear so many, of course. Perhaps that is the definition of the human being, a mammal able to alter its face. Only one person in all of history went entirely without mask, was always His very self, come betrayer or killer. He was murdered by power, on a tree.

Soon afterwards, I noticed the décor of Hauptmann's cell had begun to change, gradually at first, but noticeably, calculatedly, postcards of the saints and martyrs had been taped to the walls. One sees this often enough in a prison. One morning I arrived, reluctant as always, to find a photograph of myself in their midst.

'You are where you belong, Monsignor. I pray to you, daily.' Here he paused. 'Forgive my English, I meant *for* you.'

It will be obvious to you, perceptive Jo, where matters were heading. Soon, I was proven correct. Hauptmann asked if he could be received into the Catholic faith, as I had known from the very outset he would. No doubt it is cynical to notice that the discovery of the Lord by murderers and liars happens with predictable regularity once the judge passes sentence, rarely beforehand. With an eye on the Parole Board, the killer arrives at realisations the Sermon on the Mount did not provoke. Hauptmann insisted he was sincere, wrote long letters to Rome, saying he wished me – and me only – to be the priest who would prepare him.

The decision brought me agonies. In the end, I agreed.

We went through the required formalities, I gave him a Catechism, which he studied most assiduously, often asking deep, knowledgeable questions, as the sly faker and the truly earnest both must.

The morning came for his baptism, which took place in his cell, the prison chapel having suffered a collapsed ceiling. Hauptmann and I were alone. He had not shaved or washed. His lank hair was greasy. He had a bad cold and felt unable to face the shower block, he said, but his lack of proper deportment seemed to me a way of transmitting his contempt. Perhaps it was not.

He snuffled and mock-solemnly stared, misremembering the vows. The moment arrived at which the priest must summon two witnesses to the sincerity of the person entering the Church. He had hoped I would find a couple of guards to fulfil the role, but, without telling him, I had made a different arrangement.

'*Bitte*,' I called.

Two young people entered the cell. His daughter, now aged twenty, and her brother, seventeen. Both attempting not to weep. Neither able to look at him.

'Your children will witness your solemn oath,' I told him.

He was taken aback and did not address them, which I thought was strange, and he waited a fair while before nodding his head. As they watched, I concluded his baptism.

Perhaps he was not duping me. Perhaps he was. So be it. I do not understand or even like several of my Redeemer's teachings. Think yourself not much better, offer good to those that hate you. Like many of my sex, I have often felt

273

profoundly that God made a terrible mistake in not making me God, that the world would be without darkness or difficulty if only I ruled it. Had I been the Almighty, I would have put several matters rather differently. But I wasn't.

God was.

And is.

The moment the baptism rite was complete, his children departed the cell, his son having shaken hands, the girl still refusing to touch him. He asked if I would hear his first confession. This I would not do, but I summoned a confrère, the prison chaplain, as I left. In the end, the priest later told me, Hauptmann declined to confess.

The day of his baptism was the last time I saw him, I am happy to say. Some years ago I heard that his wife had applied to dissolve their marriage. She may since have remarried, but I don't know.

These are the painful events I should have told you about in London. I am not certain as to what prevented me from doing so. Perhaps I thought you might be angry that I had given him any attention at all. Often, I was angry with myself for that reason. More recently I have found that I do not wish to think of him, and there are many days when I do not, for which mercy I thank the God of Silences. As I come closer to the Light, I have grown uninterested in the Dark. Always I used to fear it, and fear is a connectedness.

I am sorry that I hurt you. When in this world I ever doubted the existence of anything good, I thought of you, your kindness, compassion and grace, the love you showed a friend who was prideful and mean, your forgiveness, ardent bravery and guts. Many people never meet a hero. I met heroes. I loved them.

Arrivederci, my friend and comrade. I did many things wrong in my life. But my Father's house has many rooms.

Be kind to yourself, bellissima. You're not kind enough to yourself.

Sing your song, taste the wine.

With all love and respect.

Che Dio ti benedica sempre,

Your H

Caveat, Bibliography, Acknowledgements

While real people and real events inspired the work of fiction that is *My Father's House*, it is first and last a novel. Liberties have been taken with facts, characterisations and chronologies. Incidents have been concentrated, characters amalgamated, renamed, adapted or invented. The Hugh O'Flaherty, Sam Derry, John May, Delia Kiernan and D'Arcy Osborne in these pages are my versions and are not to be relied upon by biographers or researchers. This novel is not intended to be a source for students of wartime Rome or the Nazi occupation of Italy. The letter reproduced as epigraph is quoted on page 197 of Sam Derry's memoir *The Rome Escape Line* (1960). The writer's surname is not listed. He was 'a Glasgow boy'. All other sequences of *My Father's House* presenting themselves as authentic documents are works of fiction. Readers in search of nonfiction on Hugh O'Flaherty and the Rome Escape Line, or reportage on life in wartime Rome, are directed to the following works, which of course do not agree on every aspect, and to the references, notes and bibliographies they contain:

Fergus Butler-Gallie, *Priests de la Resistance!* (2019), Victor Failmezger, *Rome, City in Terror, the Nazi Occupation 1943-44* (2020). JP Gallagher, *Scarlet Pimpernel of the Vatican* (1967), republished as *The Scarlet and the Black* (2009), Stefan Heid, Johann Ickx: *Der Campo Santo Teutonico, das deutsche Priesterkolleg und die Erzbruderschaft zur Schmerzhaften Mutter Gottes während des Zweiten Weltkriegs* (2015), Robert Katz, *The Pope, the Resistance and the German Occupation of Rome* (2003), Borden W. Painter, *Mussolini's Rome* (2005), William Simpson, *A Vatican Lifeline* (1995), Stephen Walker, *Hide and Seek: the Irish Priest in the Vatican Who Defied the Nazi Command* (2012), M. de Wyss, *Rome Under the Terror* (1945). This list is far from exhaustive.

I express heartfelt gratitude to the Monsignor's nephew and namesake, retired Judge of the Irish Supreme Court, Hugh O'Flaherty, and grand-niece Catherine, a filmmaker, for granting me an interview and making available to me their collection of Monsignor Hugh's unpublished papers, including his letters, diaries, notes, telegrams and other writings and his published journalism (for some years he wrote a newspaper column) as well as audio and other recordings that Catherine O'Flaherty found while researching her documentary about the Monsignor (*Pimpernel sa Vatican*, 2008), including a full audiotape recording of the 1963 *This is Your Life* programme for Sam Derry, a fictitious version of which concludes this novel. I thank archivist Mark Ward for the skill and professionalism with which he facilitated the family's sharing of this material with me. I thank Flor MacCarthy for alerting me to a letter to the Monsignor that I had not seen before, from Irish president Sean T O'Kelly, and for sharing an inherited collection of remarkable unpublished 1930s and '40s Rome photographs. All the book's errors are my own.

I thank Liz Foley and Mikaela Pedlow at Harvill, and Isobel Dixon and Conrad Williams and their colleagues at the Blake Friedmann Literary Agency. The closing chapter's threat that false teeth will be provided on the Day of Judgement is borrowed from the work of that virtuoso of storytelling, the late Dave Allen. I have altered it a bit for my purposes. A special pleasure of writing this book was the warm helpfulness of Ireland's former ambassador to the Holy See, Emma Madigan, and her husband Laurence Simms. I thank them and their son Cormac, whom I first met when he was a tiny Roman, for their friendship. The arrangement on page 101 is by maestro Brian Byrne, to whom I offer heartfelt gratitude. I thank John Bowman, Bert Wright, Prof Diarmaid Ferriter, Monsignor Stefan Heid (see list of reference works, above) and the librarians at the Collegium Germanicum in Rome, Monsignor John Kennedy in Rome, Kathy Rose O'Brien, Mariachiara Rusca, Anna Loi, and my sister, Dr Éimear O'Connor. As ever, I thank my sons James and Marcus, and my wife, Anne-Marie Casey. *Vi amo, dal profondo del mio cuore.*

Joseph O'Connor was born in Dublin. His books include *Cowboys and Indians*, *Inishowen*, *Star of the Sea* (American Library Association Award, Irish Post Award for Fiction, France's Prix Millepages, Italy's Premio Acerbi, Prix Madeleine Zepter for European Novel of the Year), *Redemption Falls*, *Ghost Light* (Dublin One City One Book Novel 2011) and *Shadowplay* (Irish Book Awards Novel of the Year, Costa Novel of the Year shortlist). His fiction has been translated into forty languages. He received the 2012 Irish PEN Award for Outstanding Contribution to Literature and in 2014 he was appointed Frank McCourt Professor of Creative Writing at the University of Limerick.

www.josephoconnorauthor.com